Raja Alem was born in Mecca and now lives in Paris. Her works include ten novels, two plays, biography, short stories, essays, literary journalism, writing for children, and collaborations with artists and photographers. She has received many awards in the Arab world and in Europe, including from UNESCO for creative achievement in 2005, and from the Lebanese Literary Club in Paris in 2008. In 2011, she became the first woman to win the prestigious International Prize for Arabic Fiction, also known as the "Arabic Booker," for her novel *The Dove's Necklace*.

Leri Price is a literary translator based in the UK. In 2017, her translation of Khaled Khalifa's *No Knives in the Kitchens of This City* (Hoopoe, 2016) was short-listed for both the American Literary Translators Association (ALTA)'s National Translation Awards and the Saif Ghobash Banipal Prize for Arabic Literary Translation.

Sarab

Raja Alem

Translated by
Leri Price

hoopoe
AN IMPRINT OF AUC PRESS

First published in 2018 by
Hoopoe
113 Sharia Kasr el Aini, Cairo, Egypt
420 Fifth Avenue, New York, 10018
www.hoopoefiction.com

Hoopoe is an imprint of the American University in Cairo Press
www.aucpress.com

Quotations from the Quran on the following pages are taken from the English translation by Muhammad Asad: p 85 (55: 46–47); p 86 (55: 27); p 91 (2: 125); p 95 (5: 31); pp 101, 111 (5: 32); p 106 (2: 114); p 112 (55: 37)

Exclusive distribution outside Egypt and North America by I.B.Tauris & Co Ltd., 6 Salem Road, London, W4 2BU

Dar el Kutub No. 26600/17
ISBN 978 977 416 876 5

Dar el Kutub Cataloging-in-Publication Data

Alem, Raja
    Sarab / Raja Alem.—Cairo: The American University in Cairo Press,
    2018.
        p. cm.
        ISBN 978 977 416 876 5
        1. English Fiction
        823

1 2 3 4 5   22 21 20 19 18

Designed by Adam el-Sehemy
Printed in the United States of America

Day One

THE GAS BOMBS FORCED THE revolutionaries to abandon their positions guarding the huge gates and retreat to the cellars of the Grand
Mosque. There, they hunkered down and prepared for the fight to
the death.

Squadrons of paratroopers poured in torrents from the helicopters until they covered the courtyard of the Grand Mosque.
They reminded the city of the flock of birds described in the Quran
which cast handfuls of death on Abraha's army as it marched with
an elephant at its head to destroy Mecca, but this modern flock
proclaimed an unparalleled, modern horror. Soldiers in gas masks
fanned out instantly to comb the halls and corridors of the mosque
for pockets of resistance, and they opened the gates to the troops of
the National Guard who were waiting outside.

That was on November 29, 1979. Thanks to the clouds of
gas that hovered in the air over the Holy City, the National Guard
had successfully regained control of the rooftops and halls of the
Grand Mosque, despite the heavy losses they had sustained earlier
in the battle.

Utter chaos gripped the revolutionaries when electrified water
gushed in and swamped the cellars where they had taken refuge.
With distorted vision and blood spouting from their eye sockets, the
remaining members of the resistance scattered to seek out some
form of protection in the network of cellars and prayer cells. The
men stumbled away like blinded insects, defeated by the length of
the siege and the severity of the battle. Its impending conclusion,

and their own end, was clear to all; they were aware their desperate war was only a postponement of the inevitable. The interconnecting cells hindered the spread of the electrified water, lengthening the hours of endurance—or, more accurately, prolonging their demise—but the fighters weren't permitted to catch their breath.

On December 3, they were woken by a thundering over their heads, and at once realized colossal drills were consuming the ceiling above them, creating a pit so deep and dark not even the sky would be visible. Soon containers of poisonous chemicals armed with timed detonators were dropped through these holes, one after another. The fighters were dispatched in pieces—fragments of darkness, limbs, the smell of warm blood, and remnants of skin stuck in the teeth of anyone destined to escape that rain of bombs.

The soldiers continued to vary their drilling sites, distributing holes like musical notes on a stave and dispatching containers of chemicals that blinded the revolutionaries. Even so, the resistance rushed to discharge fountains of bullets upward, riddling the workers' bodies with holes. The soldiers crawled forward to extract their bodies and free up the entrances to the hell below, but despite their caution a soldier's eye exploded here, another's skull there. A bullet hit a package of poison and gas erupted among the soldiers. The streams of blood and poison pouring downward were answered by renewed volleys of bullets rocketing upward, creating a violent and terrifying pandemonium, but it didn't take long for the chemical powder to resolve the battle to the advantage of the soldiers, and the hail of gunfire from the resistance disappeared. The coughing of the choking men escaped from the holes, along with hisses of rage and the souls that had perished by the dozen. Below ground, the sense of defeat was tangible. Truly, it had been the most elegant, ingenious move in the battle since its beginning; the bombs propelled the terrified combatants out of the cellars like puppets and hounded them through the maze of subterranean vaults pumped full of poisonous chemicals, bullets, and hand grenades. Hell itself was driving them out from behind their impregnable barricades in the cellars, and as soon as they emerged into the courtyard, they were met by the sniper bullets. Stunned by daylight after days of darkness, the revolutionaries fell to the ground even before the hail of bullets annihilated them, and they died in total blindness.

All the while, Mujan continued to hold out in the hidden vaults. He mowed down attacking soldiers without mercy until the siege was concluded and he was seized.

The prayer cells belowground had become a fermenting slaughterhouse, its shadows reeking of human bodies. But in one of the sections the National Guard had already liberated from the revolutionaries, behind an abandoned minbar, there appeared a ghost, masked and smeared with blood. Suddenly it perceived a blue light piercing the screen of darkness like a scalpel and cautiously approaching the door. The ghost froze, eyes sparkling maliciously. It held its breath, waiting for the prey to approach its inevitable fate. The strip of blue light widened and a huge ghost in a blue military uniform appeared in the doorway, casting an interrogatory look inside. He advanced a step into the pitch-dark room, and directly in front of him, in the heart of the darkness rent by the blue light, he caught sight of the ghost squatting on the ground. At that moment, a body fell from the ceiling. The squatting ghost watched in terror as a supple piece of darkness detached from the ceiling of the pitch-black prayer cell and landed on the giant officer. As their bodies collided there was a sound of stone hitting stone, and the officer fell to the ground unconscious, as if struck by lightning. The light went out and darkness closed over the scene once more. It hadn't been a human body, but was more likely a piece of ceiling, or maybe one of the angels of punishment come to dispel the gas clouds and the darkness. The ghost was certain of this as the small piece of darkness disappeared within the greater darkness and its rescuer vanished as if it had never been. While the officer was incapacitated, the ghost seized the opportunity to leap up, confiscate his FAMAS rifle, and point it at his head. The ghost forced the officer to lift the drain cover, pushed him through first, and closed the cover behind them. Their masks were plunged into darkness.

As they set off in the pitch black, the ghost kept the gun aimed at the other, huge shadow. The slim ghost, lost inside in a stained National Guard uniform, urged the huge blue-suited officer forward. They hurried on like a stream bubbling in silence, fleeing the horror of Judgment Day, lost in the bowels of the earth. They panted, inhaling mold and the putrefaction of death as they stumbled blindly through the suffocating network of sewage tunnels that seemed to branch off at random.

At any sign of hesitation, the slim ghost would drop the rifle onto its victim's shoulder, threatening to blow his brains out and forcing him to hurry up and flee the death pursuing them both. Bombs were still falling from the ceiling according to an infernal plan, cutting off communication lines within the network of prayer cells. The last straggling remnants of the revolutionaries were isolated from their leader and exterminated one small group at a time. The stench of charred human flesh and mashed body parts made the shadows of that underground hell even darker.

The two fleeing ghosts burst out of the sewage tunnels to find themselves in the middle of Suq al-Mudaa, outside the confines of the Grand Mosque and the hellfire of battle within. They reeled as clean air rushed into their lungs, under the confused impression that the stinging sensation was the effect of the gas.

The two ghosts fled, groping their way through the narrow alleys of Suq al-Layla. The ominous silence of the normally bustling marketplace absorbed their footsteps, which seemed deafeningly loud here. Compelled by sudden panic, the ghost shoved forward its prey, still staggering from the effects of the gas, so that they disappeared into a narrow alley that turned off the suq. They entered a wooden doorway and walked into the shadowy vestibule of the abandoned house. Every door facing them on the lower floors was closed and they were driven up the stone stairs. An upper floor opened, welcoming them to a kitchen and one other room.

"God forgive me . . ." The slim rebel opened the door of a room that seemed like a playroom. The wall was papered in lemon yellow and decorated with photographs of a girl about seven years old. She appeared to have been photographed from different angles as she leaped gleefully upward, and her short red skirt sailed through the air in harmony with the flying tendrils of her short black hair.

In the middle of the room a rocking horse stood a meter high. It neighed enthusiastically and soundlessly, facing the terrifyingly huge television screen. Row upon row of huge plastic dolls, in striking contrast to the smaller handmade cotton dolls, were scattered around the room. The gleaming white cotton faces stared ahead expressionlessly. They had large bulging eyes, decorated with large black buttons sewn on with black thread, and their eyebrows arched upward in mockery of the two ghosts who had rushed panting and uninvited into their forgotten world.

The ghosts trembled, thunderstruck by the peculiarity of the scene before them, and they drew closer together. Death rustled over the rebel like a second skin; like death itself, the ghost directed a powerful blow to the head of its victim, which sent him to the ground. His unconscious body stoked the rebel's kindling anger, and the stiff boots of the National Guard, which seemed a little too big for the feet wearing them, began to aim a series of kicks at the center of that masculine body. Vicious sadism overwhelmed the slim rebel, who appeared so overcome with bliss that he shuddered with every blow to the male member, so delicate and so vulnerable to violence. Every hatred, every fear that had disturbed the rebel while among the fighters was embodied in that organ; pulverizing it meant surviving the death that waited belowground.

The kicks escalated into a frenzy that could only be satiated by the annihilation of that masculinity.

A boot flew off the small foot of the rebel, who proceeded to kick the prone body with bare feet, giddy with the pleasure of crashing a foot directly into that symbol of masculinity and virility. He kicked in a feverish trance until woken by splashes of blood on the blue uniform; blood was gushing from wounds in his feet, which had been slashed open from wading barefoot through death, even before losing that shoe.

The rebel felt the huge body had surrendered like a bag of clay, and the satisfaction of kicking it abated. Driven by bloodlust, he knelt beside the body of the enemy, gazing at it blindly, unable to control the fingers that were trembling from his hunger to tear at his opponent's virility, at the chest webbed with muscles, to drink this enemy's blood and extinguish the hatred kindling within. But instead of ripping the officer to shreds, the rebel began to rip the clothes from the enemy's flesh, beginning with the blue military trousers.

Somewhere between unconsciousness and delirium, the French officer perceived the humiliation his body was being subjected to while a brutal hand ripped his shirt and peeled it away from his hidden survival kit: his wireless radio, his compass, headlamp, maps, grenades, ropes, emergency rations, and most importantly, his pride and the internal war machinery that kept him calm. When the claws reached his underwear, they froze suddenly. Without logic, they allowed him that last shred of dignity. The officer was inflamed; with a desire that tore deep into his guts, he craved more of the humiliation meted out by this violence, which was unlike any sexual gratification he had ever experienced before. Then, at last, he passed out completely.

The rebel knelt there, overcome with confusion by what he had done to that body; its splendor and perfection had been unexpected. The officer lay nearly naked, and the rebel's turmoil increased; none of the other revolutionaries had had these fiendish muscles braided with vice, or these slim hips. None of the other revolutionaries' bodies had borne this ominous danger, its inherent wickedness unalleviated by being unconscious. It occurred to the slim revolutionary to fall on those muscles and tear them apart fiber by fiber, to send them back to the hell they had come from. That would be a magnificent sacrifice to add to the victims left in their wake; that would make him worthy of joining the comrades who had achieved martyrdom in the past few days and doubtless found the gates of Heaven open to them.

Suddenly, the rebel was snatched from this blissful fantasy by the array of staring eyes; row upon row of doll's eyes were watching the scene without blinking. With a colossal effort the rebel dragged his body upright and, careful all the while to avoid looking at the dolls, he moved forward defiantly to close the door and the four windows overlooking the walled roof terrace.

Gathering what remained of his flagging strength, the rebel dragged the captive to a wooden column in the middle of the room by the television set, sat him on a flowery quilt, and began to tie him to the pillar using some electricity cables he had found. Feverishly, even hysterically, he covered the dolls' faces with anything he could find at hand: scraps of paper, napkins. At last the rebel allowed his body to fall onto a spongy exercise mat that had been left in the room. The two men were sunk in a stupor, surrendered to the paralysis of the gas. The smell of the sweets in the piles of cartons in the corner wafted overhead, a delightful scent that contributed to the strangeness of the scene. Around them there rose a droning sound as giant flies, of a neon color somewhere between blue and green, buzzed among the cartons of sweets and the faces of the two men.

Day Two

THE OFFICER, RAPHAEL, WAS WOKEN by the twitching of his extremities and he released a string of curses in blunt French when he failed to free his hands from their restraints. With an iron will, he ignored the agony in his crotch, which had been crushed by the vicious kicking he had received. His eyes rested on the unconscious body lying on the tattered blue mat, and he was struck by the long black plaits slipping out from beneath the red-and-white head covering.

"Either these rebels are growing their hair to be like their ancestors or I've been tortured by an extremist fag."

He felt he was floating in this unreal reality, as if his naked body were immersed in self-contempt and mockery, incapable even of sweating and drawing out the fever building within. He was blinded by a splitting headache from the blows of the rifle butt; the numbness creeping over his genitals indicated that he might have been made impotent; the gas was making his brain ring with frightening absurdity. His throat was as dry as ash, while his heart and lungs erupted with lava, promising the destruction of that skinny rebel who had wounded his colossal ego and then tied him up like a broken-down dog.

Prodded by the thunderous glare of the officer, the rebel suddenly emerged from sleep. He hurriedly covered his braids and tucked them inside his head covering as he jumped up from his bed. With steadily increasing attention, the giant officer observed the graceful movements of the rebel's slim body, stoking his anger toward himself and his adversary.

Under the eyes of his captive, the rebel headed to the roof terrace the room looked onto. He walked doubled over so that his head was no higher than the wall, careful that no watchful eyes from the surrounding terraces should catch sight of him.

Fear and rage flared up inside him whenever he looked toward the Grand Mosque through the holes in the wall made by the decorative brick pattern. He was hunting desperately for information about the outcome of the siege, but the only indication he had that the siege was over was the cooing of doves mingling with the police and ambulance sirens; the gunfire at least had definitely ended. He could no longer prevent his body from convulsing as he realized that all his companions had been silenced forever.

Deranged with terror, Sayfullah rushed back to the room and headed straight to the cartons piled in the corner. Maddened by an attack of hunger, he tore off their covers blindly, dug out their contents, and began to gulp down the various sweets and biscuits. Officer Raphael was shocked at the contrast between the elegant little biscuits and the death manifest in the face of the rebel, the result of the long siege, starvation, and the final counterattack of gas and electrified water. Sayfullah's wandering gaze seemed unable to settle on anything, haunted as it was by the corpses of his fellow rebels and the piles of hostage victims.

Raphael glared at Sayfullah in fury; how the hell had such a worthless nothing managed to knock him down and strip him of his weapon?

Those Bedouin are possessed by jinn when they fight. He recalled that phrase from the hasty training sessions he and his comrades had attended in France before they were transported to break the siege on the Grand Mosque. That day, they had greeted the idea of jinn with roars of laughter; he and his iron-hard comrades considered the jinn an insult to their rock-solid Superman muscles and their sophisticated weaponry. The Groupe d'intervention de la Gendarmerie nationale, or GIGN for short, were sent all over the world to negotiate counter-terrorism and hostage rescue missions. They laughed at the idea that they could be scared by invisible beings.

When they don't fear death, they fight like demons. Their trainer warned them of underestimating the jinn and urged the GIGN officers to take them seriously.

As Raphael sat and watched the rebel devour sweets, he was consumed by a craving to rip the flesh off him with his bare hands, to uncover the jinni inside and tear it to pieces. If given the opportunity, he wouldn't stab or shoot; he would plunge steely fingers into those soft muscles.

Suddenly Sayfullah raced to the bathroom and vomited up everything he had swallowed, as if he were vomiting his very bowels.

When he returned to the room he seemed at a total loss, unsure what to do about his captive or the situation in general. With no particular aim in mind he brought a carton of biscuits to Raphael, freed his left hand from its restraint, and stood watching him eat. At the same time, he was angered at being so nerveless he was feeding his enemy.

"J'ai soif." Raphael mimed drinking water while Sayfullah stood watching him impassively, reveling in his thirst, aware that he had probably vanquished his victim, this Western infidel. In an outburst of fury, Raphael flung the box of biscuits away from him; immediately Sayfullah responded with a series of violent kicks to his chest and thighs from his bare feet. With his free left hand, Raphael abruptly seized the attacking foot and launched Sayfullah into the air so that he landed on his back. Feverishly, Raphael turned his attention to the cables that bound him, and was on the brink of freeing himself when Sayfullah hurled himself upon him, yelping, "God curse you, you filthy infidel!"

It was a losing battle between the half-bound French GIGN officer and the slim rebel, who wasn't haunted by jinn, but by the will of death itself; his spine and muscles were accompanied by hundreds of others—the spines and muscles of the murdered comrades he had left behind.

"I am nothing unless I am Sayfullah, the Sword of God, and I slice with the will of God," Sayfullah panted, regaining the upper hand and viciously retightening the cables around his opponent's wrists. "Try to escape again and I will throw you back into the hell pit you came from."

"You mad shit, you should be buried in those sewers with your cockroach friends!" the GIGN officer exploded in Arabic marked with a strong Algerian accent, much to Sayfullah's surprise. Petrol had been poured onto Raphael's hostility; he had felt the full insult of being called a filthy infidel.

"I'll starve you to death, dog, and I'll feed you to Hell piece by piece," Sayfullah said.

"The police dogs will hunt you down soon, and I'll enjoy watching them tear you limb from limb."

Verbal abuse gave Raphael a brutal pleasure. He felt his words sinking into the flesh of the infuriating rebel, leaving behind fissures impregnated with his hatred.

Spitting in Raphael's direction, Sayfullah headed for the stairs leading to the lower floors. Nervous, spasmodic movements revealed he was troubled in his mind and soul.

He descended the stairs, examining every floor. Like most houses around the Grand Mosque, the house was made from volcanic rock, and it was illuminated by a subdued light that crept in from windows covered with wooden latticework. All the ancient wooden doors had been replaced with iron doors, which were firmly locked, effortlessly mocking Sayfullah's desperate attempts to force them. Sweat was dripping from the rebel's face when he was forced to go back to the roof terrace. He felt he was falling into the trap of that warped playroom; it was a crude and derisive incongruity, a total discord with the scene of death he had wasted no time in escaping.

Hunger led Sayfullah to the kitchen connected to the playroom, where he was confronted with a farce: in all the drawers and on all the shelves, he found nothing but box after box of sweetened oatmeal for babies and high-fiber multi-seed Quaker Oats. He felt the insult to his comrades' martyrdom when he gave in and prepared the porridge. Every spoonful deepened the pit buried inside him. He sat opposite Raphael and silently ate the bodies of his comrades. Without preamble, he surprised his adversary by offering him some, and it was accepted without hesitation. The French officer obediently ate a spoonful of porridge, then another, faithful to his GIGN training to survive at all costs.

"I'm fattening you for the slaughter," Sayfullah muttered, justifying this generous impulse to himself and his opponent in an attempt to avoid focusing on the other's diabolical nakedness—the sinful nakedness that filled the room with hot, slick steam.

Although fear gave him a mounting lust for murder, Raphael was aware of the unreality and weirdness of the scene around him. He attributed it to the effects of the gas and the blows to his head. There was something ambiguous, something he couldn't explain in the body of his opponent who had deprived him of his metal armor. Was it the beating he had undergone at the hands of this nonentity, this skinny extremist? Or was it the humiliation he was savoring now, after years of moving through battlefields like an untouchable god, taking and bestowing life according to his will? Or was there an invisible force in this country of jinn and ghosts; something that shattered the armor surrounding his pride and stripped his ego of its grandeur? Raphael was deeply troubled; of all the emotions hatching inside him, terror was the most prominent. Human frailty was a betrayal of the image he had created for himself: he was a tank, a war machine with legs. With every passing minute, Raphael had the increasing and uncomfortable feeling he was a tortoise that had been stealthily and involuntarily pushed outside its steel shell.

There was something in Sayfullah's body and movements he couldn't explain. It reminded him of his own body in its adolescence, before he joined the GIGN and surrendered his body to brutal training, bodybuilding exercises, and anabolic steroids, until the moment came when he incorporated his mother's despotism and was able to kill the ghostly body of his father latent within him. Raphael's body had thrown off its leanness; it bulged and swelled like a magical giant released from a bottle. He had succeeded in burying his skinny body so deeply it could never emerge, but now this Bedouin nonentity had come along and brought it out of its grave. It had been returned to life, and with it a temptation to give into the vulnerability he had denied for so long. Raphael felt like a modern Narcissus, falling in love once again with an old image of himself.

Without realizing it, he was allowing something odd to weaken the killing mechanism constructed inside him by years of fighting on battlefields where people were worth no more than insects, where breaking a person's neck held the same satisfaction as smoking a cigarette after a rich meal, and where a human body crushed beneath your boots was a signature on a picture drawn in blood. The course of his life had been driven by anger till this point, but toward whom, or on account of what, he didn't know.

With profound self-contempt, the two enemies seemed to be floating inside a surreal hallucination, in a slippery, emotional nakedness, in such a way that the world, which had baptized them in blood, didn't touch them. Very gradually, their rhythm slowed, and they had no choice but to surrender to this snare, contemplating the world from above while they were separate from its laws and its restrictive templates.

The insurgents finally surrendered, more than two weeks after the first attack on the mosque. Clouds of dusty, disheveled, bearded ghosts were flung into the shadows of a locked truck. They were consumed by lice and filth, by starvation from the long siege and by the rage of the open-mouthed bodies all around them. They heaved a sigh of relief to be leaving a hell of their own making. The houses surrounding the Grand Mosque watched intently and in silence; none of the remaining inhabitants dared to feel safe or break the curfew until it was announced officially that the siege was over. News of the insurgents' surrender hadn't spread through the city yet, and whenever a bird landed, children and adults started in shock, deeply disturbed by the bullets, sights, and memories of those terrifying weeks; many residents still expected to be felled by a crazed bullet from one of the snipers who had been hunting them for a fortnight.

The courtyard of the Grand Mosque was sunk in total silence, spattered with blood and body parts, and human limbs blocked the path of the attacking soldiers. Gas clouds hovered over the scene, protecting the troops in blue and khaki as they scoured the halls, corridors, cellars, and minarets of the Grand Mosque, purging them of the last pockets of resistance.

The houses trembled from the influx of armored cars and tanks crawling along the roads. From peepholes and cracks in windows, eyes peered out onto a string of military trucks carrying the bodies of the dead, thrown into indiscriminate piles; they had not been covered with khaki canvas. The vehicles proceeded along al-Khalil Street then turned south to Bir Yakhour, where their cargo would be thrown into a mass grave and forcibly forgotten.

Flocks of doves watched from the rooftops, unsure whether it was safe to resume flying over the Grand Mosque alongside the giant birds with metal rotors. Their memories still held images of bearded snipers in the minarets who had fired on every moving shadow.

Presently, a group of families overcame their terror. They rushed to assist in cleaning up the mosque, eager to hurry the moment when the minarets would shower them with the call to prayer, rather than random bullets. However, most houses remained paralyzed by rumors that some of the rebels on the outskirts of the mosque had escaped. These rumors were corroborated by the gunfire that broke out in various districts of the city, the result of attempts to capture them.

Day Three

Sayfullah walked through the room barefoot, his face and arms shining from his ablutions for prayer. He glanced around, looking for a spot where he could pray. Raphael watched, seeing Sayfullah's anxiety when he was unable to find a spot where he could escape seeing the girl who hunted him from the walls. Raphael closed his eyes, vanquished by the strong emotions swelling inside him. Growing rage was mixed with an attraction to the self he saw reflected in the mirror of that slim body. He was ashamed of admitting an intolerable need to squeeze and rend those arms, hairless and elegantly molded, and those long fingers, soft and as far from the fingers of a fighter as they could be; but despite their softness, they had left painful bruises on his body from their last struggle. The water from Sayfullah's ablutions softly illuminated his delicate features, and there was something in his movements while praying that unsteadied and hypnotized Raphael. The humiliation Raphael's body had endured, and the destruction of the steel shell that had protected him, had left him raw, and now he was in a state of excessive sensitivity; his senses were whetted to such a disorienting pitch that no movement or smell, not even the crawling of an ant, escaped him. His state of vigilance was painful.

Sayfullah stood as if nailed to the floor. He became conscious of the dolls, which he had pushed into the background and forgotten about. Now he felt the outlines of their faces were slipping out from beneath the covers he had placed on them and peering at him. Plastic arms and legs began to raise their coverings and writhe lasciviously, with a sinuousness that was almost liquid, scattering the angels who had descended to witness and receive his prayers. The plastic nakedness filled him with horror, the more so as he felt the Devil in those malignant gyrations which mocked him and his attempts to be purified of death, to evoke God in this room so He could apportion the reward of that lost battle.

Rapidly, he turned around so he could pray at the entrance of the room overlooking the terrace, offering his defenseless back as a target for the stares of the dolls and Raphael, which focused mockingly on his round backside. As Sayfullah performed his prostrations, his entire abdomen quivered, his blood rushed burning to his ears, and he lost his balance. He tumbled onto his hands and knees and the moment his forehead touched the ground, his dry eyelids exploded with scorching tears that blinded him as they fell onto the cold floor, and his limbs plunged into a long prostration, while he yearned for a hole or a grave in whose dust he could find peace.

"Oh Lord, I am Your broken sword if You do not guide me with Your mercy. The Devil is filling me with doubts; God, do you see me fleeing from him? I am nothing but Your slave. I surrendered to Your will for us there, when You struck us with an earthquake in Your sacred house, and You were our witness when we fought to the last breath, and our hearts were in our throats and we looked into the eyes of Azrael the angel of death. I ran away so I could continue fighting, and here I am, in Your hands, but I am too weak for this test. It is beyond any test You sent me before."

Something bombarded Raphael's heart when he caught Sayfullah's faint wail. He could hear the explosion in senses that for years he had thought impregnable, incapable of being moved or softened. The sight of Sayfullah squatting on his prayer mat made Raphael quiver uncontrollably. He had a vision not of Sayfullah's body, but of his own, Raphael's, squatting in exactly that position while he was mounted by countless destructive human monsters. Long-repressed memories escaped from the bottle where he had imprisoned them all these years, and here he was, confronting the incident that had occurred during the second month of the hellish exercise he had embarked on in order to join the GIGN forces. For two months they had driven him beyond the limit of endurance; for two months, which lasted an eternity, he had been tempted to throw himself into the path of a stray bullet or an exploding bomb so the torture would end. Inevitably, his trainers caught the scent of his desperation, and it pushed them to ensnare him in even more violence so he would be driven to exceed his capabilities. It had happened during a survival exercise in the wild, when they were flown to the rainforests of Madagascar. Each of them was left to battle nature and find a way to survive. Raphael had found himself in a lost world, haunted by fabled creatures and turbulent conditions. This primitive theater had been carefully selected to pluck out the last roots of gentleness and humanity hidden within them, on both a physical and a psychological level.

Raphael had hardly jumped out in his parachute when he was swept away by a tropical storm and flung thousands of feet down a precipice into the flooded rainforests. Caverns ran underground where sunlight couldn't penetrate. Even if there had been light, Raphael wouldn't have been able to see; his senses were dulled after hours spent wandering through intersecting caves filled with darkness and damp, foul-smelling algae, and calcified rats. A hostile, implacable world snatched him up and he plunged deeper and deeper until he finally hit the bottom, shackled by mud and tree bark and creatures it was impossible to imagine.

Raphael stumbled on, trying to discover a path, any path, but he couldn't get far or even follow his compass. Every piece of equipment he was carrying proved ineffectual in his hands; he had fallen victim to his inner lack of direction. He was like an insect in the face of the forest of never-ending trees and rivers that suddenly gushed forth and then dried up, and vicious traps that multiplied all around him. Numb, Raphael curled up under a mass of roots that had grown into a sort of canopy, and he lit a sluggish fire that emitted no light or warmth and only succeeded in lengthening the threatening shadows all around. He didn't dare to move as his shadow bulged and spilled over everything, in every direction. Wherever he turned there was nothing but his own self, lying in wait, engorged and attracting the endless monsters who roamed this island. Raphael couldn't lie down. Everything was slipping under his feet; the earth was covered with a carpet of lizards like miniature omens of misfortune, and over his head hung a bower of boas, of every snake from the seven continents, hissing and twining and staring at him. He didn't dare leave the canopy; all around his refuge he had been able to hear the bellowing of that mythical bull which moved relentlessly, fast as lightning, devouring everything in its path. Those myths provoked none of the mockery now that they had in the training programs. He and his comrades had laughed at those beings, those imaginary creatures that had risen from the heads of the primitive and naive Malagasy, but in these lethal forests those myths were more real and dangerous than the sophisticated weapons on his back.

An age seemed to pass while Raphael hoped the forest would retreat and leave him alone to rot—or that all its demons would descend on him and rip him apart. He was in the perfect place to give up and die, but the wait became more oppressive than dying itself. He had to move on through this nonexistence. Sometimes at a crawl, sometimes at a blind gallop, he began to push through cavities and hollows that contained no distinguishing features other than their skin-flaying humidity. It was difficult to determine whether it was night or day as sunlight couldn't reach the bottom of the trees, and Raphael spent days in the several caves he came across, letting his body slip from one humid womb to another even more dank and dark. Bladelike plants left deep wounds in his aching body, and once he turned away from a human corpse that had been dispatched to his pit to rot. As he walked, burdened with revulsion and despair, some ghost came between him and the discovery of a way out of this hell. Things had lost all meaning; the lines and the knowledge of the maps he carried were useless. He began to be convinced that all human life had vanished, everything had drowned in the darkness, nothing was left but ghosts hatched out of the nothingness that dug into the wounds he had unknowingly buried since childhood. He sat in the undergrowth and probed the scars made by his father's suffering, itself caused by his mother's repeated betrayals. He plunged into the depths of his father's despair; the same despair that had possessed him as an adolescent and driven him to join the army with the aim of taking revenge on life in general. His father's anguish was infinite and it ate away at Raphael in the same way bones are crumbled by humidity, so that he was no longer sure how much time he had spent on this island. Minutes? Hours? An age? There was no time of any kind here, nor any will to go on. He didn't care about time. All his attention was concentrated in finding a ray of light, any light, even if it was the light of death, but he kept roaming through a nihilistic slice of pitch blackness. Minutes swelled into hours without noticeable alteration, like a fat black scorpion hiding from view.

Except for the moment when his heightened senses caught the sound of a twig breaking, a faint *tick* almost beyond hearing, and hope of survival re-awoke in Raphael. He wheeled around impatiently, only to find his body crushed onto a giant root that rose from the earth like a platform. He had been thrown so he was kneeling face downward, like a sacrificial offering to the demon now sucking his body, pinned down and open for desecration. His trousers were torn away, his guts congealed when claws scoured them, countless claws were plunging into his flesh; against all logic, he was certain they belonged to the demons of this forest, given physical form in order to punish him, and at the same time he heard wails breaking out all around like newborn babies. Faintly, a memory came back of their trainer telling them about Malagasy children born on inauspicious dates, who were left on anthills to be eaten alive. He could feel the soft flesh in his belly being gnawed by the fangs of a ruthless ant. However much he struggled, he couldn't succeed in freeing his body. It was pinned down for what seemed like an eternity while dry stalks burrowed into his guts and lecherous spears tore his anus mercilessly, answering his deeply rooted need to destroy his being and self beyond hope of repair, until the pain brought him to a climax that burst his heart and soul like a blister.

Afterward, he was left alone. A trail of blood trickled behind him as he walked, and not an insect, beast, or shadow dared to follow him. The entire forest was revolted by the rot of his bowels that had been infected by a demon's sperm.

The smell of semen guided him while he was at the summit of pain, beyond pain. He left his weapons behind, along with the state-of-the-art survival kit they had armed him with when they dropped him into this hell. Half-naked, he began to grope his way forward. He didn't bother with concealment; his feverish wound gave him additional senses that helped him decipher the darkness.

At some point, an enormous apparition appeared in front of him, layers of pitch-black wrinkles flowing over gleaming white bones. This skeleton was the first light to appear on his path; its burning eyes were like live coals, illuminating slack lips drawn like a short veil over long teeth.

The vision beckoned to Raphael, but its feet gave Raphael cause for doubt; they pointed backward. Raphael wanted to turn and run away but the giant clothed with wrinkles wouldn't let him retreat. It pointed, indicating that Raphael should cross the sea of crystal blades spreading out before him, sharp blades nature had formed so close together there was no way of passing between them and no way of walking over them. Raphael wanted to escape, but wherever he turned the wrinkled giant was there, guiding him deeper and deeper. Raphael followed, trampling the crystal knives in a state of numbness. He didn't care whether the apparition was leading him to his destruction. He followed automatically, as if he were following an instinct, until the vision brought him to the entrance of a huge cavern, a pit of nothingness like the depths of his soul at that moment, and invited him to enter. At once he was swept away into its flooded and endless tunnels, and although he couldn't see anything, he was sure that the walls of this cave were lined with corpses. A voice in his head affirmed that it was a mass grave left over from some colonial war or other, and he remembered his trainer's warnings of the taboos of the Malagasy. He had said, "Never point your finger at a grave, or that finger will fall off." It was a ridiculous superstition, but nevertheless Raphael was careful to keep his fist closed and avoided pointing at the graves arrayed close together around him. He wondered whether he had been forced into participating in famadihana, the ritual of bone-turning, when the Malagasy dug up the bodies of their dead relatives and wrapped them in new shrouds to keep them happy. He was lightheaded at this moment of nonexistence, and wondered whether he should re-shroud his father; his mother deserved no such satisfaction.

Raphael realized he was surrounded by skeletons, white lined with black, crowned with skulls leaning at contemplative angles as they watched his passage and illuminated the cavern with their bones. As soon as Raphael exchanged a glance with them, their eye sockets began to resemble his father's eyes, gouged out by humiliation, and they sucked him in.

It was a moonlit night when he was launched back into life like a missile, and he found himself floating on the Indian Ocean. The night was calm and his feverish body, flayed and wounded, was gathered up by its cool touch. Tranquility eased his passage from the earth's crushing bowels to its surface, made resplendent by the reflections of the stars. He abandoned his body to the salty waves and the wind, realizing that he had found his way out of the forest at last.

When he was reunited with his division, he resisted all attempts to submit him to treatment. In silence, he endured fever, bowel rot, and the suspicion that it was his comrades who had raped him. They had overpowered him and bullied him since he joined the forces, seeing something twisted in him: the fragility created by his mother. It was a half-invitation to violation, and they had responded to that invitation, making sure to cure him of that fragility by their actions. But Raphael, newly formed by Madagascar, had severed every link with his past and his human weakness, aware that wherever he went, those forests and its demons would be carried living in his belly.

Afterward, he never allowed a single ray of sunlight to pierce the rot inside him and heal it.

Fury, inconducive to healing, caused him to excel at his training in extermination and turned him into something exceptional. One look at him no longer revealed a mortal man, but death itself.

Now this young, graceful rebel was praying and kneeling in front of him. It was his own past, violated body made manifest, and yet, like a mirror, it reflected his confusion about his true sexuality and the mask of brutality that protected his fragility. The mask had fallen now, that mask of a GIGN killing machine, and out of the deeps, like a radiant bubble of humanity, the delicate adolescent he had buried in the caverns of Madagascar had emerged. He didn't know why, but he found himself ensnared in feelings of tenderness toward Sayfullah; or rather, he had fallen victim to the need to protect him.

Suddenly, Raphael was struck by the insight that he had once again succumbed to the idea of destroying himself. He realized that in surrendering to captivity without seriously attempting to escape, in allowing this rebel to bewitch him, he had betrayed the military training that had turned him into a machine driven by commands without reference to his own logic. He wondered whether, by disobeying commands, he had committed the suicide he had postponed for so long.

He sat there, observing the transformation he had submitted to. It was not merely a psychological transformation; even his muscles seemed to be contracting in his body's attempt to regain the grace he had lost when he joined the army. Was this the effect of the gas? Or had the jinn in this rebel's body cast their nets over him and put a spell on him?

Sayfullah remained still for a long time, his forehead touching the ground, his heart burning to repeat his prayer, while he trembled from the unbearable coldness in his soul.

"O Guide, O Path, guide me with a miracle, or help me to kill this infidel and surrender myself to the fire of my pursuers with a heart of stone."

Finally Sayfullah finished his prayers. He turned to the rearrangement of the room. Frozen in flight on the walls, the little girl watched him while he began to clear the empty biscuit boxes and line them up neatly against the wall. As an ominous darkness fell on the room, Sayfullah seemed hypnotized, staring blankly ahead while his hand twisted a napkin. He began to gather up the dolls, trying not to touch them with his bare hands or look directly into their bright blue eyes. A gasp ran around the walls when he cut off the first head and threw it into the nearest box. A second head followed, and a third, and for a long while he was absorbed in decapitating the hypnotic dolls. He filled three boxes to the brim with heads, but the imprisoned blue eyes bored through the boxes to witness the rest of the slaughter. When he had finished, Sayfullah piled the headless bodies in a corner and covered them with a red blanket. Then, full of revulsion, he began to rip the cotton dolls apart, one after another, emptying their cotton stuffing and filling the place with white dust as he threw their empty fabric skins and withered faces into the bin.

The girl on the walls quivered when he turned to face her. He took up a knife and began to scrape her off the walls; his violent blows left deep wounds on her joyfully flying feet, but he only succeeded in scraping the surface layer of color off her neck and face, which were too high for him to reach. A long way from the knife, the girl closest to the ceiling watched the disfigurement befalling her feet and her reflections nearer the ground in terror. But however much he scraped and stabbed, specters of the girl remained, perfectly whole and engrossed in the ecstasy of her unrestrained flight over the wall; she was wounded but still sparkling with joy, and free.

Raphael felt his demons reflected in these slaughtered dolls, but he resisted the temptation to fuel his disgust at the rebel who had been occupied with breathing life into the powerless dolls and turning them into an enemy army.

Mocking Sayfullah was Raphael's only way of reclaiming what he was: an officer of exceptional ability, master of the destinies of individuals and countries, capable of exterminating every living thing on the face of the earth.

Sayfullah felt Raphael's eyes on him. He stopped abruptly and turned a sullen face toward the officer. "Get ready to join them in Hell."

"You're hunting a girl on a wall? God, you're a nothing." He wanted that word to strike like a lightning bolt and reduce his enemy to ash. "Nothing."

But when no lightning bolt hit the room and his enemy was still standing, Raphael couldn't bring himself to continue the abuse.

"You're nothing but a hostage to demons of your own invention, and the weapon you hold is tempting you to play God."

Sayfullah closed his ears in the face of this blasphemy, murmuring, "Astaghfir Allah, astaghfir Allah, may God forgive me . . ."

Day Four

THE SOUND THAT FLARED UP in the silence caused Sayfullah to rush out of the bathroom, only to be blinded by the television screen. Having profited from his deep sleep, Raphael had succeeded in reaching a foot to the television and switching it on.

"This group, composed of the enemies of God and the corrupt of the earth, are sentenced to . . ."

The voice of the broadcaster quavered, heralding doom. Sayfullah found himself suddenly facing a huge screen filled with the faces of his comrades. He stood there, paralyzed by the shock of seeing the people with whom he had lived for over a year, with whom he had shared food and fear during the siege. Surely every country from east to west was frozen in front of their television screens, following the investigation? The television continued to show and reshow lengthy clips of the surrendered rebels as they confessed their crimes and claimed the ultimate punishment as their due. Their eyes were vacant, staring directly into the next world, and the death sentence hovered over their matted heads as they confessed in the hope of avoiding further torture. Even their faith in Paradise had been shaken, but as they had no choice but to cling to that promise, they were keen to leave this life. Hours of interrogation and torture had wrung their bodies and souls dry, and words like *justice*, *equality*, and *faith* had turned to ashes in dry throats clogged with blood. To onlookers, they seemed to have fallen into a trap, having utterly lost faith in everything.

Sayfullah trembled, wresting himself away from the horror of this shock. He smashed the television screen with his rifle. "Satan's eye! It's cursed Satan's eye!" he spat, aiming a blow of the rifle butt at Raphael's head. Blood poured from the wound in the GIGN officer's temple, and he released a string of curses.

"You idiot, they're hunting you down while you hide here like a blind bat pretending that the siege has ended and you're a heroic survivor." Drained, Sayfullah dragged himself to the darkest corner of the room, and a wary silence settled over the two men. Time passed slowly while Sayfullah remained in his place, barely breathing, looking at nothing. His face was a dead man's, mirroring the devastation on the faces that had appeared on the television screen. He didn't know whether he fell asleep or whether time simply dropped him and he sank beneath the city's notice, but when he got up, the blood on Raphael's temple had congealed and turned black. Mechanically, Sayfullah moved to the kitchen and began to prepare porridge, mixed with the bodies of his comrades. A thought stuck to his skull: they had all gone to Heaven and left the flimsiness of the body to worms like him. He kept stirring and swallowing feverishly, as if the scene on the television were just a nightmare that had now vanished from his mind.

"Listen, we can't keep torturing each other like this," Raphael said. "We're at a dead end, and we should find a way of settling this situation. I have a deal for you . . . Face facts: you're a captive here just like me . . ." Sayfullah's twitching jaw indicated to Raphael that he was suffering from overstrained nerves, and he went on: "Believe me, we can leave this house, and each of us can go our own way. We don't have to meet the same fate your friends did; no one has any way of knowing your role there, or even that you exist. I promise you, I'll forget I ever met you."

Sayfullah broke into laughter, which infuriated Raphael. "You laugh like a woman," he exclaimed in amazement, staring hungrily at the slender figure in front of him, its slim hips threatening to shatter under the pressure of that appetizingly round backside. Something in the air around them shifted at that moment, a tacit but dangerous change. Sayfullah blushed, and he moved outside the range of Raphael's disconcerting stare.

"Wait! Think about it. I can guarantee your safety . . ."

Like a whirlwind, Sayfullah hurtled back into the room, grabbed Raphael's throat, and began to squeeze. He hissed, "Infidel, you and your like worship the vain life of this earth, because it's your only chance. You will all fall into Hell as soon as you die as a punishment for the sin of worshiping life."

Raphael was shocked to find himself aroused by Sayfullah's hands around his throat; despite the pain, he felt a pleasurable numbness trickling down his spine, and he was blinded by an inexplicable sadistic thrill at this violent connection with his enemy.

Sayfullah leaped away from the muscled neck, stung by the perfection of that naked body. He moved away, disconcerted and self-conscious, rebuking himself for having undressed the man. But there was no longer any way of covering up the enemy, neither this Frenchman nor the enemy inside himself.

"Someone like you can't guarantee anything to someone like me. I am a jihadi—we left our homes and our families and promised to meet them again only in Paradise. There is no life for us on your vain earth."

Raphael resisted the desire to laugh out loud at this idiot who was determined to ignore the struggle inside him and like a tape player kept repeating that Paradise was reserved for him and his comrades. The sardonic smile on his face provoked Sayfullah, and he snarled, "Until now, I haven't done anything to fulfill the pledge of eternal life in Heaven, but you were sent to me as a miracle. Either I use you as a hostage to negotiate for the release of my comrades in prison or, if that fails . . ." His voice betrayed him. His confused mind struggled to know what to do with his hostage. "If I kill an enemy like you, God will give me a palace in Heaven."

"Fine. Let's get it over with. Shoot me and get your throne in Heaven. Because I won't help you get what you want on earth. You can't exchange me for anything. And soon you'll be facing some very angry people all by yourself. As you saw on the television, there won't be an easy death in store for you at their hands. You'll endure horrific torture."

Somehow his words succeeded in shaking Sayfullah's mask.

"Whoever fights in the path of God will never be alone. God is with me. As for what you think, I'm not so naive that I'll end your torment so easily. You have no hope of reaching Heaven—not in this life, and not in the next."

"Ah, so now you're Heaven's doorman, and my word, what an egotistical doorman you are! Tell me: who are the lucky ones on your list worthy of Heaven?" Raphael greatly enjoyed quarreling with Sayfullah. "Look out, boy; maybe I deserve to be in Heaven more than any of you. Consider that I've converted to Islam, and pronounced the Shahada—'*I testify that there is no God but God and Muhammad is His prophet*'—and I was allowed to enter the Grand Mosque. You, on the other hand, had to skulk inside with your insurgent friends." Raphael was maneuvering to crumple Sayfullah's mask; he considered this as important as killing him.

"Speaking Arabic and pronouncing the Shahada don't make you a real Muslim. My ancestors are the Ikhwan. They helped found this country, and didn't hesitate to go to war with it when it established diplomatic relations with the foreigners and allowed them to come to our country." Sayfullah was shocked to hear himself automatically repeating Mujan's sermons, which had bored into his memory.

"What does a boy like you know about international politics? Your ruler was building a state while Mujan was brainwashing ignorant boys like you in that godforsaken desert camp." Sayfullah was mortified and Raphael pressed on: "What's so shameful in dealing with other nations? To my knowledge, the Prophet said, 'Seek knowledge, even in China.' He didn't say, 'Boycott the Chinese and kill them.'"

Sayfullah closed his ears against this logic, which threatened to disrupt the beliefs he had been living out for months. But the discussion forged a new, human space between the two men; it seemed to have stripped them of their mechanical impulse to kill and left them as mere humans, faced with each other and their own weakness and limitations before all else.

"You think you are the authority that can grant a certificate of faith? Who decides who is the believer and who the infidel?" Raphael exploited Sayfullah's silence and went on: "Look, I spent time in North Africa on a mission for the forces. I learned Arabic and the fundamentals of Islam, and the most important thing I learned was that faith is in the heart, and only God knows the truth of it. What makes you think you know what's in my heart? But still you put me on trial and pass a death sentence on me?"

Turmoil overwhelmed Sayfullah, and he rushed to attack: "You're a sinful demon, I know that much." He spoke in a tense voice, betraying weakness.

Raphael took advantage of it: "Can you explain why you destroyed the television yesterday when you need to know what happened to your friends outside?"

They looked at each other, the traces of desperation evident to both. Fissures were gradually widening in their hearts while each tried to penetrate the defenses of the other, one aiming to escape, the other aiming for martyrdom and a throne in Heaven.

"Television is the false messiah," Sayfullah said. "It's the secret agent of you Westerners, and you use it to invade the world and program our people with your iniquitous messages. You make us addicted to the temptations of naked women and devilish music and promises of eternal Heaven on earth. You use it to train people and enlist them in your army against our creed, and those who are naive and whose hearts or faith are weak fall easily into your trap, while our destiny is to fight your deceit. Everything shown on this screen is nothing but a delusion you have fabricated to ensnare us."

"Do you really consider yourself worthy of Heaven while you hide here and do nothing but threaten me, instead of continuing the fight out there and being defeated with your comrades?"

Raphael knew he was taking a chance by challenging Sayfullah in this way, but the young rebel suddenly sank to the ground, the ultimate expression of despair and exhaustion.

"You sound like a frustrated mother," Sayfullah said.

Raphael hadn't expected this sudden change in tone, but he hurriedly encouraged it: "Yes, our mothers' words are probably the first nails in our coffins. If they don't believe in us, it distorts us for life." Raphael sensed an inward shift in Sayfullah as his cruelty subsided, leaving room for cynical indifference.

"My mother raised me by wrapping me in white, like a shroud. She couldn't stand anyone who stayed in the shadows."

The bitterness in Sayfullah's words didn't escape Raphael. "No?"

"It's beyond belief, how strong my mother was. She's the type that can't die." Sayfullah's confession was almost inaudible. "She was molded from the kind of steel that can't bend. Or perhaps it can only bend in God's hands." The insolence with which he was treating his mother terrified him, but he couldn't control himself. "Now, finally, my poor mother is freed from the greatest of her sins: the shadow she raised as the twin to her favorite child, the shadow that mourned over her grave for days in agony, wondering whether she had been tormented by raising that ghost, that nothing." Sayfullah stopped talking suddenly, his eyes glinting madly as he looked straight into his mother's grave.

"Was it a curse to be born from a steel womb, the ghost of a steel twin?" Raphael took no chances in imitating Sayfullah's words, fearing to shatter the crystalline transparency, so very unexpected, of his dialogue with himself.

"You know, twins are the cruelest creation. You share the fate of a single person, and most of the time one gets the best of everything, and the other becomes a freak." Sayfullah kept talking to himself. "We mustn't burn the dead with our tears. That is how we were raised; they hammered it into us that wailing scalds the dead in the graves. Why did I wail so much? Did I really mean to burn her with every tear and every sob?" His eyes wandered over the objects around him in an attempt to avoid the open grave in front of him, the fire he had touched to his mother's body. "Dying as a martyr would have been like a medal for her. But I chose to escape like this, so I've deprived her of a medal yet again." Immediately, Sayfullah

32

regretted having allowed these words, all this hatred and rage, to escape from their prison. He hurriedly restrained himself and amended his admission. "May God punish me for this disrespect."

Realizing it was his turn, Raphael succumbed to confession. "You could say that my mother was also an iron woman. She killed my desire for all women. Toughness in a woman is a matter of pride for us—a mark of equality between the sexes. But a mother's cruelty turns us into distorted creatures nothing like our real selves." Raphael resisted a sudden burst of rage, suppressed since his youth, at his family's allusions to the femininity he had shown as a teenager. There was more sensitivity and grace in him than femininity, perhaps as a reaction to his mother's controlling personality; but even so, they tormented him with their insinuations.

"Mujan and the people in Wajir, the settlement where I was born, all know that they nursed at the ghoul's breast; that's why every attempt to wean us from this milk, and to get us used to civilization in the settlement, has failed." Sayfullah paused, listening to the echo of his words, which he had never dared to say out loud before. "The ghoul's milk creates iron women, but they exist behind a veil; they only dare to reveal their iron faces to their children. Now I can feel my mother's soul burning with her curses, she never stopped cursing me and the fate that had allotted her such a child."

"After my father, my mother moved onto three other men," Raphael said. "None of them was able to live with her so they pulled away, and we paid the price."

The resentment of Raphael's confession infected Sayfullah. Seemingly incapable of curbing his ramblings, he declared bitterly, "In the desert, they sent us out to nurse from the ghoul, the ferocious spirits that roam the sand, so that their milk would make our hearts into iron. I was lost in the desert for a whole night and they found me in the morning, suckling from a gazelle. I failed where my iron twin succeeded; there is no doubt he drank the blood of the ghoul."

"Your iron twin?" As soon as Raphael asked the question, he

realized his mistake.

Sayfullah twitched like he was waking up from a nap, realizing he had veered off course. He threw Raphael a look of doubt that was more like hatred, tempted to kill him then and there to obliterate everything he had revealed about himself. But instead of picking up his gun, Sayfullah went out to the terrace and stood there staring at the sky. He was waiting for a shooting star to annihilate him and end his torture, or for a miracle to descend on him.

A faint creak turned his attention again to the room, and he remembered what the old men in Wajir had declared: "When the furniture creaks, an angel is present." He turned to inspect the room. He sighed, his aching heart plunging as it sought to escape him and his burden.

"What is stopping the angels from touching my heart?" he said. "But what can I expect—a heart molded by gazelle's milk can only be crushed." He had no doubt the creak came from the boxes of severed doll heads.

Raphael followed Sayfullah's tentative gaze and took advantage of it to continue chipping away at Sayfullah's confidence and composure. "They're watching you. You know very well that they never stopped. Boxes can't cover Satan's eyes."

Sayfullah didn't smile; he took Raphael's sarcasm seriously. He hurried into the kitchen, unearthed a sharp knife from the drawers, and went back to the room. Wrenching open the boxes, he began to stab the plastic heads one after another, gouging out the eyes. He gathered the eyes into a blue pile and began grinding the glass under his rifle butt. But however much he pounded, it was difficult to avoid their gaze.

Here and there a cracked eyeball escaped and struck the wall, watching him from a distance. Another violent blow sent one horrifying monstrosity flying under the kitchen cupboard where it lurked ominously, observing Sayfullah's desperate attempts to retrieve it. He lay prostrate in front of the cupboard, trying to use his rifle to penetrate the narrow gap and draw out the eye, but he failed; the eye and its wrath plunged further into darkness.

"Now I've no doubt you were the sniveling twin," said Raphael.

The sneer opened old wounds in Sayfullah's heart. His eyes gleamed madly. "Swords were not made to snivel," he said, and he struck Raphael's face, inscribing those words in both their heads. He was discovering the profound unspoken pleasure that came from unrestrained violence, the same inclination that had deserted him during the occupation of the Grand Mosque.

Strewn about the room, the fragile blue eyes continued watching Sayfullah's madness with a mixture of defiance and terror.

Day Five

THERE WAS NOTHING BUT DARKNESS. A ray of moonlight stole in from the terrace and swept over the shattered blue eyes. Sayfullah was sleeping like the dead. For an hour that seemed like an age, Raphael continued to pant in his struggle against his restraints, until he finally succeeded in freeing his hands and sank to the floor, unable to believe his luck. Cautiously, he crept toward the rifle lying to the right of the sleeping Sayfullah, and his hand seized it at the same moment his gaze fell on Sayfullah's full, parted lips glowing in the moonlight. Raphael's fingers closed around the weapon. He was ready to rush down the stairs and out of that place, but his body wouldn't obey him. His insides contracted, his eyes fogged with heat, and his trembling hands sweated with an unnamable desire. As if in a trance, he pressed his burning mouth to the lips falling open in the shadows. At the gentle touch of his lips, Sayfullah's opened deeper, responding hungrily to his hunger, and the two bodies cleaved together in a feverish embrace.

Time stopped, but Sayfullah was floating, his body torn away. The fog of naked desire and hatred in his eyes tore at Raphael.

Shaken to the core, Sayfullah didn't know what to do. Both were lying there, each staring at the belly of the other.

Raphael had pinned Sayfullah's body to the ground like a terrified animal, using his lips swollen from his enemy's bites and the rifle pointing at his head. "Listen," he said. "Mad dogs are roaming the city right now looking for escaped cowards like you; there's an attractive bounty on every head collected. Even if you don't hang around here to be tortured and put out of your misery by the state,

I only have to drag you to the street. As soon as the mob sets eyes on you, they'll tear you to pieces."

Like two beasts, they stared at each other, eyeball to eyeball. Sayfullah seemed relieved at having ceded control to his enemy, and Raphael wondered whether his ties had been left a little loose on purpose.

"Fine. What are you waiting for? Kill me." The barely audible words quavered like echoes in Sayfullah's head.

"Oh no, it's not that simple. A worse fate is waiting for you at the hands of the Lord."

It wasn't the threat, but the trembling smile in Raphael's eye that made Sayfullah's jaw quiver.

"Maybe I don't seem like a soldier to you," Raphael said. "Actually . . . it's not usual for a soldier to have the thoughts I have now. Since I saw you I've been haunted by one temptation: to hear the shell you've built around yourself shatter. A moron like you presents a challenge I can't ignore. You're a terrified piece of shit, a juvenile fool who doesn't know anything about the world apart from the clichés dug up by his own perverted mind."

Sayfullah spat in his face and was startled when Raphael licked it up with provocative pleasure. Nonchalantly, he pushed away Raphael's hand, the one pointing the gun at him, and then lashed out suddenly with a kick to Raphael's groin.

They fell into another struggle; Sayfullah seemed to have lost his earlier ferocity, as if the rage which had driven him had been wrested away, and it was easy for the Frenchman's flexed muscles to crush his slender body into submission. Raphael pushed Sayfullah's face into the wall and secured his body there between his thighs. He took Sayfullah's head between his hands as though to break his neck, but instead his right hand crept forward of its own accord, sliding the length of the arched back to the slim hip, where his touch softened, sliding sensuously over the round backside, and found its way between the slender thighs.

"Merde!" The Frenchman exploded, shocked by what he had touched. At once, his hand began to tear the clothes away from the skinny body, which had begun to resist him desperately, only to end up pinned to the wall like a statue while its sex was exposed.

"A woman?" Raphael spat in fury. "All this time, I was defeated by a woman? Me? A GIGN officer?"

A vein in his head exploded from rage and blood gushed from his nose. Defeated, furious with himself, he surrendered to the fact that the doubts about his sexuality that had followed him all his life had come to this: a woman disguised in male clothing. What an utter farce; here was life presenting him with another betrayal.

"I am Sayf, a man like the other fighters."

Her uncowed haughtiness ruptured Raphael's latent aggression, and he blindly aimed blows at her face, at his mother's face, at his comrades with their bared teeth, at his father, at himself.

The girl received the blows without trying to shield her face; she struggled fiercely to free her hands in order to cover her nakedness. Being naked in front of a man overpowered any hell she feared to face in the afterlife.

Suddenly Raphael grasped what those small hands were trying to do; they were absorbed in pulling a coat around her to cover her sex, leaving her bloody cheeks exposed to his slaps.

This pitiful idea paralyzed his hands. The stupidity of such a reaction had floored him. A trail of fresh blood streamed from the left corner of the woman's mouth and down her neck, and her dark-red cheeks were an indication of his own weakness, which he had masked with cruelty. He felt more feeble and squalid than he ever had in the darkest hours of his life; he had never felt so young, even when he was raped.

He ignored the blood gushing from his nose and the convulsions deep within. He trained his savage gaze on the black triangle between her legs, aiming rays of hatred and contempt like a knife at the figure responsible for his degradation. If he didn't want to rape her physically, he wanted to wound her deeply, to perforate the virginity of her pride and dignity. She welcomed this humiliation; her pupils dilated madly and her body was paralyzed under the masculine gaze penetrating her very bones.

I am dead. A suicidal wish clamored in her veins, inciting her body to disintegrate and escape this disgrace. In one way or another, she was relieved to have surrendered control of the situation to this man who called himself a "jijin" officer, even though the word didn't mean anything to her. Would killing him have meant something? Had she missed out on a heroic deed? What was the importance of all this?

Suddenly Raphael's strength ebbed. He smashed his fist into the wall and received a jolt of pain, which eased the self-hatred overwhelming him.

Pointing the rifle at her head, Raphael began to search the pocket of the National Guard uniform she had used as disguise. He came across an identity card thrust into the chest pocket and compared the picture on the card with her face, reading the name Sayf al-Qutaybi. He aimed a vicious blow at her midriff, asking, "Who did you steal this from?"

Her resistance collapsed at seeing the bloodstain on the card. As if trying to control a fit of hysteria, she slapped her own cheeks: what had she done to Sayfullah's identity card? Terror froze her and she felt the knife of the past at work in her brain, scraping away the layers of pretense and the armor she had built around unbearable pain.

For the first time, she grasped the shocking truth she had tried to ignore: she was Sarab, a girl, and Sayf was the name of the twin brother she had revered, but as soon as the opportunity offered itself, she had pounced on it like an eagle, stealing his name and his identity. Of course she deserved to end up naked in front of this infidel; a mere woman lacking brains and religion, in thrall to this jijin officer who was probably a sort of infidel jinni; a woman ready to go to Hell for her nakedness.

She longed to snatch that card from under Raphael's contaminating stare. The pain of discovering a spot of that beloved blood on the card overwhelmed the pain of her sinful nakedness. She felt her brother's blood point an accusing finger at her, and the picture on the card nailed her to the spot with the same exasperated look he always gave her. That look of displeasure was the only comment he ever passed on her existence, and as she accepted how much she deserved it, the dam broke in Sarab's heart. She collapsed to the ground, not caring to cover herself, perhaps even wallowing in her humiliation. She sat gazing blankly at the opposite wall. She stared unblinking at the little girl. She was hypnotized by the unrestrained frivolity of that figure, who hadn't been slow to take advantage of Sarab's sudden surrender; the girl had dared to resemble her, and declare her resemblance with the same cheerfulness that had always been categorically denied to Sarab.

Sarab sat there at the mercy of her captor. That mercy allowed her, a girl, to confront the atrocities of the past three weeks, and everything that led her to where she was now, naked.

To Medina

WHEN HIS MOTHER DIED, SAYF fell into an abyss. He searched for consolation in the desert, hunting bustards as if pursuing the ghosts haunting him. He seemed deaf, but would instantly explode at any attempt to try to pull him out of his sense of loss.

Sarab was aware that her brother savored the state of mourning, immersing himself in it. Whenever he shot at a bird and missed, she felt the bullet hit the sky. But however much she understood the ferocity of his grief, it didn't lessen the shock when she woke up one dawn to find him gathering their father's guns and preparing to disappear from their hometown, Hijrat al-Wajir. She quelled her breathing and the terror that coursed through her veins like poison, turning her face purple, and she didn't dare ask him why or where. She followed him on tiptoe, hoping not to anger him in case he turned her away and made her return to Wajir. Hidden by the shadows of dawn, they slunk away; even the dogs, which usually were pleased to see her, watched them in silence. The two boyish figures were almost identical: dark-faced Sayf with the beard he hadn't shaved in months, followed by Sarab like a faithful dog, disguised in a man's clothes with the bottom half of her face wrapped in her father's famous red-and-white head covering. They walked for days, and Sayf never turned back once to look at her; he simply didn't care, as indifferent to her as a man to his shadow. He had been hypnotized by the news circulating through the settlements about the dissident preacher Mujan al-Qutaybi, descended from the Ikhwan, whose fame had spread as he called for reform.

After what seemed like an age of traveling, they arrived at Medina. After they asked for directions in the mosque, a guide led them to where Mujan was staying in a large house in al-Hara al-Sharqiya.

Sarab would never forget the day they arrived in that house. The moment her feet stepped into the large courtyard she felt that she and her brother, previously like Siamese twins, were being forcibly separated. Beards reached over the chests of the men seeking knowledge here. The sky erupted ecstatically with cries of "Allahu akbar!" as the men lined up in neat rows in front of a slim figure, a tall man in pure white interrupted only by a black beard, with a piercing gaze that bored straight into the hearts of his audience.

"Mujan!"

Her body echoed the tremor that ran through Sayf when he breathed that name and bowed deeply. She was struck by the fever that broke out in Sayf upon seeing this leader, a fever that made it clear they would survive what was to come.

Sarab stared, not at Mujan al-Qutaybi, but at his companion, a graceful man also dressed in white. Mujan was laying an arm across his shoulders, declaring his affection and pride for him.

"My brother, Muhammad bin Abdullah, and I are practiced in uncovering the sinful arts of Satan's envoys, who strive to rally their power over us through calumny. We defied the interrogators to prove that we have an arsenal of weapons. We were freed due to the lack of proof. Through God's will, we will uncover the identity of these traitors who offered up these sly doubts with the aim of hurling us into prison." He raised his hand up high and his voice trembled as he warned the crowd, "No mercy for traitors!"

And the crowd fervently repeated after him, "No mercy for traitors!"

Sarab and Sayf understood that it had not taken long for the two men to be released from prison on the charges of inciting fitna and stockpiling weapons. The authorities had been careful to avoid a direct clash with Mujan and his band of zealots, who were mounting the pulpits in many cities and spreading their radical message through sermons and free classes. Although Mujan and his brother-in-law Muhammad bin Abdullah had been arrested for stockpiling, it was the ulema who had questioned them, and on charges of blasphemy and sacrilege. After questioning, these religious authorities declared the men innocent on the basis that they were conservative, traditional preachers, like all the Qutayba tribe, and posed no danger to the state.

"But, Sheikh, do we have the weapons we need to fight Satan and his demons?" The eager question raced through the crowd like wildfire, and was answered by a reassuring smile from Mujan. It kindled his audience's hidden hopes, and dangled the possibility of war like a tempting fruit.

Emboldened, the crowd shouted "Allahu akbar!" as loudly as they were able.

Mujan enjoyed widespread fame as a rebel, a utopian religious reformer, and a contemporary development of the Bedouin group the Ikhwan fi Taat Allah, known widely as just the Ikhwan. They had been formed earlier in the century from the most zealous of the newly converted nomadic tribes who wished to purify the practice of Islam. In his sermons, Mujan would echo their rejection of modern society and culture, and exhorted his followers: "We will stop this Satanic wheel they call 'progress' although it is nothing more than a regression to the lowest steps of Hell. We who bear the absolute truth will sacrifice everything to take this truth to the world, which will have no choice but to yield to it." Mujan's ambiguous smile sent tremors through the faces hanging reverently on his every word.

He went on: "My beloved brothers in God, time has passed and God is choosing those of His worshipers who are most devoted, those most ready for sacrifice. This is the test, and you are the chosen who will fight Dajjal, the false Messiah who will lead the righteous astray with his evil lies.

"My father and grandfather and the best men of the Qutayba tribe scorned Wajir, the settlement founded by the ruler to tame us: us, the Ikhwan, the Bedouin who fought in his army, who brought him victory and made him ruler of this desert and its riches. The fearless men of the Qutayba did not hesitate to revolt against him and sacrifice their lives in the great Battle of al-Sibala when he brought the modern, infidel Western world to our country and encouraged our women to participate in what they call 'development'; to leave their homes and join schools and universities." Mujan took a deep breath, allowing the heroism of his ancestors to sink into the crowd's minds.

"I was raised on the stories of their heroic deeds and their fierce battles to establish the truth. From 1955, for eight years, I worked in the National Guard and was trained in their methods of fighting. Thank God—at last, in compensation for the slavery I had endured, God liberated me and my brother Muhammad from our slavery of the heart. So, by the grace of the Almighty, we were expelled from the mockery of working for the state, because as long as we continued to be in its debt, we could never truly oppose it."

"Allahu akbar!" rang out from the crowd, hoarse with excitement.

Mujan and his brother-in-law Muhammad bin Abdullah were the ideal pair to captivate a crowd. Muhammad was the star who blazed with elegance, the absolute embodiment of a divine prophet, while Mujan was the true innovator who presented his followers with fascinating visions of grace and Hell—and he advised what would attract the former and repel the latter. In him, the crowd saw both Malik, gatekeeper of Hell, and Radwan, gatekeeper of Heaven.

"Don't close your eyes and feign innocence. Open your eyes and look upon the Hell we have allowed to open on our earth, the cradle of truth. We turned this virtuous cradle into a temple of money worship, where we are slaves to the evil West and its Satanic modernity." Despite the heat that coursed through her from the crowd's fervor, Mujan seemed to Sarab to be a little deranged by his own private Heaven and Hell on earth.

"Look at us, brothers. From every nation and color, there is no division between the Arabs and the non-Arabs, only piety. We are the seeds from which the Ikhwan will grow, the only bond between us that of truth. We are the bearers of absolute truth."

He watched his men, drilling into their minds his idea of what that constituted.

"And now we are together, brothers. Let us put our trust in God to lead us on the path of our pious ancestors in our fight against atheism and modernity."

Sarab turned and found her brother in a state of rapture that bordered on mania. He left her and moved toward the preacher like he was in a trance, heedless of the guards who were blocking his way and pushing him back, fully prepared to fling him to the ground. He kept forcing his way through the guards, attracting the suspicion and concern of the crowd. Something in Sayf's suicidal behavior and his look of utter adoration halted Mujan as he was about to retire to his room. He gestured to his guards to step aside and reached out his hand to Sayf.

"Come here, my young brother."

Sayf moved forward, entranced by this face carved from rock. He kissed the proffered hand and introduced himself. With childish enthusiasm, he placed the bundle he was carrying at Mujan's feet and opened it, displaying the collection of his father's rifles. "I am the son of Sheikh Baroud. Here: I present his guns to you to help reach the goal you are leading us to, Sheikh Mujan. I have come here from Wajir to follow your path of absolute truth."

The name of the legendary Sheikh Baroud did not escape Mujan.

"Blessings on you, for you are the heir of the Ikhwan, the true mujahideen. We need men like you. God preserve you, and may He welcome you into Heaven."

That was how Sarab began to part ways with her brother Sayf, in the shadow of that large house. It was made up of several rooms circling a courtyard; some were used to house young, destitute followers, while others were used to hold small study groups where students were instructed in jurisprudence and Mujan's teachings. Mujan profited from the legitimacy granted to him by the Grand Mufti, who had rented this house for Mujan to signal his blessing of the jamaa, the religious and educational community gathered under Mujan's leadership. The Grand Mufti approved his calls for a return to strictly religious teachings and, along with other members of the ulema, often attended lectures there.

However, the mufti didn't know this jamaa and its advisory council were making covert plans. They convened secret meetings to debate their most important aspirations, of which he was not kept informed.

Sarab watched her brother closely. The moment his eyes fell on Mujan, a meteor struck him; it left a crater in his head into which the whole world had toppled and disappeared, except for Mujan. Even Sarab was among those missing from Sayf's mind, along with his father's rifles that he used to glory in, and had now forgotten in the courtyard. Sarab hurried to pick the bundle up and hold it against her like another spine.

Two sponge mattresses were brought, and Sarab and Sayf were led to the room where they would stay. They were greeted by five mattresses lying on the ground; evidently, five other seekers of truth slept in here side by side, and Sayf didn't hesitate to accept this room of single men over the family rooms. Enthusiastically, he unrolled his mattress next to the other five and Sarab realized she would have to sleep close to these men.

Trying to create some kind of boundary, she took refuge in a small cavity in the corner, a hollow in the wall intended as a sort of cupboard, two meters by half a meter. She pushed her mattress into this tomb-like cavity and put the bundle containing her father's guns at its foot to guard her from the masculinity dominating the room.

On her first night in that house, the room was fogged up with stifling fumes of sweat. Sarab burrowed into her mattress and cocooned herself inside her woolen blanket, and despite the heat she began to shiver with bone-wracking cold. She felt her soul leaving her trembling body and standing in the air, observing her pityingly. She closed her eyes. She couldn't bear to read what her soul would reveal of her future: that what she had thought was just a visit to this place would turn into a home and a destiny. Most frighteningly, it might show her that from that moment, her fate had diverged from her brother's.

In the house in Medina, in her body of ice inside that cube of fire, Sarab realized for the first time that Sayf had never in his life displayed feeling toward another living thing. Only after their mother's death had he showed he felt something, and the sentiment he displayed was hatred toward life.

To do him justice, Sarab thought that perhaps he could only have strong feelings for one person: himself. And yet here he was, granting that entire self to Mujan, dissolving into him. Sarab had been raised not to approach Sayf; not even to show him affection of any kind. She was molded into his ghost, copying all his actions and gestures, just a mirror of that emotional void. Confined to following him with equal coldness and negativity, she was nevertheless frightened by the poisonous mixture of servility and envy, even the compulsion to protect him, planted in her by her mother. She had to protect him; he was the secret of her existence, and if he ceased to exist, so would she.

Like a cog in a huge wheel, Sayf automatically started turning. Sarab, meanwhile, found herself like an alien creature, moving among people who couldn't see her and who spoke among themselves in cryptic riddles. Panic mushroomed. She would wander between the study groups and the students, exhausted from discussions that conveyed nothing to her despite buffeting her head like burning meteors. She suffered from a fear she didn't want to name.

Gradually the stream of newcomers increased. They fed the classes and plunged into fiery discussions about the impending end of the world and the salvation embodied in Mujan. Mujan's arrest had fortified his image as a jihadi and he was attracting more followers from other communities under different leaders. Rumors of his intentions for an armed struggle were escalating, along with the gradual recklessness of the jamaa in using their sermons to advocate for such an approach.

At its core, Mujan's jamaa was influenced by two schools of thought: the first was represented by Sheikh Muhammad Nasr al-Din al-Albani, who refused sectarianism and called for rigid adherence to the Quran and the verified hadith, while Mujan adopted the principles of tawhid, the nature of God's indivisibility, from the writings of Sheikh Muhammad ibn Abd al-Wahhab, Ibn Taymiya, and Sheikh Ibn al-Qayyim.

These names resounded in Sarab's head. Wherever she went she found a group of students clustered around a tape player, ardently listening to recordings of sermons that condemned all signs of urbanization and adherence to this vain life. Sarab was haunted by a nightmare of this behemoth infected with the voracity of urbanization and civilization.

The endless debate convinced everyone, Sarab included, that "outside was evil."

Month after month, she, along with everyone else was tamed by the idea, and the house became her only refuge. Her greatest fear was that the jamaa would throw her out and she would find herself "outside," where she would be swept away in the currents of Hell and "urbanization" rampaging through the country.

"Welcome to freedom, welcome to safety." Sayf's voice trembled, cautioning the group of newcomers who had gathered around him. The sins of the world burned within them like the fire they hoped to avoid, so painful they were tearing their clothes in despair. Meanwhile, Sarab was arrested by the voice she no longer recognized as her brother's as it recited Mujan's apocalyptic essay "Innovation and Clock Signals," which he had learned by heart.

Every night he lay on his mattress like a corpse, staring blindly into space, while the tape player whirred beneath his pillow and warned that "the Devil raises his head and reaches out to make them worship banknotes. Banknotes are the modern Antichrist, enslaving them."

Whenever Sayf opened his mouth Mujan's words would gush out. "Who will lead us to salvation? Who other than Mujan and our jamaa?"

Sayf exuded authority, and he roved about distributing tapes of Mujan's sermons to the new arrivals, particularly avid that they listen to the sermon called "Removing Confusion," in which Mujan outlined his stance on the other groups. "Do not trust the Muslim Brotherhood; their work in politics has led them astray.

And do not trust the Jamaat al-Tabshiriya, for they are deficient in preaching tawhid."

Sayf would walk around questioning the new followers. "What sermon did you listen to today? God bless you. Did you listen closely? Did you play it twice? Or only once?"

Sarab herself would have forgotten she was female were it not for the shared bathroom. Her period was the first challenge she faced there. The situation remained forever carved into her memory, and she would be haunted by the smell of that bloodied rag between her legs, which became increasingly slippery. It couldn't absorb the deluge of blood that flowed from her body as it faced its fears and the unknown future. She had to change the rag so it wouldn't brim over and stain her clothes and reveal her as a woman. She knew this, but was bewildered by how to deal with this necessity. What should she wash it with? She and her brother were destitute, utterly without livelihoods or possessions; they were living on the shared funds of the group—donations from rich, anonymous followers.

One day she knew she had to find some soap. She waited impatiently for the end of the meal that the poor members of the jamaa shared in the courtyard, and as soon as she could she slipped into the main kitchen and volunteered to help clean the plates. The cook glanced at her in surprise, but allowed her to clean the huge copper pot. She was drowning in grease and the blood was sticky between her legs. When the cook took out the rubbish, she seized her chance and hurriedly poured some soap powder into a cup.

Her heart pounding, she rushed to the bathroom and locked herself in for over an hour, dealing with her ridiculous problem. The others knocked on the door irritably and shouted at her to hurry up. In that confined space she felt suffocated by the rag's stubbornness. It was almost impossible to get rid of the blood and the smell; it was like rotten fish, guaranteed to draw the attention of the men who shared the bathroom with her.

Washing the blood wasn't the end of her tribulations; now she didn't know where to spread the ignominious rag to dry. The tiny bathroom had no space where she could hide it, so she had to take it with her. She carried it around in a plastic shopping bag, secretly begging it to hurry up and dry.

Sarab was wandering among her male comrades, who were exempt from the humiliation of menstruating, when she noticed a room in the corner of the courtyard. She hadn't noticed it before; no one went in or out of it, and not even the air moved the open door. It occurred to Sarab that she could hang her rag in that overlooked place, certain that no one would notice her, and she hurriedly slipped through the wide-open door. As soon as she stepped inside, she was stunned by the equipment surrounding her, chugging away in darkness. She saw a vast number of seemingly endless recorders, their red buttons staring at her, along with a young, dark-skinned Pakistani man whose beard reached to his navel. Facing every recorder were two openings like gaping mouths in which cassette tapes were spinning. Sarab couldn't turn her gaze from these mouths, realizing that the room around her was crammed with shelves to the ceiling, all laden with cassette tapes filled with preachings and warnings about Dajjal. The young man was making countless copies of every title. Sarab was stupefied, not daring to leave. After what seemed like an age, the young man handed her a bottle of glue and a pile of thin stickers the length of a finger.

"Take these, and stick the titles onto the tapes. Be careful; God loves someone who excels at his task."

The bag dropped from Sarab's hands like evidence of a crime. She didn't confess her humiliation, or how this task elevated her from it. Mechanically, she began to stick the thin strips of paper to the front of the cassettes. Mujan's name was repeated under her fingers; she felt it was burning off her fingerprints. As she stuck the titles down, her eyes widened blindly in the darkness. All the while, the cassettes made her head spin like giant mills of fire, but a fire fueled by an unknown source. Her terror increased at the thought that it might consume her and her brother, and her whole body trembled.

"Watch out!" The dark hand grabbed hers, and her fingers cracked inside the iron fist. "Don't you realize what you're doing? You're gumming up the tape!" She looked down, and was horrified at the sight of glue spreading to the insides of the cassette. She didn't say a word. She bent over, snatched her bag of shame from the ground, and disappeared under the young man's glazed eyes.

She retreated like a hunted animal, wondering whether she had ruined the tapes on purpose to silence the mill grinding out its threat of Hell. Sarab wandered to her room, feeling the soaked rag weighing it down like a mountain of sin, twice as heavy now because of the wickedness that had made her gum up the tapes. Guilt prodded her to return to the room and finish her task submissively, but she was deterred by something she couldn't explain. She began to wander through the courtyard, aware of the enormous compass inside that room, with its ability to break out and swallow up the world she knew. She resorted to hiding under her blanket, sinking into her corner in the wall.

Soon the courtyard was swept by a new wave of cassettes entitled "Demons Find Their Ideal Dwelling Place within Women."

"Thanks be to God, I've been saved from being female," Sarab sighed, congratulating herself on her disguise. She was deeply attached to the white male clothing that draped her with superiority, exonerating her from any hint of femininity.

But the problem of the bloody rag remained unsolved because, while she was waiting for the washed rag to dry, the second rag got the better of her and was saturated with blood, threatening to compromise Sarab and tip her into the ranks of the hellish female sex.

During her next period, she hit upon a brilliant idea. She began to cover the rag in plastic to stop excess blood from leaking onto her clothes. But it wasn't long before the rustling sound and the touch of the bloodied plastic between her thighs drove her mad with every footstep. So, in another burst of ingenuity, she added paper padding over the plastic layer, which made it more absorbent and lessened the slipping sensation. Paper was available in abundance, and was easy to dispose of by putting it in one of the many plastic bags around and tossing it into the rubbish.

Absorbed by these petty daily torments, Sarab was oblivious to the rising tide around her, a current of arrogant hatred circulating among Mujan's inner circle—especially her brother.

*

Human weakness was another factor that shielded Sarab from the development of hatred in her brother's heart.

One morning, the two leaders accompanied their followers on a sudden journey to the desert outside Medina. The convoy of Land Rovers forged deep into the desert, leaving all traces of the city far behind them. Sarab found herself in a Land Rover with Sayf and the two leaders, and couldn't believe her luck.

The refreshing morning breeze brushed their faces and threw back their head coverings, making their long hair fly out jubilantly. They looked like a gang of young men out for some fun.

Responding to the temptation of the men's released hair, and for the first time in months, Sarab allowed her head covering to slip to her shoulders, uncovering her long braids. At once, Muhammad's eye was caught by that shining braid, so like a woman's hair, and he stared at it for a while. Everyone else had curly hair that snaked to their shoulders, but Sarab's hair was different: it was soft, and had a luminous tinge.

Sarab noticed the men's astonished glances, and Sayf's glare that would have liked to turn her into stone for her boldness. But she didn't care; the morning breeze had goaded her to rebellion and she succumbed to the high spirits that had stormed her being and threatened to launch her out of the hurtling car. She had never felt such happiness as she surrendered to the rapture of the morning and the wind and the rush into the unknown, far from captivity inside the house that was her only defense, and that she had only imagined leaving to go to her grave. Once inside, she hadn't dared to cross the doorstep again for fear that the river of demons outside might sweep her away. But now she was outside, pushing deep into the hidden heart of things, protected by the presence of the two untouchable leaders.

Finally the convoy reached a military camp that had sprung out of the huge dunes; it seemed to have been waiting for them.

"Allah, Allah, Allah . . ." Mujan's voice shook with childish glee at seeing the well-appointed camp. "God bless our loyal followers in the National Guard who conquered this camp to invite us here." In the heart of the huge and austere void, the camp welcomed them with every facility for civilized living, including powerful generators, cisterns, running water, and air conditioning that blew cool air through the camp like a breeze from a heavenly oasis.

An officer of the National Guard quickly emerged from the central tent, welcoming them with visible reverence.

"God's greetings, dear Sheikh Mujan. It is an honor to welcome you and your jamaa to our humble camp."

"May God bless you, brother, and may He further the trust between us."

"All our hope rests in you, Sheikh."

"May it please God." They embraced warmly.

"Please, extend our thanks to our brothers and supporters in the Guard, and confirm that their service will be a boon to us as long as we live. May God reward you all handsomely." The officer went on to greet each individual warmly, placing rapid kisses on the foreheads of Mujan and Muhammad, and on the cheeks of the other members of the jamaa. He led Mujan to a canopy in the middle of the camp, where the ground seemed to swallow them from view. They had gone through a door in the ground of the camp that led to an underground bunker. No sooner had Mujan entered the bunker than he was struck dumb by the quantity of supplies piled up there.

"This is all at your disposal, Sheikh Mujan," the officer said. "Your loyal supporters smuggled everything they could for months, and the supervisors at the National Guard's supply warehouses didn't even notice."

Sarab relaxed on the dune, surrendering to the heat of the sand beneath her and the coolness of the shadow descending over the desert. Her senses were entranced by the thrilling contrast between cold and heat, between the opening up of space and the obscuring of it, and by the spasm that had peeled her away from the stagnation of the courtyard where she had been confined for months. A young man from the Guard passed by and lit the campfire a few steps from where she lay. At once the smell of firewood wafted toward her and she was encircled by the searing heat of the invigorating flames. She buried her body deeper into the tranquility of the sand, and was suddenly ravenous, with both a physical and spiritual hunger, for life. Driven by the ambiguity of this mysterious new craving, she plunged into the smell of barbecue; the freshly slaughtered animal's blood was clotting in a small pond behind the camp. The scent of burning meat called forth a beast hidden in the heart of the desert, and in her own heart. An irresistible appetite for blood and escape was pumping through her veins, giving her face a seductive glow. Spontaneously, her fingers unfastened the buttons of her male garment and she allowed the night's coolness to flow like the holy spring of Salsabil over her throat and her breasts, thwarted and frustrated from the endless disputes and evocations of Hell that had surrounded her for months.

From where she lazed, she could see a sudden transformation come over the leaders. Like snakes shedding their scales to reveal a succulent new skin, the two leaders shed their armor. She was struck by the smile that split Muhammad's features like a lightning flash, and her heart was crammed into her throat. Muhammad's smile was answered by Mujan's and, like an infection, smiles ran freely over the stern faces around them. Everything in the camp suddenly softened and freshened, and the two leaders exchanged jokes with their followers.

"We'll have to hide you, Sarab—our enemies won't take us seriously when they see our fighters have such attractive braids." Muhammad sprang this praise on Sarab as he approached to stoke the fire. He had turned his back to her so she couldn't tell whether he was joking or serious; had he discovered her identity? But calling the jamaa's members "fighters" made the comment even more peculiar. As he knelt by the fire, the rising flames drew her attention to his handsome face. Sarab's heart stopped for a moment, and the heat of the blood rushing to her face rivaled the heat of the fire. On his knees, illuminated by the fire, he turned and stared into her face. She was confused; he was like an angel or a mythical bird flashing from the flames, and her distress was increased by his ambiguous smile. A tremor in his depths was reaching her through the distance that separated them. Without further comment he chose a piece of the lamb shoulder and threw it gracefully onto an empty plate. Sarab choked with tears; she felt like a beggar desperately entreating more of that human contact. The pain of that need goaded her until she had to escape her weakness. She moved off like a dog with its tail between its legs and sat at the foot of a sand dune, chewing on meat salted with tears. She couldn't stop thinking that Muhammad bin Abdullah was the first person to notice her, or to offer her something other than criticism and indifference.

At dawn the following day the 4x4s appeared, carrying three officers from the National Guard. A halo of authority surrounded them as they prepared to train the group to use the weapons that were stored underground. The awestruck men lined up under the critical eyes of the officers, who scrutinized their fitness for duty and proceeded to assess their latent capabilities as fighters. The weapons were brought out of the cache and an officer began to distribute them according to the possibility they saw in each man. They asked her brother Sayf to try the M240 sniper rifle.

"You're skinny, and light as a feather." The officer regarded Sarab with a keen eye, and sweat broke out at the back of her neck and traveled down her spine. "A heavy weapon like this will fling you through the air with one shot," he said, as he followed her gaze, which was hovering longingly on the automatic rifles beside Muhammad bin Abdullah.

Without hesitation, Muhammad handed her an M60 machine gun, although he directed his words to the training officer. "Our grandfathers were as skinny and light as bolts of lightning; they also killed like bolts of lightning," he said, oozing authority that curtailed the officer's searching, sardonic glance at Sarab, and he handed Sarab an automatic weapon.

The first round she fired almost blew off her shoulder, or so she imagined from the intense pain the gun discharged into her body as it flung her to the ground. She lay there dumbfounded, laughed at by the superior males. Muhammad watched her anxiously while she struggled to stand up again and tried to endure the pain. Gradually her shoulder became a map of bruises, but while she could bear the pain, it seemed impossible for her to hit a target unless it was by accident. All her bullets strayed shamefully off course and left her the butt of everyone's jokes, Sayf leading the mirth when he wasn't ignoring her. That day seemed endless; she was afraid that the training would continue forever, until her trembling arm was so completely shattered there would be no hope of hiding it. More than once she had to resist an urge to throw her gun into the faces of those disdainful men and turn her back on them, but Sayf's scornful glare gave her the strength to last until sunset.

That night she sat far away from the fire, hidden from view by the wall of a tent. The men's voices reached her but she stayed out of sight. Only Muhammad bin Abdullah noticed her dejection. She had the idea of seizing her chance and running off into the night, letting the desert swallow her while the men were lying down. She heard Muhammad bin Abdullah's voice approaching, and drew back, plunging into the tent covering while Muhammad stopped and called, "Masrour, will you . . ."

"Sum." The huge servant didn't let him complete the sentence before pronouncing the traditional word to say, "Order me, I obey."

She could hear a smile in Muhammad's voice as he went on: "God bless you. Turn down the fire under the coffee."

"Tum." The servant spent no more time over this word, which he used to say, "It is done," and he sprang to carry out his command.

The two words *sum* and *tum* formed the entire lexicon uttered by the slave who had accompanied his master Nasir al-Kharaymi, the most important member of the council after Mujan and Muhammad bin Abdullah.

Hearing the two words echo into the desert night, Sarab realized exactly what it was she was lacking: the will to intentionally annihilate herself and vanish within the two leaders.

From her hiding place, she saw Masrour swiftly carrying out the order, dragging his teenage son Kasir behind him. Masrour and

Kasir were like two rods, the father with his giant's body and the son with his long, gangly body that looked like it might snap in two. They had turned heads in the Medina house because of the padlocked chain that linked Masrour's leg to his son's. They walked and slept chained together, and it was only unlocked when they used the bathroom. Before the father went to relieve himself, he chained his son to the window bars; when the son went, Masrour sat guarding the door, waiting for him to come out. There was nothing in Kasir's appearance to suggest he might run away, and neither father nor son were heard to speak a word of complaint, but everyone was convinced of Kasir's escape attempts. He didn't listen, not even to Mujan, and took no notice of anyone. He seemed to be deaf. Kasir was crushed at being deprived of the ability to use his outstanding intellect; that year, he had advanced from being an average student to one who could compete at state level, but Masrour had denied him a high school education by dragging his son behind him to the house in Medina.

The day of Sarab's disgrace in the camp was a day of pride for Masrour; his son Kasir had roused widespread admiration. The moment they put a machine gun in his hand, a commotion broke out in him. His mask of indifference collapsed and his face gleamed with a child's glee as he began to move it in a circle around himself. With the first hail of bullets, the fury in his eyes was replaced with lust and his whole being shook with the ecstasy of annihilating the target dummies. Drawing everyone's attention, he straightened up and carried on shooting without batting an eyelid. Suddenly he was no longer a boy, a crushed fifteen-year-old son; Kasir had become a lethal tool of correction. He circled and fired, annihilating flocks of bustards. He never missed a moving target or made a single mistake, winning the approval of the leaders and his father Masrour. Sarab didn't envy Sayf as much as she envied that infatuated boy, all his senses awakened, who had just fallen in love with his machine gun. He sparked a rivalry in the jamaa, as his skill detracted adulation even from Sayf. Suddenly Sarab noticed Kasir staring at her defiantly, waving his gun in front of her as if he had smelled the female scent in her male clothes.

"Give me the order and I'll tear out my eyes for you, my lord."
With a deep sense of service, Masrour abandoned his silence and
added that phrase to his lexicon. That night, with unwavering resolution, he unfastened the chain on his son's leg. He released him,
sure of his loyalty to Mujan, and above all to the machine gun that
had become part of his flesh.

Training, which stretched out for almost a fortnight, formed a series of
continual humiliations for Sarab. One moonlit night she confronted
a hopeless truth. The grains of sand seemed to be stinging her from
below while the campfire hissed, the heat accumulating on her face
weighed her down with defeat, and tears shone in her eyes. She had
grown used to the pitying, lofty glances of her comrades; this was the
first time she had appeared on their radar, only to magnify her failure.

Sayf avoided her like the plague while he wallowed like a puppy
in Mujan's praise of his genius: "You're a born sniper!" Sayf was
wrapped up in this commendation. For a week he never paused,
even for a moment, to commiserate with or mock his sister; she
simply didn't exist for him. His laughter rang out each night as he
challenged Kasir to a competition to eat the bustards they had shot
that day, now roasting on the fire. Sarab hadn't swallowed a morsel
of it, stupefied by the delicious fragrance that traveled into the night,
exciting the hunger of the desert and its predators.

"Take this." Muhammad said, handing her some of the meat.
"You need to gather your strength for the next round. We certainly
haven't lost hope in you yet."

Muhammad's sympathetic glance made her bruises ache even
more. It simultaneously paralyzed her and provoked her to run out
into the night and never return. How would she explain her failure
to keep pace with the jamaa's successes? Everyone else was progress-
ing in their training, while she only demonstrated a high tolerance
for overcoming obstacles and the rigorous morning exercises, and
continued to be an abysmal failure at target practice.

Would she be thrown out of the camp and the jamaa's house in
Medina too? She trembled with the horror of finding herself outside

the protection of the two leaders and away from her brother. She was convinced that his rejection of love linked her to him like a halter. She secretly wished she could break the halter and flee.

"What path do you have other than this? Align your resolution with our path and you will hit the mark. I think your only barrier lies in the will to aim your heart; you haven't yet summoned the will to fight." Muhammad had evidently seen straight through her.

Sleep eluded her for a long time as she lay on her blanket in the open air outside the leaders' tent. Everyone slept outside, wrapped in the refreshing darkness of the desert, muscles aching from the day's rigorous training. Before she fell asleep, the last person her eyes settled on was Muhammad on his blanket, his eyes boring into the night and the unknown fate in store for them.

Explosions rocked the night and pitched the men from their sleep, terrified. They leaped from their blankets and seized their weapons, ready to return this unexpected attack on the camp.

But there was no trace of an enemy. The echoes of the firing led them to make out the skinny figure of Sarab, firing demonically at every target with astonishing accuracy.

She seemed unaware of their approach.

"God's blessings on you," Mujan said. "Allahu akbar!"

But Mujan's congratulations left her unmoved.

"My brother is apparently shooting in his sleep. This is the courage of dreams; if he wakes up he'll turn tail and flee." A glare from Muhammad curbed Sayf's supercilious comment. Meanwhile, Sarab continued to shoot in a trance, and the men were captivated by her silvery appearance under the moonlight.

"All right, that's enough. There's no doubt you can shoot."

Muhammad took her by the shoulder and led her back to the camp. She walked beside him like she was hypnotized, confirming the suspicion raised by her brother that she was merely sleepwalking.

In the following days, the trainees competed using the most sophisticated weaponry, and Sarab oscillated between her failure at target practice when awake and her success when asleep.

"Awake or asleep, we need men like Sarab here; they have night vision that pierces the darkness and hits the target," Mujan declared. This settled any doubts of Sarab's value to the jamaa, but had no effect on their determination to view her as a source of amusement. A frivolous spirit sprang up in the group; the desert's wide-open spaces and their preoccupation with violent training seemed to have exhausted their bodies and stopped Hell from pulsing through their minds and veins. It allowed their programmed minds to clear and their theories to stagnate, letting their souls reveal themselves. The hardness in their faces dispersed, and smiles began to creep over them. They surrendered to life, and Sarab was a font of entertainment. They began to take turns watching her at night, and concocted elaborate jokes about what she did when she was sleepwalking. There was a wager on whether she was asleep or dreaming when she fired clouds from her weapon that rivaled even their capabilities.

Sarab wasn't aware of their jokes or their bets, impervious in the state that seized her between waking and sleeping when her overpowering fear slackened its grip on her body and mind.

During the day, despite her failure, she hovered in rapture. She bloomed, her vitality bursting free in the open spaces of the desert and its gentle breezes, which diminished her memories of her childhood and the father she had lost early on. He had passed away when she was two years old, and she no longer remembered him. She was dumbstruck that Muhammad had unconsciously begun to play the role of her lost father, filling the void he had left in and around her all these years. But Sarab's response to Muhammad wasn't that of a son or daughter; inevitably, she had become infatuated with him.

While the hearts around them were hardening like stones through their growing intimacy with weapons, her heart was softening from this secret crush. She made sure to join his team for training but, dazzled by his proximity, didn't wonder why they were using machine guns. Why had they been placed in the jamaa's hands? What had they been recruited for? Where would their next steps take them? To her, this was merely another hunting trip.

Her whole desire was to be shoulder to shoulder with Muhammad as he supported her delicate body when she fired. The twinkle in his eye whenever she hit the target and her hunger for that encouraging look drove Sarab to improve until the weapon was like a natural extension of her intoxicated body. Sayf was envious of her unexpected skills, and refused to acknowledge her proficiency. But Sarab's aptitude couldn't save her from being viewed merely as Sayf's shadow. As if their male hormones had caught a whiff of her female hormones, they took aggressive aim at her. Not content with her given name—which meant mirage or delusion—they took pleasure in distorting it, and nicknamed her Khayyal, a shadow without substance, something that can't be dispelled. They saw her as an appendage to Sayf, whom Mujan honored with the appellation Sayfullah—Sword of God.

On their return to Medina, Sarab was bereft by the leaders' renewed seclusion. Opportunities to meet them dwindled, reduced to the secret meetings that were heading toward a point of no return. Rumors abounded and the house was struck by a wave of suspicion about "the end," whatever that might mean, although Sarab welcomed the prospect of it if it meant the end of her separation from Muhammad. In fact, for the first time she could remember, she gave her heart free rein to beat madly while she struggled with the indomitable desire to be near him. It was fruitless to declare to herself that her desire was foolish, to scold herself for not preferring to be near her brother. But Sayf's blindness when it came to Mujan was no different than hers for Muhammad; she was ready to give her life in exchange for one moment near him, for a touch of his hand on her shoulder. She ignored the fact that Muhammad was the husband of Mujan's sister, and they shared a room connected to the room of Mujan and his wife.

Mystery cloaked these women, who almost never left their rooms. Sarab knew that there was a door that linked the leaders' rooms and the wives moved through it, in their own private cocoon. As long as the women were merely ghosts who didn't appear in daylight, Sarab could convince herself they were just in her head, giving her an excuse to sink deeper into her infatuation with Muhammad.

1979: The Savior

THE JAMAA'S SECRET ACTIVITIES CAME to a head in 1979. The group had swollen as it collected students from private universities, institutes of the ulema, and an institute of studies subordinate to the Grand Mosque. It had also gathered fanatical followers among houses founded by the Ikhwan in other cities.

Sayf spent six months blindly devoting his heart and soul to Mujan's aims and developing his combat skills before he was allowed to attend the council's secret meetings. This mark of favor surprised the older followers. After a string of arrests among the jamaa that year, Sayf had been brought into the inner circle at a time when they needed to exercise more caution, not less, in who was allowed direct communication with the leader.

Mujan's confidence inspired optimism in men like Sayfullah; their readiness for martyrdom in pursuit of their goals was cemented as a result of one decisive meeting of the council. It had been convened in total secrecy during the winter, and the door remained locked on the council members for two days. The cold gouged their exposed ankles like razor blades, but they avoided lighting a fire even to heat a coffee-pot. There was no alleviation of the cold intended both as a test of their toughness and as an introduction to the sufferings that awaited them if they abandoned these plans. Before the door shut on them, Sarab tried to catch a glimpse of Sayfullah whose back clung to the wall like a barricade, his eyes fixed on Mujan as he hung on his every word.

The men were not permitted to sit. The metal chairs and primitive wooden table were left ice cold while the men stood, anticipation hovering over them. Mujan presided, shoulder to shoulder with Muhammad. He looked deeply into the eyes of each of them before disclosing the revelation he had received. It was the first spark, preparation for the step of resorting to an armed struggle in pursuit of their goal. Mujan's features glowed in the dim light of the room as he presented a dramatic retelling of the vision that had appeared to him in his sleep.

"This year, in 1399, I felt God speaking inside me. His great hands seized my heart, but not to burst it with His majesty." His eyes pierced the breasts of the men around him, their hearts burning with immense yearning. "There was nothing but light, and in that light He revealed to me His might. He raised the face of my brother Muhammad, and said, 'You have received your Mahdi.'"

Encircling Muhammad's shoulder with his right arm, Mujan pushed him forward to establish his rule over the hearts and eyes in the room. With a faith that struck an answering fire in the hearts of his audience, he went on: "Muhammad bin Abdullah, you are the Mahdi, our savior, the redeemer of humankind." The flame of his words blew through the frozen air and flowed over the men's exposed ankles. The atmosphere suddenly ignited, and on that cold January morning, Mujan appointed his brother-in-law Muhammad bin Abdullah the long-awaited Mahdi.

Wrapped in Muhammad's halo, their hearts thumped in awe of Mujan's iron will. In him, they saw the true search for martyrdom, which didn't run after power but scorned itself, wishing only to serve the Mahdi, God's emissary. Nasir al-Kharaymi, known for his oppositional stance within the council, remained solitary in the corner of the room, watching. He was divided from the glow cast over the rest of the gathering; while Mujan's words set their faces alight, his was shadowed with doubt as the gravity of the situation escalated. He scrutinized Sayfullah, who throughout had stood to attention like a physical manifestation of Mujan's will. He was the first to make his way through the transfixed audience and bend over to kiss Muhammad's hand, paying homage to him as the anticipated Mahdi. This drove the rest of the company to do the same, and they lined up to follow his example.

"Why him?" The words cracked like a whip, splitting the silence moistened by the sound of lips kissing skin, and all eyes turned terrified to Nasir al-Kharaymi.

Mujan froze for a moment but, pushed by this opposition to his announcement that the Mahdi had taken bodily form in this very room, he invoked the description of the Mahdi that appeared in the apocalyptic books of judgment and signs of doomsday. In a trembling voice he recited a hadith:

> The Mahdi will appear between Rukn and Maqam, and three hundred and thirteen men will be his companions and pledge their allegiance. They will be like lions emerging from the forest, their hearts like iron. If they cared to erase a mountain, they would erase it from where it stood. In appearance and attire they will be as one. Gabriel beside him will call on the people to pay homage to him, and his followers will come from all the corners of the earth to bow before him in secret and pay homage, among them the Abdal from the Levant, the Nujaba from Egypt, the groups from Iraq, the groups from the east, and the defender of the people of Yemen. Then an army will come from Tabouk to wage war on him and it will be destroyed.

The threat in Mujan's tone didn't succeed in quelling al-Kharaymi's opposition. His raised voice took on a steely gloss.

"I'm not convinced. I don't see any signs of the Mahdi in Muhammad al-Qahtani, and we cannot determine his legitimacy merely because he shares a name with Muhammad bin Abdullah. Most important, this Muhammad is not descended from the Prophet's line (peace be upon him), and that is the primary condition of the Mahdi."

"We, the people of true faith, have been chosen to receive the Mahdi," Mujan said. "He has emerged from desperation and despondency. Blessings be showered on those who recognize him and support him, and woe to those who oppose him and his orders.

May God fill the earth with justice, as it is now filled with oppression and tyranny." Though Mujan magnified his threats, al-Kharaymi didn't show a tremor.

"What is all this talk about destroying the army from Tabouk?" al-Kharaymi asked. "It is forbidden to carry weapons into the house of God, if that is what you are intending us to do. God knows we have followed you to fight Dajjal, Mujan, not to set our most sacred site on fire."

Outside, the eyes of the followers were fixed on the door. It was guarded by comrades notable for their size. There were whispers of a disagreement between the two groups in the room, and the followers had split into factions according to their predictions. The atmosphere in the courtyard weighed heavily while they avoided clashes and kept watch in solemn silence. They knew that Mujan was leading a fateful meeting in that room. They waited for hours, none daring to leave. No one wanted to risk missing the rise of the legendary leader and his announcement of the council meeting's result.

At last the door opened, and Nasir al-Kharaymi was the first to appear, anger shadowing his face. He had confirmed his position as the leader of the opposition. He was quickly followed by three other opponents of Mujan, who hurriedly left the house. Although Sarab retreated a few steps from him and his supporters, he looked so dreadful that she felt sorry for him when he turned to her as she stood by the door. In a voice laden with grief, he told her, "The innocent should save their skins now and leave. One goal is no longer to be found here: the pursuit of truth."

Before he left, he turned back once more to send a vehement warning to the others. "God leaves us to ourselves when we surrender to personal ambition."

His words sent a ripple of aversion through Mujan's loyal followers. The air of the courtyard clouded over. Suddenly the dispute between the two factions broke out into uproar, and it wasn't long before some of Nasir's own followers broke away from him. His stormy departure was blocked by the prizefighter build of his most loyal guard, Masrour.

"My master, how can we leave like this?" Masrour was pale with shock. Explosions were rocking the goal in whose service he had sacrificed his life, had even dragged his only son to serve. Kasir had hurried behind them, his face ashen.

"What if he really is the Mahdi?" Kasir asked.

"He's not the Mahdi. God as my witness, we don't believe in his legitimacy, or in the legitimacy of carrying weapons into mosques."

"Forgive me, master, but I am afraid of facing my Lord on Judgment Day and explaining that I missed the call of His envoy, the Mahdi." The savage gleam on Kasir's face made it plain he agreed with his father.

"You are wrong, but you are a free man. I pray God will guide you to the truth."

Nasir al-Kharaymi patted Masrour's shoulder affectionately, and embraced Kasir.

"But you will be asked about Kasir; remember he is a minor."

He left them and walked out, never to appear again in that house. Sarab suffered sleepless nights over the rift in the jamaa created by Nasir al-Kharaymi.

War: June 1979

SIX MONTHS AFTER THIS RUPTURE, Mujan announced the next stage of his plan. He convened a meeting calling together the influential heads of each branch of the jamaa which had been established in other cities, and when they gathered in the courtyard of the house in Medina, they saw for themselves the rapture that stirred Mujan's followers every time he appeared. Most of them had never seen their leader in person before; he had gone into hiding after his name appeared on a list of people wanted by the authorities, and the arrests of his rank-and-file followers had escalated.

"Allahu akbar!" Ecstatic cries rose when Mujan revealed his plan to occupy the Grand Mosque, aligning his plan with the description of the Mahdi found in the books of Hadith on the end of the world.

With a grave and pious face, Mujan repeated the hadith.

Sarab's heart began to throb; she could hear hearts fluttering all around her, but theirs were pounding from rapture.

Mujan went on:

Then the chosen one will depart from Mecca, taking the road to Medina, where he will wage war on the enemies of Isa bin Maryam . . . he will journey to Palestine and defeat the Jews and sunder them, and he will continue to Syria and pray in the Umayyad Mosque to proclaim Judgment Day.

A wave of tension swept the courtyard and Sarab sensed the bodies around her swaying and bending in the air.

The Mahdi will only appear amid a great terror. Earthquakes will afflict the people, and the plague and the sword will divide the Arabs. Great conflict will take place between the people, and corruption in their religion, and a great change in their state, and they will wish for death morning and evening . . . When the Mahdi appears, righteousness and justice will reign over the earth after it was filled with injustice and terrible oppression, and he will spread blessings and charity and knowledge, and the earth will bring out its treasures, and the sky will rain down its blessings.

The watching faces rose in fear.

"And so, we have been chosen to attend the appearance of he who will purify the earth of its afflictions, and to gift humanity with the blessings of earth and sky."

With these words, Mujan announced war on the world. His words ran through the brainwashed crowd like fire through dry straw. They were ready to explode, programmed to do so, and emboldened from being chosen as the first to receive the Mahdi, the Redeemer, unaware of the twist their fate had taken.

Fever coursed through the council over the following months. The number of secret meetings increased, and new followers scrambled to join the group. Weapons were distributed and several trips were organized to the desert camps so the new adherents could be trained in their use.

Sarab was responsible for serving the leaders; from up close, she could observe the transformation that came over their features, mirrored in the transformation of her brother's. They were placing metal armor over their faces and hearts, preparing for the ultimate sacrifice.

Muhammad had forgotten her existence. Now he was the pivot on which everyone turned. His followers found the vengeful, piercing light in his eyes utterly bewitching. He was the generator Mujan used to kindle the fire of zealotry and the desire to seek martyrdom, attracting more and more to the jamaa.

Sarab was entrusted with the maps they were studying; it was like a bone to a hungry dog. Sarab found it challenging to shut herself away to study these maps; for six months they had had no occupation other than weapons training. These secret documents mapped out the engineering of the Grand Mosque; the exits and entrances, the branching cellars like a maze of subterranean vaults, the hundreds of cells for prayer and retreat—it all set her head spinning.

"We thank God that our brothers in that company are proving useful." Mujan was referring proudly to the architecture firm and its offshoots, which were responsible for expanding, developing, and renovating the Grand Mosque. Adherents of his who worked in the company had equipped him with these secret maps of the mosque.

"Not even the authorities themselves have access to these maps, but the will of God has placed them in our hands."

Mujan consolidated his plans, focusing on the cellars and labyrinthine vaults of the Grand Mosque.

"Rejoice! Our brothers have laid up large quantities of provisions and ammunition in this city below the mosque. As soon we walk inside, it's finished; we need only hold out and time will be in our favor."

Few members of the council knew the names of the followers supplying this food and ammunition. Even the intermediaries' identities were secret, known only to Mujan. His associates had grown bolder and they began to expand their smuggling operation from the warehouses of the National Guard to the cellars of the Grand Mosque. The countdown to the deadline made them reckless, and they had no fear of being caught.

An engineer from the architecture firm volunteered to explain the maps and charts to the group, and Sarab took advantage of every opportunity to listen to him. As soon as they finished studying for the day and the maps were entrusted to her for safekeeping, she would bring them out of the safe and go over what she had heard; she traced Mujan's plans over these intersecting slices until their smallest details were drilled into her memory. In her dreams, she rifled through this complex, hidden network formed by the service entrances and exits. For some mysterious reason, she was haunted by the hidden tunnels that led from the holy fountain across the vaults and outside the mosque, surfacing in a faraway part of the city near the Maala Cemetery.

"Perhaps we will not need to fire at all; we only have to walk inside and the Grand Mosque will be an impenetrable fortress. It will fall into our hands, and they will have no choice but to surrender and carry out our demands. They cannot defile the house of God with our blood, and they will never be able to extract us from that underground maze." His tone deepened and intensified. "Let everyone understand that if it is so demanded, then this maze will be our grave. Unless we are victorious, we will not leave alive."

Mujan's words had an intoxicating effect; the jamaa seemed ready for obliteration, to be sacrificed for the salvation of humankind.

The speech put fear into Sarab's heart. Memorizing those maps became an obsession occupying every waking and sleeping hour.

One night while she was sleeping, a choked murmur rose from her intermittently, until it resolved into jerky kicks and broke off with a cry. This made her surface from sleep, rescuing her from a bottomless nightmare. She sat up in bed, frenziedly shaking an invisible blackness from her body, and the black dissolved before her eyes. The room was empty, as the others had left for a round of training in the camp. Only Sayf was getting ready to lie down. He ignored her soft cry; he was used to her nightmares.

"If you have to keep on with this garbage, at least train yourself to scream like a man," was his perpetual comment on her nightmares.

"You have nightmares because you lie flat on your stomach. That's how Satan sleeps." Those were her comrades' comments on the nightmares that lay in wait for her every time she lay down. "That's how Satan sleeps," her roommates jeered whenever she went to bed, and Sarab bit back the question: When have you seen him asleep?

Without looking at her, Sayfullah lay on his mattress, setting the tape recorder under his pillow. Sarab leaped from her bed and leaned over him like an axe.

"Sayf, are we caught up in something much bigger than us?"

He pulled away from her and sat up on his bed, staring at her blankly.

"A black sandstorm was hunting us both in my dream just now."

His eyes widened in disapproval, but she went on: "Don't be angry with me, but it was horrible. Sayf, Mujan frightens—"

He interrupted her before she could articulate her fear of Mujan: "You have a heart like a rat." He spat contemptuously. "Pack your things and go back where you came from."

"I'm afraid for you. Let's leave here, and pray to God that He will grant us a good life."

"What?"

"Please, let's go. Don't worry, we won't go back to Wajir; the earth is huge. We can go to the mosque and stay there. We'll put ourselves in the hands of the Prophet (peace be upon him) and he will guide us to the right path."

He struck her in the chest, pushing her away from him.

"From now on, I don't know you. Your heart is made of air; mine is made of rock. You're a disgrace to me, to all of us here."

She crawled toward her bed and his voice followed her, freezing her to the spot.

"Look, just pack your things and go. Don't ever show me your face again."

She hid in her bed, trembling, and never again dared to voice her fears.

Everyone was beginning to notice the countdown secretly taking place in Mujan's head. A month before their fated day, followers began to gush from all corners of the country toward the Holy City. They descended on it as individuals or in small groups, so as not to attract attention. Around two hundred weapons were hidden in anticipation of the dawn of the Hijri year 1400. But one morning, two weeks before the end of the year, something unexpected occurred.

Sarab was returning from the dawn prayer in the mosque attached to the house when her attention was suddenly caught by a fine black thread coming from the door of the recording room in the corner of the courtyard. It wasn't that remarkable; just a small piece of darkness added to the darkness of the night, and it didn't seem to have been noticed by anyone but her.

She went closer and was struck by a strange rotting smell. Her first thought was that it was the urine of Satan. She approached the door cautiously, and her chest tightened from the stench. She poked her head through the open door and gasped. The room was entirely turned into soot; it seemed as though acid had passed through it and silently burned everything. There was no trace of the young Pakistani man and she didn't dare to look behind the desk where he had been working in case she saw a deformed lump melting there. She slammed the door shut and ran away, feeling acid burn away the whorls of her brain, and every tape that wouldn't stop whirring away inside it.

Dawn, November 20,
1979 / 1 Moharram 1400

SARAB FOUND HERSELF IN A small bus heading into the dawn of the Hijri year 1400. They were threading through the sleeping streets of the Holy City, heading for the Grand Mosque. Six of the most loyal fighters surrounded the two leaders, buoyed up by the adrenaline that came from the knowledge that at dawn they were going to present the long-awaited Mahdi to the world.

Suddenly Sarab noticed they had all performed their ablutions for the dawn prayer; the water was still soaking their beards but it failed to extinguish the fire smoldering inside them. She was the only fighter with a veiled face. Her head rang with Mujan's intimidations.

"The Mahdi will bring red death and white death, and locusts at the appointed time, and locusts at the unappointed time, like the colors of blood. The red death is the sword, and the white death will be plague, and five out of every seven will fall . . ."

Her eyes swiveled, seeking a trace of these deaths, but they met nothing but the tranquility of the Holy City and its inhabitants, still unaware of what was in store for them.

Her gaze turned away from the vehicles speeding through the slumbering streets and she contemplated the bearded men around her on the bus. Inside their heads she saw, not modern buildings, but tents and camels. She thought she was looking at the face of the cosmic clock, and was about to force its hands to turn counterclockwise; they were dispatching the modern era and ushering in another, one of unknown identity.

Their departure was like the opening shot of an eternal war, and Sarab didn't know how she would be able to keep her brother safe; in contrast to the men around her, her battle was not against any monster or demon, but the ghosts hidden in her brother's head. Him at least she had to extract from their clutches; Muhammad seemed out of reach to her and beyond any attempts at rescue.

As soon as they got off the bus and Sayf banged the door closed, Sarab felt an invisible door slam shut behind her. The jamaa encircled its leaders and made its way inside the Grand Mosque with forceful strides, their hearts calcifying with every step. They regarded Muhammad bin Abdullah as the embodiment of Muhammad (peace be upon him), for the simple coincidence of their names.

Mujan watched like a hawk as the squadrons of his army infiltrated the mosque from all sides. He confirmed the men were stationed in the positions he had assigned to them, scattered throughout the mosque and around the thirty-nine doors. They were waiting for the starting signal: the moment that the imam concluded the dawn prayer.

The Grand Mosque was thronged with inhabitants of the Holy City and a hundred thousand pilgrims who had traveled from all over the world to perform pilgrimage. The crowds joyfully celebrated the start of the Hijri year and a shudder went through Sarab's body.

The imam of the Grand Mosque took up his position directly in front of the Kaaba to lead the prayers through the microphone. His voice was permeated with solemnity as he began the Chapter of Repentance.

"Disavowal by God and His Apostle is herewith announced." The first word struck Sarab like a physical blow. She staggered and almost fainted. A hundred thousand souls repeated the statement of disavowal, and Sarab felt disavowed by them. And all repeated after the imam, "Amen."

The word overlapped with the fluttering of a flock of doves that hovered overhead, tracing circles in the sky and prophesying the awe of what was to come. However much Sarab gazed at the Kaaba to calm her heart, it wouldn't be still. It outstripped the fluttering of the doves' wings as the prayer neared its conclusion. Suddenly a herd of men appeared, each of their heads wrapped in a red-spotted head covering, carrying coffins on their shoulders. They began to move forward through the rows of praying people and placed their burdens in front of the Kaaba so the prayer for the dead could be read over them after the dawn prayer was finished. It wasn't anything out of the ordinary; it was the custom of the inhabitants of the Holy City and the surrounding towns to bring their dead for the crowds to pray over in the Grand Mosque. Mujan watched his men carry fifty coffins concealing their huge arsenal into the mosque. Sarab felt suffocated in her disguise of male clothing. She fingered the cold weapon hidden under her clothes and her soul was racked when her brother broke away from her. She watched him desolately, her whole being shaken, while he walked unnoticed to the back and took up his position at the top of the minaret over Bab al-Malik, the principal entrance to the Grand Mosque.

The plan required that she take up a position close to the imam. The moment the prayer was completed, the peace of the dawn and the prayers was shattered by a shot fired from the direction of the mosque's main entrance. It seemed that one of their fighters had gotten confused and fired too soon, killing a nearby guard. The shot terrified the crowds. Sarab leaped up to snatch the microphone from the imam but he raised his hand as a barrier and blocked her way. As she fumbled for the weapon hidden in the folds of her clothes, his wise eyes stared into hers warningly. She felt God nailing her to the spot from the depths of those ageless eyes. The imam instinctively perceived the danger in the air and the gravity of surrendering the microphone to the young man who had pounced upon it; such a small act might play a decisive role in the uproar unexpectedly breaking out in the peace of the mosque.

And so, endangering himself by raking Sarab with reproachful eyes, he intoned gravely, "Fear God. Let us pray for the dead brought here today."

Sarab quivered, retreating while the imam led the prayer for the dead in total serenity.

Four times "Allahu akbar!" rang in Sarab's ears like knocks on the door of a grave the size of Heaven and earth. "O God, forgive the living and the dead, the present and absent." The words solidified in Sarab's heart, so heavy they almost broke her spine.

The prayer did not take more than three minutes. During the third "Allahu akbar," total chaos broke out in the arcades around the doors, and the worshipers wavered between attending to the imam or the sound of the bullets.

" . . . O God, give him a home better than his home and a family better than his family . . ." The prayers were like a prediction, and Sarab's heart broke from the certainty that she and her brother had no retreat now. No sooner had the imam pronounced the fourth and final "Allahu akbar" than the horror around the doors was made clear; the insurgents were struggling to close the thirty-nine colossal, enormously heavy doors while the terrified worshipers rushed to escape. Weapons glinted in different sections of the mosque, and the sight of them struck the crowds like a lightning bolt. Sarab's attention was distracted by the sound of shots coming from the minaret where her brother was positioned.

The murder has begun. This thought struck Sarab, and the taste of blood and bile rose in her throat.

"Hurry, take this out of the mosque." The imam pushed the microphone into the hands of his stupefied guard, who automatically began to run and disappeared in the panicking crowds.

The imam was driven back by the men from the jamaa, who rushed forward. Revealing the weapons hidden in their clothes, they began to shoot at the small number of security guards, who were not permitted to use weapons inside the mosque, and they fired shots in the air to control the unruly, terrified crowds. The men screamed into the frenzied torrent with voices hoarse and cracked with tension: "The Mahdi has appeared!"

When Sarab noticed the imam had disappeared and there was no trace of the microphone, she was devastated; she had failed in the first trivial task she had been charged with. She was supposed to deliver the microphone to Mujan to broadcast his declaration of war and the appearance of the Mahdi to the crowds.

Dozens of insurgents gathered quickly in the courtyard of the Grand Mosque and they began to open the coffins and bring out the weapons hidden there. They brandished these at the crowds, which began to push and shove at the sight of them. Thousands of terrified bodies threatened to swamp the handful of rebels, and they opened fire. The bodies that fell to the ground smeared with blood only magnified the shoving, the madness, and the torrent of random shots.

Sarab went deaf. Everything was taking place in slow motion. She couldn't see anything but her comrades, their darting eyes widened with terror as they tried to stem the onslaught of the panicking crowds. Fear swelled in a cloud over the Grand Mosque as the snipers occupied their strategic positions at the summit of each of the nine minarets, and they began to fire on anyone attempting to approach the mosque.

Finally, by some miracle, the enormous heavy doors were closed and chained shut, sending a current of madness through the crowds trapped inside, who were stumbling over and crushing each other in their blind rush to escape.

As the situation threatened to spiral out of control, Mujan issued his orders: "Let the foreigners leave. Only keep nationals as hostages. They are our audience and our objective, and our trump cards in negotiations with the authorities."

The rebels herded the horrified pilgrims toward the tunnels used by service lorries to enter the mosque. Sarab and a group of her comrades were assigned to carry out the dispersal orders swiftly.

Hundreds of dumbstruck faces of every nationality left under Sarab's gaze, clouded with doubt at what was happening. Suddenly her attention was drawn by a pilgrim in a simple white garment, a head covering lying haphazardly on his shoulders. He was looking at his feet, avoiding everyone's eye. She knew him at once; it was none other than the imam of the mosque, hiding in the clothes of an Indonesian pilgrim. He looked up suddenly and caught her eye; he knew she had identified him, but he didn't stop or stumble, and he continued making his way out. This was Sarab's second test on the first day of the battle and she hesitated, unable to make herself stop him and disclose his identity to her comrades. Disregarding everything her leaders believed, she felt that releasing the imam was a sincere act of piety. She looked away and allowed the imam to escape. Nevertheless she worried that her comrades had lost a trump card for their negotiations while a hail of bullets was launched over the mosque in a salute of the first decision she had taken in her life independently of her mother and brother.

Mujan clung to the Kaaba near the Black Stone, believed to have been formed from the pearls of Paradise. He was standing a meter above the ground on a narrow edge that barely offered a foothold, in a desperate attempt to appear to everyone in the courtyard and quiet them. His ringing voice was futile and unintelligible to the crowds as he announced the demands to be conveyed to the authorities.

"The ruler of the country must look to our demands, which are as follows: We demand a boycott of the secular West; we demand the termination of education for women; we demand the termination of television broadcasts and the repudiation of Dajjal, the demon of the West, which is found inside its screen. And above all, we demand the expulsion of foreigners and the closure of their embassies."

The faces of the imprisoned pilgrims stared at Mujan, overwhelmed with confusion by these riddles.

"It is a disgrace that we belong to this state, which pledges allegiance to the West. It is lawful in the eyes of God to spill the blood of anyone who carries its identification papers." Mujan flourished his identity card and began to rip it up theatrically in front of everyone, and his men followed suit. Fear coursed through the hostages; they hurriedly imitated the rebels, taking out their identity cards and tearing them up so as not to be punished.

Sarab stood three paces from where Mujan clung. She avoided looking at the Kaaba, trying not to increase the crushing weight of her weapon. Her eyes were glued to Mujan's profile as she stood in front of the panicking hostages, aware of the mistakes of that unsteady beginning. The hostages couldn't see them; their weapons loomed too large. She found it difficult to believe that this skinny man was really there, under the Kaaba, clutching the veil covering it in his left hand and a trembling machine gun in his right. He raised his voice louder, his lips grown rigid from the tension of conveying his electrifying current to them. No one knew or cared what was being declared. One idea occupied their minds: survival.

Even Sarab hadn't realized the truth of what it meant to accompany that deranged leader. It was the first time she had seen or set foot in that sacred place, and she had instantly been cowed by its vastness, its sanctity. Even though she was a just a simple girl from Wajir, she realized the enormity of the place. They were no more than five hundred fighters, and despite the weapons waiting for them in the cellars and in those fifty coffins, they were lost in this space like a handful of sand. It covered perhaps five hundred thousand square meters, had more than thirty doors, and contained a forest of hundreds of marble pillars interspersed with 244 pillars of red sandstone; more than enough to swallow four hundred thousand men. Even so, Mujan had brought them here in their puny numbers and with their primitive weapons, confident and ready for a siege in the Grand Mosque, which might last till God alone knew; and now, added to their own feebleness were hundreds of hostages, all besieged with horror. The rebels were destined to stay with these hostages until the end, which seemed to Sarab to have been determined from the first instant when the venerable imam stared at her sternly and said, "Fear God. Let us pray for the dead."

The prayer had been for them; they were the dead, and the empty coffins their own, ready for them in the unknown future.

Mujan seemed to have finished spitting out the flame of his demands and had now relaxed, assured that his words would circulate through the crowds. He leaped down and roamed among his men, inspecting their capacity for dealing with the siege now it had become a reality. He moved like a black cloud and his wide eyes seemed bottomless, exposing the battle he had plunged his entire soul into, as he aimed to bolster his men's belief that the dawn of the empire of truth was breaking at their hands.

Mujan concentrated his men around the doors and all over the roof of the mosque, and he distributed groups to keep watch on the courtyard and the open sky above it, anticipating an air attack by countering forces. At a glance, the five hundred fighters seemed like grains of dust swallowed up by the infinite house of God.

Snipers

BULLETS POURED INTERMITTENTLY FROM THE nine minarets in response to shots from outside, where the police had initially rushed in, desperate to break through the doors, break the siege, and regain control of the Grand Mosque; but they had underestimated the scale of the armaments of inside. Bullets thudded savagely, covering the sky with an apprehensive silence that deafened fighters, hostages, and nearby residents alike. The mountains and the stone houses of the Holy City resounded with the echoes of that unexpected horror; no one could believe that death was emanating from the house of God instead of the melodious call to prayer.

Sarab retreated to the darkness under the arcades and took up position behind a marble pillar, aiming her automatic rifle and preparing herself to shoot any attackers. Behind her, she heard a recitation of the Quran in a soft, lilting tone. It seemed to her that an angel had descended to pray, to remind them of God in this house of worship. She didn't dare to turn around for fear that the enchanting recitation would disappear.

"But for those who of their Sustainer's Presence stand in fear, two gardens of paradise are readied—which, then, of your Sustainer's powers can you disavow?"

It was the Chapter of the Most Gracious, its soothing rustle echoing throughout the arcades. When at last she was brave enough to turn around, she saw a hostage. The small, thin man had the look of an Azhari scholar; his eyes were entirely white, blinded to the things of this world, and he was absorbed in his recitation. The sweetness of his voice gave the impression he was floating in midair, untouched by the murder all around.

For a moment Sarab slipped into the melodious lilt. Closing her eyes, she felt her body uplifted up when he recited, *"But forever will abide thy Sustainer's Self, full of majesty and glory."*

Suddenly a giant body fell from the sky in front of her, slamming into the earth like a bomb. She froze, staring at the open wound ripped through the stomach wall. The man's chest rose and fell in a rattle. Without thinking, she reached out a hand to him and was scorched by heat. Something exploded in her head and she hurtled away like a missile, blinded by the sight of the hostage's bowels snaking toward her.

She was still running when her foot struck a shinbone. She looked down and saw the bare foot of a plump woman leaning against a marble pillar, facing the Kaaba.

Sarab was shocked by the inhuman whiteness of that female hostage. Her face was round as a snowball, drooping over her huge chest. Her head was shaved at the back and sides, the locks remaining on top were disheveled and soaked with sweat, and a thick, nest-like clump of hair was gathered on her forehead. Her silky black abaya had slipped to her waist, revealing the shock of a lemon-yellow dress. Bloodstains blossomed on her right shoulder from the bullet that had left her arm dangling at her side like a dead branch. Her left arm gripped the body of her baby. Sarab's eyes fell on the smashed skull of the child, and the shock sent her off running again, blinded by pain. Wherever she went she was greeted by a pitiless scene of death, the work of her comrades' bullets during their dawn assault on the mosque. The brutality magnified the innocence of these hostages caught in their trap.

She ran, racing against the thudding of her heart until her breathing was labored. It offered her no relief, as once again the sound of bullets and explosions thundered, seemingly even more dangerous. She heard the roar but didn't realize that, this time, a massacre was taking place outside the walls of the Grand Mosque. A squadron of soldiers had charged and were being driven back by the rebel snipers in the minarets before they got anywhere near the huge, heavy doors of the mosque. Bullets and explosives rained down on them from her comrades inside, and the soldiers were mown down without exception. The circles of peace around the mosque were soiled with blood, the manifestation of a desecration that had never occurred to anyone before.

All at once, an unexpected silence descended while the stench of blood settled over the scene.

"Allahu akbar!" A ragged victory cry broke the silence, and Mujan moved along the arcades, carrying the news of the victory won by his snipers.

"Our snipers have succeeded in mowing down an entire battalion of the police and Special Forces." At once, this early success eliminated their horror at the reality of the language of weapons, and the rebels' morale was boosted afresh. From their positions, most were unable to see what was happening outside the mosque, but their blind faith in Mujan made them capable of imagining and justifying the massacre.

Sarab stumbled when the cry of "Allahu akbar" informed her of the news. She suddenly stopped running, realizing there was no escape. *We're trapped.* The phrase pounded inside her head like a hammer, but the only thing she cared about was her brother.

Now Sayf has achieved the aim of his existence: war. Bitter tears sprang from her eyes, welling up out of the fear she had repressed for months. *And it will be impossible to wean him off the taste of blood.*

The Holy City was torn between terror and excitement, unsure whether or not the Mahdi had really appeared. It could hardly believe the murder, which had begun to spread out from the minarets until it reached the houses surrounding the Grand Mosque, and random victims began falling victim to rebel sniper bullets.

Hundreds of hostages were led to form an audience in the courtyard, and Muhammad bin Abdullah al-Qahtani, the long-awaited Mahdi, was brought to stand in front of them. He rested his back against the Black Stone in the corner of the Kaaba, while the hostages were driven forward one by one to kiss his hand and repeat after Mujan, "We pledge allegiance to you, O Mahdi, sent by the mercy of God, and we swear obedience to you."

Simple men clustered in deference to the weapons leading them to slaughter. They kissed the hand with its long fingers, murmured the words unheedingly, and were herded back to their seats in the northern arcades, paralyzed with fear. They were not in the least interested in the inauguration of a new empire, or in the declaration of war on the present age; they merely crouched down to wait for the miracle that would save them and restore the peace the mosque was renowned for.

While the fighters were wandering among the hostages, a spiritual void had settled on the Grand Mosque. Time was paused, like the gap between one second and another when everything could be heard draining away, and in this gap, ravens were speaking; they had come from nowhere to circle over the Grand Mosque. In that ignominious silence, Mujan stood behind his Mahdi, watching the hostages' submissive masks. He realized the stupidity of forcing them to pledge their allegiance. Doubt about what exactly was lurking behind those masks made it impossible to recruit even those hostages who had exhibited enthusiasm for him and his followers; putting weapons in these hands could mean the definitive end, should they revolt against him.

He contemplated the ten men he had appointed to guard the hostages. If these faces began to stir, they would be dealt with summarily. He issued an order to his assistant: "Double the guards on the hostages."

All the same, he was aware that sacrificing this number to guard them was a risk. Meanwhile, a fiercer enemy presented itself in the terrain of the mosque; it defied the maps he had pored over and had easily swallowed up the five hundred fighters he had brought. It wouldn't be long before this enemy took shape outside in the resourceful authorities who would soon regain their equilibrium and try to attack. The blood of so many had declared: *There's no way back.*

"But Sheikh Mujan . . ." The assistant suppressed his caution and drew Mujan's attention to the huge number of hostages. "How are we going to feed them?" This question circulated in everyone's heads—how were they going to prolong the limited supplies they had smuggled into the Grand Mosque?

Before long they realized the authorities had cut off all water and electricity to the mosque and the surrounding areas, muting the loudspeakers in the minarets so the rebels couldn't use them to call for allegiance to the Mahdi.

Amid all this chaos, time flew by and they didn't realize they had missed the afternoon prayer. Time had shut behind them, and in front of them was a void. The calls to prayer, which had wooed the sky of the Holy City five times a day, had suddenly fallen silent.

A mute city without a call to prayer was like a true curse. It seemed as if the angels had fled the Holy City. Mujan realized this suddenly, and so he ordered the muezzin of the jamaa to raise the call for the evening prayer. The man stood by the curtains of the Kaaba, holding his rifle to his mouth like a microphone, and he embarked on a powerful call to prayer, protesting against the chaos. It inflated into the dense silence enveloping the Grand Mosque.

"*Hayy ala al-salaat*—"A stray bullet from an unknown source struck the muezzin dead. Uproar broke out around his body, and Sarab wondered whether the confusion and bloodshed of their first prayer in the Grand Mosque was a reflection of the true essence of the jamaa.

Mujan collected himself. He covered the body with his red-striped pilgrim's garment and stood behind the Mahdi, who hurriedly congregated a group of fighters in the northern arcades. They recited the prayer for the dead over the muezzin and all the casualties of that day. One group after another embarked on prayers in different locations within the arcades, remaining alert for any reaction.

The dead and wounded are working against us. The truth hit Mujan as the sun rose on the third day of the occupation, when he began the morning with an inspection of his men in the different quarters of the mosque. Before long, he was struck by the stench. He lifted his head and carried on, unwilling to wrap his pilgrim's robe around his nose to block the smell. The corpses of hostages and fighters were scattered about indiscriminately and had begun to decompose in the extreme heat, dispersing unbearable waves of decay and besieging his men with nightmares of the battles awaiting them. He had issued a command on the first day that all medical efforts were to be devoted to his own men, and another command forbidding the fighters from communicating with the hostages.

"Get rid of these bodies," he ordered hoarsely. Under the eyes of the terrified hostages, the men began to drag the bodies away. They piled them up at the entrance to the sewer tunnel and left them there to finish rotting.

Mujan contemplated his men, who were marooned in sluggishness as they waited for a reaction from outside. Everything seemed silent, as if their existence had been forgotten. They couldn't guess what was planned for them, or whether or how the authorities would assent to their demands.

After the first attack, anticipation had a detrimental effect on the men's morale. Even Mujan found it difficult to concentrate; he could only focus on his men who were still living; the dead were out of his control.

The fourth day passed, then the fifth, and nothing happened other than the continued decay of a new batch of casualties, the wounded who had breathed their last during the night. The men's thirst for battle found its only gratification in the courage of the snipers in the minarets, who were firing on unseen targets, firing at nothing, firing at time itself to move it along, firing at silence, and at the endless waiting. Nothing bolstered the resolve of the insurgents apart from those random shots. Even the call to prayer was absent after the muezzin was killed. Guilt settled over the fighters at every prayer time; each group began to mumble their prayers, the words lost in the abyss of the arcades.

Sarab would select the dawn and sunset prayers to face the Kaaba, gazing at the sky, wondering whether there was any angel who would care to descend and move time and assist them with the miserable hostages.

On the sixth day, the fumes of putrefaction intensified. Eyes began to grow a film of doubt, and they avoided Mujan's so he wouldn't see the betrayal lurking within.

Even the urine and excrement are fighting us. No one dared to voice this trifling omission from the plans, an oversight discovered to be dreadful in reality: Mujan had failed to consider the most basic functions of the human body. Due to the limited number of fighters in that atmosphere of charged suspense, it was no longer possible to spare any of them to accompany the hostages to the bathrooms at the edges of the mosques. And so it wasn't long before the large number of hostages became factories expelling waste, which began to silently accumulate—something Mujan hadn't expected would be a deciding factor in the scales of battle. It was not merely urine and feces; it was urine and feces in a sacred place of worship. That inescapable violation of the mosque's sanctity began to silently crumble the men's faith in the value of their fight. The waste lying everywhere became an obsession for them; wherever they turned, they were hounded by the echoes of God's call to Ibrahim and Ismail: *Purify My temple for those who will walk around it, and those who will abide near it in meditation, and those who will bow down and prostrate themselves in prayer.* Here, there was no one circling the Kaaba, no bowing, and no prostration in prayer—just open graves and human waste and flies drunk on their feast; belowground there were no devoted worshipers on retreat in the prayer cells, just a sea of weapons.

From the first week, Sarab was no longer able to ignore the widening gulf between herself and the other fighters. She froze whenever an order came to fire on a living target, and in the first attack she hadn't succeeded in firing a single bullet. That day she had stood holding her machine gun like it was her own broken spine, and her mother's perpetual complaints reverberated around her head.

"We hear of twins born with one skull but I—praise God, we thank you for our troubles—I was suffered by my Lord to bear two children with one spine. Sayf is our backbone. Perhaps God is making him strong enough to live long and be victorious in all his battles."

For the first time, Sarab didn't resent her mother's description of her as a spineless freak. She accepted it humbly. Despite her highly developed combat skills, she had withdrawn to work in the supply lines, moving between the cellar vaults and the fighters on the frontlines. She was careful to stay close to Muhammad, inclining toward the human weakness that had begun to reveal itself with perplexing brilliance. She avoided Mujan, who seemed imprisoned in a constricting coat of armor called "victory at whatever cost," trying to force the rest of the world inside with him. From Sarab's infatuated and heavily biased vantage point, the tacit division between the two leaders grew deeper by the day. Muhammad seemed inclined to peace and, in a state of semi-surrender, lacked the will to complete their goal. He answered the description given in the texts of the divine envoy, and could be excused as bewitched by his faith, while Mujan was the vengeful, intolerant sorcerer. Muhammad's surrender to divine commandment equaled Mujan's resolve to impose surrender on the world around him.

Sarab profited from her observation post to steal moments where she could offer help to the wounded hostages. She knew it was against orders, but she couldn't ignore the increasingly grim suffering all around her.

One night she finally succeeded in gathering her courage to return to the giant with the ripped-open belly. She shuddered as she knelt beside him and helped him sip some water. She was careful not to look at the gaping wounds in his abdomen; his guts were pouring out of his belly onto the ground beside him, and they gleamed a nauseating, phosphorescent blue.

In a burst of unthinking heroism, she fought her revulsion and reached out for those intestines. She was paralyzed by their cold, sticky touch, but kept trying to gather them up with trembling fingers. She strove desperately to push the leathery guts back into the abdominal cavity, while they resisted her like muscular snakes. At last she succeeded in vanquishing them, and buried them deep inside until she felt her fingers brushing his spine.

Sarab sank down on the ground there and then, her shoulders spreading out over the cold, congealed blood. The gelatinous intestines were bulging out of the belly walls and the open wounds, and she didn't know how to keep everything closed. She tore a strip from the giant's white robe and was trying to tie it over the stomach when she felt a shadow hovering over her. She froze, expecting a bullet to burst her skull. When a few seconds had ticked by and she was still alive, she plucked up courage and looked up, terrified, to find Muhammad, the supposed Mahdi, looking down on her, watching her struggle to keep the bandages on the wounds that were impossible to close.

"It's just a little water from the well," she stammered, trying to exonerate herself from a charge of smuggling. "He's dying."

Muhammad's face radiated an unearthly translucency. The angels' compassion must be reflected on the face of the Mahdi, she thought.

"Yes. And who, in your belief, bears the sin of annihilating this soul?"

Was it him speaking these words and pointing at his chest? Sarab doubted her hearing; had he really said, "God knows it is a battle to establish the truth, and we implore God to accept our sacrifices on the path to do so"?

Hastily, he helped her bind the wounds. They were both certain that it was just a farce; nothing could save that giant from dying of wounds at such a late stage of gangrene.

Sarab drew strength from Muhammad, who began to crystallize into a true redeemer. Something godlike radiated from his gaze when it settled on her or the other fighters; it was a look of encouraging faith that dispensed goodness. As silent death grew alarmingly all around them, so did her conviction that he was without doubt one of the heavenly envoys. The fighters were looking to the Mahdi and Mujan, entreating them to shore up their faith, and both moved tirelessly among the fighters scattered throughout the vast expanse of the mosque. Both demonstrated superhuman strength in scaling the minarets and the roof of the Grand Mosque, and in moving among the arcades and the vaults. They were everywhere, encouraging the fighters' stamina and affirming that victory was near. Whenever a fighter was weary, Muhammad sprang from nowhere to massage his shoulders; whenever a fighter allowed his weapon to droop, Mujan materialized to restore his aim. One look into their eyes would kindle the embers in the fighter's soul.

Mujan and his fighters were certain, in a way that surpassed Sarab's simple understanding, that they were winning the battle thanks to the attackers' reluctance to use lethal force inside the Grand Mosque, in case it exposed hundreds of hostages to danger.

"Time is on our side. We will achieve our goal if we succeed in regulating our consumption of resources, and if we avoid dissension within our ranks and defeat from within." With this phrase, Mujan made his cruelest decision.

Sarab stood paralyzed, watching Mujan supervise the implementation of an order that chilled the blood in her veins. Her comrades hurried to herd the healthy and unharmed hostages to the prayer cells at the farthest point of the cellars, where they were locked inside.

These unharmed hostages were the potential defeat from within, and they were imprisoned in darkness in order to stymie any potential rebellion. She, like everyone, was aware that the prayer cells intended for worship had been turned into rooms of slow, silent death. None of those hostages would the leave the room alive.

That night seemed the darkest. She couldn't lie down to relax or sleep; she couldn't bear the touch of the earth underneath her. For hours she wandered like a caged lion, preyed on by nightmares of people buried alive, their bodies slowly decomposing, unseen in the shadows. Her feet drove her to the Shahada Gallery, where she had heard the hostage reciting the Chapter of the Most Gracious. She expected him to have disappeared into the cellar along with the other hostages, but to her surprise she saw he was still there, shaking with his recitation. She approached cautiously so as not to interrupt the sweetness of his verses, but when she was a few footsteps away, she was halted by doubt. In his gray robe and white keffiyeh the man seemed no more than a wisp of smoke, something she had dreamed up in her need for peace. As soon as she took another step, the gallery filled with the susurrations of numberless Qurans, their pages turned as quickly as lightning by dozens of unseen reciters as they delivered their verses in interweaving whispers. Sarab stood stock still, not daring to draw closer in case she dispersed the comforting vision. But she was surprised when the reciter in the gray robe paused at the verse of Cain's murder of Abel in the Chapter of the Repast: *Thereupon God sent forth a raven which scratched the earth, to show him how he might conceal the nakedness of his brother's body.* And the darkness of the arcades intensified to the blackness of a raven.

As a meager form of penance, she went back to the woman in the lemon-yellow dress and found she had mummified in her position. She hadn't moved a finger, still leaning against the wall in a state of clotted horror, still facing the Kaaba.

Sarab stood watching her with a mixture of fascination and dismay. Her face was so pale it was almost transparent, the sweat dripping on her face had dried, and the red rose of blood on her right shoulder had turned black. Her right arm was completely immobile, and her left arm clutched the body of her baby, which was rapidly beginning to rot. A stream of maggots crawled in a chain from the infant's broken skull to the mother's chest. The woman's breathing was labored and her crazed face leaned over, absorbed in watching the maggots. Sarab thoughtlessly reached out to take the infant's corpse, but the arm clung on fiercely with an inhuman grip; it was impossible to extract the body, which seemed like an extension of the mother.

Sarab stood there at a loss. The mother froze, terrified, not allowing her to get near her shoulder. Sarab backed away, aware that she was delirious. The dryness in her eyes caused the arcades around her to widen and splinter. She chose a remote corner where she could hide away and sleep a little. With some difficulty, she forced her eyelids to close, but no sooner had she closed her eyes than a lemon-yellow blaze erupted over her body. She noticed that she was wearing the same dress as the woman, but this one was decorated with prints of the stiffened body of her child, and whenever she moved the edges of the bodies printed on the dress clacked against one another. Suddenly all the faces of the printed corpses wheeled around and revealed the same face to her—the face of her brother Sayf. She woke up, horrified, and rushed to the courtyard, hoping that a stray bullet would peel the nightmare from her skin. Wherever she turned, behind every pillar, a lemony blaze outwitted her, bringing out the decomposed body of the baby with her brother's face. She began to wander, aware that she was embracing death of some kind, and that she had to relax her grip on it.

Sarab moved away from her comrades, pursued by the choking feeling of falling into a trap. Suddenly, a hidden desire to keep living pushed her to review the maps of the Grand Mosque buried in her memory. Without realizing it, with an aim she couldn't define, she strove to follow the details of those maps over the real terrain in an attempt to locate the secret tunnels leading outside the mosque, and the passages leading from the roof to the vaults. It wasn't easy but she kept going, determined to discover the entrance that led to the sewers.

Her memory of the absent maps led her at last to a narrow cell in a far-flung and abandoned part of the cellars, used to store broken minbars. There was no source of light in the cell, and Sarab groped around in total darkness. Patiently, she continued to feel her way over the walls and the ground. But it was in vain; however much she tried, there was no trace of an opening or a secret door, just the touch of cold dampness and the utter silence of the grave. She wasn't prepared to give up yet, however, and repeated her secret visits to that cell over the next three days.

On her fourth visit, she concluded that she had wasted her time and energy in a delusion of escape when she should have dedicated all her energy to helping the wounded.

She was about to give up when a mysterious intuition caused her to pause next to what felt like an old minbar; she had ignored it in her previous search, believing it was the last place an exit would be hidden. Squeezing herself beneath it, she began to search the ground, which was covered with spiderwebs. Almost immediately, her hand found a small metal circle. She gasped; this must be the secret entrance to the sewers she had been looking for. Sarab was flooded with a feeling of victory, and she felt giddy at the mere promise of escape. She sat there, her outspread hands clutching the metal door. She didn't dare raise it and confirm there was an opening underneath. Suddenly her heart stopped as she realized the implicit betrayal of having discovered a way out. She stood up and backed away, and as she left the cell she vowed to forget this door existed.

Falling Demons, Fleeing Angels

A LOUD EXPLOSION ROCKED THE Grand Mosque and Sarab's heart. It was the moment they had been waiting for. A terrifying quantity of dynamite had succeeded in blasting open the Riyada Gate in the gallery on the eastern side of the mosque, and a throng of soldiers rushed through the breach. At the same moment, the sky over the mosque was suddenly covered with helicopters dispatching armed paratroopers into the courtyard like a heavy shower of rain. Everything seemed to happen in the blink of an eye, and rage and terror exploded in the arcades around the courtyard. The rebels emerged from their stagnant state of anticipation; their machine guns broke out with fierce intensity, discharging all the doubt and loss that had accumulated over the interminable hours of watching and waiting.

Sarab looked around. All of a sudden the courtyard behind her had been surrounded by a ring of flames, and the occupiers' hand grenades flew through the air, reaping harvest from that human rain.

With reckless courage Muhammad bin Abdullah was positioned at the heart of that hellfire, totally exposed in the shade of the Kaaba and mowing down paratroopers with machine gunfire. Like a sleepwalker, Sarab broke through the ring of fire to take up a position next to him. She didn't fire, but with the same rash courage as his, she circled the doors of the Kaaba, abandoning her wounded comrades as she watched the Mahdi. Although it was illogical, she was convinced that her all-encompassing gaze was guaranteed to keep him alive.

In less than an hour, the marble floor of the courtyard was covered with red and khaki stains, an absurd tableau of attackers' bodies, lifeless and staring at the Kaaba. Stray bullets had hit some of the wounded hostages and rescued them from the unendurable torture of a slow death.

Sarab woke from her ardent protection of the Mahdi to find herself mired in a deluge of blood. Jubilant cries of "La ilaha illa Allah!" and "Allahu akbar!" rent the chests of her comrades, pricked by the same doubt regarding the legitimacy of their war that had troubled her since the beginning. A second loud explosion interrupted the victory cry; all of a sudden, the minaret overlooking the suq collapsed; it had been bombed by a circling helicopter. Sarab's heart throbbed, and she offered a prayer of thankfulness that it wasn't the minaret where Sayfullah was positioned.

Despite the loss of the snipers in the collapsed minaret, the rebels were bursting with zeal; the Holy City had fallen under their control. Wherever Mujan appeared in order to examine his troops, the rebels rushed toward him, congratulating him, kissing the Mahdi's hand, and cheering the bloody result of the ambush.

"Now those who have strayed from the true path know that we have a response for every trick of their armies, and they have no choice but to surrender to our demands." Mujan congratulated himself, readying his forces for the next massacre and ignoring the fact that they had passed the point of demands; there was no path forward but blood.

Sarab kneeled in the Kaaba's shade, besieged by the staring eyes of the corpses littering the courtyard. "It's a real war, a plague of locusts and lice and frogs and blood." With chattering teeth, Sarab feverishly repeated that peculiar phrase; she didn't know why it had possessed her. She stood, creaking from the icy cold she felt, facing the shattered, still-bleeding bodies. The human body bereft of life left ice in the soul, and she could hear rustling coming from these bodies. She finished her monologue, perhaps freed from her greatest fear. A column of smoke, swollen to gigantic proportions, rose from the spot where the ghost of the reciter had stammered the verse of Cain and Abel and overpowered the noises coming from the bodies.

"*If anyone slays a human being . . . it shall be as though he had slain all mankind.*"

Sarab felt that they had all died in this massacre, had all committed suicide. Something inside her had died even if she was still breathing. This was more abhorrent than any hunting trip, or any battle plan worked out on paper.

At the same time, Sarab battled with a feverish bitterness that pulled her out of her kneeling position. She was consumed by an obsessive thought: *You are too wretched to prostrate yourself in the presence of God.*

She raised her head and suddenly saw a skinny black ghost springing out of the courtyard. For a moment she was positive it was Azrael come to claim her, but the flash of white teeth in the bellowing mouth restored her to reality. It was Kasir, Masrour's teenage son.

Kasir was holding his machine gun in his right hand and a machete in his left. She saw that he was bending over a body. He clamped his thighs over its torso and plunged his cleaver into its lifeless chest. He continued to stab lustily until the chest was ripped open and its ribs exposed; crazed elation split his face and he carried on hacking, savoring the sound of the ribs shattering with each thrust. His hunger escalated until it could no longer be satiated by that lump, and he rose and began to stalk the bodies. A torrent of bullets finished off the weakened soul of a soldier, another burst tore at a pile of bodies and turned them into shredded flesh. Kasir couldn't believe his luck when he saw a wounded soldier trying to crawl away. He let out a whoop of savage joy and pounced on him, stabbing him in the neck and hacking at the back of the man, who was still writhing to escape. Sarab was more shocked by the sight of the knife plunging into living flesh than she had been by all the bullets. She felt as though her own arms were plunging into that human flesh, and she began to retch. Kasir was aghast and turned toward her with a roar. The fire in his eyes warned her that he would plunge his knife into her guts.

"*Phtu!* Son of Baroud!" He spat contemptuously.

"You should fear God. What pleasure do you get from killing the dead?" Her voice came out weakly, anointed with bile.

"What does a weasel like you know about it?" It was the first time she had heard Kasir speak. His voice was high-pitched, like a knife blade boring into her ear. He turned his back on her and began to roam among the bodies in the courtyard, butchering the wounded and mutilating the dead.

She followed him and pushed him. "Stop this! You're just an imbecile boy."

"And I've been watching you. You carry your weapon like a lady in her panties."

Sarab was stupefied by this malice.

"You're the son of a sheikh and a slave to your fear and cowardice," he said. "I'm the son of a slave but I'm a master thanks to this." He waved his machine gun in her face. "Here, the gun separates the slave from the master."

"Master over the dead?"

"Anyone who saw me now would spit on that stupid question."

"Where does a boy like you get all this rage?"

"When we wipe out these infidels and start a new state, a boy like me will be minister of war, while a spineless nothing like you will find something at the bottom of the ministry of health; somewhere boring just like you." Whenever Kasir spoke he silenced her with an unexpected torrent. He bent down, mounted the body of a soldier and wrenched at the corpse's neck, shearing it off with evident satisfaction and a stupefying smoothness. He seemed drunk as he joined in the victory cries coming from the rebels' fortifications in the arcades.

The breach in the Riyada gate gaped like a wound in Mujan's guts. He was clearly furious, and moved restlessly while he supervised his men as they reinforced the door with anything they could find, mostly the Grand Mosque's furniture and bookshelves. He appointed the most zealous of his fighters, and the most suicidal, to take up position around the door in readiness for any renewed attempt to break through.

Sarab fled, withdrawing from her comrades' celebrations of this nightmare. She took refuge in the shadows of the cellars and stood there shaking, her back to the piles of dates that formed their provisions. Suddenly, she felt something sticky around her neck. Fumbling at it cautiously, her fingers touched a bloated worm. She threw it away in horror and wheeled around to find maggots squirming through the bags of dates, leaving blood trails behind them. The sight of the maggots was as horrifying as the bullets. A Bedouin saying rang in her ears: "Dates are determined. Scorpions and snakes and time pass over them and they don't spoil. Dates are eternity." What had corrupted this eternity?

She closed her eyes and felt the maggots swell to the same size as the bags. She realized the futility of feeding the fighters, when they were merely soon-to-be-rotting corpses. The massacre she had left behind her gave her the feeling that Judgment Day would soon swallow up everyone. The moans of her wounded comrades made her incapable of forgetting the hideousness of the scene above her. But she couldn't retreat. The voice that obsessed her with survival had fallen mute, and so she hurried to help the Sudanese doctor who was moving in a flurry among her suicidal comrades, amputating limbs and plunging into guts in an attempt to save whomever he could.

Only a week had passed since they first occupied the Grand Mosque, and it was the first real attack they had faced. They soon realized the grave mistake of not bringing medical supplies, which would at least have guaranteed that those terrible wounds wouldn't fester. The doctor was extracting shrapnel and amputating extremities and dressing them with holy water.

"Mujan, prepared for everything, wasn't prepared at all for this many wounded fighters," Sarab thought while she was struggling to dam the blood fountaining from the stump of an Egyptian fighter's leg. His constant howling had made her pulse race wildly ever since they carried him in, and when he suddenly fell silent from the shock of the amputation, her heart almost stopped. She staggered, and the world would have blurred had the scalpel not sunk into her hand and woken her.

✳

That night a red shadow descended over the Grand Mosque. Sarab was facing the minaret where her brother was positioned when suddenly, from the pit of darkness, she spotted a gleam creeping through the arcades. She watched it closely and made out the face of Masrour glistening with sweat. It was the first time she had seen Kasir's father since they entered the mosque.

She noticed that Masrour was holding on to a bound man and pushing him along, but she didn't understand who his captive was. Why had Masrour left his strategic position as a sniper at the top of the Taysir Minaret to creep around down here? And where was he going? A mysterious excitement made Sarab follow him from a distance, and before long she realized that he was heading for the entrance to the sewers. Her pulse raced at the thought that he wanted to escape and that he might be able to help her kidnap her brother Sayfullah and take them both out of this hell.

When Masrour reached the tunnel entrance, he stumbled and his prisoner freed himself. Masrour rushed to grab him and a silent scuffle ensued. At once, Sarab realized that the silent captive was Kasir. Masrour continued to struggle with his son, and both were careful not to make any sound that might attract attention. Masrour tried to drag his son to the tunnel and Sarab realized that Kasir was refusing to escape. His love for weapons had healed the pain of his abandoned education; he had dedicated himself not to Mujan, but to the pleasure of murder.

Finally Masrour succeeded in gaining the upper hand over his son; pointing his gun at Kasir's head, he forced him to yield, hissing, "I'm the one who threw you in here and I'm the one who will save you. You will follow me whether you like it or not."

Kasir put up fierce resistance, aware that his father wasn't able to kill him.

"You're only responsible for yourself. I'm my own master." Kasir tried to push away his father, who proceeded to bind him using his pilgrim's clothes.

"It's the weapons that are tempting you to this false machismo. You are a boy; you weren't born for this."

104

He picked Kasir up like a sack and threw him over his back, carrying him to the tunnel entrance. Suddenly, to his father's shock, Kasir let out a piercing scream like the whine of an ax blade. The cry rent Sarab's heart as it leaped into her throat and choked her. From nowhere, shots were fired and ghosts swooped down on father and son from the darkness.

Masrour stood dumbstruck. A bullet had left a hole the size of a coin in Kasir's forehead, killing him instantly.

The ghosts didn't waste time. They threw Masrour to the ground and fell on him. Sarab backed away, blinded by the blood pounding in her head as the battle between the giant and his rebel comrades disturbed the night.

"You damned worm!" Their curses lashed him as he struggled against them desperately, without saying a word. He was on the verge of overpowering his five attackers when more arrived, attracted by the sound of the fight, and succeeded in wrestling him to the ground. Now Mujan appeared, and without comment he supervised the removal of Masrour to the southern arcades, where he was bound between two pillars.

"You will be left to die slowly of hunger and thirst, as a warning to anyone else with thoughts of weakness."

From her hiding place, Sarab watched as they left him there and disappeared into the darkness. Masrour sobbed bitterly when Kasir's lifeless body was thrown in front of him. Perhaps he had been more shocked by his son's betrayal than his death. For a few moments, Sarab couldn't move; longing and horror silently goaded her to move forward and break the ropes, and then to surrender to whatever happened afterward. But however much she gathered her strength, she couldn't take a single step in Masrour's direction.

"When we are resurrected on Judgment Day, we will pay for this bloodshed!"

Sarab trembled as Masrour directed his ravings toward her through ragged breathing.

"And we won't be forgiven for ignoring the truth," he went on. "My master al-Kharaymi was right: how can we have ignored the most important condition for the appearance of the Mahdi? He must be descended from the Prophet, peace be upon him. This Muhammad is an al-Qahtani, not a blood descendant of the Prophet! And I sacrificed the most precious thing I had to a delusion." His weeping overwhelmed him. "My son wasn't the type to slaughter the dead. Perhaps I made him disloyal and death-loving when I ate the lizard's testicles." He waited for her to exonerate him, and when she persisted in her silence, he carried on talking to himself.

"Since I was a child, it was my dream to have a son like me. I got married when I was fifteen so I could have a family quickly, but I spent fifteen more years without children. For years I took a fertility potion, a mixture of ground lizard testicles and palm pollen, until I had him. I called him Kasir so he would have a lucky name, a beautiful flower planted in rock, since he split the rock of my infertility. I named him Kasir, the destroyer, and I intended him to grow up to be a great hunter, like an eagle or a falcon. He charged up against death and disease, but he didn't die or even get sick. When he was born I swore I would only reply to the world 'sum' and 'tum' to acknowledge my gratitude for that gift. And I kept my promise, to discover now that those words were the bombs that broke my heart."

The two were silent, listening to his words echo into the night.

"I made him join this hell, thinking it would lead to Paradise. What kind of a father am I, to wish my son to grow up in Heaven by throwing him into Hell."

When she didn't reply, he began to recite the Quran, his recitation mixing with his tears and the verses of the blind reciter pilgrim, as if they were one person.

Hence, who could be more wicked than those who bar the mention of God's name from any of His houses of worship and strive for their ruin, although they have no right to enter them save in fear of God? For them, in this world, there is ignominy in store; and for them, in the life to come, awesome suffering.

A shudder ran through Sarab, but she resisted the impulse to reply to this provocation. She remained there for a long time, victim of her own weakness and self-hatred. She mocked herself for being too cowardly to assist not only Masrour but also the healthy hostages imprisoned in the cellars, while she affected compassion for the dying hostages, neglected and strewn among the arcades.

Death, the Final Separation

THIS IS THE WASTE THAT propagates death, and death that propagates waste. She didn't know how this phrase instilled itself in her head, but it began to haunt her while she watched her comrades struggle in misery; not only against the attackers and the weapons, which were beginning to run out, but with their own human bodies. They were being brought to their knees by trivial needs they couldn't avoid, like the need to defecate and be rid of the result. A week had passed since their first victory, and as the attempts to storm the Grand Mosque intensified, the rebels could no longer leave their positions to use the bathrooms. They resorted to exercising their need behind the forest of pillars, turning the galleries of worship into an open sewer. The stench of this waste, heightened by the hot sun and combined with the increasing attacks, caused the fighters' faith in their end goal to teeter.

Her brother in particular seemed to scorn his body for the mere fact of its humanity. He pushed it mercilessly beyond its limits in order to become a superman, capable of killing ceaselessly day and night. But his poor body, however much it struggled to do so, wasn't able to escape its humanity and it weakened him. It caused him to sleep where he stood, snatching a few minutes of rest, or forced him to leave his weapon and evacuate his bowels in the bucket which Sarab emptied every morning, reassured her brother was still human.

Sarab felt her brain dry up and shrivel with torpor as events beyond imagining began to come thick and fast. She carried on with her tasks, all the while feeling that the sky was silent and indifferent. She craved to see any sign of clemency there in the form of a cloud or a lightning bolt, but the sky remained absolutely clear, never tempered, confirming Sarab's deepest fears that God had abandoned them to the horror they had created.

Wherever she looked, Sarab was faced with corpses rotting in hidden rage and frustration.

"How will we justify all of this before God?" Muhammad appeared suddenly, voicing this unexpected condemnation of himself. Both he and Sarab listened to the ominous silence around the Grand Mosque, their heads sunk into the thick black cloth covering the Kaaba, and for a moment its dull perfume covered the stench of death around them.

He went on: "I am haunted by the Prophet's order to his army not to cut down a tree on their march, and not to kill women, children, and the elderly."

"But you are the Mahdi. It's your destiny to save the world," Sarab said.

He looked at her for a long time and the purity of his face was split with an inexplicable smile; it carried suffering and pity, for her and perhaps for himself and the whole world. His face had a beauty that struck her like a lightning bolt, and she hurriedly hid her embarrassment.

"You are the Mahdi and you will lead us out of this bloodshed."

"Will I? Can we ever survive this bloodshed of our own making?"

"I didn't mean that you will lead us as a jamaa; perhaps we have lost any hope of survival by now. But the important thing now is what we brought with us. You must lead this to the end."

"This is the end." His voice exuded a despair that admitted no rescue or conclusion.

Sarab was furious. "Don't be angry with me, but what did you expect by coming here like this and starting a war in God's house?"

She bit her tongue at her bluntness, but instead of the angry reaction she had expected, Muhammad said bitterly, "Nothing like this."

She thumped the wall softly and added, "Perhaps you believed that the doors of this mosque would just close on you and your men, and the world would respect you and pledge allegiance to you as the Mahdi. And the world would be filled with justice after it was filled with tyranny." Despite her respect for Muhammad, she was surprised by the bitter sarcasm filling her voice as it repeated Mujan's promise. She couldn't believe that the Mahdi himself was frankly declaring doubts that she had been too afraid to even whisper in the presence of her brother.

"I never imagined war would break out. Perhaps it was naive of me to believe that they wouldn't dare fight us here, although history tells us the opposite. The Ummayads bombarded the mosque twice using their catapults; the second time, in 73 Hijri, they set fire to a part of it."

"You could throw away your weapon any time and say 'enough' to this path of blood." She realized the naivety of this suggestion.

"*If anyone slays a human being . . . it shall be as though he had slain all mankind.* The murder of just one person recurs endlessly. There's no going back," he said.

He stared at her, hawk-like, and her whole being shuddered from the tremors along her spine. She knew she was staring into the eyes of a dead man, and falling in love with him. The truth shook her then and there, in a place and time that were inappropriate for love, or for any feeling other than despair and terror. Her feelings were incompatible with all this death. Not even the fact that he was married to Mujan's sister had hindered her capitulation to these blissful, terrifying feelings. She looked around, trembling, for fear that someone might be eavesdropping on a conversation that could only be described as betrayal. She was astonished that he could read her thoughts.

"Veil yourself well."

She was confused. Did he mean the veil of a woman? Could it be, by some miracle, he had uncovered her disguise?

"Throw away your weapons, all of you!" A voice like thunder exploded behind Sarab. Mujan had been passing when a giant shadow pounced on him and, to everyone's shock, held a knife to his neck. It was Masrour the giant, who had succeeded in breaking his chains and charging the leader.

"This slaughter must end. Order your men to surrender."

Mujan remained silent, but he bared his teeth in a smile as the knifepoint dug deeper into his neck. A drop of blood trickled to his chest. The violence arrested the fighters and, bewildered, they wavered between surrender and hesitation, hoping for a miracle.

Sarab froze; she didn't dare to turn around to see what was happening behind her. From the corner of her eye she caught a glimpse of Muhammad's shadow as he crept around Masrour, who had protected his back with a pillar.

"Give the order to these miserable wretches, and save those whose souls can still be saved." A bullet exploded in the giant's arm and Mujan wheeled around on his adversary, freed by the bullet.

"Fear the day of reckoning, Mujan. On that day, you won't be helped by money or—" A hail of bullets silenced the cry, which tore the red glow of the sunset.

Sarab froze. Behind her, she heard the sound of a human skull cracking and blood fountaining into the air, before she saw it gushing over her feet. Sarab was certain that a bullet had pierced her brain and burst the tumor of doubt swelling there. Her veins throbbed with the sound of the pilgrim's voice announcing Judgment Day: *"And when the sky is rent asunder and becomes red like burning oil . . ."*

When she didn't fall down dead and her head was still on her shoulders, she summoned up the courage the dead man had shown and turned around. She saw Masrour's body, its head mashed, lying a couple of meters away. She saw the gaunt, rigid apparition of Mujan hurrying away from the scene, ignoring the blood still dripping from the wound in his neck where the knife had twisted into him.

The nearby rebels were dumbstruck, their gaze fixed on the heap of bodies; the giant had fallen and covered the body of his son. The pure red blood of the father mixed with the blood of the son, which had already turned black. Wings fluttered in the air, and Muhammad stood in the middle of the area between the arcades, watching with a brooding expression as a breeze blew through the arcades and buffeted their faces.

The angels of death are here, Sarab thought, too frightened to look up and face them. *It's the angels driving hell over our heads.*

"Allahu akbar! Allahu akbar! La ilaha illa Allah!" The sudden call to sunset prayer disturbed them. It came from a location no one had been expecting. Eyes swiveled to the bearded fighter who had taken up position among the arcades to perform the call to prayer, for fear of stray bullets. His loud voice was agitated, like a lament, and he wasn't qualified to lead the call to prayer, so it echoed feebly in the forest of pillars. The sound caused the outlines of Grand Mosque to expand beyond the planet's boundaries, to where the sky disappeared, leaving them to tumble into a hell of their own making.

Sarab hurried away from the mangled lump, formerly the bodies of Masrour and his son. She quickened her pace, avoiding the eyes of her comrades. If they shone a light inside her head now, they would discover absolute sin, embodied in the absence of the call to prayer.

She groped forward blindly, losing herself in the darkness, imploring the earth to open and swallow her up. She felt fragile, and avoided al-Mutawwaj Minaret where Sayf was stationed. He had started this by exterminating an entire battalion of the National Guard with his unerring bullets. He had repelled and demolished that first counterattack, playing a decisive role in transforming the path of their jamaa's venture. Since that massacre, whenever Sarab looked up she saw the minaret drenched in blood, a nightmare that haunted her even when she was awake. She stopped suddenly, arrested by the fact that her brother, Sayfullah, was responsible for turning the call to prayer into a call for war.

"If not for Sayf, I would never have ended up here." This sorrow erupted in fire. "Or at least I wouldn't have been too cowardly to release Masrour and follow him outside." For the millionth time, Sarab asked herself, "What is it that shackles me? Why do I loiter here around death, unable to cut the cord with a brother who hankers after blood?" Was it because of the physical resemblance between them? Because it was her duty? Or maybe there was a hidden appetite for suicide in her? Inside, all was a blur; she couldn't make out a glimmer of feeling other than increasing revulsion, and a sense of loss that she and Sayf had remained there and sacrificed everything to the abyss. In that massacre, when Sarab came face to face with death, its face transmuted; it became seductive. Her body was stimulated by its numbing pleasure; her tingling flesh responded easily and instinctively to the bottomless chasm.

There had been another wave of deaths, and the rebels had still had no opportunity to dispose of the bodies. Wherever Sarab went, her senses were violated; everything she took in, the smells, sights, sounds, and tastes, was like death.

Rage blinded her and she quickened her pace. She ran aimlessly, and came to her senses in front of the Riyada gate, exposed to the reproving glare of her comrades. As she stood there, bile began to gush through her veins, a compulsive, inhuman force pumping through her delicate body and whetting her senses. With some difficulty she controlled the yearning to hurtle forward and tear down all these barricades as if they were made of paper, allowing the soldiers inside the Grand Mosque while her supernatural body absorbed a hail of bullets from her brother's machine gun.

She returned to the cellars. Involuntarily, her feet took her toward the prayer cell where the minbar hid the door to the outside. The darkness was condensing, welling up from her sense of being adrift, torn as she was between escaping now and holding out to ensure her brother survived. As each day passed, she realized her ability to save him was a delusion.

She pushed on, and the darkness sucked her up until she reached the cell, one of a row of similar rooms. She was sure it was the same prayer cell, although she was confused by a perfume she hadn't noticed before. She advanced cautiously, thirstily drinking in that fragrance.

As she entered the room she couldn't make out anything at all; rather, she was guided by the scent. There was no trace of the minbar, and in its place there was a body clinging to the back of the room, a gleaming lump of smooth, brown flesh.

At first, Sarab thought that it was the body of one of the hostages who had been imprisoned there, although she smelled perfume, not decomposition. But as she approached, she saw a barely perceptible movement of slow breathing.

She pointed her machine gun at the broad chest and heard a sigh.

"What use are weapons on a figment of your imagination?"

It was difficult to judge whether the voice came from the body or if it was the darkness whispering inside her.

"Even so, it would be a shame if the perfection of this body was marred by a bullet."

Sarab stayed silent; but she pointed the gun away from the man's chest.

"This is a body I have kept alive in these shadows for a hundred years and more; when I reached a hundred, I stopped counting. I might be older than any cloud or revolution that has settled or will settle over this mosque." Sarab's eyes had become accustomed to the darkness, and she began to make out the features of the body that didn't move. Its bottom half was dressed in black rags covered in writing that fluttered in a wave, until it appeared to Sarab that they were in perpetual, living motion.

"Have you come to escape from the decay, girl?" His eyes glimmered like two stars, resting upon her face compassionately. " Everything has its moment, even escape. But the time for that perhaps has not yet come."

Sarab trembled: he had read her intention.

"Let me show you something." He pointed. "Open that cupboard in the corner."

Sarab obeyed, feeling her way to the corner on the right, where she discovered a wooden cupboard reaching up to the ceiling. She opened it cautiously and was taken aback by a gust of perfume. Gleaming bottles of every color were lined up inside.

"Since the house of God was established its blood has run pure red beneath its skin, but it soon turns black when exposed to human desires."

She didn't understand what he was trying to tell her.

"So, whenever the year changes, we wash the house, and we peel human desires away from its skin."

She didn't move her gaze from the vials.

"Those are the scents I collected for the ritual of washing the Kaaba, year after year." Sarab couldn't resist; she opened the first flask and inhaled the scent of sandalwood, and caught the rustle of wings in the air.

"I am a eunuch, one of the oldest. I vowed to serve the Kaaba as long as I lived, until its perfumes ran in my veins. My fellow eunuchs respected my age and said that I was the same age as the Kaaba. They thought of me as Adam, devoted to this tent. My clothes are made from the covering of the Kaaba; whenever they removed a curtain from it they would place it on my body, which I have indulged so that only goodness has touched it. If I were in your place, I wouldn't pollute my exterior with clothes of departure. With patience, the clothing will fall away and remove me from the void of my earthly existence."

He closed his eyes and light disappeared from the room.

"Everyone who departs above is departing from a void of earthly existence," he said.

Sarab wondered what this strange being knew about the events taking place above.

"You are carrying a machine gun," he went on, "but even so, you are not one who kills, nor are you a murderer. Why should the disintegration of the clothing terrify you or cause you to doubt the inevitable journey?"

Sarab contemplated the man, certain that if she fired at him, perfume would spray out instead of blood and the hue of peace on his perfectly round face would be undisturbed. Perhaps this was one of the souls that lived in the Grand Mosque forever, made incarnate now to battle wits with her and postpone her escape. He was not much like a body vulnerable to destruction; he seemed to be beyond it. What message was he giving her? That she should trust death?

"Look at the truth: what is decay? What is perfume? Decay is nothing but a state of the body, of clothing. The soul remains untouched; that is perfume."

Sarab took a step back.

"You people came here demanding death. When you summoned it, it terrified you, and you forgot that dying is not death. You, here—sooner or later, you will realize that there is no death."

She was frustrated by his speech, and disturbed by its untruth. She turned and left, sure that it was no more than a hallucination conjured up by her fear. His mysterious words followed her: "We are all the children of Adam; if your destiny is to live, the darkness itself will reach out to save you, even from the lion's jaw. One day, in your darkest hour, you will hear the shadows roar and you will remember my words."

After that encounter, life for Sarab lost its gravity. The possibility of losing her life was no longer a source of horror, but of liberation. In facing death, Sarab felt that she had turned into the lightest of bubbles, freed from the weight of despair all around her. Suddenly, she no longer needed to embody what her brother emulated, nor what excited Mujan's approval; rather, she aimed not to overstep the truth of what she was, to reveal this buried self; the self that accepted annihilation, without the sense that this fragility made her inferior to the others and their aspirations. And so she completely forgot about the dead machine gun dangling from her shoulder; she enjoyed unleashing the unsuspected recklessness springing up inside her like a wild seedling. She had disguised her depths for fear that someone might notice her or she might harm the people she loved. Now, the damage would fall from and onto herself alone; she was the one who would pay the price for her rashness, because in the Grand Mosque she had become a single individual. Freed from the fear of death that terrorized everyone else, she didn't care whether or not she survived, as long as Sayf shut himself in the minaret till the end. Sarab allowed herself to be guided by her lightness, or her recklessness, which the others called "a sleepwalker's courage." They watched her pass nonchalantly through gunfire while moving the wounded to the cellars, where she helped the Sudanese doctor patch up whatever was left of their shattered limbs. She participated tirelessly in stitching and amputations, never losing sight of the irony of doing their best to save bodies destined inevitably for Hell. Sarab kept running through the dense bombardment, looking at the sky, imploring God to see her and accept her small acts. It was an offering, a way of cleansing a conscience weighed down with sin and exonerating herself from the ongoing fighting.

When Ghosts Pray

AT MIDNIGHT, AN HOUR THE rebels had begun to dread, the only source of light in the forest of pillars was the moon, which began to retreat as the siege entered its third week. Midnight turned the paralyzed mosque and the surrounding mountains into a gulf of ominous darkness, from which profound doubt bombarded the fighters. Wherever they looked, their comrades were falling, and what they had thought was merely an occupation had become a hell beyond anything they had planned; their Mahdi would lead them into the red death instead of dispelling it from the earth, and their dominance over the vast area of the Grand Mosque was shaken.

That night, the houses around the mosque seemed to have become demonic eyes firing meteors, as the attackers focused their bombardment on the roof of the mosque. Mujan realized that the army's strategy was to break his control over the rooftop. Machine gun after machine gun silenced his men and laid the courtyard bare; it wasn't difficult for him to foresee that they were preparing a devastating attack.

In a suicidal plan, Mujan began to move fifty of his best fighters from the arcades to fill the gaps between their comrades on the roof.

From her hiding place in the arcade Sarab watched the men, their black clothes now hanging loose on them, leap up the stairs while total silence awaited them above. No sooner had the first fighter appeared than the silence was torn apart and he was felled by a government sniper. His vacant-eyed body rolled down to the bottom of the stairs. Another followed, and another, accompanied by a frantic volley from the rebels in the minarets, who began firing indiscriminately at the houses around the mosque.

"They must have night-vision goggles!" Mujan cursed; fifty of his best fighters had been annihilated in ten minutes. He was forced to abandon his plan to cover the rooftops, and had no choice but to rely on the snipers in the minarets. He hurried to boost the morale of those stationed in the arcades, where he showed up like a flash of lightning in the white robe he still wore in disdain of the attacking snipers. He moved among the pillars like a hundred ghosts, and could be found in multiple places at once, materializing among the men to fortify their resolve.

"Stand by to defend; if it comes to it, we will fight them from pillar to pillar." His words chilled the blood in their veins. "Don't even blink. They might use the darkness to take us by surprise. We mustn't let them." Death no longer seemed glorious to the men, as they stood staring into their graves.

Sarab didn't usually sleep during the night. From time to time, whenever the snipers fell silent, terror wormed inside her and she craved reassurance that her brother was still alive. She would climb to the top of the minaret without breathing. Sitting on the edge of the narrow step, she'd watch Sayf's back convulse over his machine gun with inhuman strength and, relieved, she'd doze off for a few moments. Then she'd get up and blindly stumble back into the nightmare below.

That night, in despair at the thought of an imminent massacre, Sarab avoided climbing the minaret. She was kept reassured about her brother's safety by his hysterical gunfire, which never abated. He alone howled in the sky over the Grand Mosque, making the darkness even blacker. She kept moving among the pillars, following the apparitions of Mujan and the Mahdi. Wherever she went, the Mahdi's eyes seemed to follow her in perplexity; more than once they tempted her to reveal her true identity as a woman.

She walked until she couldn't feel her legs and dozed as she walked. She didn't notice when Mujan disappeared to inspect his snipers in the Minaret Tawfiq, or when the Mahdi went down to his fortifications in the holy well. Sarab swayed; she didn't know if she was waking or sleeping as she observed her body moving of its own accord, leading her to the cellar. She avoided looking at the eunuch, who didn't open his eyes and perhaps wasn't even breathing, but went back up carrying vials of perfume and a long-handled spray. Her path took her across the middle of the courtyard toward the Kaaba. She stood in the darkness, spraying perfumes onto the coverings that were now scorched and stained with blood. The fragrance of sandalwood, musk, and oud mingled with the smell of burning, and for what seemed like an eternity she continued to sprinkle the perfumes in the hope they would summon the angels.

When the flasks were empty, they fell from her hand, and the sound of them smashing against the ground roused her. She looked up, but no angel wings were fluttering around her, only an erratic hail of bullets, which knocked over the row of lanterns hung around the well. There was no longer a trace of the curtains, or the perfumes, on her hands. There was nothing but the heavy breathing below her feet, and she was filled with the conviction that the eunuch and his perfumes were only an illusion, and belowground there was no night, no day, no pleading. There was nothing but an uninterrupted slice of black tar with human bodies clinging to it like flies, dying slowly.

Heedless of stray bullets, perhaps even welcoming the prospect of being hit, Sarab made her way back and climbed the steps to the balcony that had been erected over the courtyard to allow teams of television cameras to broadcast prayers from the mosque. It was after midnight now, the hours crawling by so slowly that every second seemed like an age to Sarab as she sat staring into the night, her eyes bulging in her effort to distinguish the outline of the Kaaba from the darkness surrounding it. She was horrified at the thought that the House of God had suddenly disappeared and abandoned them. She couldn't see it no matter how she stared, but she didn't despair. It suddenly became vital that the Kaaba reveal itself to her while she felt so forsaken, but she couldn't go over to feel its existence for herself; she was convinced that if her feet trod on the ground, she would fall and be swallowed up by the bottomless tar underground. She sat and stared, hoping to see at least something of the gold girdle encircling it, hoping it would proclaim, with a small glimmer, just one of the names of God inscribed on its walls.

But, unexpectedly, Sarab saw her father emerging from the shadow, his beard dripping water just as it had the only time she had dreamed of him. In the dream they were washing his dead body while Sarab, still a child, approached the table where he lay. Her father's kind face seemed to turn to her. He smiled and encouraged her to come closer, and the men absorbed in washing his body didn't notice the skinny child who ran like a bird toward her dead father. She stumbled and fell, and her face landed directly on the soaked, bushy beard. She was confident that she had seen this when she was awake, not while asleep, and now, from the depths of the shadows, that dream emerged vigorously alive, along with the touch of the soaking beard on her face and the taste of roses on her tongue, bitter as gunpowder, before they carried her away.

Sarab closed her eyes, casting away the vision of her father. But the ghost of her mother followed, welling up and baring her teeth in a laugh, revealing her barren heart. There wasn't a speck of emotion in those dark eyes; with a single, scornful look she ripped the peace from Sarab's heart.

"Ya heef! You disgrace!" It was the accusation Sarab was used to hearing from her mother, and it bore a handful of contemptuous meanings in one breath: *you shame, you iniquity, you who aborted all my hopes.*

Her mother's ghost rushed through the shadows of the Grand Mosque like a wave of fire. Evidently, death had only succeeded in calcifying her uncompromising nature, her resistance to brokering a truce. Sarab could see everything turning inside her mother's head, all the wheels and twists and plans. At that moment, there was nothing in her mother's head but a smoldering excitement at plunging into the hell they had established in the Grand Mosque.

Sarab thought: *If my mother could bargain for an additional day of life, and she chose today out of all days of the siege, then she would be truly a terrifying tool in the fight. Or perhaps she has struck a deal and has been sent to take up her share of the killing.* The rage that had propelled her mother's ghost from the grave was palpable; no doubt her mother had been infuriated by Sarab's capitulation to her own unreliability, and her calm in the face of pandemonium. She had come with the aim of demolishing the surrender Sarab had discovered within herself; she had come to force Sarab to raise her moribund weapon to her shoulder, aim it in unison with her brother in the minaret, and shoot everything that moved. Nothing but blood would satisfy her mother, the descendant of heroes, whom the tribe had crowned with the description "the wolf-woman worth a thousand men."

"What a fate, to be born as Tafla." Sarab's mother had earned that name when she was born, the eleventh child of a man renowned for fathering only sons. By being a girl, she had destroyed his reputation. So she was called Tafla, "spittle," because, through her, time had spat in his face.

From that name sprang her mother's fierce struggle to surpass the men in cruelty, to erase the shame she had handed to her father for having been born female. Tafla was fourteen years old when her father died and left her as a burden on her brothers. The seventy-year-old hero Sheikh Baroud volunteered to take her as a wife; it was the final heroic act of the old warrior, to take on the liability of this spittle. Tafla felt that Heaven was smiling on her at last, to end up the wife of an admired sheikh in the Qutayba tribe; he had earned the name Baroud, or "gunpowder," in recognition of his legendary heroism in the ruler's army when it subdued the Jazira and unified it under his command in 1902.

No sooner had Tafla moved under the old warrior's protection when her penetrating intelligence led her to realize where to invest the ardor that would never be destined for the sheikh. Despite his heroic past her passions scorned his person. Instead, she focused on the collection of rare rifles given to him when he retired from the army in recognition for his service. Tafla convinced the aged warrior to train her to use them, and at once her fierce eagerness for the weapons kindled the sheikh's memories of his past deeds. In record time, Tafla became a miraculous shot. She never missed a target and could effortlessly shoot down whole flocks of birds on their daily hunting trips. People quickly forgot about "Tafla" and instead began to refer to her by a new name, Bunduqa—the rifle hunter.

The elderly hero's bed was kept alight by the she-wolf's ferocity, which stemmed from her bloodlust. He succeeded in discharging the last of his gunpowder into her and fathered two children, despite her self-contempt for being female. When the second child turned out to be a girl it was an unexpected defeat, inconsistent with the legend of Bunduqa.

"That's the price for opening our bodies to moldy gunpowder." Bunduqa never forgave herself or her husband for this blow, and in revenge she named the girl Sarab, "mirage," in the hope she too might disappear. But when it appeared that the newborn would keep on kicking vigorously, Bunduqa made a decision: she would ignore the sex of this baby and would raise her as a male. It would be easy to disguise her sex in her brother's clothes.

"My two sons—God in his mercy has bestowed these two boys on me." This phrase was repeated without the slightest restraint or twinge of conscience, and it carved the maleness of her two children in the heads of everyone, including her husband, whose great deeds were enhanced by having fathered two sons. At last, at the age of seventy-five, perhaps because her will to keep him alive had run out, or perhaps because it was inevitable that the curtain would close on his great performance, Baroud passed away and left Bunduqa a widow.

Her husband's death shattered Bunduqa, the eighteen-year-old girl who had avoided considering even the possibility of his absence. She no longer benefited from his status as a hero of near-mythical renown; once again, fate had defeated her and she was no one, left alone with two children, one of doubtful quality. So she pledged to herself that her husband's death would not touch his legend. The elegy for her husband on the day of his burial came as a flash of inspiration to Bunduqa; she was arrested by the word *controversy*, which brought her husband's legend to an abrupt end. At once,

Bunduqa seized on it as a revelation and a message. She clung to the word *jihad*, and it took the place of her broken spine; she swore to employ the soul and the child in the service of that abstract goal. As there was no actual enemy threatening them, Bunduqa went to great lengths to create its specter. She breathed life into it and it remained in the background wherever she and her children went, even in their bedrooms. Bunduqa created a freakish monster, ready to swoop down on their creed and lead them to perdition. She instilled terror in her children, making their lives full of dread in order to keep them safe from the sinful heedlessness that sank its fangs into the other children others. She implanted in their heads the fact that they had been dedicated to waging war on Dajjal, which lived in the stories she told them before they went to sleep and in the dread they awoke to every morning.

"You should both eat camel and stand up like men. Weakness won't help us if the worst happens," she would say, stuffing pieces of leathery meat down their throats and forcing it down with fortifying camel milk to strengthen their hearts.

"Perhaps we will wake up tomorrow and Dajjal will have come. What will we do? Will we run away like pampered women? Absolutely not—we will fight to the death!" Or another time: "On your way to the market, or to the mosque, do not trust even the most trustworthy citizens. Keep your eyes open; it's not impossible Dajjal will cross your path."

Bunduqa was a terrifying storyteller, and she succeeded in planting Dajjal not just in the heads of her two children, but also in the heads of all the women of the tribe, who went on to instill it in their own children.

She was totally serious in her ominous stories, so her children saw Dajjal in every shadow that moved, and in every sandstorm that approached their path. They passed their whole childhoods in a self-created war camp, where they were trained as fighters in the army against Dajjal. Bunduqa's faith in this war became a source of inspiration to the tribe, and it strengthened her position as a "woman worth a thousand men."

Her fortunes would have improved if not for the shadow hanging over her: the female buried deep within Sarab, which was determined to breathe despite all her efforts to smother it. This feminine side came upon her unexpectedly, ruining her dream of mothering heroes and killing machines. In contrast to her older brother Sayf, Sarab didn't show the same affinity with weapons—a flaw that shocked her mother when she discovered it as Sarab turned six.

No one could have known that Bunduqa wasn't absolutely fair to both her children. She gave them both the same opportunities to realize her ambitions and carry their father's legacy. So she began to train them like two princes from a race of kings. She dressed them both in the same pure-white robes, cut off above the ankle as a sign of piety, and over their shoulders she would throw a head covering belonging to Baroud, white spotted with red from their father's wounds in battle. Whenever they went outside she would make them walk in front of her while she followed meekly behind, in order to accustom them to leadership. The tribe observed her in amazement while her children walked ahead of her, puffed up like two young cocks, and she followed them, dressed in black from head to toe. In contrast to her children clad in blazing white, she was like a ghost. She encouraged them to borrow her light to eclipse her. It was thought they were twins who shone with the same wondrous halo, until that fateful day when Sarab was six.

The day began with a promising sunrise, the horizon revealing all the hunting targets like a magnifying glass. They only word for it was "perfect"; it could have been made on purpose for them to hit a record number of targets. Bunduqa had carefully selected that day to train her children in desert hunting, and, with Sarab's first shot, a bird fell at her feet.

"Yooohooo! You little warrior, you're the apple of your mother's eye, Sarab!" Bunduqa exploded with pride, incredulous at Sarab's luck, while the girl stood rigid with fear, having only just realized what it meant to fire a gun. She stood goggling at the torn wings and the blood dripping on the sand, and the bird's agonized spasms made her burst out crying.

"You coward. Come on, shut your mouth—hurry up and wring its neck," her mother hissed, hurrying her along, but she didn't manage to wrench Sarab out of her stupor. At once Sayf stepped forward, bellowing with laughter and stung by envy. He knelt beside the bird, whose chest had started to rattle, took hold of its neck, and snapped it cleanly.

"That's my man!" Their frustrated mother applauded encouragingly, while Sarab broke into a hysterical howl. Turning to Sarab, Bunduqa pointed an accusing finger at her. "You're nothing but a girl!" she screamed. "You didn't come from this belly!"

Sarab had ruined the trip for them all.

In the following days, whenever Bunduqa tried to make Sarab fire the gun, she would start trembling and burst into a frantic fit of wailing, almost turning blue.

The mother despaired utterly of Sarab when she discovered that she had hidden a bird with a broken wing and was secretly nursing it in the hope that she could get it to fly again. Her face pale with exasperation, Bunduqa stood in front of the box where the bird lay. She saw Tafla's ghost rising before her, dragging the fate of defeat she had so nimbly escaped.

"Weasel heart!" She rammed a finger into Sarab's chest with the utmost contempt, resisting an urge to sink her claws into it, tear out the heart, and remold it from steel.

From that moment, Bunduqa severed herself from Sarab. Her daughter was an encumbrance that hampered her star from rising. She dedicated her princely care to Sayf, who was proving to be an unadulterated copy of her own self.

"You disgrace!" Sarab never stopped hearing this lament; the words swelled until they encircled the frustration the child bore. Bunduqa never wearied of exacting perpetual revenge on Sarab, calling her attention every moment to the fact she would never be forgiven for being born a girl and one with a mouse's heart.

Above all, Bunduqa resolved to keep referring to Sarab as a boy, as if she was trying to imprison the girl in the other sex. She developed a way of talking about Sarab in her presence as if she weren't there, as if she were invisible or nonexistent.

"I am a true martyr. It is decreed that we face the scales of our sins on Judgment Day, but God has already sent me the scales. Here are my sins, walking on two feet in this world." Her eyes flickered to indicate Sarab, but she avoided looking at her.

Sarab didn't realize she was female until her first period came, when she was ten years old. That morning they were in the desert and she had bent down to gather some wood when the silence was rent by Bunduqa's crow-like scream.

"Stand up straight, you filthy idiot. Turn around and come here. Hurry! We're going home—stay in front of me. Hurry up, now." She pushed Sarab ahead of her and walked close behind, hiding her backside with the ferocity of a lioness. She kept responding to greetings as people passed them, even when the door of their house closed behind them. She fixed Sarab with a baleful glare, ripped the white clothes off her body, and hurled them into the trash. Picking up a strip of elastic and a square piece of fabric from a special cupboard, she began to fold the fabric into layers, making it into a long, diaper-like pad.

"As many layers as possible." She kept folding the fabric until it turned into something like a cushion. "We won't let a drop of blood betray us," she muttered doggedly.

The girl mastered her shock and asked, "What blood?" Her frightened question went unanswered.

"Tie this elastic around your waist like a belt, you idiot, and hang this pad from it."

Sarab obeyed, not understanding what had roused her mother's anger. What sin had she committed? Why the pad?

Bunduqa supervised the positioning while Sarab tied the elastic around her waist, and she instructed her how to pass the long pad between her legs so that the ends hung out of the front and back of the elastic belt. Sarab felt the primitive, many-layered pad like a stone between her delicate thighs, a punishment for her disruptive femaleness.

"We won't let any stain appear on your clothes like it did today. We were sullied by this blood."

Sarab stood there trembling; fear amassed heavily on her thin shoulders, sending a thick trickle of blood between her legs. A cramp tore through her pubic area, and tears fell down her cheeks. She felt very small under the weight of her mother's disdain.

Bunduqa went on: "Wash the fabric when it is soaked in blood and change it for this other one." She handed Sarab an additional strip of fabric. From that day, Sarab carried the two strips of fabric, but however much she washed them, they were still stained with faint traces of blood. She carried them like a banner of her nullity. She would see them hanging in the small bathroom, hidden behind a curve in the bathroom wall, and was overwhelmed with violent hatred for the faint smell that no washing could remove, even if she scrubbed till her hands were raw. She hated the blood that defeated her every month, without delay or truce. It confirmed that she was female, and roused secret envy toward her brother and his superior sex. Every month it brought hatred, envy and humiliation, and intensified her feeling of sin.

The blood on the white, male clothing formed an additional badge of shame for Bunduqa. She faced it with resolute denial, burying it in layer after layer of pads, as if by ignoring Sarab's femaleness, she could make it disappear and invert the girl into a boy overnight. Sarab submitted to being despised, as punishment for having failed to induce her body to swap its gender.

Countdown

AT DAWN THE DARKNESS WAS split by a roar of rotors; black metallic bodies were hovering in the skies over the Grand Mosque. The helicopters managed to land a team of paratroopers, trying to spread them out over strategic positions on the roof of the mosque. The machine guns in the minarets fired wildly, but while they mowed down large numbers of the suicide teams, another group of paratroopers succeeded in securing control of the courtyard.

The courtyard of the mosque turned into an inferno, surrounded by silence. Muhammad assumed his strategic position in the well amid the chaos, secure behind piles of furniture and prayer rugs. He was an open target there and, afraid for him, Sarab crawled in his direction. She made her way under the bombardment until she reached the top of the stairs leading to the well. She saw him standing there, aiming his machine gun at a helicopter. Despite his absorption, he spotted her and beckoned her closer.

Day after day she had been gnawed by the struggle between her attraction to Muhammad and the doubt that he was really the Mahdi, but in that moment her only thought was fear for his life. The only thing she cared about in this fight was keeping him and her brother alive. Their safety came before hers, and she was ready to sacrifice everything to achieve it; they were her battle.

Heavy fire from the helicopters forced the rebels to retreat inside the well. Bullets scorched the barricades they had erected, and the government forces intensified their assault on the well, aware that the most important pockets of resistance were there.

"If we are defeated, please don't let them take you alive. God will be merciful . . ." She didn't know how she could have uttered those pitiful words; she seemed to be begging for Muhammad's attention. But as soon as she spoke them, the words lost their triviality; they hung in the air like a premonition.

"It's up to God whether we are destined to remain or to depart this world." He couldn't help staring deeply into her eyes, a look that pierced her like a spearhead. Usually he avoided her gaze, but at that moment, when death was tangible, he wanted to fix his faith inside her.

"You truly seek martyrdom, and by God's will you will be called on for it."

She lost all control of her senses and began to drown in those thickly lashed eyes, her body ablaze and melting in the flames kindled by his gaze, while his husky voice rushed tremulously through her veins.

"Don't think of victory or defeat—fix your heart on Heaven, whether in this life or the next. And if the opportunity comes, get out of here. Don't think of it as cowardice or creeping away. You were made for a different fate, something beyond all of this."

They were interrupted by a thunderous explosion, and Sarab was blown from the top of the stairs to the bottom of the well. Muhammad rushed toward her as she lay there in shock.

"Are you wounded? Answer me!" He searched her body in terror, looking for wounds, and her shock was made worse by this unexpected and thorough handling of her body. His hands encountered her bound breasts, and his eyes gleamed when he realized what he was touching. His suspicions were finally been confirmed and, trembling, he withdrew his hands. Her voice came out as a squeak when she was finally able to speak.

"I'm fine . . ."

His chest heaved in a sigh and he helped her sit up.

"Are you sure?"

She nodded, and his hands sprang away from her shoulders as if they had been stung. Hoarsely, he ordered, "Stay here. Don't move until the shock has worn off."

He left her to take up his position in the battle to block the army's attempts to land another wave of paratroopers in the courtyard. At last she managed to gather the strength to heave up her body and leave.

She crawled away, shaken to the core, propelled by a need to disappear and hide the delicacy and fragility that had suddenly appeared when least expected. She felt naked, as though she had uncovered herself in front of him, unveiled her attraction to him, in the midst of this massacre. No doubt he had seen the truth of how she felt, and now she couldn't continue denying it to herself. She couldn't face additional anxiety—her brother and now this man. Intuition told her they were hurrying to their graves.

At sunset, without warning, the intensive attempts to land troops slackened. A few individuals from the government forces had succeeded in descending to the southern arcades and were now trapped there by the rebels. It seemed that a new game plan was being drawn up outside. Sarab slipped out of the firing line to another gallery and hurried up the narrow spiral stairs of Sayfullah's minaret. Exhausted by the stairs and her fear, she arrived panting at the top of the minaret and stood there behind her brother. She watched his face, colored red by the setting sun, and his eyes seemed to have widened into two pits of shadow, occupying most of his face. He seemed demented from lack of sleep and from having played the greatest role in eliminating the teams that had been dropped over the courtyard since dawn.

He was still firing while darkness slowly descended; he seemed unaware of his sister's presence, or perhaps, as usual, he was nullifying it. Sarab could see nothing but him, while the features of the city were submerged in darkness made thicker by smoke from the continuous explosions. She could swear Sayf had stopped breathing while he scanned row after row of the surrounding rooftops and windows, waiting for any sign of life. The windows seemed to be playing a trick on Sayf's overstrained senses, expanding and contracting and dwindling into the sky, luring him into firing eagerly and at random on any twitch of movement or tremor of light. The battle had moved on; it was no longer about establishing the Mahdi, but had become a bloody struggle between Sayf and the obstinate city that refused to surrender to his unerring bullets. Where there were no living targets, he aimed at the city itself. Sarab suspected that he was, as usual, aiming at the ghosts in his head. Standing there, for an instant she felt anger that verged on distaste for the two men who had violated her life and her peace of mind.

Sayf's body was like a live wire, exposed and ready to shock, and Sarab was overcome with tenderness. She resisted the desire to come closer and stroke that jerking shoulder; she withdrew a step instead, convinced that his skinny body would explode if touched by even a mosquito. Like the rest of his comrades, Sayf was aware of the dangerous development in the attackers' stance that day. It was clear that they had abandoned caution in attacking the Grand Mosque, ramping up their attempts to land fighters on the roof and apparently unconcerned by how many fell in their ranks. They concentrated fire on the arcades and the courtyard, aiming to force the rebels to abandon their fortifications and end the siege. Moving in the arcades was now suicide, and the makeshift muezzin had to take refuge in the cellar to raise the call to the evening prayer.

Sarab couldn't bear to look at the muezzin; he was like a mole, lost in the infinite darkness of the cellars. Terror turned his voice into a screech, as if he were begging for salvation in return for raising the name of God in that hell. Sarab heard the call to prayer like a dirge accompanying them straight to Hell for having colluded with Mujan.

As the siege entered its third week, both the rebels and the attackers seemed to have reached a suicidal climax; all were determined to purge the scene and reach any end, as fast as possible, no matter what it might be and whatever the victory might cost.

Steel Clouds

As NIGHT FELL OVER THE insurgents, so did a profound sense of despair. The ground was trembling under their feet from the tanks that had begun to congregate around the mosque. It seemed that the hesitancy that had granted the rebels victories in the previous weeks had come to an end. The army had arrived. Heavy armored cars took up position around the mosque, tanks lumbered forward, fighter jets shrieked as they tore through the night, reconnaissance helicopters hovered ceaselessly overhead. It seemed clear that a colossal army had been amassed to destroy them utterly and completely. The rebels knew that their days were numbered; before long they would be wiped off the face of the earth. The darkness amplified their terror, and the sense of being surrounded gave their faces an ashen hue. When Sarab woke up that day, she was unsure whether it was dawn or sunset. A thin red line encircled the horizon, and despite the cold light she felt unnaturally warm; she was sure she was in Hell, and below her, bodies were melting in fire.

Sarab braced herself against the earth, trying to raise her body, but felt no solid ground. Wherever she placed a hand, it slithered over disintegrating flesh until she fell prostrate.

Helicopters roared overhead, their rotors covering the sky over the Grand Mosque with a steel cloud like devils' wings. The ground simmered and boiled, explosions thundered, and shredded bodies flew through the air. From where she lay, Sarab could see dozens of her comrades scattered around, dead.

It was without doubt the long-anticipated attack. As armored cars and heavily armed legions of the army rushed forward, the National Guard and Special Forces tore open the huge doors simultaneously. Sarab made her way step by bloody step toward the Sa'a Gallery, where the principal attack was expected. Around them on every side the sky rained down human frogs, who opened fire as soon as their feet hit the ground, and more and more bodies fell in the arcades and the marble passages. Again, Sarab felt like she was in a theater of torture where lice and frogs and blood rained down on heretics. Great strain wrapped the unreal scene, where everyone seemed to be moving in a dream; souls detached themselves and floated in the air, dispassionately watching their bodies fight on ferociously without them, while the army, with growing impatience, intensified the attack until it seemed like Judgment Day had come.

"Retreat to the cellars!"

Sarab ignored Mujan's sharp order, which had been given so late that withdrawal was now more or less impossible.

"We will fight on from our graves!" Mujan's cry rang out in the infernal chaos, and his order moved along the barricades. The great retreat began. Two days previously, when reckoning on the worst, Mujan had appointed twenty suicide fighters to cover their withdrawal should they be forced to it. Five of the most committed fighters had been stationed on each side of the mosque, their machine guns trained on the courtyard to block the advance of the state forces, while the others retreated with a feeling of ignominy and Mujan's shining words rattling in their throats.

Mujan looked back once at the men, the Mahdi among them, who continued to fight and had now lost even the possibility of retreat. Certain of his divine immunity, the Mahdi was moving among the fighters with a courage that bordered on recklessness, exposing himself to bullets in the certainty that he could not be killed. It was this faith rooted in the Mahdi's skin that motivated the fighters to voluntarily stay on the roofs and fight, sure they would eventually succeed in blocking the attack. They had even smeared their faces with tar so they could blend into the shadows and surprise the attackers. Meanwhile, Mujan reached the cellars with around two hundred of his men, who locked the door behind them.

"You disgrace!"

Under the dense hail of bullets, Sarab ran; her mother's cry of contempt lashed her onward and drove her to prove herself worthy of her lineage. She stumbled over the body of a soldier from the National Guard, and without thinking she sat back up and began to strip him of his uniform. Hands trembling, she put on the clothes saturated with sweat and smoke, which would make her indistinguishable from the torrent of attackers.

In this uniform, she hurried on and spotted the Mahdi in the Sa'a Gallery, where the armored cars had succeeded in breaking through. The Mahdi was leading the remnants of his men in desperately trying to stop this advance. They succeeded in setting fire to one lot, but the stream of vehicles was uninterrupted and shielded yet another wave of attacking troops. The moment Sarab looked out onto the arcade, a hand grenade fell directly in front of her. She made out the metallic tick through the darkness and realized she was dead. She wasn't frightened of dying so much as frightened for the Mahdi; he rushed out of the darkness to snatch up the grenade, and before she could blink had thrown it back where it had come from. An explosion roared and bits of the attacking troops were scattered around them. Sarab stood there, unable to join in mowing down the soldiers who were advancing in darkness and fighting ghosts, of which she was the feeblest. The state forces kept advancing, tossing grenades among the arcades to ensure they were purged of the Mahdi's men. Under Sarab's paralyzed gaze, the body of the Mahdi bent over each grenade, one after the other, and threw them back, killing those who had thrown them. A sigh rippled through the rebels, confident in the miracles of their Mahdi who couldn't die. Suddenly a grenade fell on the opposite side, and the Mahdi stumbled on his way to pick it up. At once Hamidan ran forward; he was a fanatical supporter of the Mahdi, and even resembled him, with his white skin and long, smooth, black hair. In the darkness, underneath their tar masks, it wasn't easy to distinguish between them. The moment

Hamidan picked up the grenade it exploded, shredding the lower half of his body and those around him. A tremor ran through the few survivors; to them, it appeared that it was the Mahdi who had been torn apart.

"The Mahdi has been killed."

The phrase swept through the company, more searing than gunfire from the armored cars, and the rebels' faith in their savior collapsed. One band disappeared to take the news to Mujan, and another lot threw down their weapons in surrender. They were mown down by government troops, wary of the tricks and repeated ambushes that had killed so many of their comrades over the previous days.

Sarab found herself with the Mahdi. The arcade had collapsed, trapping the attacking forces. Realizing the danger of his position, the Mahdi retreated toward the courtyard, rounding up the last band of volunteers and concentrating them around the well.

Sarab needed time to grasp what had happened. When she awoke from her torpor, she rushed straight for the courtyard, disguised in a National Guard uniform. She ran risking fire from the state forces that were advancing to clear the courtyard and protect the Kaaba.

From his position in the well the Mahdi unleashed gunfire on a torrent of soldiers. Sarab rushed headlong toward the well, risking fire from her fellow rebels barricaded inside, and took advantage of an attacking wave of National Guard troops to approach the entrance.

Launching herself forward, Sarab broke through the burning barricades. There was utter chaos as attackers fought hand to hand with the rebels. Sarab was looking for the Mahdi; from her position at the top of the stairs she saw him at last, standing in the middle of the entrance to the well, recklessly exposed to gunfire, aiming his bombs at the first wave of troops trying to descend the stairs toward him. She froze, blinded by fear and dazzled at the sight of him. She could swear that his eyes were sweeping the scene with an inhuman glow. And at that moment, a bullet struck his head and his body fell to the ground.

Blackness enveloped Sarab. Behind her, bombs continued to explode and further blinded them with smoke. Tear gas had been released into the inner hall of the well, forcing the rebels out of their hiding places into a dense barrage of bullets. Fear eliminated all rational thought among the soldiers, who were hoping for a quick, decisive victory.

Sarab was paralyzed where she stood; as the soldiers rushed past her they urged her to advance, believing she was one of them. She became aware of a second wave of her comrades emerging from their secure defenses in the inner areas of the well. Eyes streaming, they came out with hands raised over their heads in surrender. Blows from the soldiers' gun butts rained down upon them and they were dragged away, coughing and retching from the gas. The soldiers lost interest in the well once they had cleared it of that lethal resistance; it had been the scene of some of the most savage fighting in the whole mosque.

Sarab still stood there, incapacitated by misery. She was three meters from the body of Muhammad bin Abdullah, the Mahdi who had lost his life, whom no one had realized was the pivot on which the whole war had turned. One glance at that handsome face struck her with the realization that life had no meaning, that everything around her was senseless folly. Nothing mattered; nothing could cause pain or anger, or provoke envy or desire. It was a moment when feeling was obliterated, apart from a sense of total liberation from her weakness and her ties to the world. In those moments, when she was separate from life and its currents, her soul began to float upward and she saw everything that was happening in every part of the mosque. She saw all the bodies falling from the sky and all the bodies running and crawling, the yelling mouths, the bulging eyes, the broken hearts. What were all these bodies struggling for? What was life if it deserved all of this? Was it the devouring of everything, simply in order to reach old age and death?

Everything appeared startlingly blank. Not blank in the sense of sterility, but in the sense of renewal, a sort of rapture; the readiness to be filled again with something new.

This freedom lasted for a short while, but before long Sarab's soul descended to her body. Remnants of the pleasure she had found in that brief escape made the death coursing all around her seem less frightening. She knew, with total acceptance, that only truth had been returned to her body; that her brother Sayf was still alive up there, still stationed in his minaret, still struggling. His life was the only one that deserved incarnation; the only one, now, to keep living for. He gave meaning to the act of mindless devouring, of reaching old age; she wanted to see him as an old man.

She stood, rambling through these small, trivial thoughts. She didn't dare to approach the body of the man whom she had believed was an emissary from God. She had been so sure, and the emissary was now dead, having conveyed his message only to the bodies around him.

Sarab sensed death fanning out behind her with extraordinary speed. It would drown them all; she had to hurry to save her brother. The moment she emerged from the quietened well she was blinded by the savage sunlight, a light she couldn't ignore from behind the smoke. Suddenly the rifle at the top of the minaret where her brother was barricaded fell quiet beneath the roaring rotor of a helicopter that had just launched a TOW missile; those missiles, guided remotely by demons, had already wiped out most of their legendary snipers in the minarets. Despite the din and the smoke, Sarab's soul caught that sudden silence, and a freezing shadow swooped on her heart. Throughout the siege, she had been listening for that horror-filled silence.

She began to forge a path through the thick smoke enveloping the mosque. She couldn't see where she was walking and stumbled over bodies while bullets whizzed past her head. She leaped up the stairs of the minaret, half-blinded by the burning in her eyes. Her body outstripped her mind. At the turn of the stairs she saw her brother's rifles, the bolt-action sniper rifle DM/S-R and the M240, her brother's lifelong companion and his pride and joy. Both were just lying there. Her sinking heart nearly stopped beating, but a superhuman force pushed her up the remaining stairs to face the scene in which

140

the fears that had terrified her most since childhood were made incarnate. There was her brother, his head blackened and burnt, lying in his own feces, which were spilling everywhere because the bucket she had not had time to empty this morning had overturned.

The sun was beating down on the top of the minaret; the scorching heat fused her brain and she was roasted by the smoldering embers of her brother's body. His entire skull was shattered; if it weren't for the skinny frame whose every detail was imprinted on her heart, she wouldn't have been able to identify it as the brother who had never accepted death. Sarab collapsed, overcome with exhaustion. She couldn't even cry to alleviate the burning agony gushing through her veins; she was dried out from the same fire that had burned her brother.

She stirred and moved closer to the corpse with the obliterated head. She dipped her chest to his, sensing death in the flat silence she found there. Suddenly she became aware that their souls were clinging together in the form of a huge bird; it escaped from their bodies and soared through the sky, sucking up the burning heat of the sun, before swooping back down like a shooting star to penetrate her guts. Possessed, she let out a cry that tore the air.

She became her murdered brother Sayf, and the girl Sarab was buried inside that charred corpse. Without hesitation she plunged her fingers into his chest pocket and pulled out his identity card. Sayf had not been present at the ritual where rebels and hostages tore up their identity cards after they first stormed the Grand Mosque; he had already taken up his position in the minaret. She stuffed the card into her jacket pocket and hurtled blindly down the stairs. At last she had become what she had always wanted to be: she had become Sayf, and she sensed his vengeful blood pulsing through her veins.

She crossed the courtyard, armed with her brother's identity card and the machine gun that had annihilated every spark of life. Despite her skill at using the heavy weapon she was dragging behind her, she couldn't stop to shoot. Sarab was invincible as she ran through the gunfire, forgetting that the khaki National Guard uniform she wore protected her from their attacks. She could have made her way safely out of the mosque in this uniform, but her brother's will drove her toward suicide. Burning with pain and rage, she urgently needed to kill or be killed like her comrades.

In the cellars, Mujan had succeeded in regrouping. The remaining fighters erected barricades in the interconnecting prayer cells and labyrinthine vaults of that miniature underground city, preparing for the interminable resistance.

Avoiding the soldiers as they mercilessly combed the arcades for anyone holding out, Sarab headed toward the cellars, worming her way through the secret passages behind the loudspeakers. She slid from an air vent across some pipes and landed in an abandoned part of the vaults; she risked being shot by one her comrades if any of them spotted an unexpected National Guard uniform.

Time had stopped in that underground city, and it was submerged in total darkness. She listened but no one had seen her; the rebels had been careful not to light even the smallest torch. A suicidal spirit had settled over them, and she could almost hear huge drops of sweat crawling over their skin.

She heard someone moaning as if deranged: "The Mahdi was killed in the Sa'a Gallery. He was blown up by a grenade."

The voice exploded in the dark tunnel. A rebel had managed to survive the hell above and had brought the news with him.

"The Mahdi was killed in the well. He was shot in the head," an echo retorted from another tunnel.

Without a moment's hesitation Mujan took aim and shot both, to the shock of his men. In a voice like a knife blade, he carved his statement into everyone: "The Mahdi cannot be killed."

Those closest to Mujan clustered around him, consumed by doubt.

"If the Mahdi has died, does that mean we have sinned?"

"This fight has taken us off the true path. Our stubbornness takes us farther and farther away."

Even the most stalwart supporters were tempted to lay down their weapons.

"Don't let doubt creep in." For the first time, Mujan begged his men. "God adjures you to repress this fitna."

But despite his attempts to quash it, the grim news coursed through the shadows and into the veins of the men, who had already noticed the Mahdi was missing among them. At that moment, Mujan could not escape facing his men.

In a steely voice, deeper than the grave, he pronounced, "You saw for yourselves—here, someone saw him blown up in the Sa'a Gallery, and over there, someone else saw him shot in the head in the well. Who is this person who was killed twice? He was blown up and he didn't die; he was shot and he got up. He is living still; without a doubt he is still fighting in the open air. He is protecting us with his unparalleled courage, and even if we are wiped out, he will go on. He will break the siege, and he will appear, and he will save the world from idolatry. You saw what happened to those who told us these lethal falsehoods, and anyone who dares to circulate similar rumors will meet the same fate."

In her distant corner, Sarab choked bitterly on Mujan's words. He really was mad. He was still dreaming of being rescued by the Mahdi and refused to face the truth: that he had failed in translating his theories to the real world. His voice burrowed into their heads to destroy the phrase "the Mahdi has been killed." The Mahdi's death was more terrifying than the nightmare of being besieged in the cellars and mown down like rats by the army.

Sarab was isolated from the danger all around her by the embers of her brother's body, which had bored through to her core. Her soul was in a state of flux and her body had shed its coating of torpor; staying alive seemed a trivial endeavor. All the while, her mother's curse reverberated around her head, freezing her: "What are you waiting for? You should die. If you were made of stone like your martyr brother, you would follow him."

Despite their desperate position, the rebels were able temporarily to turn the battle to their advantage, thanks to their knowledge of the cellars. The army lacked the maps that would have allowed them to concoct a plan to break the underground resistance. The army's attempt to storm the cellars brought about disaster; both the cellars and the rebels' ambushes swallowed up the soldiers as they stumbled around in blind ignorance. They were an easy target for Mujan and his men, who were able to exploit the narrow passages of that maze, and the army sustained an enormous number of casualties.

After a week of ruinous battles and heavy casualties, certain CIA operatives were invited to join the special taskforce. After pronouncing the article of faith that would enable them to declare themselves Muslim, they were brought into the Holy City. Following their advice, vast quantities of tear gas were released into the cellars through its many entrances, while barricades sprang up feverishly below. On Mujan's orders the men dedicated themselves to constructing barricades from carpets and furniture and boxes—anything that might block the gas in the narrow passageways of the cellars. The men moved like frightened giants, each face masked with a water-soaked head covering to protect them from the gas. Their bloodied eyes receded while their skulls bulged with soaked cardboard masks; some limbs were swallowed up by randomly applied bandages and others had swelled with a rotten-looking blue tinge, a warning that not even amputation could save them now.

Those ghosts did achieve a victory from where they lay in their graves, because the light gas rose to the ceiling of the Grand Mosque, where it enveloped the army, who had not been equipped with gas masks as they could not be fastened over their long beards. An entire battalion was put out of action. The gas spread to the areas surrounding the Grand Mosque and the ensuing uproar sped up the evacuation of the area.

News of the victory could have raised the morale of the besieged ghosts in the cellars, but they were cut off in the vaults and had lost all communication with those aboveground. They were clinging to the weak faith that their underground city was able to withstand attacks and remain under their complete control. It was impossible for things to get any worse than they already were; they were effectively in their own graves and disappearing into another life, from which they would doubtless be resurrected without further consequences. Their goal was no longer to stay alive but to inflict maximum losses on their enemies.

December 1, 1979:
Assignment Number 3016

THE BATTLE TOOK A DECISIVE step toward conclusion with the arrival of two men: structural engineer Dr. Salih Barqawi and GIGN-dispatched Deputy Commander Patrice Bareille.

At the insistence of the commander heading the taskforce reinforcements had been called in: Bareille, and a group of his men to lead the planned operations in the battlefield.

"We suggest another dose of gas," Bareille announced, glancing at the military personages gathered at the table with his blue eyes and devastating smile. A heavy silence blanketed the room while Bareille waited for their reactions, especially from the admiral chairing the meeting; when he was met with silence, he dropped his bomb: "Actually, a full ton."

The American lieutenant's mouth fell open in disbelief. "Damn, that's a crazy quantity! It's enough to knock out a small city," he protested. He objected to France's interference in sending such a rogue; he construed it as a measure of his own failure and consequent lost credibility.

"So what?" Bareille didn't bat an eyelid. "If we don't, this war will go on forever and our casualties will double. Let's amputate this irritation once and for all."

The American lieutenant rose to leave the room in evident disgust. The GIGN officers fidgeted in their seats, watching the taut smile of support on the admiral's lips. The admiral breathed a sigh of relief to find someone who advocated such extreme measures, and assigned Bareille and his men the task of carrying out this mad plan on the battlefield.

However, Bareille's hopes were dashed after a telephone call with Paris. The short conversation with his superiors confirmed that "the entire French supply is just three hundred kilograms. But it will definitely be enough to drive those rats from their cave."

The second man to prove decisive in the scales of battle appeared hard on the heels of the first. He was brought to the operations rooms to be introduced to Bareille, who greeted him with palpable delight.

"You must be the structural engineer, Dr. Salih. They say you know the cellars of the Grand Mosque like the back of your hand."

Dr. Salih smiled self-deprecatingly. "Not without this," he said, drawing from his bag a map of the cellars of the mosque. "This is the end result of years of study in the Center for Research on the Hajj, which was under my management for a long time."

"You are a real find. I wonder why our American friends didn't discover you earlier?" Bareille seemed to be boasting, clearly charmed by the elegant engineer. "This time," he went on, "we'll concentrate high levels of gas on those rebels. They will sample French delicacies from French experts." Bareille bragged like a Michelin-starred chef. This plan was another lethal blow to the American's pride; the French genius had contrived the idea of using a much more powerful substance than the American gas, which had turned the last battle into such a farce.

Below, in the hell of the darkness and amid the remnants of the tear gas, the rebels took some time to establish what was happening. A sudden roar broke out above their heads and it seemed as if their graves were falling in upon them. Terrible drills seemed to bore into their ears and hearts. Countless holes were being made in the roofs of the cellars, and before they had emerged from their shock, three hundred kilograms of gas had been pumped through the holes. Simultaneously, the army launched an attack on the cellar, advancing from different sides in a pincer movement. Sarab felt like a rat in a trap as her comrades fell dead around her. The gas mask she had hidden from the previous attacks proved its worth, but the lethal blow to all sanity came when she saw her comrades rushing into the bullets of the attacking soldiers to escape the agony of suffocating from the gas.

"It's Mujan!"

Sarab muffled a cry of alarm when a soldier pulverized the door to a hidden room. Mujan appeared before them, standing in front of a number of his men who were on the ground, bloodstained, retching, and drowning in vomit. Mujan was still standing, despite the starvation, the gas, and the imminent collapse of the savage battle he had plunged into a fortnight earlier.

Sarab heard the captain ask, "What is your name?"

"Mujan." The reply came calmly, steady as a breath of truth, a verification of the self. At once, the captain and his aide surrounded Mujan and furtively led him outside, careful not to alert the other soldiers to the identity of their valuable captive so they wouldn't vent their rage on him for the victims he had culled from their ranks. To Sarab, Mujan appeared frightened, and robbed of his will; it was difficult to judge whether he was paralyzed from the effects of the gas or the effects of the defeat.

"Mujan has been arrested." The news spread, even more lethal than the gas, and it sent a shudder throughout the mosque and into the hearts of soldiers on both sides. It was followed by the surrender of those rebels still hiding. Mujan, covered in black, his beard bushy and his hair matted, was put into an ambulance, which quickly disappeared, hurrying him through the city, which was already eager to learn how the consequences of violating its sanctity would be explained to him. It was indistinguishable from the dozens of ambulances that had darted to and fro for two weeks, carrying the wounded in that city where bloodshed was forbidden. Onlookers had no idea who its passenger was, or that he was approaching the final chapter of the tragedy that had escaped from between the lines drawn up on paper and yielded fifty thousand victims, all created by this man, who had perfect faith in the righteousness of his goal.

Sarab stood a step away from the room where the massacre was brought to an end. She was paralyzed, in utter disbelief at the conclusion that was summarized in that serene response: Mujan.

The echo of that word reverberated around her head, emptied of all meaning after Mujan's departure. Everything she had lived through and fought for on his account lost its substance, and she was whirled into a void. She could neither leave nor stay; she had to do something to return to life, to substantiality.

She was terrified at the thought of being identified as a soldier as she left the cellar. Her brain was in a state of stubborn confusion; it seemed to her that any action taken to survive was a betrayal of the dead, and of her brother most of all. She took a few aimless steps and realized she was in the room with the broken minbar.

At that moment a huge soldier appeared in front of her, a response to her need for suicide. Again, she was given the opportunity to shoot and confirm she was worthy of her family name, but there seemed to be a rupture between her body and the killing machine it carried. She had been paralyzed by her feeble, feminine genes when facing her first easy prey, and now she was being swept with a horrifying sense of being cursed. In response, a piece of the blackness suddenly fell from the ceiling and pounced on her opponent; it activated her body, which proceeded to leap onto the enemy soldier and take him prisoner. Her body moved of its own accord, seeking the way out through the sewers, which she had found under the broken minbar. It was the last way she could leave honorably. In the total darkness, Sarab stumbled over the opening and, with utter self-contempt, she pushed her captive in front her and followed close behind, out of that hell at last.

If Only You Were Dead

SARAB FELT THAT SHE HAD gathered a bombshell out of the horrors of
the siege and buried it deep inside her chest. She had taken courage
and dug it up at last, and displayed its contents to the light so she
could face what she had done. She carried all those sins as if they
were her personal transgressions, convinced that she deserved to be
cursed and expelled from God's mercy.

She sat there, appreciating the light on her face, facing the jijin
officer, and thinking, "Why did I kidnap him in the first place? Why
did I drag anything out of the hell I escaped from without a scratch?"
Was it a final, desperate attempt to raise her mother's estimation of
her? An attempt to convince people that she could be an extraordinary
jihadi and succeed where everyone else had failed? God, how pathetic!

Like a scratched record, her mother's voice repeated, "You disgrace! What kind of courage is this? What did you do other than
retreat? You're nothing but a pathetic fugitive."

Sarab leaped up and shook off those voices obsessed with the
past. She looked straight at the girl on the wallpaper and, without
anger, said, "All through the siege—no. All your life, you wished your
brother was dead."

This denunciation shocked the girl on the wallpaper, as well
as the young girl buried deep within Sarab herself. It snatched her
out of her rambling capitulation. Sarab realized she was facing the
world alone at last, simultaneously her own master and torturer.

"They're all dead now." She shrugged indifferently, echoing this
fact to herself. "The dead won't have any part in our world or our

decisions. They are busy with their new existence, God help them," she said, her words verging on the malicious. "When they face the angels Raqib and Atid and Munkar and Nakir, their deeds in this world will be have been recorded."

Perhaps her brother would face the pile of souls he had annihilated without a shred of remorse, and her mother might pay for the seed she had planted in her son. Sarab felt wicked for devising punishments for them after their deaths. But most important, there was no longer anyone to pin their hopes on her for the heroic deeds she would never commit. She had survived, and not a drop of blood stained her hands. That had been her own independent decision, her first ever. And she had kept to it until the very end; or more properly, till this moment.

"And now it's you—just you. What are you going to do with yourself?"

She was struck by a rush of faith that she could exist on her own, according to her own free will. Her ready willingness to do so made her feel guilty and so she evaded it, conversing scornfully with that "I."

"First, you have to pay the price of accompanying Mujan and his men, and of helping them in the siege and the killings in the Grand Mosque." Time stopped while Sarab passed judgment on herself and her dead comrades.

She shared a harmonious silence with her French adversary. Neither of them felt the need for the rifle, which Raphael had left to one side, as if he had forgotten about it. It appeared that they were both caught in a lethal trap. They didn't know what would happen, but neither headed to the door demanding release; it was as if their fate hung on a fine thread, independent of them both. Each retreated to their usual corner, Sarab still shaking from their encounter, Raphael avoiding even a glance in her direction. A quiet space was created between them.

"My father died when I was five. He was the only person who was gentle with my heart. When he passed away, I felt that life had betrayed me by leaving me in the hands of the dragon. Yes, my mother was a real dragon, for me."

Sarab didn't want to listen. Raphael's words made him into a human, which disturbed her. She didn't want this light shone on their points of resemblance.

Raphael continued talking to himself: "My father and I were one soul. We had moments when he was the child and I was the adult." He was surprised to be reviving these long-buried memories. Since he had become a soldier he hadn't allowed his childhood to drag him back and disturb his cruelty. He had convinced himself that he had been born from the ashes of the battlefield as a grown man.

He went on: "My mother tormented my father with her betrayals and he always came to me, even when I was an infant. I recently read in his diary that our closeness was the only peace he found in his life. When I learned to speak, my words, whatever they were, gave him comfort. Everything I said that struck him deeply he wrote down in his diary, and he lived according to it. My father didn't ask for much."

Against her will, Sarab was moved. She had never heard anyone speaking like this, in a way that exhumed the heart and laid bare its suffering and joy.

"God offered you a small taste of Hell." Sarab astonished herself by this explosion of hostility, which she had intended to break the sympathy that was beginning to grow between them. Raphael regarded her impassively, perhaps encouraging her to vomit and be rid of the bile in her stomach.

"These hypocritical societies were made by your own hands." She couldn't control the violence of the words gushing from her mouth. "You created them and you will all burn for it. In Wajir, people like you and your father were wiped off the face of the earth. It is a man's duty to kill a wife who betrays him like your mother did, and he should be honored for his actions."

"Kill her? I never even saw my father get angry, let alone resort to violence. He was as soft as water. Every Sunday he used to take me to the bird market and we would buy a bird and go to the Luxembourg Gardens in Paris, and he would ask me to open the door of the cage and set it free. I would burst out crying and protest—I wanted to keep the bird. When I asked him why we were releasing it, he would say, 'Why do you think birds were created with wings?'"

Sarab felt that only an imbecile would be moved by this nonsense about birds. In Wajir, children pelted birds with stones, and broke their necks and wings; she herself had hunted them. It was all a childish game. She ignored the pain she had felt on that first hunting trip, when her mother forced her to shoot.

Raphael went on: "I was that bird. I made sure to leave all cages and all negativity behind me. Negativity is like seaweed—well, maybe you know don't know seaweed . . . negativity is like quicksand. I vowed to myself not to let this sand build up around me and drag me down. And so I always hovered high above life."

Immediately Raphael felt the spuriousness of his words, because by plunging into warfare he had avoided having any compassion for himself. He had hovered, enjoying life, by averting his eyes from the harm he caused. He had merged with the currents of life, like death itself, like disease, like an indomitable virus. This was what he had become in his blind obedience to military orders. His revolt against his father's weakness pushed him to join the army, and the army pushed him to become something like a god, wreaking vengeance on all who thwarted him.

His comment troubled Sarab, who had been caught by the picture he had drawn of himself as a bird. The vulnerability of his confession touched her, and perhaps she even envied him that early awareness of freedom.

"You talk about freedom," she said, "while you infidels are enslaved by your blind love for this world and its pleasures. That is the biggest cage that surrounds you, and you don't want to leave it, even though it will close in and crush you." She couldn't believe she was saying these words, reviving her brother's convictions. She felt he was haunting her through his identity card, and she was powerless to prevent him. "You are terrified by death and the thought of leaving this vain earth behind you, and you will always be enslaved by your sins and by the clay within you, unless you believe that death is another life where there is no death."

To the surprise of them both, Raphael burst out laughing. "You know what?" he said. "Your cage is your eternal obsession about sin. Poor little bird, you dare to criticize me? Life was given to us so we could live it truly, doing good and bad. Otherwise God would have been content with creating angels free from sin in Heaven." He paused to let his words sink in, then went on: "This desire for suicide is the greatest sin of all. A reverence for life is the faith He cherishes, and that's what I fight for, while you fight for death, either your own or someone else's. I don't think your Lord will look kindly on you or on this bloodlust that possesses you now."

He despised himself for his determination to change this girl, to extract her from the desire for self-destruction that was the mirror of his desire to destroy. Why not leave her alone, secure in her beliefs? But without realizing it, his attempts to destroy her convictions were in fact destroying his own.

"Talk about your demons, but take care when you talk about my Lord," she said.

"You're right. Who can predict God's will? Let's relax. Let's leave Satan and God's justice out of our discussion. Let me tell you something about life; or really, about flying."

As soon as he made this hollow offer, he realized that he didn't really know how to save himself, now that he had revealed his deepest secrets. How could he reconcile the fighter and the bird inside him?

"I don't have anything to exchange with you other than bullets," she said, "and you have the last word as long as you have the weapon, so go on: shoot."

"What kind of believer are you, ignoring the opportunity to offer guidance to an infidel?" The question startled her, and he capitalized on her confusion to continue his encouragement. "Yes, now you're thinking outside the cage of clichés."

Sarab looked away.

"For the first time since we met," he continued, "I feel you're listening with your own ears, not with your brother's. You know, you weren't yourself; you were just a cassette player reeling off something it didn't understand or believe in. This is your first real encounter with life. Not there, facing bullets, but here, facing the truth. With every day, with the truth of life, you've lost all the clichés that enclosed you like a shell."

Raphael moved closer and reached out an open palm to touch Sarab under her collarbone, but she slapped it away furiously.

"My father used to put his hand on my heart," Raphael said, "and I could feel all my pains and doubts and worries dissolving under it. Then, when he lifted it, it was as if he had scraped them away. I always felt renewed afterward."

"Your father seems to have been a spineless weasel." It shocked her that she was using the same description her mother had used. "In Wajir, men like that were only good for pouring coffee," she said, defensively.

Cut off from the world, they were little by little wrapped within another sphere, another time. The events outside, and the last days in particular, seemed unreal.

"Move!" Raphael dragged Sarab upright and pushed her in front of him to the roof terrace. "Let's take a look at your world. Is this what you were fighting against? Or what you were fighting for?"

On the surrounding rooftops, life had resumed. Women appeared, cleaning up the mess created by the days of siege and their evacuation from their homes.

Long, flowery robes were scattered over the rooftops, rolled up to the knee and tucked into belts, revealing beautifully molded legs and bare feet, dappled with henna or wearing brightly colored plastic sandals, immersed in soap bubbles. Women were sweeping water in smooth movements as sweat gleamed on their foreheads under the morning sun. A fragrance concocted of soap and cooking aromas reached the two enemies in their hiding place on that distant rooftop. Sarab stood entranced, watching the joy on the rooftops; after days of hunger and fear, her taut senses were engulfed by what Raphael called "life." She was overwhelmed by the loud "ah's" exhaled by a female singer on a nearby cassette player, mingling with a man's voice singing a love song for a gathering in the next alley.

A scene guilty of being composed of pure joy, washed clean of the horrors of the previous days. She watched it intently.

"Is there any life—or rather, is there no life—planted in you?" He swept a pitying, curious gaze over Sarab's body.

She shrugged and moved away disapprovingly. Raphael stood and stared, aroused by the smooth, sinuous movements of her slim hips and round backside. As the days passed, Sarab could no longer ignore the glances loaded with meaning and desire. She didn't seem to mind them, and perhaps even enjoyed falling victim to them. In fact, she could deal with the appeal in those glances, and the thought that he was looking at her, with more equanimity than his sympathy and compassion. It was making them both soften, threatening to topple their beliefs, leaving them prey to their humanity.

Unseen Ghosts

THAT NIGHT, IN HER SLEEP, Sarab was slowly drawn out onto the rooftop. Bewildering whispers made her look down at her feet, and she saw a large, dark stain sticking to them like a second shadow. At once she knew it was traces of dried blood she hadn't noticed before. Something in the air was making her eyes sting and she wiped away tears as she tried to focus on the stain, which slowly began to turn dark red, then to pulse and gradually condense, until it took the shape of human bodies. Seven girls ranging in age from two to twelve years old poured forth; laughing and holding hands, they formed a circle and began to go round. The youngest snatched Sarab's hand without warning and dragged her to join in their game.

Suddenly, gunfire broke out around them; it came from the tallest minaret in the Grand Mosque, where Sayf had been stationed throughout the siege.

Sarab knew beyond a shadow of a doubt that it was Sayf who was firing. She shouted at him over the rooftops to stop. She raised her voice as the bullets rained down and the girls fell, screaming, into their own blood. Everything was happening in slow motion. Their round-faced mother loomed in the background, bearing witness to the scene while voices urged her not to look, to leave the girls to be buried.

Sarab was screaming hysterically, surrounded by the still-bleeding bodies, when Raphael's hand pulled her out of the nightmare.

She sat up, staring at the blackened spot where she still saw the girls writhing. The bodies she had seen in the Grand Mosque were nothing in comparison with those young girls, bleeding to death forever. Their blood stirred and became a wave, which descended on the quivering Sarab as she finally emerged out of the nightmare.

"There were children in this house . . ." That meaningless comment remained on the tip of her tongue. She wanted to convey what she had seen to Raphael, what that spot represented. She needed someone else to share the ghosts that haunted the silent roof terrace.

Suddenly she caught a nauseating smell; it was the smell of bodies rotting, and it came from the boxes where she had imprisoned the butchered dolls. Sarab turned delirious, imagining bodies inside those boxes, whispering and accusing her and her brother of murder.

"I never killed anyone!" she burst out, to Raphael's surprise.

He wanted to tell her how many people he had killed, in case it was some consolation to her, but Sarab pressed on with her denials.

"I have betrayed my comrades. I carried a weapon like a medal on my shoulder, just so they would admire me. How am I a real believer? Even I doubted my faith, so I decided to kill you to make up for my cowardice during the siege. But I failed again; you're still alive."

"I don't understand. Why kill, when a girl like you is supposed to create and nurture life? If war is necessary, it's the trade of men like me."

"Infidels like you sow doubt even in the nobility of dying for a belief."

"What is your definition of a monster or an infidel? Is it someone different from you? Or is it, for example, someone who lives outside Wajir?"

Sarab looked at him doubtfully. She thought he was making fun of her.

"Listen, I'm a believer," he said. "I started out Catholic, and when I was a child the priests made me join the choir." He stopped suddenly, gripped with an urge to laugh at the contradiction; he was nothing but a killing machine shamelessly pretending to have emerged from Catholic roots. Astonishment showed on Sarab's face.

"According to my father, singing in church was the highest ritual of faith, like prayer."

"God forbid!"

"Is it a duty in life to kill those who aren't an exact copy of ourselves?" His words were directed more at himself than at her. He expected her to substantiate this but she kept listening passively, as if what he said could have no relevance to her. All the while he kept striving. He wanted to save her, even if he failed to save himself; he wanted to wash the creed of murder from his brain.

He went on: "God gave us the right to choose. He is the one who will judge us."

Her silence made him try a different kind of bait.

"We're just people of the Book, along with the all the other prophets they sent with holy books to countries we don't even know about. Didn't they teach you that?"

"All I know is that you Westerners are the army of Dajjal, the Messiah who carries Heaven in his right hand and Hell in his left hand to tempt you, even though both are false. They're both eternal Hell."

"On this mission, they emphasized respect for other religions," he said. "There is a verse in the Quran that describes the people of Abraham, Moses, and Jesus as Muslims. Why do you ignore this?"

Sarab was caught off guard. "Stop asking me questions like that."

"Why? I know—it must be torture for you to be forced to think."

"It's nothing to do with you. Just remember that I won't pass up the opportunity to kill you if it comes. So better keep your eye on the gun."

"You know, I could surrender that weapon to you and I very much doubt you would use it to kill me. You hide your doubts behind that word—'kill'—like it's a barricade."

Raphael's doubts made Sarab murderous, and pushed her further into her delirium. She wasn't aware of Raphael and the play-room where they were imprisoned; instead, she saw her childhood in Wajir, when she and her brother Sayf moved like two shadows split off from their mother and her powerful stride. It was easy for Sayf to match their mother's pitiless march, while Sarab stumbled and kept falling until she could no longer even wish to get up.

Raphael perceived her utter helplessness and her lack of guile.

"Listen," he said. "Let me take you home. I mean, to somewhere far away from here, where you can purge your mind of all this war, where you can start a new life . . . where you can belong to something new."

Her eyes widened incredulously at his offer. Without a word she rose and disappeared into the bathroom, fleeing the humiliating suggestion.

Raphael remained seated. He could barely believe his offer, made in a crazy rush. It would mean the end of his life as a soldier, but he didn't care. There and then, a belief came to him that everything he had been building until that moment was finished, and now he wanted to find a way out for them both.

Berry Red

THEY HEARD FOOTSTEPS CLIMBING THE stairs and a head suddenly appeared through the door. Its terrified eyes widened and swallowed up most of the face of a woman swathed in a black veil. Shock paralyzed any reaction.

The plump woman rushed into the room, and Sarab was struck by her resemblance to the woman who had appeared in her nightmare about the seven girls. The woman's eyes flashed crazed sparks as she screamed, "You, with the weapon—you drank the blood of my seven daughters!"

She lifted the hem of her abaya, revealing the berry red robe underneath. "The day you entered the Grand Mosque, the blood came up to here." She lifted her abaya to her knees, revealing more of her red clothing, her whole body trembling.

"And then it came to here." She lifted the abaya to her hips. "People who have no fear of God, they dragged me outside to save me, and they buried my poor girls, day after day. For ten days my poor girls were alone in a single grave in Maala."

The woman ignored Sarab, turning instead to the muscled soldier whose machine gun had agitated her. She struck him lightly and pushed him backward toward the roof terrace, uttering a laughing sound like a bird.

"Hoooyaah, hoooyaah," she cooed manically. She flapped the edges of her abaya like wings, using them to drive him backward; it was hard to tell whether she was sane. Raphael went along with her out of pity, and perhaps out of astonishment at the novel noises she was making. He put his gun on one side to calm her.

"You waded in their blood, hoooyaah." She herded him toward the dark bloodstain on the roof. "Seven girls in a hail of bullets."

Sarab felt the mad woman's stab of agony; it was possible that the girls were her brother's victims. The darkness she had lived through in the Grand Mosque came back to her and swept her away, along with the girl on the wallpaper and all of her cheerful red clothes; the dark bloodstain on the terrace obliterated them all. In that moment of darkness, Raphael was driven to a corner of the roof terrace covered with a thick canvas sheet, which neither had noticed before. As soon as he trod on the canvas, the ground opened beneath his feet and swallowed him up, and the woman's breast split in a joyful cry of "Hoooyaah," followed by a savage bark of laughter.

Sarab gasped, and before she could think she flew to save him. With savage glee, the woman bent over the hole that had appeared under the canvas, only to find her hopes dashed; instead of falling seven floors to the foot of the demolished staircase, Raphael had seized a piece of broken wood from the roof and was still dangling in midair. The woman hurried to snatch up a chair, cushions, and whatever else she could lay her hands on to fling at him and break his grip.

"Stop! Stop!" Sarab shouted as the woman kept up her frenzied attack. "Stop, or I'll blow your head off." She pushed the gun's barrel into the woman's skull, trying to carve some rationality into that insane head.

The woman snarled and slowly backed away from the hole, submitting to Sarab's order. She swayed from side to side while Sarab drove her to the bathroom and shut her inside.

Sarab locked the door and secured the handle with a broom, then hurried back to Raphael. Winding a nylon cord around the roof pillar, she hastily twisted the ends together and threw it to Raphael. He caught hold of it with difficulty, holding tightly to the wood with one hand and using the other to try to drag his heavy body upward. It was impossible for his sweaty hand to grip the plastic cord, and he kept slipping. The endurance tests he had undergone to join GIGN were nothing compared to the struggle with this cord. Sarab watched him in despair. At last, he succeeded in jamming his foot into a crack in the wall, and she used all her strength to help raise his phenomenal weight onto the roof.

They lay there panting, in a state of discomposure—and even awkwardness, seeing as she had rushed to save him. In the flood of embarrassment, they both forgot about the woman who had vanished, leaving the broken bathroom door as the only proof of her peculiar visit.

Raphael mastered himself first, his soldier's intuition reading the danger inherent in their position.

"That woman will most likely rush off to inform on us, and as soon as she does this place will be surrounded."

Sarab appeared drugged, incapable of understanding him.

"Let's get moving," he urged her. "We have to leave at once."

He felt his fate was entwined with the fate of this skinny girl, although he was still confused by why she had rescued him. Nevertheless, he felt a profound sense of gratitude, and was resolved that she should follow him.

"The soldiers will be here any minute, and they will execute you without mercy."

"I won't go anywhere," Sarab stammered, her heart fluttering in her throat. "Let them come and take me. It was cowardly to flee the Grand Mosque, and even though I failed in killing an infidel like you, I should face what my comrades faced."

"Are you mad?" Desperation seemed to have erased the girl in the wallpaper from the wall; the wall had transformed into a flat, bare surface, while Raphael frantically tried to convince Sarab.

"Some of your comrades escaped when they had the chance, and even Mujan didn't pass up the opportunity of fleeing and resuming his fight somewhere else." His words struck a nerve and she seemed to hesitate, so he went on. "Look, your death won't serve any purpose. It's suicide to stay here." He looked desperate, and she was embarrassed; she couldn't believe she had really saved this infidel from the fate he deserved. When she didn't budge, Raphael pointed the gun at her head and said, threateningly, "Now, move! That's an order."

She was propelled less by the gun than the despair in his voice.

He made her search the room for anything they could use as a disguise. They hastily dug up a bundle in the corner containing women's clothes and black abayas. Raphael ordered Sarab to put on the loose, flowery cotton clothes, probably belonging to the plump mother. She retired to the bathroom, and as soon as she started undoing the buttons of the military shirt, she felt living scales shedding from her skin. She trembled with fear at the protection, the habitual identity, that was falling away from her; hastily, she re-buttoned the shirt. She put the women's clothes over the National Guard uniform, doubling her sense of schizophrenia. For the first time in her life, Sarab appeared as a woman. Her body rejected the female clothing like an emasculated man, and she hastily wrapped her body in the black abaya to preclude any possibility of inhaling that vulnerable femininity. When she came out of the bathroom, Raphael was wearing a long green satin robe that barely reached his ankles and slithered oddly over the coarse military uniform. He too hurriedly wrapped himself in a black abaya to conceal the pleasure he took in this feminine form. Both were engrossed in this playacting, following Raphael's instructions. They covered their faces in black chiffon veils and Raphael crammed his large feet into women's shoes; the shoes Sarab chose were loose on her.

They hurried down the stairs, but heard footsteps tramping quickly through the entrance hall in their direction. Raphael retreated and turned into a corridor on the second floor. They reached a window on another corridor and found that it opened onto the roof of the neighboring house. Without hesitation, Raphael pushed Sarab, so that she had to jump through, and he followed after her, and they slipped from the open window onto the roof of what seemed to be an animal pen. They jumped down among the goats, which rushed about in consternation and then withdrew to watch them doubtfully from the far side of the pen. Sarab and Raphael slipped out of the pen, taking the risk of running into someone who might reveal them to their pursuers.

In front of them was a narrow passageway, and a small boy stood watching them with a gleam in his eye. They froze, trying to guess what he would do. His smirk made Raphael even more aware of his jumbled and amateurish disguise; the boy seemed to know he was a man under his satin dress, and a hairy one at that. Raphael hurriedly covered himself up, and without a word the boy pointed to the dark lobby leading to the back door of the house. They plunged into the narrow passageway as the boy watched them from the doorway. Behind them, police sirens laid siege to the house they had just left.

Hurriedly, they adjusted their veils and disappeared into the alleyways of the suq. Despite her suicidal state, Sarab's senses were refreshed by the vitality around her, while Raphael felt lost among the unfamiliar items spread out around them. Tables arranged in circles were loaded with gleaming fruit and vegetables brought in from the meadows around the city. Boys in colored clothing were calling out their wares and dusting the display piles, and small shops were opening up on both sides of every alley and small passage. The market seemed to be exploding with life after the three-week paralysis imposed on it by the snipers in the minarets.

As Raphael hurried on, he was dominated by a single thought: How could he get this girl out of here, and out of this country? He would manage it, even if he was forced to abduct her.

He could leave her in the middle of the suq and disappear; he could go back to his life. But, against his will, he was fascinated by his captive and the danger staring them both in the face. He was well aware that she was a danger to everything he was and had built. However, he no longer cared about that, or about anything other than getting her out of there. But how? His mind raced, and then lit upon a ridiculous rescue plan.

He moved, trusting in one thing: to keep up the male identity she had assumed. Sayf's identity card might form their only means of escape. Perhaps it would be easier to forge a passport, visa, and the chance of a better life for a man than it would be for a girl. Sarab should continue to disguise herself as a man; the man who had kidnapped him in the mosque.

Ending Number One

MUJAN REMAINED SILENT AFTER HE was arrested on December 4. However much he was tortured and cajoled, not a word escaped him. He already seemed to have moved on to the next world, and he endured pain, starvation, and interrogation in silence and utter passivity, letting them do what they liked to his body. He was a corpse in their hands, untouched by suffering, however intense.

He didn't raise his head when his cell door was opened, but the scent of the Kaaba's perfume filled him with a crushing certainty that the end was near. His eyes gleamed, illuminating the death he was facing. For a moment, he thought he had died already and was in the presence of the angels. He lifted his eyes and was taken aback to see a group of the ulema who had taught him as a student in Medina, headed by Sheikh Hamid Amin al-Mauritani. Mujan thought he was hallucinating and didn't move, afraid that the faces he had revered would evaporate.

Sheikh al-Mauritani approached him, embraced him, and burst into bitter weeping. "Brother Mujan," he said, "give us an argument to justify what you were bold enough to do."

After days of silence, Mujan's lips parted. The deep voice said only a few words: "My brothers and I were propelled by the whirlwinds of this era. We hoped that if we took refuge in God and asked for His forgiveness, perhaps He would pardon us." He said nothing after that, and sank into the silence of the grave.

The ulema came forward one by one to embrace him and repeat, "May God forgive us all." And then they left.

Mujan was tried in a secret court, along with sixty-seven of his men who had surrendered, and the mufti pronounced their sentence.

"Frivolous overconsumption and worship of money are not unknown in this country, but these rebels have erred on two counts: first in defying their rulers, and second in announcing the appearance of the Mahdi."

And so Mujan and his men were condemned to death.

Back in Paris, Raphael attended an evaluation meeting with the operations team. It concluded with a videotape of the punishments and executions that had been carried out at dawn on January 9, 1980.

Mujan was the last to be taken to the execution site in the Holy City, in the large square in front of Bab al-Malik, the main door of the Grand Mosque, directly below the minaret in which Sayf had been killed a few weeks earlier.

Mujan kneeled before the executioner like a bow, taut with disdain. The sword, raised resolutely in the black-gloved hand, sliced the air. It hovered, traced a half circle, and then fell. In a moment, the head of the legend was severed from his body. It flew high into the air before falling at the feet of the officer supervising the condemned men's sentences. A gasp went through the huge crowd that had gathered to witness the end of that unprecedented tragedy. Within ten days, a series of heads had flown in every direction in each of the principal cities. In accordance with the court rulings and on the orders of the ruler, sixty-three rebel heads were cut off: forty-one state nationals, ten Egyptians, seven Yemenis, three Kuwaitis, one Iraqi, and one man from Sudan. The heads were sewn back onto their bodies and buried in an unmarked grave.

Raphael walked to his car, his mind still full of the ruling authorities' official report. "The battle, which lasted over a fortnight, resulted in large numbers of casualties: 117 rebels during the siege, comprised of 87 casualties during the battle and 27 who died after reaching hospital. Nineteen rebels were sentenced to death, subsequently commuted to life imprisonment. The local authorities sustained the following losses: 127 killed and 451 wounded." The report also mentioned that 255 pilgrims had been killed and 260 wounded.

Raphael didn't notice his colleague running to catch up with him.

"Raphael, wait a moment!" The man blocked Raphael's path to the car park. "Hold on, are you serious about resigning?"

Raphael smiled. "It seems impossible, but yes."

"But why? After everything you've achieved with the forces?" The man stared at Raphael, his words boring into him. "You're the best we've got! You've got the killer instinct."

Killer instinct! Raphael was shocked at this description of himself. His whole being contracted painfully, bringing on the despair that had become marked in him recently.

He couldn't believe it had been over a month since the suffering he had endured with Sarab after their return to Paris.

They had arrived in Paris one early morning in December. An intense silence had descended on Sarab for the whole journey. Her eyes strained open all the time, barely blinking, during the seven-hour flight. He glanced at her furtively, certain that she was replaying the horrors of the siege in her head. However, wherever Sarab looked, she saw only her shorn locks of black hair. In her head, the scene loomed of the day Raphael had begun the preparations for her travel, when he cut off the first lock and threw it on the ground. To his surprise, she hurriedly bent over, picked it up, and put it on the table in front of her. She hesitated to do the same with the second lock, but he placed it on the table next to its companion.

Her eyes bulged when he bent her head forward and she felt his electric razor denude the back of her skull. The buzzing noise drilled a cavity in her brain. She raised her head and gasped when she saw the woman in the lemon-yellow dress staring back at her from the mirror. With the locks that Raphael had left on top of her head, she had become the woman who had embraced her child's dead body. She wrapped her shorn hair in a towel and put it in her coat pocket, and on entering the airport, she laid it like a corpse in one of the large blue basins. All her mother's attempts to obliterate her paled before that act of shaving, and the hair that had previously meant nothing to her suddenly, with the first snip of the scissors, became a symbol of absolute negation.

Now, the glass window of the airplane reflected the face of the girl on the wallpaper. It occurred to Sarab that with her short hair, she embodied all her victims, beginning with the woman in the lemon-yellow dress and ending with the girl on the wallpaper. Raphael didn't sleep a wink as he watched Sarab hiding inside the heavy black coat and men's trousers. He was familiar with the signs of mental breakdown and knew one wasn't far away, so he kept silent, afraid to break the fragile shell holding her together. When she didn't touch her meal, he opened the tinfoil covering without being asked, took the knife and fork from the small wrapper, and tried to feed her pieces of chicken. She refused them coldly, but when he put the fork in her hand, she took it automatically. Since they left the Holy City she had been no more than a puppet, with him moving the strings. It was the first time she had seen a fork. He watched as she began to stab at pieces of potato in a daze, trying to convey them to her mouth before they disintegrated. She started to shovel food and drink into her mouth with the mechanical gestures of someone filling in a pit.

When they left the airport in Paris, they were startled to see snow flying through the air. Sarab's eyes were dull. She stood stock still in front of a taxi, its door open and waiting for her, as the snowflakes glittered in her black hair and eyelashes and on the tops of her ears. She turned to Raphael in terror and almost asked him, "Can you hear it?" But her voice betrayed her, wounded by the sudden assault of cold. The tufts of snow carried a whisper only she could hear; she was tempted to think the snow was a message meant for her alone.

It was clear that the souls of the dead were communicating with her.

She was unsure how to respond to the snow. Gently, Raphael placed a hand on her shoulder and urged her into the taxi, and she shivered. The snow had gone under her collar. He wrapped her neck in his scarf as he took a seat beside her. She was staring fixedly at the road, and he was unable to tear his gaze away from her. He would have given half his life to be able creep inside her head and share the anxiety that nested there. She was absorbed by the thick layer of snow covering the fields and the sides of the road. It was a shroud . . . she was piercing through a shroud. From Charles de Gaulle Airport to the center of Paris, her gaze swept over cars and rooftops robed in snow and people on their motorbikes, all the black driven away by pure white.

This is the barzakh. She was sure she had died and was crossing over from this world to the next. She was filled with contentment, all her senses muffled by the snow; the smell of smoke, which had never left her since the siege, had subsided, and with it the taste of fire and gas and gangrene and corpses. Everything entered a tranquil state of suspension.

The fountain was frozen in Place Saint-Sulpice, which could be seen from Raphael's apartment in Rue Bonaparte in the sixth arrondissement. She crossed the distance between the taxi and the apartment in a state of peace, like a delicate snowflake.

"This will be your room," Raphael told her, leading her into his bedroom. "You have absolute freedom in this space . . ."

The concept of "absolute freedom" wasn't in her lexicon.

He went on, inscribing the fact into her head. "This is the key. You can lock the door whenever you want and no one will go in but you."

The thought of a key and a lock appealed to her.

He led her to the bathroom barefoot, went to the ancient, high-backed bathtub, and opened the taps. Speaking to himself, he explained which tap held the hot water and which cold, and then he added bath salts and soap balls scented with green tea. She just stood at the door, watching the fragrant clouds of steam and the velvety, pure-white towel waiting for her on a heated rail. She compared it to the single towel she had shared with her mother and brother in their house in Wajir. Raphael gestured to her to step inside the bathtub and then he left, pulling the door closed behind him. The look in her eyes begged him not to go far.

Trancelike, she took off her clothes and stepped into the bath. She froze for a moment with her left foot in the water, while the perfumed steam ran over her body.

At last she put both her feet fully into the water and stood there, bewildered by the water reaching to her knees. She was bending over to splash her face and shoulders, when her foot slipped and she fell on her backside. She sat there, stunned by how the smooth bath and the fragrant water felt on her backside and over her breasts and under her arms. Slowly she slid her body down until she was lying in the water, and then she let her face sink. She held her breath for a few seconds, and time stopped. Her past detached and rose to the surface of the water, to float there like a second body.

Raphael was packing his clothes into a suitcase when she sprang into her bedroom, wrapped in a white towel. She didn't look at him. Without a word, she slipped into the king-size bed and sank into the fluffy covers like a caterpillar. She had never been wrapped in such softness, apart perhaps from the womb before Tafla wrenched her out. Her body had never known anything but the hardness of the ground through thin strips of sponge, or the bare marble of the Grand Mosque. As she fell asleep, a thought snagged in her head: "This bed would do for a whole family in Wajir."

Raphael stood there for a short while, gazing at her slow breathing, and then he went out. He only came back when he grew worried that she was dead, but she was still breathing. After a while, very quietly, he carried the suitcase to the living room and closed the door to Sarab's room.

The following morning there was no sign of her. In the evening, he knocked at the door and she didn't reply. He pushed the door open, apologizing: "I'm sorry, I was worried."

He found her lying on the bed, her eyes fixed on the ceiling. At once he knew that something was wrong.

"Sarab." Her pulse was slow and her body was in a state of suspension. Her eyes were glued to the scene behind him, on the snowflakes falling past the window onto the treetops of the Luxembourg Gardens.

"Sarab, please, what is it?"

She didn't respond.

The doctor he called to examine her gave her an injection to prevent seizures. "She is probably suffering from panic associated with severe stress. It seems to be the result of some psychological trauma." He prescribed some antidepressants and left.

For three days, Raphael devoted himself to caring for her. As if tending to a child, he fed her, gave her the medicines, and left the door open to watch for any relapse. His life hung on hers.

On the fourth day he woke to find her in front of the bathroom door with wet hair; she had gotten up early and bathed.

"I don't need this drug now," she told him serenely, taking the box of pills from the side table and throwing them away.

It was plain to him that she had passed the point of crisis.

"You see, I have no control over myself," she said, more to herself than to him. "My body is here and my soul is there . . ." She pointed at the door to the street. Looking at her, Raphael was surprised by the violence hatching within him. At that moment, he knew that if worse came to worst, he was ready to stuff medicine and food down her throat to force her to live. She had no choice, because if she lived, he would also join the living, having been among the dead. Through this girl, he would be saved from everyone who had died at his hands throughout his military career. But she avoided this, returning to life with the same suddenness with which she had withdrawn from it.

"You have the killer instinct." His colleague's phrase returned him to the present, and he confirmed it bitterly.

"Yes. But you could say I'm addicted to change."

"You've never given us that impression."

"True, but we have to burn certain bridges in order to move on."

"It's not just me; all your superiors agree you can go far in this field."

"Not far enough."

His friend burst out laughing. "Ah, so it's never enough! Not even if you were nominated for president?"

"My resignation was a leap in the dark, but perhaps it's much simpler than that. Perhaps now I will try to become a chef."

They both laughed at this.

"Really?" his friend said. "You were always the joker, even on those missions that turned everyone else's hair white."

"No joke this time. I'm serious."

His friend felt almost insulted. "It's weird to imagine eating something made by hands that are used to breaking necks."

The quip hurt Raphael; he seemed painfully trapped by this fact.

"Please, rethink your decision, my friend," his friend said. "Be sensible. Don't let this whirlwind blow you off course. We're in an era where war has become the only way of keeping this little globe balanced. The world needs an iron fist on the reins to lead it in the right direction. We're just keeping it balanced."

Raphael looked at him sympathetically, but he went on.

"They've only postponed accepting your resignation because they're giving you an opportunity to review. You should thank your lucky stars they didn't punish you for disappearing at the Grand Mosque; they were prepared to forgive you, considering your past service. Please, just take a holiday; take a few days to reflect on what you're sacrificing by resigning."

In some way, that trivial exchange convinced Raphael that he was right to hand in his resignation. He sat behind the steering wheel of his silver Peugeot, contemplating his outstretched hands. "You were made to kill; you were made to cook." He was accustomed to finding his fingers cocking a rifle or pulling a detonator, but an age had passed since he had cracked an egg.

His fingers felt fragile, like those of a child who shared his father's passion for cooking. Raphael punched the steering wheel when he remembered his father's lame words: "Your mother can't bear a man in an apron."

This was the mother whose pride and monstrous egotism was only nourished by a businessman husband; his father had acted the part, but it sucked the life out of him like a vampire.

Raphael made a mental note to search for his father's notebook containing his own recipes, probably buried somewhere in his bookshelves. He heaved a sigh of relief to be leaving these bloodied years behind him and paving the way to facing his demons.

Despite his fears and doubts, he suddenly felt light, as if catching sight of a new life he had never reckoned upon. It was as if he had broken an invisible siege that had been imposed within and around him, and around the truth of what he had wanted all these years.

He drove toward Saint-Germain-des-Prés, the car making its way through the crowds of tourists wandering into the bus lane, and he stopped in front of a café, Bar Saint-Germain. A girl hurried toward the car, her coal-black hair cropped á la garçon in striking contrast to her clothes, a white linen dress that reached almost to her ankles. He watched the wide, lily-shaped hem flapping freely and gently brushing her legs. The neckline was like a crack across her shoulders, revealing their grace and drawing attention to her long neck. Her walk contained the appetite of someone touching the world with her bare body for the first time. He remembered how, in the second week after they came to Paris, he had surprised her with a parcel, which he had left on her bed. From where he stood in the doorway, he watched her open the bundle enthusiastically and fall suddenly silent when she pulled out three dresses of silk, lace, and delicate cotton. He hadn't chosen short dresses or daring necklines for her, guessing she already found her sudden transformation difficult.

At the bottom of the parcel lay some lace underwear sets in blue, white, black, and red. Her fingers trembled and she didn't dare even to touch them. She sat, staring at the small red rose on the belt of the small red panties. He quietly closed the door and left her alone. He didn't know how long she remained sitting there.

Sarab felt a thick skin peeling off her, and she thought of the wound the snake makes in itself when it sloughs off its skin. This was that wound. Calmly, she stood up. She took off the male trousers and shirt in which she had left her country, she took off the body her mother had forced over her own for all those years, and she stood naked in the middle of the room. Defiantly she avoided the neutral colors and picked up the red lace panties. When she slipped them over her thighs she shivered, and she allowed the red rose to dig into her with exquisite pain, like a live ember. She stood still for a few moments, feeling the burning sensation of the rose spread through her veins. That rose touched her like nothing had ever touched her before; no bullet, no wound, had hurt her this deeply. Aiming for more, she struggled to work out how to put on the red bra, looking for help in the picture drawn on the box. Finally she managed to put it on, and another red rose burned between her breasts. She didn't know what devilish impulse had enticed her to choose the red set. She contemplated her body, a statue of gold draped in red. She was haunted by the thought that she was embodying the apex of sin, but delighted in it at the same time. Her body moved spontaneously, reveling in its feminine nakedness, glowing throughout the room. She gently stroked its softness, unprotected by rigid or coarse coverings. She crossed the distance from the bed to the window and stood there; she couldn't believe how the breeze stimulated and invigorated her body, now open and breathing. In those two strips of red, the womb of iron that had imprisoned her had been shattered and now ejected her, reborn. She trembled. Hurrying over to the blue cotton dress, she lowered it around her body and sat there, feeling a nakedness that couldn't be covered up. When she finally opened the door, she felt like a drop of water.

He lifted his eyes, entranced by her lightness. He had felt her presence like a burden weighing him down, and here she was, so light she was almost flying; and he was profoundly aware of the red at the heart of the water drop.

But this was only a foretaste of what was to come. Two days later, without warning, Sarab's mood flipped. It was almost nine in the evening; the sun had set at quarter to five, cutting the day dramatically short and giving the impression that there was no time for living.

Raphael was shocked when he opened the door and found the apartment immersed in darkness. He could have cut the curtains of depression with a knife. He had spent a long day in a series of meetings, repelling relentless interrogation about what had happened during his sudden disappearance from the Grand Mosque.

Despite the darkness, he spotted a pile of clothes on the sofa. All the clothes he had given Sarab were carefully folded and left there, returned to him probably. For a moment he stood frozen in the doorway, stunned at the thought she had left him and gone away. But the bedroom door opened suddenly and she appeared, silhouetted in the doorway. Rays pierced through her body, alleviating the tragic darkness of the living room. Even from a distance, Raphael could sense the tension in that slim body; it seemed suffocated in her austere, male outfit. He felt threatened by this recurrence of the same outfit in which she had fled to France. His tired eyes washed over her. They stood, her hair bound tightly inside a scarf; in that soft covering, he sensed the barrier that had been erected against him, keeping him out. Stifling the anger that had erupted along with his fear, he called sarcastically, "So, it's back into the breach?"

She was shaken by his sneering tone and responded in kind: "In these clothes . . ." Words failed her as she pointed in disgust to the pile of clothes on the sofa. "I feel naked." She could sense the violence pounding his veins. "It drives the angels away when I leave my skin exposed to strangers in the street."

"You're afraid of liking it?"

His scornful tone stung her and she shouted back defensively, "You've come between me and my fate!"

"If I were in your shoes, I would be down on my knees right now, thanking God for giving me a second chance at life." Each seemed compelled to hurt the other. "Anyway, I've already seen your hair—I cut it myself. So what good is it hiding it from me?"

"Of course, what would it matter to you if I left my hair uncovered to men's eyes and fell to the deepest pit of Hell?"

"So now covering up your hair is your biggest worry?"

Sarab paled. His words bored right through to her hidden self-contempt, the fanatical soldier latent within her who enjoyed practicing the utmost aggression against the self.

"Of course!" She flared up at his attack. "You Westerners encourage women to go outside naked. It's one of the weapons you use to tempt the world into sin." Once more, Sarab was shocked to hear herself repeat Mujan's recordings.

Raphael stepped forward until they were eye to eye. He took a lock of her hair and rubbed it defiantly between his fingers.

She shoved him in the chest and raced to the door, and before he could react she had left, leaping down the stairs ten at a time.

He hesitated a moment before running after her.

When he came out of the building there was no sign of Sarab. There was nothing but Place Saint-Sulpice bathed in a melancholy, dramatic light. Drizzle fell, obscuring and fragmenting his vision, and a feeling of doom squatted on his chest. He ran to the middle of the square, hoping to see her on one of the roads that led away in every direction. Suddenly he spotted a slender apparition running up Rue Bonaparte toward the Luxembourg Gardens, and he raced after it. Like a wounded animal, she needed to hide, and the small park called out to her; she turned into it, blending in with the darkness of the trees. Raphael swung after her, bounding up the six steps with a single leap, but there was no trace of Sarab in that narrow walkway—nothing but bushes and the long, dark-green benches, and he was tempted to think that she had entered one of the buildings lining the path. But she burst suddenly out of her hiding place between two shrubs, and in a flash she was back on Rue Bonaparte. He caught up with her again in the middle of Place Saint-Sulpice. He grabbed her shoulders and pushed her against the wall of the fountain, trying to subdue her resistance.

"Sarab, please calm down. I'm sorry."

She punched him in the chest, trying to escape. "Let go of me!"

Tears mingled with the streaks of rain on her face, and her scarf fell down. Raphael hurriedly caught it and clumsily tried to cover up her hair by way of apology. But she pushed his hand away angrily and the scarf fell to the ground, soaked.

Raphael's voice came deep and quiet: "Please, slow down. Where do you think you are going?"

"To Hell . . ." Like a suppressed flame given oxygen, that wail shattered the barricade she had erected around herself.

"Please."

"I will hand myself over to the police," she stammered. "Maybe they'll send me back to my country."

"Come here, please. Let's understand each other."

"Why did you drag me here? You kidnapped me!" she screamed hysterically. He was forced to smother her mouth with his hand, and she tried to bite him.

"You claim you've given me freedom, while you want to control even what I wear. What you really want is to convert me. I am a Bedouin in a form that is not me—I'm not a Western woman, and I'm not a toy you can dress up in whatever clothes you please. I am Bedouin." She said this in a voice devoid of anger; it was flattened, drained, empty of blame or protest.

"You think that a few shreds of European clothing can erase who you are and where you come from?" he asked. Her body shook with sobs, and his right hand stroked her hair soothingly while he whispered, "I think what's most important is your heart."

They stood there under the rain, which suddenly began to pour down, their faces illuminated by the misty lights of the square, while the birds hidden in the surrounding trees watched two people engaged in a ritual of purification.

And there she was that morning, all in white. A feeling of alarm stirred in him. Her breath smelled of coffee as she took the seat beside him. Raphael stared at her, and she avoided his searching gaze.

"Who could believe that a little girl like you wrestled a GIGN officer to the ground and took him captive?" he joked, to lighten her nervousness.

"Thanks to the rock that fell from the ceiling and knocked him out. But it wasn't long before the jijin recovered the machine gun and stripped his captive down to her underwear."

He burst out in sincere laughter, making her heart beat wildly. Suddenly Sarab remembered the miracle that had come to her aid that day. She recalled the blackness anointed with the perfumes of the last remaining eunuch, whose presence had filled the prayer cell. His words about the blackness that would save her from the lion's mouth still lived and resounded in her head. Was it the ceiling that had fallen that day, or was it the eunuch who had leaped out of the shadows to bind her fate to this foreigner, sending them both on this long journey?

"You know, I always called you jijin. I was sure that you were a sort of infidel jinn that had possessed me."

He laughed incredulously.

"And now, Sarab, the time has come for the jijin to throw away some of your fears. Let's ease your mind."

He drove along Boulevard Saint-Germain toward the fifth arrondissement, passing the Institut du Monde Arabe by the River Seine, turned right alongside the Jardin des Plantes, and then left onto Rue Georges-Desplas. In front of them rose the Grand Mosque of Paris, its architecture inspired by the Qarawiyyin Mosque in Fez.

The tranquility reigning over the mosque provoked a feeling of guilt in both of them, as if someone might deny them entry, so Raphael hurriedly said, "This beautiful building came about as the result of a bloodbath."

This shocked Sarab, and pulled her out of the melancholy that had enveloped her when her gaze fell on the minaret. It had been influenced by the minarets of the Zaytouna Mosque in Tunis and was nothing like the minarets of the Grand Mosque of the Holy City, but even so she still felt the warmth of her brother's blood as it oozed over her body.

Raphael went on, trying desperately to dispel the agony on her face. "It was built in 1922 after the First World War to honor the seventy thousand Muslims who fought and died in the French army." Raphael swamped her with information to distract her thoughts from the task which awaited them.

"It seems like a paradox, but during the Second World War, when Paris was occupied by the German army, the imam of this mosque used it as a secret hiding place to shelter Jews from Europe and Algeria. He supplied them with forged birth certificates confirming they were Muslim, to protect them from the concentration camps."

At last they found the car park and he took her toward the mosque; when she realized his intention, she stopped dead in the middle of the street.

"I don't think I can go into a mosque."

"But it's one of the most beautiful places in Paris, and you'll find it reassuring."

She was embarrassed to say that she was menstruating; she had never spoken about that shameful topic to anyone before.

"I'm not clean."

"But we haven't come to pray. We won't stay long."

She found herself with no choice but to follow him, painfully aware of the delicate cotton towel between her legs, although it was like a breeze bearing her up by its lightness. She was recalling her first period in Paris. It had arrived suddenly, on the day she threw away the antidepressants. She had woken that morning with the sensation that her nether regions were exploding; when she rushed to the bathroom, she was startled to see a stream of blood. She undressed and stood in the bathtub to bathe, but whenever she washed, the effusion would return and run down her legs, and it didn't stop. She was sure that an old, hidden wound inside her had started to drain and she would surely die of it. Exhausted, she sat naked in the bathtub and waited for death while the pool of blood widened around her frozen buttocks. It didn't seem possible that such a torrent could come from her wasted body.

When an hour had passed and she was still fully conscious, she was tempted to think it was nothing but the blood she had waded through in the Grand Mosque, leaking out of her in thick clots like pieces of liver. She recalled that she hadn't menstruated at all during the siege; her cycle had been interrupted by her fear of dying and her dread of polluting the house of God. Was it reasonable to think that all this filth had been trapped inside her? She dismissed the idea as nonsense.

She had completely forgotten that she was female and obliged to undergo such squalor. Here she was now, in this Parisian bathroom, without even her mother's rags to help her. She looked around her; there was nothing but a hand towel. When the stream eventually stopped, she folded the towel and pushed it between her legs, sorry to pollute its snowy whiteness, and directed a spurt of water to wash away the clots of blood collected in the tub.

Before the end of the day, Raphael noticed the washed towel hanging to dry below the bathtub. That same evening, he presented her with some sanitary pads, and her face flushed dark red. They made her feel as if he had opened her legs and was pointing at the blood, mercilessly emphasizing that she was female and irreversibly marked with sin.

In a pathetic show of stubbornness, she left the pads in the bathroom cabinet on the shelf, a declaration that they didn't concern her, she would never use them, he had no right to creep into the red zone of her privacy. The pads had robbed her of her biggest secret, her shame, and in retaliation she furiously regarded his interference in such trivialities as her period as proof of his lack of manhood.

But during her next period, she found herself driven to try the pads. As soon as the strip was settled between her legs, she felt it sucking up all the ooze that had accumulated for years in that secret region of her body; the resulting feeling of lightness eased and smoothed her step. It was the drying-up of the shame represented by her monthly flow. A piece of her past was stolen from her, easing her burden.

Sarab and Raphael entered the mosque silently, followed by the eyes of homeless women from North Africa who had rolled out their blankets on the steps of the mosque, their huge bodies wrapped in long, loose robes. Sarab was struck with guilt at seeing their veiled hair; hers was uncovered. On entering, Sarab and Raphael were immediately swallowed by the calm blue of the surging sea of tiles, a startling miscellany of intricate mosaics that merged the soul and the genius of master craftsmen from North Africa. The gardens were laid out in welcome in front of them, their water channels and azure fountains a haven of peace hidden in the heart of the City of Light. It was not yet eleven and not a prayer time, so tourists were scattered around, wandering peacefully through the mosque and taking pictures against the celestial blue background.

Raphael led Sarab to the door to the left of the entrance, where the mosque's offices were situated. He greeted a Moroccan guard and asked where they could find the imam. The guard led them to the last room of a narrow corridor of offices, where the Moroccan imam sat sipping tea with two Arab men.

"Excuse me, Imam, I would like speak to you in private," Raphael said.

The imam darted a quick, searching look at Raphael; the aura of authority in Raphael's body language did not escape him. He gestured to his two friends, who stood up grudgingly and left the room.

"Please sit down." Although his greeting had included both of them, the sheikh studiously avoided looking at Sarab, as if she didn't exist, increasing her consciousness of the sin of being uncovered.

Raphael and Sarab sat side by side, careful to leave a gap between them.

"How can I help you?" The question was pointless, as the imam could foresee what would be asked of him.

"We want you to draw up a marriage contract according to sharia."

The imam had probably lost count of the number of times he had heard this, and he had a ready reply.

"Very gladly. But we need official papers to complete the process. Are you both French citizens?"

"It doesn't matter what nationality we are. All we want is for you, as the imam of the Muslim community in France, to join us as husband and wife."

"Are you both Muslim?"

"Yes," Raphael replied without batting an eyelid and Sarab fidgeted, remembering the previous night in his apartment. They had been eating takeaway pizza in the kitchen when she surprised them both by blurting a question that came out of nowhere.

"Can you convert to Islam?" She bit her tongue with remorse as soon as she asked.

But he smiled and replied simply, "It's been done."

Her eyes widened happily, and he added, "In front of the appropriate authority."

"I'm sorry, Sir, but our hands are tied by the law." The steely refusal in the imam's tone pulled her back to the siege and the other imam's refusal to give up the microphone to her. "We can't grant a marriage certificate unless we receive sanction from both your governments."

"We're not asking for a marriage certificate. We're not trying to get official documentation; all we want is for you to witness a verbal marriage contract to give our connection legitimacy before God. Just like the marriage contracts in the days of the Prophet, when he was married by word without the contracts imposed on it by the needs of modern society."

Irritation showed plainly on the imam's face, and he repeated with icy courtesy: "But now we are a part of modern society, and we must respect its laws safeguarding individual rights. I am sorry, but it is not in my power—nor is it appropriate for me to do what you ask."

"Can't you just witness our marriage before God?"

The imam turned away, refusing sympathy or understanding. "I cannot get involved in situations that might create problems or complications. What about your children? Where will they be raised? Or will you bring misfortune on me by saying that I have married you?"

"There won't be any children. All we want is peace of mind about living under one roof. I want this girl to feel safe and pure in front of her Lord."

Sarab squirmed.

"*Her* Lord?" the imam asked.

Raphael lost his temper. "Her Lord, our Lord, what's the difference? You're our witness. We came to you and you know now . . ." Raphael recognized the futility of what he was about to say. "Please, Imam, recite the Fatiha and bless us as husband and wife."

The dry look on the imam's face made it clear that he wouldn't relent. Finally Raphael resorted to the last card in his deck.

"I have brought you a special request from Captain Davos."

At once, the steely conviction melted from the imam's face. He reined in his irritation and asked, "Tell me, what exactly does he ask of me?"

"This girl lost all her relatives in the war, and she doesn't have anyone to act on her behalf. So, according to the law, you are now her guardian and it is your duty to see she is married. Please, be gracious to us and recite the Fatiha, and marry us before God and according to the Prophet's example."

Without further comment, the imam invited his two friends into the room as witnesses, and under their suspicious gaze, the imam humbly held Raphael and Sarab's hands within his own and recited the Fatiha, the opening chapter of the Quran, so they all could hear.

An hour later, Raphael and Sarab were wandering through the Bois de Vincennes. Nothing in their appearance suggested they had just gotten married.

They walked peacefully, side by side, avoiding brushing each other's hands, and allowed the spaces of infinite green to seize them and lead them toward the beauties of its hidden lakes. They approached a sort of walkway, a great passage between two rows of towering trees, its ground covered with golden autumn leaves. It reached all the way to the horizon and had been split down the middle by a pale line from all the feet that had walked along it. Sarab was rooted to the spot, captivated by this dazzling passage of light. Suddenly, a red bicycle appeared on the horizon and raced toward them. At first the rider alarmed Sarab as he bowled toward them like a black lump, but as he got nearer she became aware of the details of his flowing black woolen robe and wide sleeves, his black hood, and the ragged scarf flung over his shoulders. He ignored them as they stood watching the magnificent scene he presented: the vivid red bike rushing over the regal gold of the earth, and the pale face of the young priest brimming with vitality, framed by the ragged black clothes, flying through the air as he shot past them and shifted into a higher speed.

"That priest was from the Minim order. They live in this forest and dedicate themselves to a life of isolation, vowing to live in poverty, chastity, and obedience," Raphael said.

Sarab whirled around, her gaze following the flying monk until he disappeared in the dense wood. "I'm trying to comprehend that I just saw a priest flying along on a red bike!" She could never have imagined one of the sheikhs on such a bicycle, and felt as cheerful as if she herself had been flying along on it. They left the golden passageway and plunged into the vast lawn that suddenly rolled away before them.

Raphael took advantage of that moment of levity to reassure her: "Sarab, I want you to know that what we've done today—I mean the contract—doesn't mean I'm going to impose any physical demands on you. It's just a measure we've taken so you feel it's lawful for you to live with me."

The cheeks of both flushed, and he avoided looking at her. They were as embarrassed as if they were naked, and an electric charge crackled between them.

"I pray that God accepts this. He knows how fear blinded me there. And here, I have no way of making a living. I can't even work as a maid or go back to my country, seeing as I have a man's identity card."

"You can't leave your country as a woman with no male relatives; as Sayf, you're an independent person." He needed to justify having pushed her to keep using her brother's identity card.

"Sometimes at night, I leap awake in terror. For a girl like me, from a desert tribe, the sense of being alone in the world is horrifying. Sometimes I wake up screaming. I've never felt anything like this terror. It's worse than anything I felt in the Grand Mosque. It's not of this earth. I'm certain it's the sound of terror after death, and I can't stop shaking and wondering whether I was mad to stay alive and leave my country and put myself in a situation where there's no going back."

He watched her silently, and she went on: "I know you're trying to help me."

He was perplexed by this loneliness of hers he couldn't keep at bay, and they sat in silence.

After a few moments, he said abruptly, "I've resigned."

That moment, when the barriers fell, Sarab realized what had drawn her to this stranger. There was no doubt he had been a professional killer, but he'd had the will to stop and question himself, and here he was now, striving to change. He reminded her of tilled ground, ready to sprout seedlings at the least hint of rain.

He was confused by her glance, in which pleasure, longing, pity, and fear fought one another. He went on: "Not because you need me, but because I'm the one who needs you."

Sarab felt she was resisting an invasion of her innermost thoughts; for the first time in her life, all the obstacles with which she had stopped up the channels in her brain had been swept away, releasing a deluge of her own reflections and ideas. She was alarmed at the sudden, instinctive craving that exploded within her.

"You shouldn't depend on me. In the desert, when the snake sheds its skin, the Bedouin call it the moving wound, and they avoid it in case it lashes out at them. I am that moving wound, and I don't know what I will do, or why I did what I did, or where I am going. I am afraid and naked, and I don't know what I will do to you. I might be dangerous to you; I will be in constant danger if your country finds out I'm hiding here under a man's stolen identity."

"Don't deceive yourself. You are strong."

She ducked her head bashfully under his admiring gaze.

"And please, don't worry about your legal status in France. Let's pray the storm around the siege will quiet down. Later we can find a way of getting you a real refuge . . ." He put his arm around her shoulders.

"Don't do that!" she gasped, moving away.

In a revolt against the serious discussion, her body took over. She removed her shoes and sank her bare feet into the grass; her face shone with pleasure at the unexpected sensation. They sat on the grass, looking at the Temple of Love gleaming across Lac Dau-mesnil. The overwhelming pleasure of the grass brushing against her legs and through her clothes whetted her senses; she had a vision of her body lying naked on the grass, and the flush on her cheeks deepened. She felt herself sucked in by the beeches and oaks, by the Temple of Love perched on its humpbacked rock sunk into the lake, forming a grotto that invited her to disappear inside.

"For twenty-one years in the desert, I never saw houses made from anything but mud and sand and palms."

He stayed silent.

"I could never have imagined that I would be sitting here, in this paradise on earth." She was astonished to see him turn away from her and wipe away a tear.

"Are you crying?"

He stopped trying to hide his tears.

"But a man should never cry," she said. "If my mother had seen you crying, she would doubt your virility."

"Not you. I suppose you don't have any doubts on that score?" He teased her to lighten the tension, and they sat in silence. From his bag Raphael took out some bread and cheese he had bought on their way to the forest, and divided them up.

"The lunch of ascetics. It used to be a ritual of mine to have Comté cheese with seeded bread. Bread and cheese are an art form in France."

Sarab compared the taste of the bread with the treasure that was oven-baked bread in Wajir. She had no words to describe the difference; there, the bread tasted of earth and salt and fire, more ascetic, perhaps like the bread of the prophets. Here, bread was a work of art with a glorious taste, like the bread of kings. She scoffed at her own naive comparisons.

"You could say that we French are haunted by the idea of art."

"Just as we're haunted by the idea of Paradise after death, where something is waiting for us that no eye has seen and no ear has heard."

He almost asked her: "Was that why you were so keen for mar-tyrdom?" But he held himself back.

Finally Raphael took out a grapefruit. It had sparked her interest in the market, and when he saw she had noticed it, he put in their shopping bag immediately. He brought it out, huge and rosy and glowing in the sunlight. Peeling it, he offered a slice to Sarab, unaware that it was the first time she had seen one.

Raphael watched the tip of her red tongue pass doubtfully over the segments of grapefruit; she wrinkled her nose, and he burst out laughing. His laughter had a stimulating solidity; she had never heard a man laugh with such abandon before. She felt years of apathy flaking off her tongue from that bitter taste and her thwarted senses were sharpened into life, demanding more.

The taste of the sun and the morning with its hint of bitterness loaded her with something reckless. His gaze followed her tongue as it chased the drops of grapefruit juice that had slid along her fingers to her wrist. His soul had been stolen by this girl from the desert who was tearing each segment of grapefruit apart, looking inside them as if she were seeing a miracle.

"After my father died, this was my secret refuge." This slice of his past surprised him; accompanying Sarab had opened up more memories about his father, which had been buried in oblivion for years. He went on: "I was fascinated by Mata Hari, who was imprisoned in the fortress here during the First World War."

He didn't know what had driven him to bring up this funereal topic, but he kept going. "I used to come at dawn and stand next to the moat, imagining the soldiers leading Mata Hari in front of her executioners. She refused to be blindfolded or to have her hands bound. She blew a kiss to the firing squad and said, 'Strange habits you French have, to shoot people at dawn.'"

Ending Number Two

SARAB WENT OUT FOR ONE of her walks along Saint Germain. She was dawdling, glancing furtively at the art galleries on either side without daring to go in. They showed a completely different world from the one she knew, one where serious men opened their doors to display colorful canvases to invisible people. In their house in Wajir, the only wall decorations were her father's rifles and a small tapestry woven with the Throne Verse. She saw the city around her like some huge, decorated doll, the River Seine running through it like a magical illumination, its banks brimming with life and lovers who adored each other openly in front of every passerby. There was a lot to discover in an open city like this.

She was engrossed in watching two lovers kissing in Café La Palette when she heard a car screech behind her. She retreated to the pavement to let it pass. Suddenly the white Renault Alpine speeded up and hurtled onto the pavement alongside her. She hurled herself backward into the doorway of a gallery that fortuitously appeared next to her.

She stood in the middle of the exhibition. The abstract paintings tracing endless whirlpools on the walls reflected the roiling flood inside her. She reeled, dizzy, as the gallery owner rushed over to her.

"That crazy man almost hit you . . . are you all right, Mademoiselle?" Sarab was overcome with a fit of shaking. She recognized the gallery owner as Arab from the black circles around his eyes and the luxuriant black beard; a strange color, as if it had been dyed with shoe polish. It was the third time such an occurrence had happened; always the same driver, but in different cars.

At first Raphael was inclined to believe that they were harmless coincidences. "Calm down, there's no need for all this panic. The siege is in the past now."

He treated the accident lightly, like an ironic joke, but his levity failed to wipe the pallor of fear from her face.

"You must have been distracted by the city. You're always walking around with your eyes glued to the buildings and the changing light in the sky and the florists' displays and the bakers in the boulangeries and the shop windows. You never pay any attention to where you're going, or even to the road. So what do you expect? Paris has a lot of traffic and you have to keep your eyes open if you want to avoid getting run over."

But now she was half-confident that it was in fact a pursuit, and the driver really did want to kill her.

"But why?" Raphael wasn't convinced. His eyes ran nervously over his medals, which were lined up on the living room wall over his small desk.

"What if I've been discovered?"

"Who would care about you? They might think you deserve to be punished for escaping, but it defies all imagination that you would be run over like this in broad daylight." However, he was instantly assailed by doubt about this logic.

"I'm a fugitive, don't you understand?"

"Are you saying that Mujan's followers are after you?"

She trembled.

"But why?" Raphael realized they were still standing at the entrance to his small apartment. The door was still open; when he had opened it for her, she had immediately blurted out her fears. Calmly, he led her to the comfortable sofa and sat next to her. From the broad, open windows the trees of the Luxembourg Gardens looked down on them, spying on their bewilderment and filling the room with a refreshing smell of verdure.

"You're not the only one who escaped the siege. There are reports confirming that a number of your comrades managed to escape, and they were never found."

Fear still pierced Sarab's eyes, and he asked again, "Why you? Why look for a simple girl like you? Excuse me for saying so, but you're nothing and no one to them."

His question sparked a memory Sarab had ignored till now. She closed her eyes, hiding her sudden realization. She got up and fled to her bedroom; Raphael now slept on the sofa in the living room, as he had done for the two months they had been in Paris. She sat on the wine-colored bed and he followed her, standing in front of her, waiting for an explanation.

"What is it?" he persisted. "Do you know something that might make them follow you?"

Her hesitation confirmed that she was hiding something, and he kneeled down in front of her.

"Sarab, if you are in danger, you have to let me help you. Our lives are united; you are a part of me. Next time maybe you won't be quick enough or lucky enough, and you could be killed. Are you hiding something that might put you in danger?"

She looked at him with a mixture of fear and utter confusion, unable to speak. She couldn't find the words to begin.

"If there is something, it might be what happened in the well of the mosque, when the Mahdi was shot," she faltered at last.

He waited patiently, determined to hear every detail.

Her face turned gray as she looked back into the terror she had striven to bury. She had to exhume that fear and display it to the light, so it could be examined.

Her voice was as faint as an echo from the distant mosque: "I was standing at the top of the steps leading to the well when he was hit in the head by a bullet and fell to the ground. I was sure he was dead."

Raphael seized on every word she said, listening intently. She was silent, aware she had said more than she should, sure that she would never be free from whatever she revealed now of her past.

She was still staring into Raphael's eyes, overcome by the hell she had lived through, the last hours of the siege, and the moment in the well when the Mahdi was shot.

Sarab coughed violently as she came back to life, her eyes burning and her heart exploding from the smoke and the teargas. She flew down the steps of the well to where Muhammad's body lay. She knelt next to him, but couldn't look. His face was covered with blood, which oozed over her feverish hands. She brought her face close to his chest and realized he was still breathing, and she was flooded with a joy that gave her extraordinary powers. She tore off his turban, revealing the wound. The bullet had pierced the turban and made an incision so deep she could touch his skull.

She closed her eyes with a mixture of joy and revulsion. Suddenly two hands of steel clamped her from behind like a vice and lifted her bodily from the ground, crushing her ribcage and lungs. She gasped for air, and the grip on her body slackened when the attacker recognized her voice despite the National Guard uniform she wore. She recognized Muhammad's personal guard, a tall Yemeni. He was like a man returned from the dead; blood drenched his left shoulder. Quickly, without speaking, they dressed Muhammad's wound. They knew they had to get him out of there.

The Yemeni took his master onto his right shoulder and carried him as though he were a weightless puppet. Automatically, Sarab led the way; the maps she had studied for months glowed in her head, indicating every secret passage. Her body took over and she easily led the Yemeni to the mouth of the well. It was difficult for them to find the entrance to the tunnel Sarab was looking for, located close to the well source. The door was probably identical to the stones of the wall. But at last they distinguished its outline low to the ground, marked with larger stones. In the smoke and darkness, they groped blindly for a handle or some way to open it. Beating the door in desperation, they knocked a round stone, which fell to the ground, uncovering the handle hidden behind it. The Yemeni pulled at the heavy door; his strength was supernatural. Carrying his master effortlessly with one arm, he used his injured arm to pull open the door, which was half-welded shut. It was so low they had to crawl through it.

Sarab went forward into the pitch black, and the Yemeni followed, dragging his master with him. Sarab's body was on full alert, somewhere between total collapse and ecstasy, in a state of disembodiment. It seemed as if they were crawling through the very essence of darkness, driven by some inhuman will to reach the end of that endless tunnel. They were forced into narrow passageways, where the

Yemeni had to cram his master in front him like he was threading a needle, until they reached an open space where they could stand and stretch out the tension in their backs. But after a few steps, the earth opened under their feet and they slid deep into the mossy bowels of the earth, falling all the way to the bottom. The Yemeni slammed into the ground, cushioning his master's body. It was a miracle that Sarab didn't break a rib from the force of the fall. As soon as she reached the bottom she trembled, feeling something slippery crawling over her body. Paralyzed, she stopped moving. The crawling sensation had reached her head when, with a crack, blood exploded over her face and neck. Her gasp was lost as she stared into the cold eyes of a serpent; between them, the Yemeni's knife was sunk deeply into its skull. She couldn't see anything but those eyes, which seemed wider than the tunnel, and Sarab started to imagine that the snake was infinite, the size of the tunnel itself. Both fugitives were exhausted, but they moved forward relentlessly. They were racing against time to carry their Mahdi to safety.

At last they reached what seemed like the end, or an obstacle, and were forced to stop. In front of them, there was just a smooth stone wall. The Yemeni put his master on the ground and in total darkness they began to look feverishly for an opening. Simultaneously, they found a chink in the stone foundation. The Yemeni crammed his finger into it, and with extraordinary strength he began to pull. Sarab smothered hysterical laugher; she thought he was trying to move the belly of the entire earth like a madman. Suddenly the darkness wavered and rose, and daylight gushed into the tunnel, blinding the burning eyes of both. Sarab felt her skin was being scorched by the light. They were looking at the mountain at the end of the cemetery, and no one was around. The area seemed deserted; even the dead had abandoned this cemetery to stay in the heart of the city. The road south looked clear. Without a word, the Yemeni hoisted his master and strode off, expecting Sarab to follow him; when she didn't, he stopped and turned to her impatiently.

She urged him to keep going. "You go. I have to go back." His eyes bulged in disbelief. "My brother Sayf is still there." She couldn't believe the madness of what she was saying; that she was voluntarily turning her feet back toward Hell.

The Yemeni's eyes softened sympathetically and he tried to persuade her to follow him, but she stood as firm as the rock behind her, unable to save her own skin and leave her brother to commit suicide.

"Be sure to get him to safety." It was vital to her at that moment that she felt she was guarding the two men she loved.

Some hidden instinct told her that her brother was a lost cause, but she had to witness his end. When the Yemeni spoke, his voice was like a breeze from a grave.

"Don't worry. I have friends in the graveyard. They will look after us. And before God, I swear we won't stop until we reach our people in Yemen, where our Mahdi will be guarded and no harm will come to him."

Sarab found it laughable that he was determined to call Muhammad "the Mahdi," when at that moment it was the last thing that would have occurred to her, or that she cared about. To her, he was more than just the savior of humankind; he was the person who had cared about her, even if from a distance.

Without a backward glance she plunged once more into the darkness. The moment she reached the well, the sound of the firing from the top of the minaret where Sayf was positioned suddenly stopped. She ran up the minaret to find her brother's bullet-riddled body. Crushing despair prompted her to stay and die with him, but an inexcusable survival instinct forced her return to the tunnel. She tried to reach the well, only to find that a hand grenade had exploded inside it, closing off the path to freedom. She had been robbed of the decision to flee. She stood in the middle of the smoke, paralyzed with rage at her brother, who had died after she lost her only chance of survival. She stood there, thoughtlessly exposing herself to the bombardment while successive small explosions colored the background red and black. Her mind was whirring, reviewing the secret maps she had memorized, while an inner voice jeered: "It's no surprise you're focusing on escape tunnels. The traitor hidden in you was looking for a way out even before the battle started." There was no way of quieting that voice other than by voluntarily plunging into the hell of the underground cellars to share the fate of her besieged comrades.

Sarab felt a burden lift from her shoulders after frankly telling Raphael everything that had happened in the final hours of the Grand Mosque. But she was racked with guilt at having saved Muhammad, realizing only now that he bore just as much responsibility for what had happened as Mujan did. He was responsible for it all, to the last shot fired.

"So they've come looking for you now?" Anxiety was clear in Raphael's voice.

"Please, don't say that." She felt young, silly, vulnerable, and unprotected, like she had when she was a child confronted with a bird bleeding to death in front of her for the first time. "No, it's impossible." She searched his green eyes for a refuge from the nightmare, and kept repeating feverishly, "No, you can't be sure whether these accidents here have any connection to the Mahdi. It's another world there . . . it's so far away. . . ."

"Please, Sarab, think with me. Apart from his bodyguard, you are just about the only person who knows that Muhammad is still alive and has been smuggled to Yemen."

"Yes."

"I believe that the Mahdi has influential friends acting on his behalf in every corner of the globe. I don't know how they managed to find you, but they must have guessed that you also managed to escape, seeing as you smuggled the Mahdi out of the Grand Mosque. After you used your brother's identity card, it wouldn't be hard for them to trace you. Smuggling the Mahdi out of the siege was a momentous undertaking, and logic dictates you should be rewarded for it, but it also put you in the spotlight."

"Will they kill me for it?"

"They would see you being here with me as a threat, in case you reveal that he's still alive. So they are trying to bury the secret with you. You're their enemy now."

She shuddered. "Do you think God is angry with me? Am I being punished for escaping the siege and marrying you?"

Raphael, still kneeling, slammed his fist on the bed, enraged. He stood up.

"All the fighters surrendered, including the legendary Mujan."

"I should have been executed with the others. Why deny it? I'm no less responsible than they were, just by being there. Even though I helped nurse the wounded, I accepted the use of weapons. Bearing arms against believers is a crime. That ground is sacred, blood is sacred, and we gave Him countless sleepless nights. I am a criminal, and I deserve to be punished and to die for it."

Tears flooded her cheeks, and Raphael hurriedly took her in his arms, gathering up her pain and kissing the top of her head.

"You didn't fire a single bullet," he said, "and you offered help to everyone, regardless of which side they belonged to."

"If only you knew how afraid I am. Sometimes when I lie in bed, I see bomb shrapnel falling out of a hole in my head, and poison gas running through my veins. I'm so afraid of being punished for my sins it's like having a landmine inside me."

"Everything will calm down and you'll be surprised by what you discover about your true self."

She lifted her face to him, looking into his eyes for corroboration of his words, and accepted a gentle touch of his lips against hers. She shivered, torn between the charge of pleasure and her feelings of guilt. It was the first time he had proffered such intimate contact.

"You're the only one who makes me feel human. I feel I'm myself with you." Her voice shook from the depth of her gratitude. "Raphael . . ." Words failed her; they were both shocked by the tenderness with which she pronounced his name. It was only then that he realized she had never called him by his name before. She moved away, taking refuge in the space between them.

"I love you when I see you afraid and lost in my world," he told her. "I love you when I see you in my pajamas or in my bed, lost and not knowing where you're going or what refuge you have apart from the street. I am strong because of my training, but the strength you see is nothing but a shell. Inside, I'm still the little boy buying birds and setting them free." His words were like a breeze freshening the space between them. He respected the barriers she had put up to protect herself from him; this was his form of gratitude, an avowal of love.

"Thank you," she said. "You love me like you would a stray dog."

He laughed hoarsely and took her in his arms, resisting the desire to kiss her deeply.

"I'm not afraid of dying," she said, "but I am afraid of dying as a sinner."

His powerful embrace gathered up every objection and feeling of guilt. "You won't die," he told her. "Not before you grow old and I've seen every one of these black hairs turn white."

A tremor ran through her and she felt the Angel of Death hovering overhead. Not even in the siege had she felt it so close to her. She buried her head in his chest, filled with doubt about his promise, gripped by the certainty that she was nearing her end.

"If I die here in this foreign country, what will happen to my body?" Her unexpected question shocked him. "If I die, perhaps it would be better to send my body to my country so it can be washed and buried there and it will be pure for the next life. Would that be too much for you?"

The look in his eyes reminded her that she had saved his life; his pledge to carry out her wish was clear.

He got up suddenly, changing the course of that melancholy conversation. "Wait a moment. Let me show you something," he told her. He picked up a thick, leather-bound volume from his bookshelf.

"Look. This is the notebook where my father wrote down his own recipes, the pinnacles of his invention. Come on, I'm going to make you brandade. It tastes like the sea. And I've got a surprise for you."

He took her hand and led her to the kitchen so she could help prepare the meal.

"What do you think of opening a restaurant?" he asked. "I have enough saved to buy a small hotel. I was thinking of a beach in Spain—it's the nearest we can get to the climate you're used to. Just ten rooms with a restaurant attached, and I would look after the restaurant."

She laughed. "I could never have imagined a man cooking for a woman. You've upended everything."

Raphael held up his hands for her inspection. "Do you see? Better for a chef. Can you see these killer's hands cooking?"

She thought he was joking, but he was serious, and he looked morose.

"They seem to have been created for cooking, much more than killing," Sarab responded.

He took both her hands and buried his face in them; she felt dampness in her palms, and froze at the realization that he was crying. His tears always shocked her; she had been raised thinking that a man weeping was like the sky falling in. They remained sitting like that as night fell, peacefully darkening the kitchen around them.

The Archive of Death

DESPITE THE REASSURANCES HE'D GIVEN to Sarab, the car accident seemed to have deeply unnerved Raphael. The following morning the elevator in their apartment building was broken, and they were walking down the narrow staircase when he suddenly had a sort of fit. He stopped Sarab, and without preamble pulled her behind him for protection, then dragged her roughly down to the next floor. He wordlessly pushed her into a corner and signed to her not to move an inch. His crazed eyes flashed, his whole body was electrified, and he was ready to attack. He began to examine the wall and the shadows around them, looking for the enemy hidden there. He seemed to have forgotten her entirely.

Sarab reached out to him, trying to break through the fog cloaking his brain. Even though she was frightened and aware of a possible threat to herself, she kept trying to reach the compassionate man behind that mask of madness. But he was another man now; a terrified war machine poised to wreak havoc, and she was the potential target.

They both stood there, nailed to the landing in fear, while Raphael frantically searched his pockets for a weapon or a hand grenade and continued to scrutinize every inch around the damaged elevator. It wasn't long before Sarab's anxiety spiraled and she had the same feeling of being trapped that she'd had in the siege. But she held on, looking for a way out of the anxiety that had struck him.

At last the madness receded from his features, loss settling in its place. He allowed her to draw him down beside her so they were both sitting on the stairs, and he took a deep breath. They sat in the weak light of the stairwell for about half an hour until he had collected himself once again.

These episodes kept recurring, accompanied by regular fits of depression. Sarab would come across him sitting in the living room, apparently lost. They spent hours trying to regain the harmony and peace of the present and keep at a distance the war-filled past that haunted them both.

"They're coming back to life, all the dead," he told her.

She wanted to see what he saw, to break the terror revealed in his eyes.

"It's not my memory, it's a universal memory," he went on. "It's opening up files full of faces, the face of every victim I've left behind me. Even the ones I didn't meet, the ones I blew up from a distance. They're all here, as clear as day, right in front of my eyes." He pointed to a spot directly in front of him. "I can plant my fingers in their eyes. All those faces, without exception. I never counted them—there were too many. I can't believe how many people I've killed." He was silent for a while, then reached out as if he were scooping water from a river. "I can see a film running through all the atrocities I've committed, the big ones and the small ones. Nothing's been forgotten." He screwed his eyes shut, pausing the film reel and its barrage of images. "You would be disgusted if you could see inside my head. The torn limbs I left behind me, the charred bodies."

His tears shocked them both, but he let them fall and plunged back into the film. "I can't believe it was me." The agony contorting his features was more hideous than all the suffering Sarab had been seen on the faces of the wounded in the siege.

"What infernal logic justifies everything I did for all those years? I can't describe the horror rebuilding every cell in my body. I've been maimed forever." His eyes bulged at her, demanding a reaction, an act of retribution, and when he got nothing but sympathy, he exploded in rage: "You make me sick! How can you live with a festering sore like me?"

He was overwhelmed by the desire to destroy himself, and tried to drive her away. She was disturbed by this other man, this man who wasn't the loving, protective Raphael, but she was also aware there was another Sarab inside her. He had to find a way of dealing with his own personal archive of extremism and terrorism.

They were sharing the apartment with their shadow consorts, four bitter enemies locked in a perpetual struggle, unsure who would win the final battle.

Underground Worlds of Paris

DURING ONE OF THE WALKS Raphael took with Sarab in order to introduce to her the many worlds of Paris, they stood facing the Palais Garnier.

"I'll take you to the opera soon. It will be extraordinary, seeing it through your eyes." Raphael was in one of his changeable moods, back to his cheerful, charming self.

Caught unawares by a sudden rain shower, they ran in search of shelter. Instinctively, Raphael led them to a metro station. It was the first time Sarab had become acquainted with the concept of underground transport. Their cheerful headlong rush came to a sudden halt when Sarab became aware of where she was: the network of tunnels; the different levels and endless staircases; the silent, narrow corridors with plain lighting; the advertisements that darted past them on either side, exploding with colors.

She shuddered and asked, "What is this? Where are we?"

Raphael put an arm around her shoulders. "What's wrong? Are you all right?"

She stammered as she tried to come to grips with the fear that had struck her. As they were standing in the middle of a passage-way, blocking people flying past in every direction, Raphael pulled Sarab to one side and examined her face.

"What is it?" he asked again.

"An underground world," she said incoherently, in a small, childlike voice that was charged with dread.

"Let's get out of here." He drew her to the nearest exit, but she regained control of herself and reassured him.

"No, let's go on," she said.

He had no choice but to obey, and they continued on their journey back to Place Saint-Sulpice.

Sarab sniffed the pure air outside the station and hated the thought of leaving that open space to go inside. She and Raphael drifted to a bench in front of the Church of Saint-Sulpice opposite the fountain.

"For a moment I didn't know where I was. I felt like I was underground at the Grand Mosque." She surprised Raphael with this frank explanation. "Despite the differences between the two worlds, it's the same feeling of being in the ground, the same silence that waits and watches, the same coldness and isolation." He was listening, but she didn't know how to explain. "I don't mean there is a resemblance, but . . ."

He tried to grasp the shock she had felt when he'd herded her underground again.

"I only knew the prayer cells under the mosque during the battle, while in normal circumstances they would probably be cooling in the heat, and a peaceful refuge. But the underground world I experienced during the siege was like an endless wound. Everyone was suffering and dying, whether they were hostages or fighters." It was the first time she had opened the box of fear buried in her chest and released what was imprisoned inside.

"The last hours were the worst. The despair was beyond anything you can imagine . . ." She stopped abruptly. "It's strange. Why am I talking about 'them,' as if I weren't one of them?" After a pause, she went on: "I was arrogant about the situation there. I separated myself from it as if it had nothing to do with me."

"But it wasn't your war in the first place; it was Sayf's war."

"Perhaps. Perhaps I was so terrified, the horror of witnessing so much death paralyzed even my love for Sayf. I went numb in preparation for our inevitable separation."

She was silent for a while, then went on as if speaking to herself: "We went into a sort of trance. I'm positive we had stopped feeling, all of us. There was no more fear or pain or hope. It was a state of torpor. The body took over and kept fighting or being wounded or dying while our souls were somewhere else, watching impartially. Even the electrified water and the gas were like a game that couldn't touch us. Your body fell and it didn't matter that it fell. It was just a machine—your soul was still untouched. The only body that brought me out of that trance and made me grieve was my poor brother's. Sayf was my mother's victim just as much as I was."

Silence entered the space between them. She contemplated the untiring motion of the water in the fountain as it rose and fell, only to rise again, like souls striving to escape the material binding them.

"Life here gives me more time to think," she said. "It makes me look deep into myself, and whenever I do, I'm surprised by what I find. I've never found the time to get to know myself, and lately I've thought a lot about my mother . . ."

She seemed out of reach to him. He stayed silent, his gaze blurring over the vast square around them, as her voice came in a whisper.

"I thought . . . perhaps my mother herself was a victim, since they called her Tafla—it means 'spittle.' They made her whole life into a struggle to rid herself of the triviality and filth of that name. . . . She started a war that cost her everything: herself and Sayf and me. Look at where I ended up, homeless."

He took her hands in his but she quickly pulled them away.

"Earlier, underground, I was frightened at first, when I felt the same dampness on my face that I felt in the cellars of the mosque. I was sure I was actually suffocating, and for a moment I almost fainted, drawing my last, poisoned, breath."

A pigeon landed on the ground between them, interrupting their conversation. It pecked at their feet, picking up the crumbs of her words.

Over the next few days Sarab convinced Raphael to take her on more trips to the underground metro tunnels. They would pick a metro line to explore from beginning to end, get off at a random station, and then wander through the branching tunnels, discovering the various levels of each of the principal stations such as Gare du Nord or Saint-Lazare. They were driven by Sarab's insatiable hunger for plumbing her fear of underground worlds.

"It's a parallel city where people are crawling eternally, like ants. I imagine that when Judgment Day comes, they'll still be crawling and trying to reach the sky."

Raphael realized that the metro, which he had taken for granted since childhood, was viewed as a wonderland by someone like Sarab.

"If I tried to describe an underground city of human ants to people in Wajir, they'd think I was mad and lock me up."

"I can well imagine that."

"You know what? One city under another is frightening because it opens the possibility of other worlds we know nothing about, which you and I can't even imagine. I only moved from Wajir to Paris and here it is, a brand new world. What if we moved from Paris to some other faraway country? Would we see layers and layers of underground worlds, and other ways of living we can't picture so long as we're here?"

"It's difficult to imagine any world outside the one we know."

"But that doesn't mean they don't exist. That's just how the people of Wajir think."

He laughed, conscious that her brain was racing ahead of his thoughts, her natural intelligence incandescent. Coming from the desert, she was able to move freely between the spiritual and the material, to challenge the seen with the unseen.

"In the Quran, it says there are seven heavens and seven earths. How can all these worlds be?"

"So we have to start embracing the nomadic life. We just have to solve the issue of your official status, and I promise you we'll travel the globe and see what new worlds we can discover."

"Perhaps not in this world." Again, he was bewildered by this sudden shift into melancholy, this affinity to grief that came from isolation in the desert.

There was another confusing element to the worlds under the earth, which Sarab couldn't explain to Raphael or even to herself. One day, quite unexpectedly, while Sarab was standing on the platform waiting for the train, she felt something piercing her back. She wheeled around quickly and her whole body flinched as she looked straight into the eyes of her father, boring into her heart like fishhooks.

She gasped for air and was nailed to the spot, unable to avert her gaze or move away from those eyes. The thunder of a train arriving on the opposite platform pulled her out of the nightmare. That was when she was able to look clearly at the face of the woman printed on the advertisements; she had a strong resemblance to her mother, despite the lively, beaming smile. It was the contented smile that dug a pit of longing in Sarab; this was the smile she had craved from her mother and the world around her; the smile she had never received. For some reason, people had always seemed indifferent when they looked at her, apart from Muhammad, the Mahdi.

The train left the other platform and was followed by another, and yet another, and a tall youth in a khaki military uniform appeared on the platform where Sarab was standing. Her first impulse was to run away, but she couldn't move for fear of attracting his suspicions or attention. Suddenly she realized that the uniform might be borrowed, and then she noticed the discrepancy between the usual stance of a soldier and this young man's posture. She observed his handsome features and bronzed skin, and the stiff clump of blond plaits dangling down his back. Soon his smell reached her, an unbearable stench of decay. He had been making space for his countless bags and a colorful froth of lurid magazines, which he had probably spent years collecting. He was engrossed in digging through the bags, ignoring the people who were moving away from him, trying to escape the smell. Heedless of anyone else, within his own rotting cocoon, he started to scatter the magazines around, opening them at certain pages and leaving them face up on the ground, until he had finished creating a sort of shore of gaudy pictures around the bench behind Sarab. Finally the homeless man sat down on the bench he had selected, leaned over, and rolled up his trousers. Calmly, and to the horror of his observers, he took off his artificial legs. He put them on the ground so everyone could see them, and left the pink, shiny knee stumps exposed in confrontation to passersby. He lay back on the bench and started reading quietly, as if he were on a beach on some imaginary island, far removed from the concerns of the world.

Sarab's shock at the sight of his amputated legs made her notice the pages the homeless man had chosen to leave open. All of them contained scenes of explosions and death. He had left a small plastic cup in front of him, outside his island, blocking the way of the people passing by. It asked for donations; to war victims, perhaps.

Sarab was still frozen to the spot, stranded in the ocean far away from the island of that young homeless man.

"Sayf and I could have ended up like that." She was swept by profound gratitude to God that Sayf had died, but she felt a similar amputation in her own body. Her stump was invisible to passersby, but she was like that homeless man all the same. The fragrant soap that perfumed her hair did not make her any different from him, because inside they were both alike: lonely and marooned on an island of delusion. There was no truth other than the life she had been born into in Wajir; the life of Wajir and the idea of its heritage were like solid rock under her skin that left no room for another life to grow. She shook off this depressing idea and affirmed to herself that she was acclimatizing: only that morning, Raphael had affirmed that she was, in a way that made her proud.

Now, she huffed sarcastically: "What is this nonsense, 'acclimatizing'? All my life has been spent acclimatizing . . ." This small truth came as a surprise to her. "When will the moment come when I can stop acclimatizing and stand before my Lord as he created me: uncultivated, spontaneous, without having been pruned or tamed?"

She turned away from the homeless man and her desire for defiance worsened: "Lord, as You created me!"

She took courage and admitted to herself that she was attracted by those advertisements . . . and there was nothing sinful in that. She stopped for a moment to grasp that truth, embracing her insubordination.

A simple fact, but one that was vital to her.

Without hesitation, she moved on. Her eyes leaped to other advertisements, which showed happy people hugging their clothes joyfully or pointing radiantly to their products. Probably they were uttering cheerful phrases in a language it would never be her destiny to speak, even if she could guess at it from their smiles. Their blissful expressions, open and unrestrained, made the hypothetical world they belonged to more alive than the reality manifest on the station platform. Sarab felt swept along with it; her life depended upon sampling the joy they were proclaiming. For a fraction of a second, she was no longer certain whether she herself was just a picture on one of those walls, or whether she was a person of flesh and blood emerging from the tragedy in her past.

From that day, when Sarab decided to be "as my Lord created me," she exercised her freedom by surrendering to small pleasures. She savored the stream of images in the constantly renewed advertisements that coursed over the walls of each metro station like a river. Sometimes the advertisements were mixed with real-life figures, transforming the living world and its images, configuring them both into a single mass pulsating with life. She was aware of a separation in her response to that current; the hidden rebel like Sayf, who had smashed the dolls and erased the pictures of the little girl on the wallpaper in the Holy City, had been drowned by the pictures in Paris, a flood far worse than the electrified water that had drowned them in the cellars of the Grand Mosque and swept away their faith in the war they had started in the house of God.

These pictures formed a parallel world determined to last. She couldn't kill it; no force could kill it. She found gratification in the thought that it was eternal. Somehow, the guilt she was accustomed to feeling whenever she saw a picture had been taken away, along with her responsibility for its necessary destruction, and the fear of punishment if she failed. The world of the pictures became a world of its own. It unrolled in front her, refreshing, with its own soul, which it imposed forcefully and with discernment on the old world. The world of pictures was no longer her sin, or anyone's sin. She wasn't accountable for it; she wouldn't be asked on Judgment Day to breathe a soul into every picture she liked or that was displayed in her house, and she wouldn't be tortured when she was unable to do so.

It was a parallel world, laden with a soul, and part of God's creation and creativity; to her surprise, she began to be in fuller harmony with Him.

Jam Tomorrow

ONE DAY AS THEY WERE entering the lobby of Raphael's apartment building, they noticed an announcement on the wall. Raphael smiled when he read it.

"What is it?" Sarab asked curiously.

"Nothing important. A group of the older residents are saying they need someone to walk their dogs. The person who used to do it has quit.""Does it need a certificate or special skills?" she asked, somewhere in between mockery and gravity. "I mean, can anyone apply?"

Raphael was surprised by Sarab's evident interest. He nodded. "Anyone with the patience to be dragged around by six excited and energetic dogs every day."

"I can do this job. Anyway, it's a source of income."

Raphael laughed. "Walking six dogs, all barking and excited—they'll launch you into the air like a paper airplane."

"At least it's a language I might be able to understand. I can't speak your language, so I should take any work I can find."

She intended this statement to sting a little; she enjoyed a battle of wills, and he had no choice but to allow her to triumph and disregard his opinion. He realized her profound need to be defiant, to be intractable, and to give her views free rein.

Over the next few days, the neighbors became accustomed to the sight of that thin, haughty girl being dragged behind a pack of dogs. Sarab would take the dogs to the nearby Luxembourg Gardens and walk there aimlessly, or she would sit on one of the green iron benches by the small round pound and watch them as they chased each other and bounded back to her. They licked her hands, and their affection touched her deeply. Her mother had not been the type to translate her feeling into touching of any kind; she had wanted Sarab to grow like a wild briar. But now, the dogs read the alchemy of her feelings and gave themselves permission to lick her face and ears and neck, and the animals' tongues scraped from Sarab's body twenty-one years of neglect and emotional sterility.

She sat barefoot at the edge of the lake, touching its chilly water with her tiptoes as she observed the various facets of her character, suppressed in the past and now vigorously manifest in these free, innocent animals and their unconstrained, unconditional love.

A special relationship grew between Sarab and Zolo, a Mexican hairless who lived with the ninety-nine-year-old former psychologist on the top floor of the building. Zolo was a reflection of something rare and proud within her. There was beauty hidden inside her that she wouldn't allow to surface, but she allowed Zolo to strut, just as she herself craved to do, and she enjoyed seeing passersby admire his soft silver fur, which was like the surface of a mirror. From the first day, she decided to take him off his lead and allow him to prance to her left like an independent being, like a king.

Zolo walked beside her like a friend, intelligent and sensitive to her moods. Like her, he seemed to laugh at the naughty, purebred Löwchen who was cheerful and playful, and had an insatiable need for attention. Sarab felt herself mirrored in this small pack; each member represented one of her many hidden faces, the ones she had never dared to acknowledge in the past, and didn't dare to examine at this point of her life in exile. As an act of self-release, she began to allow these dogs off their leads one by one, aware she was courting danger and the displeasure of their owners if they noticed what she did. But she didn't care; she savored the intoxicating feeling of reckless freedom, and of being the one to grant this freedom.

The dogs loved her, and displayed a frantic enthusiasm at seeing her. In walking them, Sarab felt that instead of losing a home and a family, she was gaining more of her of secret self with every day that passed. She particularly saw herself reflected in the British bulldog, Max, one of a pair of twins; she had particular compassion for him, as his left hind leg hadn't grown properly. It was so short as to be almost nonexistent, causing the poor dog to limp and seem always a step behind. It broke Sarab's heart to see Max dragging his bulky body everywhere and falling farther behind with every step, running and falling countless times, but nevertheless continuing to press on, while his fully formed twin, Jax, lay next to her, snoring loudly. Jax never bothered to raise his heavy eyelids to acknowledge her presence, and he showed absolutely no interest in the freedom she offered them. As soon as she took his lead off, he would collapse heavily and begin to snore, reflecting the defensive indifference Sarab had learned to show to the world.

A close bond developed between Sarab and the twins, particularly on the morning when a seven-year-old boy rushed toward her with an automatic rifle and started firing. It was only a toy gun, but Sarab was paralyzed by the boy's eyes; they were the eyes of her brother Sayf, bulging at her furiously. Apologizing profusely, the boy's mother dragged her son away while Sarab sank onto the edge of the lake, shocked, her eyes welling up with tears. Suddenly Jax awoke from his deep sleep and approached her. He reared up on his hind legs, planted his left paw on her knee, and stared into her face, while his right paw gently brushed her hand. Sarab looked into his mournful eyes and knew he was saying, "Come on, stop crying, let's play." It was the first time Sarab had experienced such loyal affection, such raw, animal warmth.

The vanity she didn't dare to show was embodied in the final two dogs, a pair of cotons de Tuléar whose owner dressed them in human outfits. Their beauty felt offensive to Sarab, just as she had felt insulted by her femininity during her childhood and adolescence. As soon as she turned into the Luxembourg Gardens, she removed their silly clothes and coaxed them into running naked. She cherished the bare bodies of these dogs and found their clothes baffling. One day when walking with Raphael, she had passed a shop that specialized in dog outfits, and was shocked at the sheer variety on offer, and the exorbitant prices of the tiny T-shirts, coats, hats, and scarves.

"Two hundred francs for a silly dog hat? Why do people waste all this money just to restrict their pet's movements?"

"Perhaps their pets are an extension of themselves."

She could understand that. "The idea of my job is to take dogs for a walk so they can relieve themselves. Does that make me their poo friend?"

Raphael burst out laughing. "Don't torture yourself thinking about that. There's no difference between your job and going for a walk with a friend, and you enjoy it."

But she could only focus on that side of her job when she was hunched over with a plastic bag, picking up their waste to throw it into the rubbish bin.

She flinched at the touch of the droppings, warm and thick in the palm of her hand. Through the thin plastic bag, she could feel every detail of them. All her senses were focused on this lump of heat that had just been extruded from an animal's bowels.

"It reminds me of the waste of the hostages and the fighters during the siege. Those dried-up lumps were piled up everywhere, and I still dream about them."

The shock on Raphael's face made her wonder whether she had shamed her comrades. But his silence and lack of condemnation encouraged her to keep talking.

"The siege was an experience I can't put into words. It's like a snake's egg: if you allow it to hatch, something dead will come out. It's the little details of living through it that you carry with you, more so than the fighting. Perhaps you won't understand if I say that it wasn't the murder that upset me so much as the loss of purity."

She was surprised that the word *purity* didn't rattle Raphael as she had anticipated it might. For her, the thought of purity was all-consuming. It was her obsession day and night, and it continued to be a fundamental source of guilt that Raphael, as a foreigner, couldn't comprehend. She had been raised on the concept of purity, the water that washed the act of love, the water of prayer, and she felt defiled unless she was immersed in this water.

It was vital to her that he understand this, and she clarified: "As time went on, and escape was no longer an option, I would watch the fighters getting ready to pray. They had to perform their ablutions with sand because there was no water, so they would beat the ground, which was covered with soot and blood, and wipe their faces and their hands with the dust. They prayed next to their own filth, in trenches they had made from prayer mats and furniture, because leaving them would have been suicide."

She paused to allow him to fully grasp the picture she had drawn, and then went on. "Now the memories attack me whenever one of the dogs dawdles and goes to the side of the path. I can't get rid of the thought that those small piles were the embodiment of the darkness we were living. It wasn't just filth, it was our ignorance of the value of life that was piling up. That was our fate: to be revolting on the pretext of seeking Paradise.

"Whenever I pick up the droppings I remember my brother's bucket. I took it away every morning, and the clearer our defeat became the more his waste turned into yellow sludge. When I emptied it, I knew I was emptying out the bile that the other side's bullets had burst inside him. When the end became inevitable, I could detect Sayf's fears, all his ups and downs, as the bile began to turn green." Tears gushed over her cheeks. "But on the day I found his body, it was covered in blood and the bucket had been knocked over, and the contents had spilled everywhere. There was nothing but green urine and reddish-black lumps. All this time I've been haunted by the thought that he passed his liver that night, when he met his end at the same time as the dreams of salvation that had brought us there."

Her guilt swelled with every frank declaration to Raphael about the siege; she felt certain that her disclosure was tantamount to betrayal, a distortion of the aim that had brought her comrades to the siege. Most of them had sincerely believed they were bringing enlightenment to humanity. But Sarab had fallen victim to brooding over the real meaning of being forced into exile and earning her living by picking up excrement, and she scorned herself for cleaning streets in Paris when she hadn't done the same in the Grand Mosque.

"It reminds me of the punishment in Hell where we have to pick up animal dung." She wondered which of her many sins she was being punished for.

From her grave, her mother caught the whiff of her mental fissure and pursued Sarab in her dreams.

"It's a hell you deserve for your betrayal. You're the servant of infidel dogs, gathering their droppings instead of burning every one of their owners. Burn them, burn them!" The command haunted her, and she felt guilty whenever she met Zolo's elderly owner and his eyes twinkled in welcome. She avoided looking into them, afraid he would discern her mother's command to kill him.

But the sum she received at the end of the first week somewhat calmed this inner rift. That evening, Raphael came home to find her standing stock still in the living room in front of his desk, staring at the banknotes laid out on the table in front of her.

"One hundred and fifty francs. They're all mine."

It was difficult for him to understand the insistence and gravity in her voice. "I never owned a single riyal in my life before. My mother dealt with the money, and whenever she sent us to buy anything she would give the money to my brother. After she died he was responsible for money; he didn't trust me with it."

Raphael also couldn't understand her overwhelming concern for such a paltry sum, which frustrated her.

"Okay, what are you going to do with it?"

"Perhaps I'll keep it till I need it." After some thought, she added: "Or perhaps I can buy clothes—sleeveless dresses with a low neckline." She laughed defiantly, and he chuckled with a mixture of compassion and love.

"Or you could invite me for dinner and you could pay for once . . ." Raphael instantly regretted this, and hurriedly added: "I mean, spending it all at once might be heartbreaking."

Sarab realized he was trying to get her to see that her earnings weren't very much.

He went on: "The important thing is that it's yours, and you can do whatever you want with it."

"It's six hundred francs a month. No woman in Wajir ever earned anything close to that." She fingered each banknote appreciatively, counting and re-counting them. "Money makes me feel like a man, more than being disguised in a man's clothes."

"Ah, does that mean I have to get used to dealing with a female man?" Raphael teased her, laughing. "You know, I couldn't bear you turning back into a man again."

Storm

IT WAS NIGHT, AND A muffled sound had woken her. Terrified, she got up and rushed to the living room, but Raphael wasn't lying there as he usually was.

She stood there, heart pounding, waiting for something to lead her to the source of the moaning; she knew there was something wrong. All of a sudden, a murmuring came from the bathroom. Realizing that Raphael was inside, she ran to the closed door. She knocked frantically on the door, but there was no reply. Without thinking, she turned the door handle and was surprised to find the door unlocked. The scene that greeted her chilled her to the bone: Raphael was standing with his twitching back pressed against the wall, staring wide-eyed at his reflection in the mirror, oblivious to her presence. She reached out to take his hand but his rigid body shuddered in aversion, rejecting any human contact.

Sarab observed his contorted, clouded features and didn't know what to do. She felt naked; somehow, he was mirroring a part of herself she had been careful not to show him before—the part that relived the deaths of the hostages in the mosque. They both stood there, face to face with their ugliness, cut off from their surroundings, while the night was plunged in shadow.

Hours passed, and reality gradually began to penetrate their aching senses. Their feet were stiff from standing for so long, and his bare skin began to perceive the coldness of the wall it had been leaning against. Only then did Sarab notice he was naked, but it was an awareness stripped of sensuality or desire, laden with maternal feelings, as if she were receiving a baby still warm from the womb.

Silently she took his hand and led him out of the bathroom, back to the living room. He sat on the edge of the sofa, his head in his hands, while Sarab sat next to him, trying to gain insight into the film of atrocities turning in his head.

"Am I so hideous?" he asked. "Is this really the face that appears in the mirror every morning, and I'm still not stopped short by what I really am? The worst thing you can see is your real self. I can see the names of my nameless victims carved on my face in fire, all the piles of body parts—they're part of me. Why am I so weak now? Why didn't this weakness help me before? Is it real, or is cruelty what I really am? Who can say that I'm not acting right now?"

Sarab listened and watched while the thick skin of indifference peeled away from his body and soul leaving him raw and vulnerable, like a film reel burning up from the rays of agony he had inflicted on the world.

"Resigning has released me," he went on. "I'm free of the barricade of indifference. And I've only just started on the lonely road of guilt for all the atrocities we committed in the name of freedom and democracy. I've become a moving wound."

He raised his head, his eyes wet with tears; avoiding Sarab's gaze, he focused instead on the medals he had earned over the years. His gaze turned to the tribal dagger he had won in the Sahara, which was now a wall decoration. For a moment he found great comfort in imagining that dagger piercing his heart, puncturing the tumor of guilt swelling there. He trembled at the notion of suicide. Sarab knelt next to him, clasping his knees, and the touch of her slender arms restored him to reality. He looked at her head, buried in his thighs. Leaning over, he tenderly kissed the top of her head.

"Forgive me, Sarab."

"May they forgive us." It was an appeal to the wider world, to the ghosts hovering overhead.

They sat there until dawn broke over the Luxembourg Gardens, when the scent of the flowers wafted in through the open windows and plucked Raphael out of his abyss. He noticed Sarab, who had fallen asleep on her knees in front of him. He gently pulled her up onto the sofa and covered her with a blanket. Her eyes opened in shock, looking straight at him, and he stared at her despairingly.

"You're the one keeping me alive." What he wanted to say was: "Life—my life—is meaningless."

She knew that he would continue to suffer from these fits, just as she did, but they had to be careful. This beautiful apartment, spacious as it was, was too small to accommodate all the victims of the siege and his many battles around the world; it was too innocent and humane to absorb such horror.

Partly Overcast

FOR MONTHS, A RED LINE was drawn which both were careful not to overstep. She kept to his bed in the bedroom he had vacated for her, while he kept to the sofa in the living room. Raphael was scrupulous about this line, aware that both of them needed to face their inner cyclones before they could adjust to the changes he sought and the relationship they both craved.

But his self-restraint made Sarab doubt her attractiveness, and her warped memories sprang back to life. Over the years she had grown used to her disguise. The men in the singles' bedroom had not been enticed by the femininity buried inside her, and her body had not responded to theirs. But being with this man, even with a locked door between them, was bewildering. It roused an inner struggle she was too embarrassed even to acknowledge. Her heart thudded wildly one evening when she felt him pause behind her as she was looking out of the window; the blood rushed to her head, an engine whistled in her ears, she stammered, her legs weakened, and she stumbled away. She was cornered by a suppressed agitation she hadn't realized existed, and now she didn't know how to deal with it.

That feeling of rejection led her to close her door every night with a degree of resentment, as if she needed this barrier between them, not as protection from him but as protection from her need to throw herself into his arms, to burn every bridge to her past and throw off all the nightmares that haunted her, awake and asleep. But this, of course, was Raphael's fear; that Sarab was surrendering to him as another escape.

This pressure was on the verge of betraying her, especially at night, when she felt most fragile and the red ghosts of the siege were hatching all around and sharing her bed, or when she needed to go to the bathroom and was forced to cross the living room. She wasn't afraid of waking him, but of what would wake in her when she passed his body, its contours sharply defined beneath the thin blanket.

One night she woke up feeling thirsty. She was crossing the living room sleepily when her senses caught hold of that vision stretched out on the sofa.

She stopped in the middle of the room like someone risen from the grave. During the Jahiliya, before Islam was revealed to the Prophet, men would bury their daughters alive to rid themselves of the shame of fathering a female; in a similar vein, Sarab's body had been smothered under a mask of masculinity, but now it sprang vigorously to life. She was sure that Raphael was totally naked under the blanket that barely concealed him. She knew of no precedent for a man sleeping naked, other than Adam in Paradise. She sensed his warm breath while the night crept silently over her skin, peeling away its indifference, innocence, and sterility. Suddenly, like a tongue of flame, Sarab realized that she had a body, a female body, without a shred of doubt. She was terrified now that it was breaking loose, more fanatical in its desires than all the fanatics in her past.

Raphael lay under the blanket, nothing of him visible other than part of his left leg, which had escaped the blanket. A tremor ran along her spine at the sight of the toes sculpted with such luminous beauty, the arch of the foot, the golden hair creeping up the perfect leg muscles, the shadowy hollow beneath the knee.

"What if . . ." Suddenly, she was painfully aware of the small details of her body: her nipples, her round breasts, which she felt swelling with a fever she had never known before.

Her body pulsated recklessly, dangerous and outside her control, needing to be touched, even violated. The death she had fled had left her with a brutal need for destruction, and now this male body, lying there passive and unaware, was driving her mad. Every weapon of the siege was crammed into its masculinity, and a bottomless pit opened up in her to receive it. Her body swayed from the torrent of rage she directed at him, her arms reaching out to strike him in the chest, her teeth bared to rend the muscles of his slender abdomen. Her feet burned from the savage kicking she had enjoyed giving that male member at their first meeting in the Holy City. Her eyes blurred with the effort of staying where she was and not bringing shame on herself and her mother by crossing the short distance to where that foreigner lay, ten paces and entire galaxies away from how she had been raised. But the resistance that Raphael strengthened every day was stronger than every barrier of shame that had been erected under her skin since childhood. Since they had come to Paris, Raphael appeared to have wrapped her body in a shroud. He was always talking about giving her space; space to take stock, space to choose, space to breathe. She had never experienced this thing called "space" before; she had always been confined inside the suffocating framework of her mother and brother, and when something like "space" had been manifest around her during the siege, it had been encircled by fire, brimming with rotting corpses. Now, she was furious at this space that laid her out and embalmed her.

"You are pushing me back to being a man!" she burst out in silent accusation against him. "Is it my fate to live as a virgin?"

Her gaze fell on the dagger hanging on the wall, and she felt faint when she imagined its blade slicing those buttocks.

Stung by her thoughts of violence, she rushed toward the bathroom, knocking over a vase in her agitation. He raised his head sleepily. Their eyes met, and he saw the fear and the dawning of naked desire in her eyes.

He closed his eyes, resisting the urge to charge toward her and crush her in his arms. She stood still as the minutes passed unnoticed, facing his desk and the wall decorated with the medals he had earned from the blood he had spilled in Libya and Chad, Nigeria, Mauritania, and the Lebanese civil war.

At that moment, she was sure she was not repeating the mistake of being attracted to a sophisticated killing machine. On the contrary, Sarab remained free, a daughter of the desert; she was drawn to a man who was emerging from his iron world and trying to reach the human inside him, throwing off the military uniform that stifled his soul. He was determined to help her complete her own transformation without exacting any commitment toward himself, without any intention of exploiting her vulnerability and keeping her captive. For this reason, she had surrendered to the feeling that her home lay with him; he was her home and her country, more than any house she had lived in, including her mother's.

He gripped the blanket to stop himself rushing toward her and upsetting the natural flow of their simultaneous transformation, he toward the soul and she toward the body. He was grateful that the fates had given him the opportunity of knowing this girl from the desert, delicate and steely at the same time. Since their dramatic meeting, fresh air had been moving through the layer of ash whose embers his soul was trying breathe life into. So he allowed her to take the reins, although he could have crushed her easily, and he preferred her to every one of the elegant women he saw on the streets of Paris every day.

He got up, crossed the distance between them, and walked past her to the wall where his medals were hanging. He took them handful by handful and threw them into the wastebasket under the desk. She stopped him, pinning his hands against the wall to prevent them from plucking off more medals. They both dropped their hands, which were burning and sweating.

"No, this is the record of your work. Even if these decorations disappear from the wall, they won't disappear from you."

He lowered his eyes in shame.

"No, don't be ashamed. When you have really finished with the past it will fall away by itself, like a scab from a wound that has healed."

Bitterly, he contemplated the trifling decorations invented by humans to celebrate murder. Every medal represented a battlefield.

"This silver medal with a gold heart is the Légion d'Honneur, chevalier class, awarded to the bravest of the brave. It was given to me in recognition of a massacre; we set fire to a resistance army in

Mali. We only discovered afterward that it was an army of boys, maybe twelve or thirteen years old."

The sight of their small, charred bodies rose vividly before his eyes and the apartment was filled with the stench of burnt human flesh. He slammed his palm into the wall to destroy the medal and shattered one of its five white wings. Blood sprang from the wound, and, agitated, Sarab rushed to tend it.

"My senses were dead all those years, and now nothing can erase the smell of burnt flesh." He held his breath until his face turned dark red. "I can only block the smell if I stop breathing." He inhaled deeply, punishing himself. "I was a legend. I was never even wounded. My comrades were sure I was immortal, with more than one soul. I was proud of myself for emerging from one inferno after another without a scratch. But look at me now . . ."

She didn't know how to alleviate his suffering.

"In your opinion, how does my soul look now?" He reflected on the contradiction between the actions of his past and his current concern about his soul.

"Back then, I stood at the edge of the village watching the bull-dozers push the burnt bodies into a mass grave, and I just didn't care."

To his surprise, she took his hand, brought it to her lips, and sucked away the blood. He pulled his hand away in disgust, almost knocking her to the ground.

"You're crazy."

She was in a violent rapture. He looked at the blood on her lips. He could feel the poison accumulating in his opened veins and wanted to wipe the hideousness of his past from her lips.

"Go and wash your mouth, please. I can't bear to look at you."

She ignored him, concentrating on the broken medal; she was trying to repair the broken wing.

"You should keep this in front of you and look at it from time to time," she told him. "You'll see the distance you've traveled between then and now, from the indifference of the past to the pain of the future."

He sank down on the desk, exhausted, while she retrieved the medals from the wastebasket and hung them back on the wall. A throb of pain ran up his spine and jolted his brain as he watched her hang his disgrace on the wall of their souls like a yoke of bondage.

She woke with the taste of Raphael's blood on her tongue. Her pleasure in their emotional closeness had disappeared, and with it the armor that had held her together. Gone was the logic with which she had faced his latest panic attack, her attraction to him, and the desire to touch him. The only thing left was a burning wish to be purified so that the angels wouldn't turn away from her. She needed cleansing. She remained where she was, struck by deep revulsion.

She didn't want to cross the living room where Raphael was sleeping to go to the bathroom. She noticed the cup of water by her bed and took a sip, rinsing out her mouth which felt like a pit. Looking for somewhere to spit out the taste of everything that clung to it, she went to the window and spat out the full mouthful. The water sprayed everywhere, sending slivers of silver over the roof. She rinsed with a second mouthful, then a third, sending a thin jet of water over the sloping roof, not quite reaching the gutters. She gazed vacantly at the black moisture reflecting the lights of Place Saint-Sulpice as it carried away her sins. Her whole body was aflame with the thought of purity, and she wasn't satisfied. She rushed to the bedside table, took a bottle of eau de cologne that had been forgotten there, and took a sip, swilling it around her mouth. The bitter taste of musk and sandalwood restored her to herself. She took another sip, choked, and started to cough; frantically, she took a tissue and began to scrape the taste from her tongue and the roof of her mouth.

At last she sank down on the floor, shocked by what she had done. No water, no amount of cleansing would purify her from the taste of blood.

As she lay prostrate and naked on the floor, the first birdsong of the day reached her from the tops of the trees in the Luxembourg Gardens, interrupting her mania. She realized it was time for the dawn prayer; in the absence of mosques and calls to prayer in Paris, the birds and sun were her muezzins. Again, she crept on tiptoe to the bathroom, averting her eyes from where Raphael lay, oblivious to her internal convulsions.

Sarab realized she experienced an overwhelming sense of sin with every emotion she felt; it was a sin when she grieved, a sin when she was angry, a sin when she was happy.

Distracted, she stood beneath the shower and let it wash her, marinating every secret crevice of her body, hair, and mouth with thick foam to ensure her purification.

At last she left the bathtub and looked doubtfully at her night-shirt. Maybe it still held the sweat of the madness and the demons that had goaded her.

She avoided the shirt and wouldn't touch it even with the tips of her toes, so as not to spoil her ablutions for prayer. She wrapped her body in a clean towel instead, careful not to wear her leather slippers in case they also held traces of her sweat, although a voice in her head insisted that her impurity was unyielding and her absurd worries made no difference to it.

She slipped back to her room and closed the door. Wrapped in the clean towel, she stood to pray, reassured of being at least minimally pure, although the taste of his blood that could never be washed away still ran deep in her lungs and through her veins.

What demon made you suck the blood of this foreigner?

Ending Number Three

THAT MORNING THEY COULDN'T BEAR staying in the flat. The atmosphere was charged with desire and the tension almost drove Raphael mad. They left at dawn and walked alongside the early-morning stream of delivery lorries carrying flowers and other goods to the shops, wandering aimlessly as the sun gradually emerged. Neither realized how much time had passed until they came across Place Denfert-Rochereau in the fourteenth arrondissement. Sarab stopped abruptly, drawn like a magnet to a poster depicting a pile of skulls. She stood in front of the picture, mesmerized.

"What's this?"

After some hesitation he replied, "The catacombs."

She felt his aversion to further explanation, but persisted: "What are the catacombs?"

"It's a burial ground for skeletons . . . nothing interesting."

"Why are all those people lining up to get in? Will they be buried here?" She watched people buying tickets and disappearing inside the building.

"There are no burials here. It's not a graveyard in the usual sense; it's more like a mass grave for people who died in previous centuries. They were brought here from various graveyards and burial grounds all over Paris."

This surpassed Sarab's comprehension. She pressed him: "A mass grave? From a war? From a plague?"

"No, it's just an old stone quarry that was turned into a repository for bones. It contains the skeletons of six million Parisians.

They were brought here gradually over the eighteenth and nineteenth centuries, when the graveyards were closed because of the threat to public health."

Raphael was irritated that chance had brought them to that particular place at the very time when her life appeared to be threatened. It seemed to reinforce the feeling that death had been hovering over them ever since they fled the mosque.

"What are these people buying?"

"Entrance tickets—three francs for a thirty-minute visit," Raphael replied carelessly, trying to dispel the apprehension settling on her face. "It's a sort of museum."

"Really? A graveyard museum?" Sarab had become acquainted with the concept of museums and culture over the previous month. The museum reminded her of Raphael's medals, but more so of her father's antique rifles. The legend of her family, even of the tribe itself, had revolved around the rifles hung on the wall of their house, and everyone had drawn strength from that display every morning. She had left them behind her, buried in the house in Medina, and now they seemed like ghosts from a past century, stripped of their worth. This loss reinforced Sarab's sense of negation and nakedness in exile and, correspondingly, her desire for vengeance and defiance.

"The visitors are buying tickets to look and learn? Learn what?" He didn't understand her question and she went on: "That life is over in a flash of lightning?"

"Yes . . . and perhaps they like the tableaux made from the bones."

The peculiarity of this shocked her. She felt a mysterious threat in that warehouse of death whose essence she still hadn't grasped.

"I want to go in."

She was determined to challenge this mysterious force manifested in her and the place and even Raphael himself. She was possessed by a spirit of masochism, mixed with the living's frustration with the dead. She wanted all the skeletons to rise from their mass grave and take vengeance for her body, which had been wrapped in the shroud of Raphael's indifference when he rejected her as a woman.

"No, I don't think it's a good idea. It's twenty meters underground. There are murder victims buried here. It's a nightmare."

"Even for a soldier like you?"

"But what about you, after all you've been through? Please, let's go to the café over there; it's been preserved in the old French style, and I can take you to a graveyard another day if you really want to visit the dead. We could go to the Père Lachaise cemetery—famous people from all over the world are buried there. It's very beautiful, with paths full of flowers and sculptures on the graves and commemorative poetry here and there. It's really worth seeing."

This only increased her confusion. "What an idea, this cemetery of famous people! Death is a sort of party to you people, something to display—you clip tickets and send out invitations for it!"

Raphael couldn't understand why she was so angry, whether her words were speculation or criticism.

"Our graveyards are like anthills," she said, "just bare ground with no tombstones, no names to pin down the identity of the person buried there, nothing to lure spectators. Just piles of dust to show there are graves there. We are buried with nothing between ourselves and the earth, wrapped in a sheet of white cotton which they open as soon as we are in the grave. They uncover our faces and throw a handful of dust in our eyes so our bodies come into contact with the earth and melt into it."

Raphael raised his eyebrows, unable to picture this, while she went on: "After a month or more, they open the grave and collect the bones to bury them in a mass grave, and they vacate the grave for someone else. We don't have private graves. They're shared, because there's no such thing as property when you're dead. We are given any available grave the moment our body arrives in the graveyard, whether you're a minister or a street sweeper."

He wanted to quip: "A socialist grave?" But she went on in a reproachful tone: "And however many dead there are, the graveyards are never full and they are never shut in our faces."

The sky clouded over suddenly, and lightning flashed on the horizon. There was no rain, just a dry darkness lowering over them, but it drove them to the entrance.

"Fine," snapped Raphael. This catacomb is just a mass grave and it's not worth visiting." Her anger had finally succeeded in sparking his, but instead of deterring her, his exasperation only redoubled her determination. He had no choice but to buy them two tickets.

They walked down the steps, Sarab leading the way, rushing into the gloom.

With every downward step she took, her pulse beat faster. She was wrapped in the darkness of the stairs and it chilled her veins. But she maintained her impassive exterior, so that Raphael wouldn't take her back.

An overpowering force was driving her on, leading her to the underground entrance to the catacombs. They passed between two black pillars like the rooks in a chess game. Each pillar carried the outline of a white triangle pointing upward, symbolizing the souls still rising to the heavens, and the gateway was marked on both sides with a white rhombus inside a black rectangle.

"If I'm correct, the rhombus is a symbol of alpha and omega, the first and last letters of the Greek alphabet," Raphael volunteered. His flat tone betrayed his indecision between irritation at her stubbornness and an impulse to alleviate the somber atmosphere. "They mean that God is eternal, the first and the last, before and after death."

With his eyes fixed on her slim back, he pitied her body, burdened as it was with a combative soul that was determined to surpass its capabilities. Meanwhile, Sarab had almost forgotten his presence; like a lump of mummified will, she went forward on tiptoe. Everything in front of her was somewhere between white and black, like death and life, and she didn't know one from the other.

"Arrête! C'est ici l'empire de la mort. Stop! Here lies the empire of death." Raphael's voice exploded behind her in warning, amplifying the line of poetry crowning the door.

Shuddering, Sarab came to a halt. She was haunted by the belief that she would be destroyed if she tried to pass through the door, but the force in control of her propelled her to take a large stride across the threshold. The guard observed her keenness with a wry smile, and she went forward alone. A maze of shadowy display halls opened up before her, their mystery enhanced by the pale bones of the dead covering every wall. The arm and leg bones seemed helpless and forlorn to her, nothing showing of them but their joints in a mosaic of knee and elbow bones. Intolerant-looking skulls speckled the walls here and there, their nullifying stare emerging from bloated pillars and above walls of leg and arm bones.

Suddenly the silence thickened to a gelatinous blanket, slowing her movements. It brought her to a halt beside fourteen skulls arranged in the outline of a heart. Sarab was particularly frightened by the skull in the center, which had been destroyed so that nothing was left of it but the jaw. She rushed forward into the next hall. The catacombs suddenly seemed to have been emptied of visitors and guards, no one was left but Sarab and Raphael moving through the silent caverns where nothing spoke apart from ancient, unconcealed death. She didn't hesitate, because she had no choice; she moved forward, encouraged by the sound of Raphael's stertorous breathing as he followed her. She realized the tableaux of death had revived his nightmares of Madagascar. In point of fact, Raphael had started feeling the cold breaths of his victims, exhaled by the skulls, on every part of his body. He would have fled this horror if not for the girl who kept pushing on until she almost disappeared, swallowed up by the malicious gleam of the bone mosaics.

In an attempt to lighten the dread of those canopies of death, he carried on with his explanations: "The bodies were brought here in wagons known as 'black convoys' from different graveyards where all kinds of people were buried, from vagrants to starving artists."

He directed Sarab's gaze to three skulls lined up vertically, one dome under another. "Here, for example, it is believed these are the skulls of the Le Nain artists, three brothers who faced life as one. All their works are signed by one name, probably all by one hand."

Sarab wasn't paying attention. A red glare lured her toward a skull that rolled along and disappeared. Its haughtiness reminded her of her mother's skull; when she looked away from it, she was astounded by the sight of the hall they were in, closed off by a pillar in the form of an enormous barrel holding up the ceiling. The barrel's swollen body was paved with arm and leg bones like a riddle, and it was girdled with three bands of skulls, one close to the ceiling, the second in the middle, and the third near the ground.

"Those yellow skulls at the bottom are probably plague victims; they make up two-thirds of the skulls here."

Sarab wanted to retort that it was smallpox that emptied out eye sockets and uncovered skulls in the desert, but her voice had dried up. At the corner, she was again confronted by the skull that appeared to issue a red flame.

Raphael followed her gaze, and explained nonchalantly: "This skull, which appears and disappears, has a famous story that has inspired a lot of writers. It's rumored to be the skull of Madame de Brinvilliers. Her lover ordered a certain box to be opened after he died, and it contained memoranda and letters which they used to condemn her for adultery and the murder of her father and two brothers."

The mingling of fornication and death increased Sarab's terror. Her body was tempted to strip down to its skeleton and slip in among the others.

Raphael went on: "They cut off her head and threw her body into a fire, but they brought her skull back to Paris."

Raphael was torn between putting Sarab at ease and punishing her for excavating these skeletons. He continued with his comments, giving form to the gloom of those underground passages, even though all these strange, foreign names and stories conveyed nothing to Sarab. None of Raphael's commentary seemed to stick in her memory, but when she stood facing one particular elongated skull, out of nowhere she remembered the nightmare that had woken her the night before. In the dream, she had seen her father on a white bed, surrounded by heaving armies of black ants. Whenever he moved his hand, whole armies died, only to multiply and start heaving again. Beside him, her mother was absorbed in cooking while sewage flooded all around and began to seep into the food. The dream confirmed to her that her sins were eating away at her parents in their death; they were being tormented in the afterlife for her flight to this foreign life.

Sarab's recollection of her father's sin-laden eternity weighed her down with despair, made heavier by the gloom in the catacombs. To Raphael, still following her patiently, she seemed the embodiment of the nightmare that had kept them awake all night, and that had caused her to swathe herself in black this morning. Raphael hadn't missed this spontaneous reaction of hers; he had come to realize that whenever she was beset with guilt, she wore black clothes. And here she was, walking ahead of him in a mass of black, surrounded by a teeming sea of white skulls, while he, disturbed by his own past, was called upon to stem any evil. And Sarab was lured onward.

Suddenly she was brushed by a breeze, like a misgiving coming from the pattern under the door at the end of the corridor. A double row of skulls traced a human body with two arms and two stumpy legs open wide. Between the legs was a small skull, beginning to fall, and Sarab realized that she was witnessing a birth.

As soon as her eyes fell on that skull emerging from the womb, Sarab reeled with dizziness. Suddenly there was no more boundary between them: she was the one emerging from between those legs of ancient death. The little skull crawled into Sarab's skull and unrolled its hellish memories, throbbing and taking over her brain along with the millions of other skulls stored in this metaphysical world. Sarab's head began to expand, swallowing up the passage around her and growing until it reached the size of the catacombs. Six million arms and legs jostled and burst out of her arms and legs, and she could make out the skeletons of her fellow rebels rushing toward her from an unseen world with no border, filled with rage and coming to occupy her body. Swallowed up by her own ugliness and the emptiness of all these skulls, she fainted.

She came to in Raphael's arms as he carried her up the staircase. She looked up at him tongue-tied, watching his clouded face hovering over her, and he seemed more terrified than at any point during the battle and his captivity. Once they were in the sunlight, he leaned over her anxiously, sprinkling her face with bottled water and wiping her cheeks as gently as if she were a child. She smiled, embarrassed, and he smiled back.

"You . . ." He couldn't finish his sentence; there were no words capable of conveying what had gripped him; he was choked by horror, as well as by relief that she had regained consciousness.

"I'm what? A portable grave?" she said.

He didn't reply to her weak joke, and turned even paler; he had seen death in her.

She freed herself from him and moved away, feeling that the victims of the siege were living and breathing in her bones, and they would never leave her again. At that moment she was swamped with hatred toward Raphael for plucking her out of the siege and a fate she couldn't postpone; and she knew at the same time, in the same breath, that she loved him.

Raphael stopped a taxi and opened the door for her, but she stood there staring at it, lost in her sweeping animosity. She was dazed by her freedom to hate.

Throughout her life, she had never been able to give free rein to her feelings. Of the ninety-nine names of God, she was most enthralled by al-Muhibb—the Loving—and al-Muntaqim—the Avenger. God had announced these names to Adam, but she was on the lowest rung of humanity and had never been free to try even a drop of intense love or hatred or vengeance. She had been a humble follower and only now, in front of that warehouse of bones, did she throw off her humility.

She turned her head to look at Raphael, feeling the intoxicating hatred pumping through her veins. And he stood there, shocked at what he could see in her eyes. His senses sharpened. He reciprocated her resentment, wanting to crush her, to crush himself, to be rid of their predicament.

This oscillation between love and hatred was electrifying for them both. Still testing the patience of the taxi driver, she allowed cyclones of hatred to whirl through her, hating her mother and her lunatic brother and even her father. Above all, she hated Raphael who had brought her here to be a walking tomb.

At last she got into the taxi, where she needled him: "You people have the audacity to turn death into some sort of show!"

The taxi driver, who was Moroccan, followed this one-sided whispered conversation with evident interest. He glanced admiringly at her in the mirror, and turned an envious gaze on Raphael's rugged beauty.

Raphael's silence encouraged Sarab to persist in her provocation: "You all scorn Israfil's trumpet and ignore the fact that you've made a spectacle out of scenes like that." Sarab realized that she enjoyed conveying her feelings; enjoyed the sense that the box of writhing emotions was slipping from her control day by day.

They traveled through the city, which began to be bathed in the red light of sunset, intensifying their confusion. Sarab knew that what she had said was sheer idiocy, intended only to provoke, but she was incapable of restraining her fury and keeping silent. Meanwhile, Raphael was in another world; a Latin phrase that had been carved into that underground world was echoing through his head.

Non metuit mortem qui soit contemnere vitam—He fears not death who scorns life.

He avoided looking at Sarab, wondering why the hell he had tangled himself up with such a tortured soul as this girl, who had been raised to scorn life. Was he offering himself up to inevitable pain? But that Latin phrase echoed the vow they had taken when they joined the GIGN: to save lives without regard for their own. That was what made them invincible, and impervious to death. This girl hadn't entered his life in vain. She was the embodiment of this vow; he had to live with it, and test its vitality against his emptiness.

Ending Number Four: June 21, 1980

THE VISIT TO THE CATACOMBS disturbed Sarab deeply. The skull of the mad woman had succeeded in frightening her, causing her to doubt the blind trust she had placed in Raphael. But those qualms managed to distract Sarab's attention from the attempts to pursue her, which now stopped as if they had never been. Both Raphael and Sarab relaxed in the belief that they had been nothing but a delusion brought on by the atrocities they had experienced, which had left their marks on them both. But Sarab regretted having told Raphael how she had saved the Mahdi; her disclosure now seemed like a definitive betrayal of everything her comrades had fought for, and self-contempt began to eat away at her.

One evening she was supposed to meet Raphael for dinner at the Relais de l'Entrecôte. Sarab had grown addicted to wandering the backstreets of the city at night, when Paris was enigmatically illuminated, transforming each alleyway into a dreamland. She would walk, wondering if the people hurrying and shoving around her were aware of God like she was. Were they afraid of sinning? She would observe young men and half-naked girls congregating on the street outside cafés and bars to slurp colorful cocktails, and she wondered whether they realized that they would rot in Hell.

She would stand nearby, watching them closely; why couldn't they tell they were sinning, as she did? Did they know her Lord? Would they attack her if they knew what was whirling through her mind? That she had a God? They seemed godless, or at any rate lacking the God that had been offered to her.

If Sayf were here with his automatic rifle, would he have opened fire? She was drawn to their smiling, open faces. In their drunken state they were more awake than she was, locked as she was inside her numbing fear.

Sarab had acquired a pink silk dress. The color filled her with embarrassment; she felt her private thoughts were laid bare for passersby. The delicacy of the color revealed her heart and its craving to love and be loved, to be touched, to vigorously inhabit her body. Her arms tensed against the sides of the tight dress. All around her in Place Saint-Sulpice, dozens of buskers were gathered and microphones blasted music of all kinds into the open air—from jazz to rock to raucous Latin—till the ground shook. It was the first time Sarab had seen anything like it. She felt the air was light and her body was flying; she could barely control her lightening footsteps.

With every step she took into this dancing cosmos, her arms relaxed away from her body. She allowed the silk to brush every detail of her pelvis and backside. With every step, her body softened and opened, and she threw off the last vestiges of masculinity and hardness. With every step, she was aware of an untamed being wakening within her, ready to break out at any moment and dance wildly, to be swept away in the mad crowds and join the women and men gathered in the middle of the square. A towering woman in tight black pants danced with particular elegance, seductively swaying her slender limbs with a supple sensuality that caused passersby to pause. Sarab heard the cry of hunger in that body and was transfixed. She watched the woman enviously, aware that her body was roaring with the same seductive sensuousness. Bitter questions tore at her: *How would Raphael react to such a graceful, seductive body? Would he exercise the same self-restraint that he does with me? How would he make love to such a woman? A truly female body oozes desire, not like my normal, average body.*

The questions shocked her, and she was overcome by a sudden, unbearable desire to be possessed by Raphael; by no one but him. This desire blinded her as she was about to cross the street, and she was dimly aware of a long black limousine playing rock and roll that suddenly stopped in front of her and opened its doors. Two men leaped out of the back seat. The larger of the two grabbed her waist and swung her into the air as if he were dancing with her, then flung her to the ground and dragged her into the limousine. The music drowned out her scream, and no one noticed what had happened.

She was suffocated by the blaring music and the black bag wrapped around her head and face. She was pushed to the ground under their feet, and they trampled her and kicked her mercilessly at the slightest sign of resistance. She knew she had to stop struggling so they wouldn't break her ribs, but the needle that was plunged into her arm saved her from having to surrender, and she fell into merciful darkness.

Aden

WHEN SHE WOKE UP, HER body was stiff from being thrown onto a bare stone floor. The bag had been removed from her head. She could see a bare concrete floor, mustard-colored walls, and a single chair perched alone at the far end of the room. At first she thought she was alone, but she soon became aware of the gaunt man sitting on the chair with his back to the door.

When he stood up and turned to face her, she gasped. She kept staring at him as her voice failed her. She felt a burning thirst, her head throbbed with a painful headache, and her limbs were numb and refused to obey her. It was clear she had been here for days.

"Yes, you saved my life," the man said, "but look at where you ended up. I told you before: you were formed for a different life. But not this life of sin; you have fallen straight into its trap."

His face contained something she couldn't describe; it was marked by a darker glow than when she had known him, and the compassion had left his eyes, a slight alteration settling in its place. Despite her predicament, Sarab could only think mockingly: *The blow to his head must have caused these droopy eyelids and stony expression. Perhaps that's the price he had to pay for what he did in the siege.*

He smiled, but his smile had lost its former brilliance and was now rigid and contorted. He went on: "And so, I am committed to returning the service you did me. I am not a man to ignore his debts, and as I am resolved to saving your life, we will keep you here with us. You will enjoy the comfort we provide in abundance to our devout, honorable women. And I am confident that within a few days, you will realize the pure, honorable life you were born to."

"You're paying your debt?" She could only contradict the farce in his stately words. "Do you think you will ever pay this debt? How can a debt be paid by someone so revolting? You attacked innocent people. You were shooting and killing innocent people until the last moment . . . and for what? To become a caliph over people who were forced to pay homage to you. You wanted to issue commands and prohibitions along with Mujan. Wasn't all that murder committed so you could become king? No aim, whatever it is, could justify murder." For a moment she was muted by the disdain on his face, and then she added bitterly: "How naive we were, all of us who followed you to the Grand Mosque. How can you pay this debt, whatever you do?"

His face hardened. "So be it."

He tried to stare through her, but was incapable of seeing anything but himself. "It is a shame. I can no longer see in you the courageous, purehearted fighter I knew in the Grand Mosque. Saving me was an act that required true martyrdom. The men surrendered but you kept fighting. Don't you see what you were?" His eyes bored into her like a scalpel. "What a difference between what you were and what you have become! Sadly, your vision has clouded and you have been distorted. Your intimate association with the enemy has coated you in a thick skin that truth cannot penetrate. If you speak, we hear the voice of the enemy coming from you, and you have been blinded to our sublime goal. God sees that we did what we did to bring justice to a world infested with sin."

"How can justice be done through tyranny and hostility?" Sarab retorted. "There was clear injustice done to the victims we imprisoned in the mosque, and those who paid the price of our fight."

The change that had come over him was deeply rooted, and Sarab doubted that this was the same man she had smuggled away from the siege.

"Nothing can hold out against truth and righteousness," he said. "We will do what we can to restore truth to you, and to return you to the righteous path."

"I can't believe I once saw you as a hero."

His face contorted. "Of course, you are possessed by the Devil, and you have made this French infidel into an idol to worship. Listen carefully . . ." His wrathful look almost broke her in two. "Your flight with the infidel was a sin you should have been killed for, but I saved you from that fate, to pay the debt you hung around my neck."

The Mahdi gestured, and two women appeared, swathed in black. They blindfolded Sarab, put a black abaya on her, and drove her in front of them. From behind the thick blindfold, Sarab sensed she had left the concrete room and was being taken down a flight of stairs. Her senses picked up the dampness of being underground, and she realized she was in a cellar. She walked for some distance, and then was lifted up and set down. Under her feet, she felt soft dust, and she knew she was in an open courtyard. She realized the women wanted her to lose her sense of direction as they led her in circles away from the room she had left.

They kept her walking for ten minutes or so. When they brought her to a halt, she heard a light knock on an iron door, which opened. Sarab was pushed inside and her companions disappeared. She felt a metal device tapping her head lightly, as if someone was ordering her to uncover her face, and the blindfold was lifted from her eyes. As soon as the blindfold was removed she was blinded by a white neon light.

A woman whispered, "At last. Hah—so you're the Mahdi's woman?" It wasn't a question so much as an expression of contempt. "Nothing but skin and bones."

Sarab was taken aback by the flashlight pointed at her by a very tall woman with a strong Egyptian accent. "Oh look, here comes your devil." Shadowy women leaped behind her, scattering in alarm and spluttering the verses of protection in their hands. They rubbed these verses on their own bodies and blew them toward Sarab, to lay siege to her demon.

Sarab found herself in a primitive camp with black-robed bodies moving all around her; even she was wrapped in loss and blackness, which trailed behind her. Her name had been removed and she was known as "the Mahdi's woman," an appellation that roused envy and made her the butt of jeers and malicious comments that followed her wherever she went.

"It's the Mahdi's savior, but just look at her. They brought her back from some franji country. She's a sinner who deserves to be stoned to death for allying herself with the enemy."

"In the end, women are women; they lack reason and religion. This apostate fell from Heaven to the depths of Hell by her own doing and her own shortsightedness."

She realized that she had been housed in a wing of the camp reserved for single women. It was a type of ward: ten women were housed in each long, thin dormitory with an adjoining bathroom.

That morning, Sarab was overcome by the severity of this dormitory. After the luxury of Paris she was enveloped in despair looking at these bare concrete walls, unrelieved by any furniture apart from the foam mattresses laid out on the ground, used both for sleeping and sitting on. She didn't object to the mattresses; what confused her was the light. Instead of the shaded sidelights that she had become used to in the apartment on Rue Bonaparte, there were only neon striplights lined up over the four walls like train tracks, which followed her and spied on her movements even when she went to the bathroom. She had grown accustomed to the security of the sidelights' warm glow, and this light had an antagonistic quality. Sarab felt she was shriveling under the harsh white neon lighting, and under the gaze of the women who studied her curiously and doubtfully.

She heard a voice whispering, "Rue Bonaparte."

She remembered exactly where it was. It was carved into her head, where it crossed Rue du Four and then Boulevard Saint-Germain until it reached the Seine, full of shops selling clothes and accessories. She remembered the flowers that were renewed in the glass vase on the table to the right of the apartment entrance, wafting the scent of gardenia on some days, orchids on others. In that camp, she dwelt especially on the scent of orchids, which lingered on after the flower died; Raphael would let the fragrance recede over two days before changing it for a rose or a lily or. . . . Once, he had brought birds of paradise, and he had envied her astonishment at them; she had been certain that they pricked up their orange crowns and flew around when the apartment was in darkness, and she was sure she heard them twittering.

She was afraid that the women would perceive the conflict in her head between the scent of orchids and the choking stink coming from the bathrooms attached to each dormitory. The creaking wooden doors were always left open, allowing the suffocating smells to creep into the room.

She slept deeply that night and dreamed that the open windows looking over the Luxembourg Gardens had been closed on her, forcing her to inhale the concrete walls with tall, narrow wound-like niches gouged into them that not even air could pass through.

"Come on, there's no room here for no-good parasites. Grab a bite to eat and follow us to the workshop." Sarab noticed the plastic table laid with brown bread, a bundle of spring onions, and some tin cups of milk. She had to gulp her onion with a round loaf, like the others, who were already peeling and chewing in silence. Her throat was torn with thirst, and she sipped some milk silently under their sardonic stares.

"Let's wait and see; as time goes on she will eat her own belly fat," the Egyptian said maliciously, careful not to look at Sarab—as if she didn't exist. It was a trivial thing but it demoralized Sarab; it stirred up memories of how her mother ignored her.

The women wrapped themselves in black abayas, and Sarab followed them. Keeping together in a herd, they led her into a dusty alleyway and brought her to a building that seemed like a huge factory or a vast hospital.

Sarab was greeted by a concoction of smells that seared her head like a flash of lightning. Her eyes teared up and she was struck by a fit of coughing and sneezing. It was a smell she couldn't define, like the odor of war itself; a mixture of disinfectant and something like gunpowder. The women cast pitying glances at her then left her with Latifa, a Pakistani woman. They were swallowed up as they went down the branching passages.

Latifa led her to a desk to the right of the entrance and stood in front of the Yemeni supervisor who distributed the women around the workshop. Apart from one sharp look, she was careful not to raise her eyes to Sarab, directing her instructions instead at the red pen she twirled mechanically in her fingers.

"You will go with Latifa; you will train alongside her in the medical team."

"Wait, there's been a misunderstanding—" Sarab stammered. "I don't work here."

The official planted her pen nib in the paper and stared at the hole it left in the page.

"Go on, get moving."

Sarab was nailed to the floor, unable to tear herself away. Latifa dragged her away gently but firmly, and turned with her into the building on the right. As they walked farther inside, the nauseating smell of disinfectant increased. Sarab staggered, assailed by memories of the limbs she had helped the doctor to amputate during the siege. The Pakistani woman supported her and gave her a sympathetic glance. She urged Sarab silently to keep moving, and her look confirmed to Sarab that there was no choice, no resistance, no going back, and no way forward other than surrender.

Latifa took her through the corridors of what seemed to be a primitive hospital, and she pointed out a sign marked "Operating Room." She stepped forward and gave her name to the nurse on duty.

"This is the new volunteer. She will be joining the operations today."

"Oh, really?" The nurse gasped mockingly. "Since when did we put amateurs in charge of our wounded mujahideen? Do we evacuate them from Afghanistan so we can put an end to them here!"

The nurse seemed prepared to berate them indefinitely, but suddenly she concluded: "She hasn't passed dissection yet."

Latifa objected: "But she was the one who saved the Mah—"

"I know," the nurse interrupted decisively. "But not before she's passed the skills test."

Sarab looked at the nurse, inflexible as rock; nothing in her outward appearance suggested a healer. She was draped in a green robe which covered her from head to toe, and a green scarf wrapped her head and neck and dangled over her chest.

"She will start off stitching wounds."

Sarab was taken aback by the word *stitching*; it extricated her from the abundance of green, and tears welled in her eyes.

Latifa could only obey. She retreated, taking Sarab down more stairs to the basement and through another neon-lit corridor. As soon as Sarab stepped inside the room she was hit by a stench of blood and urine. Stretching away in front of her were long metal tables with women hovering around them. The scene was like something from a sewing factory but instead of fabric, huge cats and dogs, all drugged, were scattered on the tables. The women were burrowing inside them, removing and transplanting organs, pulling up veins and arteries, like a game of musical organs. It was a sort of primitive operating room, and the animals were used for training. The eyes of the industrious women swiveled toward her, and they whispered to each other, "She's the one who saved the Mahdi."

Suddenly everything around Sarab went blurry and then black, and she fell to the floor unconscious.

"I don't think we have room for this spineless parasite."

"She's a tapeworm. If we leave her be she'll run riot."

Sarab woke up to this whispered conversation.

"I was so mad I almost exploded, but the Mahdi entrusted her to us, and it was a red-level command."

"Just cool it till things clear up."

"This is a real mess, but if we don't solve it we'll get the blame. Everyone thinks she's some kind of savior."

Before long, Sarab was led to a department at the back of the huge factory, where there was an acrid smell of gunpowder and chemicals.

"I'm warning you: this is your last chance, in the bomb workshop." Sarab's hands shook as she resisted the urge to laugh hysterically.

What a farce—as she was unable to stitch up wounds, she was being forced to create them.

The supervisor led her to a wing containing an army of women who specialized in making different types of homemade bombs.

"Try not to get yourself blown up," hissed the worker, trying to strike terror into Sarab as she backed away. Meanwhile, the supervisor pushed Sarab forward and she was met by female faces whose noses had been bound with their black veils to protect them from the acrid fumes of the chemicals.

Sarab realized she was looking at multiple small teams distributed throughout the cubicles of that infernal cistern with rigid screens separating each group from the others. The screens blocked sight, but they were not successful in blocking the various smells which mingled together in an abominable brew and gradually remolded the workers' features.

Sarab turned away in disbelief at the turn her fate had taken. She wrapped her veil in thick layers over her nose to shield it from the fumes which accumulated and condensed every second. The primitive teams were divided into groups: one group decanted benzene into bottles covered with fabric; another made bombs from medical-grade antiseptic; and another used plastic bottles to mix vinegar and baking soda cleaning products and metals. Sarab was added to a team manufacturing saltpeter. The smell of dung greeted Sarab, and she lost all sense of time as she looked at that black hole full of women sweating over huge pans like some sort of hallucination. She barely heard her instructions.

"You have to fix the charcoal filter onto the sieve, put the sieve over the pan, and fill it with goat dung. Then pour this boiling water over it slowly, and then. . ." A primitive, endless operation to extract crystals of saltpeter, or potassium nitrate.

Sarab was lost in the steamy cistern which was piled high with old graveyard dirt saturated with human remains and decomposed vegetation; she was manufacturing death from the ground of death. She didn't know how the day passed as she stood over that pan, until the women pulled her outside and she was stung by night falling over the camp. She inhaled deeply, cleansing her lungs from the dung, and exhaled all the saltpeter crystals, wishing never to wake up to another day of that process.

"Move, your highness!" The Egyptian woman's yell plucked her out of her deep coma. She realized it was morning, and the whole, merciful night had passed. She jumped out of bed like a steam train, thrust herself into the black robe, and followed the others to the factory; she was barely awake and her soul was still somewhere else, far away.

But before long she was transported back to a reality that she could never have imagined. There had been an unexpected transformation in her fate, and the mixture of disdain and servility with which the supervisor greeted her made her realize that an order had been given to move her. She didn't know if it was solicitude or revenge that made the Mahdi move her to another team that appeared to earn a higher wage for a correspondingly higher level of danger. Here, she was squeezed among piles of saltpeter to turn it into gunpowder.

"Joining the team making black powder is the greatest of honors; here, you will make the pipes of martyrdom and glory."

The supervisor spoke in an aggressive tone, and Sarab didn't take in anything she had said; she was floored by the irony of being back in such a terrible situation, particularly one so closely associated with her father, Sheikh Baroud—"Sheikh Gunpowder." Sarab's distraction alarmed the supervisor, who kept up her profuse instructions, carving into Sarab the dread of what she was being thrust into.

"Now you are in the service of the secret army which will spread far and wide and work in silence. They will blow up the infidel French and Americans, everywhere they have been stationed to meddle in the affairs of our people."

She didn't slow down to let Sarab fully comprehend just what it was she was being embroiled in.

The new supervisor greeted Sarab and introduced herself sardonically: "I'm Napalm. That's the most important thing you'll need to know around here." She was Ethiopian, round and compact as a ball, with a juicy smile that split her face like a wound. That smile revealed large, gleaming teeth, in startling contrast to the darkness of the vault where the dynamite was produced. "And another helpful tip: keep your mouth shut from now on."

Sarab couldn't decide if Napalm was serious or sarcastic; she never relinquished her flippancy, even when she was explaining Sarab's destructive task to her.

"You will load these pipes with eighty percent saltpeter, and the rest with charcoal, then fix this reactor to every belt." Sarab was thrown into confusion at the idea of being girdled with death. It was beyond any recklessness she had experienced in the line of fire.

Napalm's exaggerated cheerfulness perplexed Sarab. She constantly broke into peals of laughter, and she never stopped rolling between tables, doling out jokes along with her instructions. Sarab noticed Napalm had very fine fingers, like antennae, in sharp contrast to the sturdiness of her body. She would pass these probes over the pipes like insects, arousing the admiration of the workers.

"Today we raised the dosage to three grams." The hands suddenly stopped working and all eyes swiveled toward Napalm, who stood in front of the table at the back of the cellar. A worker meekly handed her the specified quantity of gunpowder and, with a theatrical gesture so that everyone could see, Napalm wrapped the powder in a green leaf and swallowed it, to the amazement of her audience. Their awe was genuine, even though it was clear that this was a show that had been repeated often, and today had been singled out to dazzle the new arrival who didn't care what was happening and didn't understand its significance.

Sarab's concern was the overarching darkness which made it difficult to guess the time. Lumps of time were heavy in that place, which was more like a graveyard.

Sarab's fingers were trembling from exhaustion when Napalm released a cheerful whistle. At once the women stopped working and moved outside, and Sarab followed.

Waiting for them in the next hall was a pot overflowing with rice and meat. Every worker spooned some into a bowl, took a disk of bread, and fanned out to sit on the ground. Sarab could do nothing but take a plate and choose a spot by the door to sit. Her whole body was shaking and she had entirely lost her appetite from exhaustion. Meanwhile, her new comrades proceeded to use the bread to scoop up the rice with relish.

"Is the local cuisine not to your majesty's satisfaction?"

Sarab was taken aback at Napalm's attack; she had been watching Sarab closely. Sarab hurriedly plunged her fingers, still sprinkled with gunpowder, into the plate, pulling out meat and potatoes and scooping up the rice, cramming whole handfuls into her mouth in order to demonstrate her enjoyment and deflect the supervisor's displeasure.

The women studied Napalm, who had positioned herself between Sarab and the rest of the group. Sarab felt all movements freeze and a watchfulness settled over the workers. The Ethiopian didn't waste time; she released a thunderous fart and burst out laughing, and the women chorused with laughter in her wake; although, coming from those wretched, exhausted bodies, it sounded more like a lament.

Sarab was hit by a foul blast that made her retch. Bile splattered over the rice in her bowl and Napalm's gloating voice came amid the women's laughter.

"That was mid-level destruction; we chose it today as a little welcome for you."

Over the following days, Sarab was inducted into the team manufacturing self-induced death and its supervisor who presented them every mealtime with a thunder calculated to shock.

Sarab was less unnerved by Napalm than by her task of destruction. She sat in between veiled women and felt the coal-blackness of her own veil seeping into her lungs. From sunrise to sunset she prepared a toxic brew while her surroundings blurred: the containers of coal and saltpeter swelled in front of her; the gunpowder smearing her hands thickened and spread. She stuffed the pipes mechanically, and the limbs that would be torn apart by each bomb formed a suffocating pile around her. Whenever she wanted to run outside and escape, she was pierced by the eye of the elderly woman assigned to watch her. The old woman's fingers worked of their own accord while her eyes remained glued to Sarab, boring into her and goading her to hurry her pace, even though she was feverishly cramming saltpeter into pipes in the hope that they might explode in an act of self-sacrifice. The old woman eventually dozed off, her fingers still briskly stuffing saltpeter as her observation slackened. Sarab gradually lagged and left the remaining pipes empty except for charcoal, hoping to minimize the explosion, and thus the casualties. She was mired in an act of betrayal either way; to carry out her appointed task was to betray herself and the victims, and to be caught gambling with the recipe in this way would see her branded as a traitor to the Mahdi, who had moved her to that position either as a promotion or a way of breaking her obstinacy.

Day by day, Sarab grew thinner as a result of her aversion to all food other than milk and a few mouthfuls of dry bread at the evening meal in the factory. Her features were tinged with gray from the nightmares that never let her close her eyes in peace. Every night before going to sleep, the Egyptian woman would sit on her bed, and her reprimands competed with sleep for control of the women's drooping eyelids. Their bodies groaned and vied for attention while she declaimed lectures of chastisement, which mainly revolved around scenes of torture and the serpents that waited for them in their graves. She would describe these beings as though she could see them physically there in front of her, and every night these monsters gained a new horn and even more toxic venom. Still unsatisfied, she would interrupt these living pictures, focusing her gaze on Sarab, to hiss, "The snakes get intimate with cowards and traitors; they bite them so their flesh falls off, and the wounds ripen and split from the pus."

Pus was the Egyptian woman's favorite topic. She dragged it into conversation every waking hour. As soon as Sarab drifted off to sleep, her body would be draped in pipe bombs and she'd wake up terrified, counting each laceration and burn on her chest. The hours she spent in the pipe-bomb workshop accumulated on her skin like layers of armor, ready to blow her up along with the camp.

She forgot Rue Bonaparte. Its scents were effaced from her mind as if they had never been. She was certain that if she was left alone for long enough to fully remember, simply thinking of it would be a curse on that street; she would pack it with her pipes full of saltpeter, she would exchange the streetlamps for clusters of gunpowder. Her greatest obsession was the detonator fixed to every pipe belt. However much she scrubbed, the smell of gunpowder rose from her black robe and the roots of her hair, lancing her veins and scraping in between her teeth. She was powerless to resist the suspicion that her father was haunting her. Her movements became cautious, as she was certain that she was flammable. She flinched at every spark, especially from the Egyptian woman's flashlight; she carried it constantly, pointing it at them accusingly, as if it could illuminate lies and evil intentions.

"God save us from those haunted by Satan," the Egyptian hissed whenever she turned over in bed, her immense height causing it to wobble dangerously. Even when the batteries ran out, in Sarab's mind this flashlight became a sort of detonator connected to her sins; one spark could set them alight at any moment and obliterate her from all existence.

"When your soul rises, because it definitely will, we will wrap your demon in your shroud and lock it in your grave with you."

The Egyptian nurtured a particular hatred toward Sarab, both for her delicate body and for being "the Mahdi's woman."

In contrast to the brutality of the siege, the rough living of the camp and the hostility of its occupants wounded her because it touched her most vulnerable, sensitive parts. The women's rejection stirred up old feeling of being rejected by her mother and brother, and she was unable to assume the detached position of an observer that had saved her in the Grand Mosque. She betrayed herself this time, and surrendered to the feeling that she was sinking, alone and reviled, into her grave. She remembered Raphael's exclamation: "Why this obsession with death?" His question resounded through her head, trying to pluck her out of this capitulation. Sarab got thinner and thinner, and lost the sense of her body she had gained in Paris. She went back to denying and distorting her body.

A moment of joy gleamed in the dormitory, radiating from the gray military uniform Latifa guarded carefully. It had been smuggled to her by the Kuwaiti volunteer who had been appointed to marry her. He had started sending his clothes for her to wash, and in the sweat of each garment she could smell his prodigious passion for her.

"Abdel-Salam slipped some dinars into the pockets for me," Latifa confided to Sarab one morning as they were on their way to the factory.

Sarab's features burst into an encouraging smile; it was the first spontaneous mark of warmth she had received since arriving in the camp.

But the situation reversed that night. When they returned from the factory, Sarab's relaxed demeanor roused the suspicions of the Egyptian and her Kuwaiti friend, another giantess who had recently joined the Mahdi. The Egyptian had taken her under her wing at once, and they moved like two dinosaurs among the cowering women. They kept Sarab under close watch. The other women did not miss the scent of open hostility, and the more peaceable among them avoided Sarab so that her curse wouldn't fall on them as well.

Sarab was on her way to the bathroom when she was stopped by a shout of, "Hey you!" The shout was like an accusation. She turned to the huge Kuwaiti with her dark lips.

"Hoity-toity, cat got your tongue? You don't speak?"

Sarab had no chance to reply.

"You look down your nose at us. Are we too insignificant for you to exchange a few words with us?"

"What should I say?" It was the first time Sarab had spoken; her voice seemed thin and weak in that vast room.

"Your story. This West that you sold your religion and your honor for—what is it? Tell us."

The Kuwaiti seemed determined to make Sarab speak. A reel of the events in Paris passed through Sarab's head. Every scene was guaranteed to incriminate her.

All she could say was, "When you are in the abyss and the world caves in on you, there are pills they give you, and they lift you out of the darkness and fear."

Indifference bordering on defiance made Sarab choose that topic over any other. Her words sounded like a silly joke; she had been silent for days and now she had broken her fast of words with that piece of drivel. She was disgusted at herself.

The Yemeni dismissed her with: "Huh, that's no different from qat."

The Kuwaiti seized on that disparaging objection. "True. Tell us something new and interesting."

"Hold on. What about these pills? Do you have any with you? If we dissolve them in the water, it'll get rid of all Napalm's revolting farts."

The women ignored this joke from the Palestinian, and their eyes remained glued to Sarab, waiting for more. She was forced to submit to the inane discussion if she wanted to break that siege of curiosity.

"They have special towels for periods, with padding made of fine cotton. You throw them away after using them once, so you're not forced to keep washing rags." She spoke with sarcastic insolence, expecting the Kuwaiti to be furious at her boldness, but sincere interest gleamed in the women's eyes.

"And the rubbish overflows with blood. Well, they deserve that filth."

The Kuwaiti woman interrupted, breathing heavily: "And do they have sex with women from behind like animals?"

Unmitigated shock appeared on Sarab's face. "How should I know?"

"And their men aren't circumcised? Do they get worms in their foreskins which gnaw at their partners?"

"That's terrible!" Sarab's gasp made the women burst out laughing.

A Qahtani woman interrupted them, saying, "Haram! She's obviously inexperienced. I can tell from a girl's manner whether or not she's still a virgin."

The Kuwaiti snorted, and the rest of the women chorused, "Here we go again! The Qahtanis know all about human nature, don't they? What gibberish!"

The Kuwaiti cut her off. "A virgin? My dear . . ." She burst into scornful laughter. "The only virginal thing about her is her brain. It's harder to penetrate than rock. Don't let her fool you—they dragged her out of the bed of an infidel."

The Egyptian appeared to have provided her with every detail of Sarab's history.

Sarab wheeled around, and her body surprised her by releasing a cry and leaping at the Kuwaiti, her chest exploding with nightmares from the Grand Mosque. She pounced like a lightning bolt, throwing the Kuwaiti's huge body off balance by striking her at shoulder-height and falling on top of her. A glow of madness outlined her features and she was on her way to breaking that thick neck when the women rushed on her and dragged her to the ground. Sarab gaped at them, and the nightmare of the mosque receded. Her senses began to take in her surroundings and her helpless companions. She was horrified at what she had been so close to doing, and her body gave up resisting and subsided, silently accepting being slapped and spat upon. Her surrender robbed the attackers of their zeal, and they withdrew one by one while the Kuwaiti squatted over her like a nightmare, trying desperately to rehabilitate herself.

"You're damned! The demons are fighting in your body. Infidels have their demons too. You're possessed by desert jinn and Western demons."

From the far corner, Latifa gazed at her despondently. She didn't dare to intercede on Sarab's behalf. All the while, the Egyptian remained on her bed, watching like an empress and pealing with malicious laughter that would continue to rumble through Sarab's guts, consuming her with its spiteful fire.

Green Turtle Procession

SHE DIDN'T KNOW WHAT WOKE her up that night, but a weak light led
her to the bathroom. She stood in that narrow area of bare concrete. There were rags hanging on the wall that still bore traces of
blood despite repeated scrubbing—the shame of their female bodies
hoisted like a flag of disgrace over all the women in that dormitory.
Between the rags, Abdel-Salam's uniform was hung up to dry. Without thinking, Sarab began to strip the black robe off her body and
pulled on the gray uniform.

My fate seems to lie in men's clothing. She wouldn't let this thought
put her off however, and immediately hurried to the door that led
to the road. The key was always left in the lock, and none of the
women dared even look at it. The idea of opening it to go outside
was unthinkable, apart from the appointed times when they left for
work as a group. Everything was left open; doubtless the Mahdi was
confident of the jailers within them.

Sarab's pulse was racing. She was careful not to make any sound
turning the key in the lock. The Egyptian's snoring rose. She opened
the door resolutely. The snoring from bed nine operated like a tonic,
sending a familiar mixture of nausea and ecstasy through her veins,
and she rushed into the darkness. It was the first time she had been
outside without any guard other than the darkness. In the tranquility of the night the smell of dynamite intensified, coming from her
hair and perhaps from the nearby factory. She hurriedly gathered
up her hair under the white cap. The rough volcanic ground made
her suddenly realize she was barefoot; in her haste she had forgotten

her plastic sandals. She resolutely pushed away any thought of going back to retrieve them. In front of her, the ascetic houses of the camp stretched away in every direction. They had originally been warehouses serving the British occupation and were abandoned when the army withdrew from Aden. The buildings were arranged in lines, interspersed with meager lamps that illuminated almost nothing at all. The aim of these lamps was not to guide walkers, but to make the camp appear abandoned.

Uncertain of which way to go, Sarab crawled forward quietly. The lamps cast the long, thin shadow of a barefoot soldier in every direction. She left the factory building on her right and turned in the opposite direction. She didn't know whether the road would take her out of the camp or toward her kidnappers, but an internal sense guided her. Time passed as she moved from one cluster of storehouses to the next until a featureless square building loomed in the distance, all its windows closed apart from one almost at ground level. A weak light streamed from this window, outlining feet in black leather sandals as they moved through the room. It was the only building that appeared inhabited. Intuition, or perhaps a suicidal impulse, prevented her from retreating. She hurried on, swept up in the ecstasy of danger, and she threw her body on the ground close to the window. She was blinded by the blood that rushed to her head. Her heart was thudding, her whole body was numb, and it was some time before she could force her head to crane upward and steal a look through the window. There were perhaps five men in the room, distributed over the metal chairs and looking alert. They were probably guards, but what were they guarding? A strange smell filled her nostrils; it was familiar, but she couldn't name it, or even remember where she had encountered it before.

Suddenly the floor of the room split open. A trapdoor opened and the head of an African man rose through it. His face was on a level with Sarab's, and for a second she was certain he had seen her, but a large grin split his face as he welcomed the men.

"Musaffar, hasn't God made you repent of chewing that rubbish?" He was speaking to a Yemeni man in a yellow turban who was slumped in his chair, his jaw stuffed with qat.

Sarab focused on the trapdoor. She realized it must be the door to the cellar where the Mahdi's room was: the room from which the two women had taken her after her meeting with him when she first arrived at the camp.

She froze, exposed to the murderous intentions of any passersby, unable even to draw back. She remained prone in the volcanic dust, her face glued to the window bars and her eyes staring at the men coming and going complacently. They were sipping tea while the man called Musaffar continuously chewed handfuls of qat, spitting them out close to where she lay. Her whetted senses allowed her to catch the scent of plants over that red-tinged spittle, something reminiscent of blood or vegetation; it was the same smell she had caught when the two female guards led her out of the ground after she first arrived. Everything in her surroundings seemed to be magnified, especially the voices. She listened to an amplified discussion in various dialects.

"We've just heard the news. Salah succeeded in becoming a martyr. He blew up his belt in southern Lebanon and took those damned Shiites with him."

"Wasn't he briefed to aim for a convoy of Israeli soldiers at the border?"

"They discovered him. Witnesses said he was stopped and questioned in front of a café in the suq, so he had to detonate ahead of time. To hell with God's enemies!"

"We will meet him in Heaven."

Sarab choked at the mere idea that it was Heaven that waited for them.

"That's the third explosion this year by our martyrs. The Japanese kamikaze in World War Two weren't as brave as us." Sarab made out an Egyptian accent. "They demanded death as a sacrifice to pride, not to God and Heaven, but when we die, our eyes are fixed on Paradise."

Sarab heard this phrase as if for the first time. She listened with the ears of someone who had experienced the streets, people, and festivities of Paris. There, life was light, joyful, invulnerable; it made the voice of this cultured Egyptian sound like it came from a different planet, one with no relationship to life on earth. A struggle broke out inside her; she wished she could exchange herself for the bystanders in that suq where Salah had blown himself up in the hope of Paradise.

"My father was a prominent member of the National Liberation Front in Aden when it began its rebellion against the British. He helped attack the high commissioner with hand grenades in 1963: one dead, fifty wounded." The one called Musaffar, in telling this story, spat his qat farther, as if he were throwing a bomb. "And two of my uncles were leaders of the revolution that forced the British occupiers to leave Aden. I tattooed the date on my arm, here." He uncovered his arm to show a date tattooed in green: November 30, 1967.

"This is what I have to live up to," he said with a sigh, basking in the admiration of his companions. "And I'm sorry, my friend . . ." He turned to face the Egyptian. "On the same date, we rubbed Abdel-Nasser's nose in the mud. We gave him twenty thousand corpses for interfering in our revolution, and this land became the eternal resting place of those arrogant show-offs."

The Egyptian hurriedly exonerated him: "Thanks be to God, we have overcome our love of leaders and nationalism. Now we are brothers in our fight against a shared enemy: Dajjal."

But the Yemeni kept boasting of his origins. "It's no coincidence we're protecting our Mahdi here. Cain and Abel are buried in Aden. Death is our destiny in Aden, and we are charged with carrying the legacy of this death on earth." Clearly, Musaffar was desperate to rouse the esteem of his comrades, especially of the huge-bodied Sudanese man who had just come from meeting the Mahdi, as revealed by his elevated status in this group.

"One day I'll renounce qat and lead a suicide mission. That's my ultimate dream." To his comrades who had come from different parts of the world, merely voicing this wish was a guarantee of pardon for using qat. To increase their acceptance of his zeal, he shouted, "Didn't you once say that the land talks? Our land produces potassium—how could it speak more clearly than that? It's obvious that bombs are our destiny."

The men roared with laughter, and this discussion pumped phenomenal energy though Sarab's body.

The outside of the building wasn't guarded. She watched the guards sitting inside and racked her brains for a way of reaching that tunnel. She looked for a way of slipping into the building. She didn't know why. To meet the Mahdi? *Why, Sarab, are you lingering around this pit of death when perhaps there is an escape route through this rugged land where humanity's first victim lies?* She thought of the belts she spent her days cramming with death. If she managed to put one of them on, then reaching the Mahdi would be of some use: she would send both of their shredded bodies flying through the air. The violence of this image appalled her, but it didn't stop her from circling the building, and she couldn't believe her eyes when she found the door wide open. It sickened her that nothing was locked in this camp; it was a testament of everyone's servility, and the relinquishment of all will to flee. She slipped unhesitatingly into the dark expanse. There was a narrow corridor in front of her leading to the room where the men were gathered, and on her left there were stairs leading to an upper floor. She didn't know what waited for her there, but her body was driven upward.

It seemed that the easy life in Paris hadn't extinguished the embers of war in her. Her heart pounded when she spotted a window in the stairwell. She crept forward catlike on tiptoe, her bare feet pressing into the roughness of the floor; when she looked out of the window there was nothing but the blackness of the mountains. The horizon was obscured by crags reaching up to the sky; at the bottom of their slopes, more huge warehouses reached up to the same height.

The stairs led her to a long corridor. Closed doors lined its left-hand side. Any of them might open at any moment, but her sense of caution had stalled. A will beyond her own was leading her, perhaps to her destruction. She proceeded warily, her entire body in a sort of trance, as if it were operating in response to some unknown external impulse. She reached the end of the corridor and turned; there was another corridor in front of her and a short flight of stairs on her left, leading downward. The corridor seemed endless, so she went down the stairs. There was a small door at the bottom which she opened quietly, and she was astonished to find that it opened onto the mountain, as simply as that, with no guard. Still guided by the mysterious impulse, she jumped the meter and half that separated her from the rock face. As soon as she landing on the rocky ground she began to run, undeterred by the pain in her bare feet, expecting a bullet in her back from some observation post. Her body seemed rarefied, to have lost its density to the extent that a bullet would pass straight through it.

She didn't know how far she ran but at last she reached a cleft in the ring of crags, and as soon as she went through it, she gasped. An endless, awe-inspiring expanse of water rolled away in front of her. The mountain was like a screen between the camp and the water. She had never seen the sea before, or the huge vessels that plowed its waters. She realized that the howls rocking the ground under their beds at night, which they had thought issued from demons, were nothing more than the horns of these enormous machines passing in the sea. They bore no relation to the women's guilt.

Facing that great water for the first time, she was greeted by a salty breeze coming from the sea, loaded with the fragrance of coffee and frankincense. For the first time she felt her senses soften; the frankincense recalled memories from her childhood, when women would burn it to break an enchantment. She felt the fetters falling from her body; she felt she could fly.

Without a backward glance she broke into a run and the ground began to yield underfoot. Her eyes were fixed on the water; she didn't notice the pearl-like bodies under her bare feet where the turtles buried in the sand stirred as she passed, or the two shadows to her left. The two men stopped in their task of tying a huge turtle to a cement truck and watched her in disbelief. Suddenly, Sarab became aware of their gaping stares, and in a second they were in her sights. She realized the danger she was in and, like a cornered animal, she looked back; there was nothing but the black volcanic crags and a half-moon brilliantly illuminating the sand in front of them. The two men came toward her and she threw herself into the water. Her legs plunged into softness, her head covering fell off, and her locks unfurled so that they floated on top of the water. The waves sucked her down, until the water reached her head. Saltiness and cold sent a shiver of pleasure through her; she felt her body shed its skeleton and turn to water. When the sea entered her lungs, she didn't cough. Her body craved more, but hands plucked her out. She resisted, but couldn't free herself from their grip. The pleasure of the salt and the water had drugged her, and in the end she surrendered to being dragged back to the sand. All around her, small, narrow eyes emerged from the sand and followed her; all at once, the sand was riven by gleaming globular bodies leaving their hiding places and crawling slowly toward the sea. Her senses had a terrible purity, and as she allowed the two men to drag her, her body remained hyper-aware of those slithering bodies creeping toward the water. When the men made her walk ahead of them, she began to cough, the water that had merged with her lungs spraying into the air. Her ear caught their Yemeni dialect when one of them said, "A turtle without a shell." They both laughed, overjoyed at this unexpected catch.

She paid no attention to the road they took her along until they brought her inside a shelter that opened up in front of her like a hospital ward. Instantly her senses took in the scene in front of her. On her right were piles of empty shells, doubtless the shells of those creatures in the sand. They glittered with engravings, some in silver, others in pistachio and dark green, and some were covered in dried seaweed. Numb to any possibility of danger, her raw senses were propelled toward the splendor of those empty shells. Sarab had never had any experience of turtles; she had never seen or even heard of them before. To her, it was the earth itself that had split open and turned into these bodies which ran toward the sea. In front of her, piles of meat were carefully packed into thick paper, probably prepared for market. To her left, a man holding a blood-stained knife was standing in front of a blood-covered table, holding a plump turtle. He was tearing the flesh from its shell, and had just finished cutting off the fourth leg. He watched her while her eyes remained on the turtle's head; it was trying to withdraw into its shell, but was too fat to be able to hide itself completely. Perhaps the turtle was dead, but the poor head was still trying to hide itself in its shell even as all its limbs had been cut off. Sarab felt a kinship with the creature, hiding her head in a great shell and contemplating escape even while her legs were cut off and her breathing subsided.

"A turtle without a shell!" The men were so delighted with their joke they repeated it for the benefit of the third man, who was evidently in charge. Sarab realized these men had no connection to the Mahdi, and felt a mixture of satisfaction and terror at the fact. The leader approached her and threw her a towel.

"Dry yourself, girl. Stay here tonight and things will be clearer in the morning," the older brother said, pointing at a corner away from the box, and he drew back. Sarab submitted to the instructions and headed straight for the corner where a pile of seaweed covered with a carpet served as a bed. It was covered with a thin cotton blanket.

Their whispers reached her: "If we had left her she would have drowned, genius. She didn't swim, she didn't shout, she didn't say a word. God knows what threw her onto our beach."

Sarab lay on the blanket. The smell of seaweed pierced her heart and made it beat faster. She didn't want to sleep. Her body urged her to continue with her escape, but where to? She didn't know. She lay there, ready. What if she got up and left? Would they stop her? She hadn't reached a decision when the sleep of the exhausted seized her body and put an end to the struggle.

The three brothers spent the night chopping meat and packing it in boxes. In the dead of night they heard the roar of a lorry and went outside to greet it. Instinct made them protect the flotsam the sea had flung onto their shore, so they made sure to carry the boxes of turtle meat to the lorry themselves, offering no opportunity to the driver and his helper to enter the hut and discover her presence. However, the helper, who had grown suspicious, distracted the brothers and rushed into the hut on the pretext of needing some water. From a distance he spotted the head crowned with black locks, and he didn't mistake its feminine features. He emerged wearing a malicious smile.

When the lorry left for the market with its cargo, the brothers went to bed, lying on the platforms ranged along the opposite side of the hut.

Nothing was left of the night apart from a sliver of blackness, soon broken by the dawn. The sea carried intoxicating gusts, and the waves reached higher and plumbed the depths of her dreams. From the depths, she was washed in this rumble, which rocked her to and fro, and she returned to being the child she had been in the arms of her mother, Bunduqa Tafla.

When she woke up, the fragrance of tea filled the place and she was buoyant from the saltiness of her body, which still bore traces of the sea. She didn't know how long she had been sleeping there, whether it had been hours or days.

When she came forward they were waiting for her, sprawled on the ground in a circle around a large tray on a low table.

"Sit and eat with us." She sat at the fourth side of the table that had been prepared for her. There was an earthenware cup of tea, and the fragrance of the mint floating on the surface sent a ripple of bliss through her. An unusual transparency had overtaken her senses; they had been sharpened by her fear of what was to come, her craving for escape, and the death lurking in every choice before her.

She sat down calmly, not bothering to cover her hair which dangled to her shoulders. It was no longer important whether she was male or female, covered or uncovered. There was nothing but perfect peace encircling this haven. Warm disks of bread were piled in front of the oldest brother. He took one and handed it to Sarab.

"It's poor food, bread and honey and tea."

Sarab stayed absolutely silent, although she thought that honey was far from being the food of the poor.

The shortest brother handed her a jar brimming with honey. "Don't worry. Stick your finger in and take a lick."

Cautiously she dipped her index finger into the thick honey.

"Deeper!" They encouraged her to push all the way to the bottom. Her whole abdomen contracted with unfamiliar pleasure. Suddenly she noticed the three faces were watching her in amazement. To them, her ecstasy was a miracle, and none of them cared about where she came from. Those three brothers were the first people in her life to receive her without stopping to wonder who or what she was. They welcomed her as they would a piece of driftwood borne to them on the sea, and they allocated her a spot in their nook.

"The honey's free, from the mountain bees." The few sips of tea along with the honey and the bread were the sweetest Sarab had ever tasted. The authentic taste of a virgin land restored her to her village. For a moment she thought she was in an earthly paradise, with the sound of the sea surging a few meters away from where the table lay. She thought she would relax there for hours, perhaps days, and then would seize the first opportunity to continue with her escape. It didn't matter where; perhaps toward the sea.

"We're in Aden, maybe twenty kilometers away from the Black Land. . . ." one of the men told her.

Sarab didn't know what the Black Land was; perhaps it was just the place she needed to hide away in and forget about the gunpowder and soot she had left behind.

"We hunt turtles and sell the meat in the suq. Don't be afraid; it doesn't taste different from any other meat."

It struck Sarab that she could spend her life on this beach, free from responsibilities, free from guilt, where no one expected anything of her. She had never felt such complete and absolute freedom, not even in Paris with Raphael, where the sense of sin followed her like a shadow. Here no one pushed her to repudiate her past; here there was no past and no future and no tomorrow, just moments of silence throughout her whole being. No one was interrogating her or asking her to subject her mind to their judgment, whether for their rejection or their acceptance. Here there was no need for any of that; just these moments of utter silence within her and the sound of the sea all around.

That morning, despite her all-consuming longing to do so, Sarab didn't dare to leave the shelter and approach the sea. Through the door, she watched as the brothers' bodies were carried away by the water. She felt a profound envy and wished she was also there. After the bodies disappeared, Sarab began to wander and explore the hut. All of a sudden, the door burst open and two men ran inside with daggers drawn. It was the lorry driver and his helper, their faces torn with lust. They surrounded Sarab and savagery cloaked the driver's face.

The military uniform seemed to rouse his curiosity. "Let's see what this shell is hiding."

Without warning, he gripped Sarab's neck and his friend lunged at her legs, and together they threw her to the floor. The driver tore the uniform with the same violence he used to split the turtle's shells; buttons flew in every direction and the shirt tore open over Sarab's breast. The suddenness of the attack left her no chance to fight back. She didn't even realize what was happening until the man turned her on her back and pulled at the shirt, leaving her breasts bare to his helper's hungry stare.

"Fresh meat for dinner tonight!" They cackled loudly at Sarab's attempts to shield her breasts from their lewd gaze. The helper reached out to pull her arms away, and she surprised with him a slap. In reaction, he drew his dagger out of his belt and advanced toward her. She was ready to die when all three were taken by surprise: the door burst open again, and this time men with machine guns ran in. Instinctively, and suicidally, the driver and his helper charged their attackers, who came from the Mahdi's camp. They hadn't noticed their guns; apparently the Mahdi's followers had refrained from using them so as not to advertise their presence to the beach's inhabitants.

While the men were fighting, Sarab turned around, looking for something to cover herself with. There wasn't a trace of the shirt. Immediately she took one of the empty shells piled up in the corner and held it to her chest like armor as she hurtled outside. She ran toward the sea, driven by an irrational feeling that reaching the water would guarantee her survival. Any thoughts of swimming and drowning were beyond her and played no part in her reckonings. The mad voice assured her that the shell, which weighed down her running, would carry her on the water just as it had carried those enormous creatures. Her legs might have been too short to run fast enough to save her, but this shell was a raft. When she reached the water, it would float. The smell of the brine and dried blood embedded in the shell penetrated her bare chest and she turned into a turtle.

Suddenly she sensed running feet behind her, and despite the heavy shell she sped up. Then the feet were tangled between hers. She stumbled and flew through the air, landing a meter away from the water. The edges of the shell pierced her shoulder blades, the sand's moisture penetrated her entire nervous system. She was like an overturned turtle, lying on her face as the barrel of an automatic rifle prodded her skull. Death by water seemed soft, peaceful. Her body didn't care about the bullets and began to crawl toward the water, separated from that blessing by such a short distance. The two men pounced on her, keeping her from the wave rushing to meet her. Apparently they were trying to avoid firing their guns. One of them threw the jacket she had lost over her body. She had forgotten she was naked, but suddenly this fact became more obvious. She stopped resisting and slipped her arms inside the jacket, ignoring the men's glances at her breasts, the nipples made erect by the chill from the water. She had to hold it closed with her arms because of the lost buttons. She allowed herself to be herded submissively as they blindfolded her, utterly shutting off the sea and the horizon, and dragged her back to the camp.

When they removed the blindfold she was once again in that bare room with the single chair, and the Mahdi was regarding her with cold fury. At a wave of his hand, the two men left the room. He stood up, walked toward her, took a handful of her hair in his fist, and wrenched her off the ground.

"Do you really expect to be able to leave like that and wander around looking for help? Are you fleeing our safe haven? To go where? Don't you know what can happen to a woman in a country like this? If we had left you to them, they would have eaten you alive." He contemplated her scornfully as brine and frustration stuck her tongue to the roof of her mouth.

"What do you want, woman? We honored you and elevated you, and the only thanks we receive is this flight to impurity." He circled her, inhaling the scent of her hair. "Gunpowder smells sweeter than musk and amber."

Every mechanism of feeling and reflection had stalled inside her. A trivial thought was lodged in her head: she wondered whether her hair still reeked of dynamite or whether it smelled of salt.

The stupor in her eyes made his fist relax its grip on her hair. He stepped away from her, looking at the jacket with its torn-off buttons, where damp patches revealed the swell of her chest. Its ambiguous outlines clearly interested him.

"Do you only have to look at men's clothes to jump inside them? This is a disease we must cure you of! Didn't Paris feminize you?" He seemed to be angrier with himself than with her. "You have a fire inside you." He gazed at her intently. "Do not disguise and deny the fighter in you. If you were committed to your savage side, you would be the greatest of our fighters. Or . . ." After some thought, his features twisted into a lascivious smile. "There is one treatment that would leave you in no doubt of the woman in you."

The look in his eyes sent a shudder through her; there was no mistaking his intention.

"Remember that I was merciful to you. I didn't denounce you with stories of fornication or depravity."

Sarab cried out furiously, "Fear God! I swear I'm untouched."

The ring of desperation in her voice made him suspicious.

"You dare to swear that you're a virgin?"

After some thought, his face warped into a smile whose significance she couldn't miss. "This is an easy enough matter to verify." After a silence loaded with meaning, he mused, "I could take you prisoner." He let the words sink in. "But I am resolved to settle my debt."

An obscure feeling of danger paralyzed her; something beyond the dangers of the siege. She implored him: "If you are really in my debt, I beg you—return me to Wajir. There is no place for me here."

He ignored her. "We will surpass your modest wishes. You will be the wife of the Mahdi."

She shuddered at the term.

He went on: "Here I am—I have forgiven you, and so you have been purified. I have been patient for a long time in the hope of taming you, but it seems you are more desirable as a savage. My patience runs out here." His laughter sent a tremor through her veins. "According to the Sunna of God and his Prophet, I will marry you myself."

He took her head roughly in his hands and raised her face to his, crushing her lips in a kiss that robbed her of all sensation. She felt his body crushing hers. The taste of salt penetrated her, and his voice came out as a hiss: "Your life is in my hands. With one movement I could crush you. *I could crush you.*"

When he pushed her away the two female guards appeared, draped as usual in black. They blindfolded her and led her through the underground passage, where they threw her on the floor of a room. The salty taste on her lips increased, making her wonder whether the passage led all the way to the sea she had been deprived of, where she wished she was buried. She felt the two guards winding a thick rope around her ankles and between her feet and hoisting them into the air. Without warning a whip lashed the soles of her feet, already tender from running barefoot. Dozens of blows rained indiscriminately on her ankles and legs. When they untied her, her bloodied feet could hardly bear to touch the ground, but they mercilessly drove her in front of them barefoot, still blindfolded, back to her comrades in the dormitory.

"From tomorrow, you will prepare for the marriage." Clear instructions had been issued, excusing her from working in the factory. A cloak of envy rippled around her, especially from the Egyptian and the Kuwaiti, who stoked the fire around her although they didn't dare to attack her again openly. From a distance, Latifa threw her reproachful glances for having ruined her fiancé's uniform.

It was left unspecified how long Sarab was to lie back and wait for her wedding to the Mahdi, which might be held on any evening. For three days, Sarab was terrified as night fell, expecting a marriage contract to swoop down on her and convey her to the Mahdi's bed.

And here she was again, alienated and exiled; like her alienation from her mother, then the house in Medina, then in the siege, and afterward the exile of Paris, and now here in this land surrounded by water. Grief washed over her at this perpetual estrangement. More than once she was tempted to slip into the factory, put on one of those suicide belts, and light the fuse so her torment would be ended. But even martyrdom was a land of exile for her; she was frightened of embarking on that rash venture.

One night, as she drifted off to sleep, she became intrigued by the thought of sleep as a lesser death. With all her being, she wished that this lesser death would take her to the greater death. With the Mahdi's lips still crushing her, she fell asleep resolved not to wake up—to be saved from all the webs that ensnared her. A final thought accompanied her: that she had never been able to choose; that choices had always been imposed on her. She longed for one chance, just one, to choose.

At midnight Sarab had a nightmare. A towering ghost looked down on her, and she realized it had come to superintend her greater death. From where she lay in her bed on the floor, the ghost seemed tall enough to reach the sky. It bent over her and placed a hand of steel over her mouth, smothering her gasp of terror.

Her eyes bulged as he removed his mask, and she shouted, "Raphael!" She gulped the name like someone taking their first breath after being resurrected on Judgment Day. Her heart pounded with overwhelming joy, and she didn't dare to move or breathe in case she dispelled this dream.

"Shh." He picked her up out of her bed and buried her in his arms, but suddenly he staggered. The Egyptian giant had leveled a violent blow to his head with her torch. Her mouth was open to let out a warning scream, but Raphael recovered his balance, grabbed the torch and struck back, hitting her head, and she fell to the ground mute and unconscious.

"Sorry for the rough treatment," Raphael said lightly, burying Sarab in his arms. The rest of the women woke up terrified, frozen in their beds and unable to move, waiting for this nightmare to disappear.

Regretfully, he threw the shattered torch down beside the unconscious Egyptian.

Sarab clung to that dream and surrendered to its force. Their bodies woke up; it was the first time they had been in such close contact since they first met. A tremor shook her while he kept examining her body; he couldn't believe she was still whole and unharmed, and safe in his arms at last. A sweeping feeling of safety overpowered her after days of starvation and desperation, and she fainted. Her sudden slump frightened him; he gathered her up in his arms and carried her out of the dormitory.

Outside, the camp was under siege from combined Special Forces. The Mahdi's guards had raised the alarm and woken the whole camp to face this unexpected attack. They were aghast at the sight of Raphael carrying the Mahdi's woman, but they hesitated to open fire in case they hit her by mistake. A black Land Rover stood waiting for Raphael and Sarab, and as soon as it set off, shooting broke out around the camp and enclosed everyone who was inside. But a group of the Mahdi's men managed to break out of the siege, and they rushed in pursuit of Raphael and the Mahdi's woman. The Land Rover hurtled forward under a stream of bullets, brakes shrieking and machine guns firing on anyone who dared to obstruct its path.

The short minutes separating Raphael from his pursuers were enough for him to reach Aden Airport, where a black helicopter was waiting. A team of pursuers rushed after him, smashing through the checkpoints to reach the airport runway. They fired wildly, no doubt on explicit orders from the Mahdi: stop that woman whatever the cost.

Sarab fainted again while Raphael fastened the belt around her and took a seat next to her, directly behind the pilot.

In a nightmarish stupor, Sarab sensed the black helicopter take off, its rotors roaring over her head. She felt she had been swallowed into the guts of this phenomenal creature, of the same type that had attacked her comrades in the Grand Mosque. It had hunted her down at last, and now she was alone in this vengeful beast, which had started to strew death all around it. She sank into the leather seat, mentally paralyzed, drowning in this hallucination. She watched the ground below where the Land Rovers were racing to keep up with them, shooting volleys of bullets into the night. Fire was returned on the cars from every direction, dispatching one car here and another there; they flew through the air and landed with thunderous explosions, scattering bodies over the ground. It was a feverish scene, but it was taking place in slow motion, right under her feet; she could simply jump out and actually experience it happening all around her. Sarab closed her eyes, shutting out the absurdity of the scene below and her pressing desire to leap into the middle of it. Suddenly the night was plunged into silence, and Sarab couldn't decide whether she had lost consciousness or whether a bullet had delivered her to the murky heavens where life was extinguished. Even the roaring rotors fell quiet, although they still milled the darkness overhead. They must be on a journey of ascension after death. Sarab waited for the fragrance of sweet basil which, it was promised, would envelop the souls of the righteous as they ascended to the seventh heaven . . . *if I am one of the righteous.*

A sudden jolt restored Sarab to full consciousness. They had landed in Mogadishu Airport in Somalia, where they were greeted with friendly smiles. Eyes like torches hurried them toward the private jet waiting on the runway.

Raphael was speeding her up the steps to the airplane when Sarab froze with sudden terror; she had awoken from the trance that had overwhelmed her.

"No!" She clung to the steps, refusing to go any farther, repeating maniacally, "No, no!"

"What do you mean, no?"

Sarab was nailed to the spot as a charge of joy and fear and rage exploded in her veins.

Raphael squeezed her hand. He realized she wanted to run away and hide; the danger of the previous months had become embodied in the gaping mouth of the airplane, and in the light streaming from it, which was blinding after the darkness she had suffered. A searchlight paralyzed her.

"I can't."

"You can't? I'm taking you to Paris, to safety." Words were powerless to break through the fumes in her head. He began to repeat, "Do you want to stay here?" while resisting the urge to slap her.

"Enough." She seemed lost, incapable of stringing together a meaningful sentence, randomly putting up words as barricades, trying to gain some time, trying to grasp the shock of having survived that nightmare.

"Enough?" Like a demented parrot, he was repeating her words.

"You, the Mahdi, from here to there . . . enough."

"Sarab, pull yourself together. I understand you've had a shock but we don't have any time to waste."

"No, please." Tears poured down her cheeks. Somewhere inside her a dam had burst and was drowning her; all the frustration and terror she had suppressed for months had exploded. "Please take me back." She was horrified to hear herself repeating the same request she had made to the Mahdi. "To my country."

Her hysterical tone blinded them both.

"What will you be going back as? As a terrorist, a fugitive from justice?"

Her whole body shook from her thudding heart, which threatened to burst; from her joy at surviving, which scorched like acid; from the terror that this dream might collapse.

"Where are your documents, your identity card, your passport?" Her eyes bulged, and the bubble of her ramblings was burst. She stood stock still, in disbelief that she was completely naked; she was no one.

I am cursed. That was her first lucid thought, but she was soon swept away on a tide of satisfaction. She sighed with relief that she was finally free of those identities dragging her down. Another charge of joy gushed through her; her whole life would begin again, with a new identity, one she wanted to be.

Sarab faced Raphael, foreigner and supposed enemy, who was dragging her into situations that dared her to choose. She stood in the middle of a sea of faces which were waiting impatiently for them to climb the stairs. She was lost in a frenzied tangle of battling emotions, unsure whether to embrace her enemy, slap him, tear him to pieces, or run away.

At last, Sarab stopped resisting and Raphael led her up the steps to the airplane door which gaped like the unknowable future. Sarab climbed those few steps, aware that the first step she took inside would mean the end of Sarab as she had known her till then.

When Raphael fastened the seatbelt around her waist, Sarab resisted an urge to seize his hand and kiss it in gratitude.

Black Crescent

Raphael sat opposite Sarab in the airplane while she was trying to grasp an overwhelming feeling of freedom. She was afraid to move in case she shattered that fragile state of being. Her tongue was dry and stuck to the roof of her mouth. She racked her brain for something to say to express her gratitude, but words failed her. She was still living the nightmare she had left behind her, and spent the journey in total silence. When the pilot announced they were preparing to land, a question burst out of her.

"How did you find me?"

He stared at her, relieved she had returned to life.

"You must know that I can't live without you."

Her eyes wandered around the airplane interior, incredulous at what was happening.

"Am I really out of the camp?" Her gaze wavered over the accumulations of cloud below her. For a moment she recalled the Mahdi's icy fist around her throat. She was certain he would follow her, even after his death.

But was he really dead this time?

Suddenly she saw the tunnel leading to his hiding place. Had the attacking forces discovered it?

Raphael took her hands and kissed them, pressing his face into them.

"When you disappeared, I lost my mind with rage. I thought of your Mahdi at once. By good luck, we have influential friends who wanted to find him, and we followed the trail you left us in smuggling him to Yemen. Swift inquiries led us straight to his camp in those warehouses left over from the British occupation. As you see, in the end it's a small world."

Her eyes bored into him. "So, you went back?"

"Went back?"

"To being a soldier."

"Ah . . . no. This was my last operation. They wanted the Mahdi and I wanted you; that was our deal. You are considered an agent who supplied us with intelligence, and now you can be granted asylum."

Terror engulfed her; her initial reaction was to refuse and plunge into her protective cocoon. But instead, she revealed the depth of her fear.

"What if I'm not ready to close all the doors on what I was, on where I come from?"

"You have to understand; you don't have a choice."

His words didn't do much to assuage the notion of total exile.

"What if I hate you for this?"

"Perhaps you will, but we'll deal with that. Even if you loathe me and reject me. I understand."

They arrived at their apartment in Paris in the middle of a summer's day. A sense of excitement enveloped them. Raphael moved through the apartment restlessly, making sure all the windows were wide open to the air, the light, the birdsong from the surrounding trees, and the sound of the fountain. The light gushing through the apartment was so radiant it seemed unreal. Sarab's body was starved from days of subjection and tension, and all she wanted was to fall into bed. But instead, she stood in the middle of the living room and, slowly but resolutely, began to take off her clothes. Raphael was rooted to the spot, his heart clenched. He observed the impulsive, flowing movement of a body emerging defiantly into life, savoring the intoxicating ecstasy of the act of baring itself. The flowing black sack that passed for clothing fell to the ground, followed by the even wider black trousers. Next there appeared the black bandages that were tied around her chest instead of a bra, erasing the swell of her breasts. The black bandage harmonized enticingly with the black crescent mark that bloomed all the way across her left buttock. That mark seemed like a wound or a birthmark, and an incitement of violent desire.

Slowly, gradually, her clothes accumulated in a black pile by her feet. She left the pile behind her and went haughtily to the bathroom. She left the door open as she stood under the shower for what seemed like forever. The sound of the water gushed over Raphael, washing his senses as he stood in the living room, turned to stone where she had left him.

At last, the water stopped and Sarab emerged from the bathroom, dripping water. She stood still and he moved. She went to the bed and curled up there, and he followed. Quietly, he lay down behind her on the bed, his body cradling hers. Their bodies lay against one another, and Sarab fell at once into a deep sleep.

Raphael lay there, paralyzed; he was hyperaware of her wet hair tracing a dark, damp circle on his chest, her calves entwined with his knees. He wasn't breathing for fear of disturbing this moment of pure being. The phrase "Perfectly content, perfectly content, perfectly content" echoed through his head, and he fell asleep.

His sleep was disturbed by an urgent buzzing. His hand convulsed involuntarily at a sharp sting in his shoulder. Opening his eyes, he spotted a bee flying away, and he felt a chuckle rumble inside the chest pressed against his own. It was morning and sunlight warmed their skin. Neither was sure how long they had slept, or even what day it was. They surfaced like two primordial beings, as if from death.

He pulled her close, fiercely pressing her against his body.

"Wait." She wasn't objecting to the violence, but she was unsettled by the sudden, intoxicating shock of pleasure. "You're stung." Her words were dazed and incomprehensible, even to herself. They were both consumed by a ferocious need to break out of their limits, a need to howl with brutality, with the specters of her mother, brother, and rebel comrades hanging in the air.

"I'm female." She took a deep breath, rubbing both their faces in this sin of her femaleness. She didn't have the slightest feeling of wrongdoing, despite the voice inside insistently rebuking her, telling her, *No one has the right to feel this bliss.*

A gasp ran through their bodies and their heavy breathing became entangled. Their feverish hands tore at the twenty-two years robbed from her life, and pulled her toward an overwhelming, overflowing vitality nothing could disturb.

She caught her breath to whisper resolutely, "I'm never going back to that camp. The women were all drowning in dynamite."

Her words fell into his ears like a vow.

"You know, I discovered there that the real enemy is this false messiah, Dajjal. My mother did what she did to me and my brother to drive one messiah out of her head; Mujan dragged us behind another. I believe that we carry Dajjal inside us—it's our own enemy that we give a false messiah's face. I touched my own Dajjal; for me, it was the saltpeter I was stuffing into those bombs. I hope I'll never come across it again."

The burning sensation and the swelling on his shoulder pushed Raphael's thoughts in a shallower direction. He raved at the bee; now that it had snapped off its sting in his body, it would surely die.

"What a petty death for such a petty insect!" He shivered. "But what death is important?" He paused that bleak train of thought, unsure whether the burning sensation he felt had its source in the bee sting or in Sarab's vow.

All of a sudden, the fire that had been spent sprang up again and blinded them. Fire was consumed by fire. Raphael plunged into her fiercely, and a taste of blood welled up in Sarab's throat. She was sure that the last bridge to her past had been burned, closing the door to her masculine side forever. It was the point of no return, sealed with blood.

Two months passed after their return to Paris. Raphael was proceeding with his plans to open a restaurant, while Sarab was still soaring in her new feeling of independence and freedom. She had surrendered the flag at last, allowing herself to be no one, without a past, looking for a new "I." She was prepared to acclimatize to her new life. At the same time, she was prey to changeable moods, swinging between her love for Raphael and the guilt that came from loving an enemy. She couldn't ignore the occasional nightmares and flashbacks; she would once again be captive in the Grand Mosque and Raphael was the attacker pumping gas into the lungs of her comrades and her brother. Often, she would be so terrified of going to sleep, she would choke and her heart would almost stop. The more she surrendered to her happiness with Raphael, the more her nightmares escalated.

Aden had been added to her nightmares, and Sarab had begun to feel an explosive belt clasped around her torso whenever she moved. She would wake from the depths of sleep, convinced that she had triggered the detonator. She sat up in bed, deafened by the roar of the blast, seeing her limbs scattered all over that room in Paris. She sat in bed for hours, afraid to sleep in case she made the mistake of detonating the belt all over again. The belt had a physical existence she could feel on her waist, and especially in Raphael's arms; when they embraced, her first reaction was fear, in case she felt their bodies explode.

Sarab had started learning French at a language institute alongside other female migrants and asylum seekers. One day, her eyes blurred and she could no longer hear anything the teacher was saying; she felt she was suffocating. She stood up and rushed to the bathroom; she needed to hide from the inferiority she felt when she compared her meager progress in learning French to the achievements of those brilliant girls in her class. Their sharp tongues contorted effortlessly into French constructions, in contrast to her tongue, which struggled to lighten the heavy letters of the Arabic alphabet, the emphatic *s* and the deep *h*.

Sarab sat in the bathroom, trying to curb her longing to surrender to a new sense of belonging. Her classmates could be the sisters she had been deprived of, but all the same she felt them hanging on her like another suicide belt. A threat lay in the increasing affection they had shown her since she started her lessons; she would become attached to them and soon, at any moment, she would leave them behind. She was used to being kidnapped and taken who knows where. So, unconsciously, Sarab kept the language barrier in place, a final defense against dissolving into those girls who came from every catastrophe-ridden corner of the globe, and losing the last traces of her links her to her past. A suicidal impulse drove her to involuntarily cling to that past in her isolation.

Sarab had hidden herself away in one of the bathroom stalls, as if she was being hunted by her own stupidity. She was at a loss, possessed by the thought of turning her back on this institute and its daily humiliation. Suddenly, from nowhere, a voice emerged, surging and receding against the tiled walls like a sea of sound:

"Padam, padam, padam . . ."

The drumming voice thundered in Sarab's chest. She knew that voice; it belonged to the thirteen-year-old Cambodian girl, Rani. The skinny girl used to escape the classroom to sit on the bathroom floor and sing that Edith Piaf song, always the same one. She had memorized it from a cassette that had played incessantly in her last pimp's house.

The voice rose like a national anthem, driving a hidden ghost out of Sarab's head, a duplicitous ghost that slipped away like mercury whenever she tried to take hold of it and name it.

Sarab couldn't understand the words, but the spirit in the song reached her, harmonizing with the ghosts in her head.

Suddenly the singing fell silent and a moment of silence unfurled between the two girls, each in her own stall. No doubt Rani was aware of Sarab's presence; she often cast a glance at her. Her eyes were like two cracks above her hollowed-out cheeks and sparkled with a fear that surpassed human understanding. However many languages Rani accumulated, she would always be the little girl who was found sitting by a mass grave, keeping watch over the bodies of her family and neighbors. Day after day she had kept to her post while the stray dogs snapped up an eye here, made off with a foot there.

Rani had never exchanged a word with Sarab although in time it appeared she had picked up some Arabic from her Algerian friend, Jamila. Rani was an ingenious mimic; she could copy any voice she heard, and languages were no obstacle to her. It wasn't long before the teachers discovered that she could speak Chinese, Vietnamese, English, Spanish and French.

The song broke out again and the drumming of the voice swelled in Sarab's chest cavity. A door cracked open in her heart, and she burst into tears at how shallow her pain was compared with Rani's.

Sarab had never seen her chatting, unlike the other girls who never stopped chirping, but Rani occasionally took everyone by surprise by exploding into a torrent of words that were never taught in their classes. The teacher would calmly take her out of the classroom, trying to quieten the hysterical flood, and when she came back, Rani would be plunged into crushing silence for days. Her closest friend was Jamila who followed Rani around like a puppy wagging its tail. If Rani was absent for a moment, Jamila would seize the opportunity to bait the other girls' interest with stories of the ghosts that haunted the Cambodian girl: the Khmer Rouge, who had wiped out her village when she was eight. The word 'red' successfully conveyed a sense of danger and reflected the oceans of blood from which those girls sprang. Aside from that, none of the girls knew or cared anything about the Khmer Rouge.

"Rani is originally a queen."

Sarab envied Jamila for the effortlessness with which she had picked up the French language, and more particularly for her ability to dazzle an audience with her trivial nonsense. Jamila herself was an expert in exaggeration and she stretched her talent to its utmost on the strength of Rani's name, which meant 'queen,' and her tragic story.

"It's not even her speaking all those languages; it's the spirits speaking through her. Rani is a mirror for all those dead people." Jamila felt the shock on their faces like a refreshing breeze, and she was encouraged to go further in her extemporization.

"The man who took her from the mass grave harmed her, he bit off a piece of her backside so she wouldn't have one, then he sold her to a Vietnamese slave trader. And he sold her to a Vietnamese family, but she ran away and found herself a French boyfriend, and they are working on her adoption papers."

The queen sat in the bathroom, at one with the freezing floor, and her heart melted into the melody.

When Sarab left the bathroom stall, Rani was waiting for her. Without preamble she said in Arabic, "Are you in danger?"

"I expect to be killed."

"By who?" Rani asked.

"By someone who might be dead," Sarab smiled sadly. "But I'm not afraid."

"It was a terrible crime, what happened to the home of the spirit."

Rani paused to allow her words to sink in.

"It's not you that needs cleansing, but the thing that happened to the home of the spirit. At sunset, wash the ground under a tree, any tree, then leave a cup of milk or honey there overnight. The spirit should forgive you."

Sarab was more shocked at the tenderness on Rani's face than her words of warning; it made the thirteen-year-old girl look like an old woman. Then, in an instant, Rani's face resumed its blank, solid innocence and she went out, leaving Sarab dumbstruck.

The Stage at Last

"Pascale and I lived in Cairo for five years."

Rosaline volunteered this statement in poor Arabic spoken with a thick Egyptian accent, drawing a smile from Sarab which did not go unnoticed by Rosaline.

"You're such a petty little thing!" Rosaline told her.

But it was clear this regal woman had taken to her at their first meeting one hot summer's day. Sweat dripped down Sarab's spine as she stood face to face with this retired actress, whose pale skin formed a striking contrast to her bloodred lips. Her nimble, upright figure was clothed in black leather, netted stockings, and knee-high boots. This gothic appearance struck Sarab as bizarre. It seemed to weigh heavily on that slight and delicate body which took a provocative stance, unconscious of having lost its youth. Time had stopped thirty years ago in this sumptuous apartment.

"If you are going to be here often, you should make yourself scarce, do you understand? I won't have you getting on my nerves or poking your nose into my things."

Disappearing was the best offer Sarab could have hoped for.

"I know I can't frighten you; you could terrorize a whole country."

It was a joke, but Sarab made no response, not even to force a smile. She simply stood there impassively, waiting for her instructions.

"And now, go."

Sarab thought she was being thrown out. She was horrified at disappointing Raphael, who had found her this job as a caregiver;

it was part of an integration program. And now just like that, she had lost her opportunity. She was aghast; a faint gleam in her eye revealed her shock, although her face retained its haughtiness.

But after a short silence, the woman said, "It's clear that you're desperate, but you're honorable; you're all right." She contemplated Sarab. "Now, take a look at the apartment, and then leave. And make sure you don't touch my wardrobes."

Who cares about your wardrobes? Sarab smothered the thought.

"Actually, just go now and come back tomorrow," Rosaline said. "After your language class."

And thus the rhythm of Sarab's tasks in that place was settled. She came and went like a ghost, cleaning the apartment and caring for the elderly actress from a distance.

Less than a month into her new job, Sarab arrived at the apartment one morning, and as soon as she opened the door she was greeted by a deep wail, like something from a wounded animal. She hurried to the bedroom to find Rosaline collapsed on the chair at her dressing table, her hands twitching, her face powder spilled on the ground and a bottle of Acqua di Parma cologne shattered on the mirror; the scent of lemon and jasmine filled the room like a cloud.

This was one of the fits of what Rosaline's son called "despair," which struck her from time to time. He had warned Sarab to watch out for them.

Sarab rushed to help Rosaline back into bed, but the woman regained her composure suddenly. She haughtily pushed Sarab's hand away and, still clinging to her chair, signaled her with a trembling, red-tipped finger to apply her lipstick for her.

Sarab hesitantly touched the lipstick to Rosaline's lips, and her whole body quivered. She watched the red color seep into the fine wrinkles in her lips and resisted a wave of pity, careful not to involve herself emotionally. She reminded herself this was temporary work; before long she would acquire a residency permit and she and Raphael would move to Spain.

During the previous month she had passed a lot of time with this woman, although on most occasions Rosaline wouldn't allow her to offer any kind of help, even when she fell victim to the fits of exhaustion she was prone to. Like a gothic queen all in black, she was resolved to carry out her own needs without assistance—especially arranging her room, which she would undertake as if caring for a sacred shrine, and cooking, when she would order Sarab to keep back and watch while she produced her miraculous recipes.

"I'm conceited, I know—I'm used to having an audience."

Little by little, Sarab's total silence roused Rosaline's curiosity and her heart warmed toward her, especially when she realized that Sarab exhibited no signs of interest or awe at her eccentricity. Rosaline did not relish this intrusion into her privacy, but neutrality bought her out of her aloofness. She no longer regarded Sarab as an alien in her world and gradually, with the vanity of a performer, she felt insulted by the girl's indifference; she was dying to dazzle her.

"Come on, take that stone mask off your face."

Sarab was disconcerted, unsure how to master her features.

"Clack, clack, clack . . ."

Rosaline accompanied the noise with stabbing motions. She spread out her palms like a curtain over her mouth, and then, with another *clack-clack*, she separated her palms, opening them little by little to reveal her laughing mouth.

"Your smile . . ." Sarab was surprised to hear her say that. "I can hear your smile hidden underneath that mask: clack clack clack."

Sarab found the noise funny, and the little smile on her face grew wider; she looked very attractive.

"See, you can laugh after all. . . wider!"

And Sarab lost all ability to smother her smile.

"Now come here and mend this."

Rosaline often gave peremptory orders, putting a torn lace glove or a silk dress in Sarab's hand and handing over some needle and thread. Sewing was a strange exercise for Sarab, who was more used to rifles and dynamite, and she was preoccupied with clumsily trying to follow Rosaline's instructions. As she sewed up the tears in silk or lace, she felt something inside her altering and relenting, despite herself.

"It's clear you haven't a drop of the seamstress in your blood." Rosaline mocked her while closely watching Sarab's progress in the art of sewing. Nevertheless, it was evident Sarab enjoyed it, even when she was pricked by a needle; it made her feel real, like a normal woman doing normal household chores.

One evening, Sarab passed the door of the bathroom while Rosaline was bathing, and she beckoned her inside.

"Don't stand there like a rabbit in the headlights; come here and scrub my back."

The regal body was laid out like a mermaid in the perfumed bathwater. Sarab was bewildered at touching the aged body of that baffling woman, the compact, firm backside and the silkiness of two slender legs in contrast with the flabbiness of the inner thigh.

Is this what it would have been like to touch my mother's body? Sarab dispelled this sudden thought.

Rosaline felt the tremor in Sarab's hand and was driven to show off.

"No one would have dared to intervene in my life if it weren't for that silly fall. My legs let me down and I fell on my back like a cockroach on the bathroom floor, and I stayed there till they found me in the morning. My son seized the chance to meddle."

Sarab listened, occupied with the body in her hands. She scrubbed her back willingly, to scrub away the pain of the fall from Rosaline's memories.

"What angers me most was my son. I could see it in his eyes. Children are cruel; they watch impatiently for us to go, but I defied all his expectations." Rosaline stopped Sarab's hand as it scrubbed her knee, to emphasize her next words. "I want to live." She was silent for a moment, to carve that wish into Sarab's consciousness. Then she went on: "I am an actress. I play at living. Do you know what? Life is precious. My husband wasn't so strong; when they made him retire he lasted a week, and I woke up one morning to find him lying dead next to me in bed." She sighed. "I didn't indulge him. But let me be clear; when men get older, they slow us down. They are desperate for an easy life, and sadly they go quickly. But maybe I prefer being alone like this, with a shining companion like you; I can suck up your youth," she added, with a peal of mocking laughter aimed at them both.

"I don't mind. I won't stop you," Sarab said in a whisper.

"That's a sin; you shouldn't let an old woman like me take advantage of you."

Rosaline watched Sarab, and her body quivered as she tried to guess the horrors she had been involved in before ending up in her apartment. There was an aura surrounding the girl which made it clear she had sampled terror so thoroughly that nothing afterward could shock her; but at the same time there was a vulnerability that was kept hidden, so she would not be wounded.

"It's all right if we're naughty from time to time. I learned a surprising fact in Egypt from some dervishes—snake charmers at festivals. When they remove all a snake's poison, it goes blind and gets weaker and weaker until it succumbs. A little poison is a good thing."

"Yes. I also have some poison."

Sarab flushed in embarrassment at Rosaline's roar of laughter at her admission.

"We're all human, in the end. The angels were ordered to bow to Adam, and it sanctified his weakness."

Sarab's hand convulsed over Rosaline's collarbone. "My brother also gave in very early." As Sarab said these seven words, she felt a mountain lift off her shoulders. She let her hands fall into the bathwater, somewhat at a loss, and Rosaline's silence encouraged her to shed more of the worries that burdened her.

"He killed many people before he reached his goal. I believe he always intended to be killed." And she added: "Me too." She fell silent abruptly.

"You too?" Rosaline's question escaped her despite herself.

"I thought I wanted him to live, whatever the cost, but now . . . I don't know," she stammered.

"Right. Perhaps you're better off alone like this."

A sense of relief washed over Sarab, as she finally summoned the courage to face the guilt that still flogged her for having clung to life when everyone she knew had gone.

"Such immature souls," Rosaline sighed. "Now, scrub my chest, and put your back into it."

Sarab was embarrassed; Rosaline must have noticed she was avoiding her breasts.

She obeyed the order and drew the sponge over the sagging breasts. She was careful not to touch them directly, but remained hyperaware of the pulse beating beneath them.

Sarab felt guilty, as if she had abused the privacy of this woman's body, and she hastily covered its sharp edges with a soft, fluffy bathrobe.

Rosaline's knowing eye settled musingly on Sarab's face while she was busy perfuming and freshening her armpits with lavender powder.

When they emerged from the bathroom the apartment seemed to be holding its breath, swimming in the blues music which harmonized with the red and black decor.

A simple activity like bathing was guaranteed to tire Rosaline out. She collapsed into bed, bare of the dark lips that emphasized her pale skin. She was like a marble statue that Sarab had toppled over.

Is she dead?

It was time for Sarab to go, but she stayed stock still in the doorway to the bedroom, unable to leave, though night was falling. She couldn't even lift her eyes from that body, struck by the shattering contradiction between Rosaline as she was now, old and impotent, and what she had been: a famous actress, wife of a diplomat, and former member of the International Red Cross.

I want to live.

Rosaline's words echoed through Sarab's head and reassured her.

*

"Come here. Breathe in."

Rosaline would accept no objection, and Sarab was afraid of opposing her. She felt that her time in that apartment was like a prison sentence, in that she had to defer completely to her jailer or guide; meanwhile, Rosaline felt Sarab needed to be forced to step outside the rigid limits inside her.

"Take a deep breath."

Sarab pulled deeply on the cigarette without coughing—it was nothing in comparison to the gas and the smoke she had inhaled during the siege. She contemplated the cigarette's delicacy between her fingers; it was an odd sight, and an even odder taste was making her head spin.

"Now paint your lips black," Rosaline invited her, watching her closely, aware that Sarab usually avoided that color.

But as soon as Sarab left and found herself outside, she twirled ecstatically, attracting the attention of the patrons in a nearby café. Cautiously, embarrassed, she pressed her lips onto a tissue, then thrust it in her handbag and hurried back home.

Raphael noticed the smudge of black on her lips at once but forbore from commenting, careful not to utter a word that might make her shrink back into her shell. He sensed a flame of excitement under her skin, and it bothered him.

Sarab didn't tell him all the details of her experiences with Rosaline. It was her secret, and by drawing a veil over it to protect it she was being another person: her true, unobserved self. And Raphael had a vague notion of what was happening to her; the black color smudged over her lips troubled him deeply.

"Your paradise," he said, placing a huge file on her knees. The first page bore a picture of the building he had just bought in Spain.

Her eyes gleamed. "No!"

"Yes, it's ours now."

Joy and disbelief battled inside her. It was an old palace in a surfing village in Cádiz. Sarab particularly adored the endless white sand sloping down to the sea. It reminded her of the sea in Aden and the total freedom she had found—and just as suddenly lost—in the sunlight and the saltwater. She felt the building was a promised paradise.

"I can imagine being naked there," she said dreamily, unruly as a child, as the touch of the sand and the seawater purified her of her sins. She vowed to reach that sea. "I will be entirely immersed in that white foam, and nothing will ever blacken me again."

Raphael realized her need to disappear without a trace, both from the Mahdi and her inner demons. "And I'm planning to renovate it all," he said, enthusiastic and proud. "We'll stay in the annex while we decide on the renovations in the main building." Even he felt transformed by this dream. "We'll choose everything together, the furniture and the decoration of every bedroom and reception room."

"But I don't know anything about decorating," Sarab said.

"We'll manage in our own way, like amateurs."

Sarab adopted his frivolity. "Everything in white?" she teased him.

"Be more adventurous."

She was haunted by the red and the black in Rosaline's apartment.

One day Rosaline surprised her by holding out a bloodred lipstick.

"Red is a transgression. It's confusing, because it's joyful and a riddle at the same time. Don't let it scare you—ride its flame."

Rosaline had changeable moods; she could be very eccentric, and flipped easily between the superciliousness of the worshiped and the lunacy of the clown; from laughter to the mysterious grief that drove Sarab to be braver; from red to black, which made Sarab triumph over her fear of revealing her long-buried femininity.

"You could be my partner in crime," Rosaline scoffed as she watched.

The moment Sarab rolled the red over her lips, a serpent of lust coursed through her blood. She hurried to the bathroom and wiped it off.

When they first met, Sarab had felt this woman was playing games with her, and she resented her for it. Then, when she realized she had underestimated Rosaline, she was appalled at the absurdity of this reaction. It was simply her way; just an actress's ploy, a game to help others escape their gravity. Sarab felt secure in shedding her seriousness, and relaxed enough to be driven further into this venture.

"Come on, take off your shirt."

Rosaline insisted on Sarab's undressing.

"Now face the mirror."

Sarab was struck by the vitality coiled in her small breasts. There was excitement and defiance that caught the eye, but she was certain that they were nothing when compared with Rosaline's.

"You should have seen them in my glory days, when I was young," Rosaline said, pointing at her own breasts. "I left a considerable number of broken hearts in my wake." She sighed deeply. "But that's life. Your body reminds me of my old figure."

Sarab faced the mirror and, for the first time, saw herself in a different light. She whispered to herself, "It's lovely."

It was the most tender praise she had ever offered to the body she had repressed and despised; merely acknowledging it sent the blood to her cheeks.

"Stop that shyness!" Rosaline ordered.

Sarab felt she was falling into a trap of that eccentric leader, who seemed to be able to read her mind. She didn't know why her mother Bunduqa suddenly burst into the apartment, a stark contrast to Rosaline.

"Yes, pull your shoulders back."

And Sarab tried to push her shoulders back.

"Ahhh!" Rosaline laughed, wagging her finger, warning her not to collapse in on herself. "Wider, wider!" Like an acrobat, Rosaline pushed her shoulders back in an exaggerated movement, imitating a bird flapping its wings, and Sarab couldn't help laughing—which was what Rosaline intended.

"And now, set these little rabbits free," Rosaline ordered her, almost touching her breasts. Sarab realized she was howling with laughter, astonished at the excess of it, but giving in to it all the same. What harm could there be in following these embarrassing instructions?

"Let them breathe," Rosaline ordered playfully, taking a deep breath.

"Breathe, little rabbits, breathe," she said rhythmically, making Sarab's breasts swell with life.

"Spread out, fill up all the space."

Sarab realized they were being ridiculous, she and Rosaline, but she was enjoying herself. She breathed deeply and was filled with pride; it made her feel like one of the female statues that had caught her eye in the parks in Paris, turning her nose up at the world like a goddess.

"And now, you Bedouin sorceress, take a look at your body." Rosaline was enjoying the role of director, guiding her ingenue in her little theater. "What land did you come from? What magic lamp did you escape from?"

She contemplated Sarab; there wasn't a shred of criticism in that all-encompassing gaze; nothing but acceptance and pleasure. It was the look Sarab had longed to receive from her own mother.

"It's hard to believe you're Arab. I learned things from Arab women I couldn't have learned from books. The art of loving the body is instinctive there. I really adored Egypt."

She surveyed Sarab from top to toe.

"This, what you have, is a gift. There's nothing shameful in the body—it's a gift, a blessing. And now, take a walk. Go and bring me a cup of chamomile tea."

And Sarab stood at the kitchen door watching the magician Rosaline arrange her music collection, dozens of records strewn around her on the floor of the entrance hall. On evenings like this, surrounded by music, Rosaline seemed like a teenager, a bundle of excitement and unruly defiance. The apartment swam in the savage voice of Mick Jagger as he sang "Tumbling Dice," which had driven Sarab mad in the first days of working for Rosaline. But gradually she, too, became addicted to his hypnotizing rhythms. The few hours each week she spent in this Gothic atmosphere slipped into the archive of Sarab's memories, effacing the files of agony stored there. Space was established between what she had been and what she was greedily plunging into.

"Hand me the scarf for parties, the one with the red roses." For the first time, Rosaline gave Sarab permission to rifle through the mysterious kingdom of her wardrobes.

Sarab faced the six huge wardrobes brimming with clothes. She opened them one by one and stood there, entranced. She was swept away on a tide of red, and black studded with silver, and all types of lace and leather, and infinite pairs of evening shoes and boots and high heels. Sarab wondered sadly whether Rosaline had enough time left to wear all this again. She inhaled the intoxicating perfumes of the wardrobe. Every piece of clothing whispered daringly, promising her a new existence. She longed to stray through this paradise, even if it was just for a day.

"What a lecherous Bedouin you are! That's enough," Rosaline ordered her to close the wardrobe.

One day when the time came for Sarab to leave, Rosaline surprised her with an offer: "Come, stay the night."

Raphael's response on the telephone was muted. He felt threatened that Sarab was spending the night away from his house, but he had no choice. He put the phone down without comment.

Rosaline offered her a bed in her dressing room, and Sarab was falling asleep when she felt the actress sit on the edge of her bed.

"If I had worked in film, do you know the role I wouldn't have minded playing?"

Sarab smiled, not caring or knowing anything about the world this woman was opening to her.

"Fanny, in *Funny Girl*. Barbara Streisand was a real star: the ugly duckling who turned herself into a beautiful swan. You remind me of her in a way. You have that tendency to happiness but it hasn't been polished yet."

"My mother didn't love me."

"Ah, I may be a senile old woman but I believe it would be easy to love you, young woman."

Sarab wanted to be sure of what Rosaline had said. Rosaline seemed prepared to spend the whole night sitting there on the edge of the bed. Sarab wanted to get up and move to where they could carry on their conversation, but Rosaline ordered her to lie back, and gently tucked the covers around her. Sarab resisted a choking desire to weep.

"And you—did you love her?"

The tears streamed down Sarab's cheeks. "Yes," she replied, almost inaudibly.

"You know, there are people who are afraid to love. I'm one of them—how love frightens me!"

Sarab stared at Rosaline, incredulous at this statement.

"I was picked up off the streets, a real gutter rat. My success on the boards couldn't drain the poison out of me—I held the hearts of the audience in my hand without having one myself, and I left many broken behind me. When Pascale entered my life he was like a sun, he resurrected my heart from the grave. He was truly a free soul. I had never seen anyone like him, and he freed me from my inner prison. He allowed my poison to evaporate, and I found myself in love."

Sarab was driven to confess: "I'm not sure if I'm in love now. Perhaps I don't have a choice."

"So what the hell are you doing in my house?"

They laughed, and Sarab longed to shout that, at that moment, she had a choice, and she loved Rosaline, through choice.

"Come here. Look at this."

Rosaline led Sarab to the window which overlooked part of Les Invalides. They stood side by side, welcoming the refreshing night breeze, and Sarab was entranced by the artful illumination of that historical landmark.

"This building," said Rosaline, pointing at Les Invalides, "heals the wounds we humans inflicted on the world. It's a graveyard and a hospital; we created monuments from our battle scars. I chose this apartment because none of its windows look out onto Les Invalides, apart from this one, which overlooks the corner of it. It's a reminder of this side of life; a reminder of its pain."

Sarab listened, distressed. She relived the sights of the siege, and the pain of it cut her like a knife. "Do you pray?" she whispered.

"Bien sûr." The reply came spontaneously in French. "Everything I do, I do to the full. I don't accept half measures. That's my way of praying." The sound of her own conceit rang in Rosaline's ears, and she added: "At least, I try!"

"Are you afraid of God?" Sarab asked.

Silence unfurled between the two women.

"I'm not sure if it's fear," Rosaline said slowly, searching for the words which would translate what the question had stirred up in her. "When I was a young girl, I never paid much attention to this." Her voice emerged as if from crushing depths, rummaging for God in every detail of her life. "But when life laid its burdens on me, even when it laid success and flashing lights on me, I felt empty."

Sarab wasn't sure whether Rosaline had understood her question, but she was content listening to this great actress speak about her past.

"I trust God. If He wasn't waiting for us on the other side, aging would be terrifying," Rosaline went on.

Throughout, Sarab had been aware of Rosaline's heavy breathing; she shouldn't have been so exhausted.

"Sorry to disappoint you, but it's true," Rosaline concluded. "We're all so busy there's no time to stop and feel God, but He is always there to pick us up."

As soon as Sarab got home the following day, Raphael exploded.

"Your job doesn't include staying the night! You have a contract that protects your rights. Don't let them abuse those rights."

She was taken aback by his hostility, and he hurriedly embraced her in apology.

"Forgive me; I get upset so easily when it comes to you. I'm so afraid of you coming to harm."

Raphael hadn't slept the previous night.

He felt he had been robbed of the girl he had plucked out of the battlefield. Some hidden instinct made him wish he could put an end to her visits to Rosaline, but he didn't dare to disturb the self-confidence Sarab was beginning to regain. Clearly she was settling down, she almost belonged to the city, but he wanted all that to end soon. The moment she got her residency papers he would fly her to Spain, to that promised paradise, and there she would find her true self, and there would be nothing to come between them, no rival affection, no one to snatch her away from him. The girl he had glimpsed kneeling in frantic prayer in the Holy City would return—the girl he had stripped of her military uniform.

Raphael's outburst left Sarab unmoved; she needed the optimism she found with Rosaline, to plumb the depths of this involvement with her, to clean her waste and trim her nails, to peel the thick skin away from her delicate anklebones. These actions, she had discovered, were an act of faith, and made her realize her humanity and her connection to God. Like prayer, it was a way of making atonement, of seeking forgiveness—but for what?

She wouldn't stop burrowing into that mask.

As summer waned, a pistachio-colored dress appeared in the window of a shop in Rue Bonaparte. Sarab would peek at it whenever she passed. It was cheerful and radiant as a sunbeam.

On the day Sarab received her first salary for her work for Rosaline, she rushed to the elegant shop.

She entered the shop with a mixture of inferiority and self-confidence. She moved among the hangers holding other dresses, but was too shy to approach the pistachio-colored one.

At last she came to the window where it was hanging and she smiled, besotted.

"It's the last piece we have, Mademoiselle. The silk is splendid," the assistant said encouragingly. "Would you like to try it, Mademoiselle? It's silk."

Sarab trembled at the thought of squeezing her body into such a short dress, but the assistant gave her no chance to object.

She took the dress off the mannequin and said, "Follow me please, Mademoiselle."

She led Sarab into a changing room, hung up the dress, and then went out and closed the curtain. Sarab found herself alone with the dress in that narrow space. On either side, below the short wall, she could see two bare female legs, and others emerging into the corridor half-dressed. The assistants were helping them, fastening a zipper here and adjusting a seam there.

"I won't buy it; I just want to touch it."

Recklessly, she took off her blouse but kept on her trousers, and she slipped into the dress. She felt the cheerful silk, loaded with sin, embrace her skin thrillingly, and without thinking she took off her trousers and pulled the dress down over her hips.

She stood there, staring at her image in the mirror. She felt like a sunbeam; she felt dizzy at the sight of her slender legs, her thighs exposed to the whole room. A dizzying mixture of guilt and joy.

She turned around, seeing how the pistachio-colored silk draped over the graceful curves of her body, and started laughing like Rosaline. Sitting on the velvet-covered chair in the changing room, she crossed one leg over the other. The sensation of direct contact with the silk and velvet made her burst out laughing again.

"Do you need any help, Mademoiselle?"

The assistant's question interrupted her lunacy.

"No, no thank you." She was afraid that the woman would pull back the curtain and peer at her shamefully exposed body.

She bought the dress recklessly, spending more than half her pay on this frivolous indulgence which she then hid in the back of her wardrobe.

She felt dizzy at starting her own collection of Western clothes.

Peeling the Pistachio

THE NEXT MORNING, SARAB WOKE early. She spent hours bathing, recalling what Rani had told her about how to make amends for a crime against the spirit. Sarab was becoming utterly convinced that purity was perhaps simpler than all the water she wasted and that never left her feel purified. *What can milk and honey offer the world?* The spurting of the water increased, and she was pleased to think that at least water might damage the ignition switch on the invisible explosive belt.

She was suddenly struck with guilt toward the pistachio-colored dress, for having snatched it out of the sun and buried it in darkness. Now she hurriedly dug it out; she reclaimed it and lightly spun around in it, allowing it to breathe. She went to the kitchen, conscious that her legs, bare from ankle to thigh, were breathing deeply for the first time. Zolo was there waiting, watching her curiously. Sarab had stopped walking the dogs, apart from Zolo. His owner, the elderly psychologist, had died the previous week and his relatives were looking for someone to care for his pet.

The dog had spent a week in mourning, and whenever Sarab took him to the bedroom or the living room he would skulk back to the kitchen, determined to stay on the margins. He lay down on the kitchen floor without showing any emotion or interest in anything, staring vacantly at nothing.

But that morning, with every sign of enjoyment, he swallowed a biscuit that Sarab had dipped in her coffee for him. It was morning and the apartment was bathed in a dazzling light, particularly the kitchen. Raphael told Sarab he had rented this apartment especially for the kitchen; the French window reached the length of the wall from ground to ceiling like another door, overlooking the Luxembourg Gardens.

Sarab opened the window as wide as it could go, welcoming the scent of flowers rising from the gardens. She was fascinated by the thought of having such a lofty door in the sky that opened onto the world, while she remained safe in a nest, occupying herself with simple everyday tasks like those she was performing at that moment: watching her coffee on the burner, taking a seat at the wooden table, sipping the coffee peacefully.

Her gaze fell on the knives arranged in the form of a star decorating the kitchen wall. A warning rang in her head: *You're wounding the angels with your nakedness.*

She hurried to the bedroom, where she put trousers on under the dress, and added a jacket to cover the delicate pistachio color.

"I look ridiculous," she thought, unconscious of her charm.

She left her hair wet and left the apartment. When her hair was struck by a cold breeze, one of her grandmother's phrases surfaced in her mind, one she used to repeat whenever she washed and combed her white hair: "A true woman grows her hair long enough to dampen her shroud when her body is washed, otherwise she will be uncovered when she rises from the grave on the Day of Resurrection and she will be naked in front of everyone. How disgraceful!"

Sarab reflected that her grandmother's only concern had been her damp shroud. She was relieved that her hair had raced ahead and grown with amazing speed in the last few months, in such profusion that it already covered her shoulders this morning.

Sarab broke into a smile. On this important day, she would be absent from the language institute for the first time. At exactly two o'clock in the afternoon she would receive her permanent residency card and her identity card. The word *permanent* carried with it a mysterious foreboding.

Sarab walked aimlessly through downtown Paris, heedless of the life blaring around her, torn between rapture and a sense of ignominy and anguish. The voice in her head lashed out at her, repeating, *Enjoy your new documents, you traitor. You're nothing but an agent of Satan by choosing to belong to this godless foreign country.*

Zolo came up beside her and rubbed his nose into her left hand. It was the first time the dog had shown her such overt affection.

Sarab was crossing Boulevard Haussmann when Zolo suddenly became agitated. Sarab felt a tremor pass through his body, and then he wheeled around and leaped straight toward the gray car that burst out of nowhere and careered toward them. Zolo's body was hurled through the air as the car slammed into Sarab's body and disappeared.

For a second that seemed like an eternity, Sarab observed her body lying on the tarmac in the middle of the street, alone. It had finally relinquished control, and was liberated from having to find a way of clinging to safety. The thing she had feared for so long had finally happened. Finally, the suicide belt around her body had been broken; she had been punished at last for her sins, both real and imaginary, and there was no more need of it now.

She lay there, observing the historic buildings on either side of the boulevard in slow motion. They were magnificent structures, made of solid stone. Hundreds of years had probably passed over them; thousands of faces, countless sensations of pain and joy had all slipped over those stone facades, and they were fully comprehensible to her in her profound relief at having surrendered to all she had feared. She felt like she was floating in the air, content rather than wretched. The shattered body seemed to belong to some other person, and its expiry meant nothing to her. Zolo was whining and hovering over her, his broken legs straining to keep standing over her as a thin trickle of blood ran from the side of his mouth and down his splendid silver neck. He wouldn't allow anyone to approach her and harm her further. His eyes, which were no longer just two but had become four or more, widened as he gazed at her apologetically. At last he lay down, pushing his nose gently against her neck as his body fell onto the tarmac, and his soul departed. She felt his last breath warm on her face, like a healing balm for the devastating damage spreading over her body.

Sarab compassionately observed the kind, terrified faces hovering over her, who were besieging her helpless body and trying to see what was happening. She watched the world spin slowly while the ambulance arrived. They put up screens around her to protect her from the curiosity of passersby. She felt cynical about this concern for her privacy; such protection would have created a greater rift in her past life. They pulled Zolo's body away and she didn't object; she had to let him go. A hand carrying a pair of scissors cut open the pistachio-colored dress, making a long tear from neck to navel. A drop of blood widened on the simple neck opening, failing to diminish its radiance, and they peeled it away from her chest.

She felt the paramedic's hand on her body, cutting a hole in her throat, perhaps to drain the blood filling her lungs and making it hard to breathe. She wanted to tell them there was no need, no need to carve more wounds into her poor body while she was still drugged by Zolo's breath. But they were struggling desperately to allow air into her crushed lungs—it was a matter of life or death to them. She felt the paramedic's lips open hers and puff air into her lungs, and his breath smelled of sweet basil. She wanted to tell him he had blessed breath, but her voice had dried up and she couldn't make it come out. In any case she didn't need a voice. Her soul communicated with the paramedics and touched their racing hearts. Sarab represented a challenge for them, liberated as she was from signs of life. They wanted her body to show some response, while the body, with its destroyed lungs, was perfectly well and felt no need to react; it was assured and finally, totally, at absolute ease.

They fixed an oxygen mask over her nose and mouth and carried her into the ambulance on a stretcher that smelled of other, perished, beings.

A siren. It ruined her liberty, and she wished they would turn it off as there was no need to hurry. But it kept shrieking insistently, driving her floating soul back to her shattered body. By the time they reached the hospital she had begun to feel the pain; agony was tearing through her lungs, and she was choking.

They rushed her into the operating room, where they pumped fluid into her and allowed her to float off once again.

Raphael clung to her hospital bed in shock. He couldn't believe he was losing her after everything they had been through, after their double escape from the siege in the Grand Mosque and the camp in Yemen. She was barely breathing as they kept repeating, "She's in pain."

"There's no way of saving her."

"Her lungs are crushed."

"She is dying."

"Her condition is hopeless."

And finally: "We must help her to let go, and depart in peace."

A woman who seemed to be a nun was brought to help her go. As soon as Raphael saw her, his heart was gripped by icy claws. The head nurse kindly asked Raphael to leave the room.

"This is the team that will prepare her to leave our world. The sister will help her feel at peace. Let's leave them alone."

"But Sarab doesn't speak French. How can I leave her with you when you can't understand each other?"

"She will understand," the austere woman confirmed with sincere faith, urging Raphael to leave. "Don't worry, we will communicate peacefully."

On a way station of her journey, Sarab was bewildered by the murmurings of the sister; for a moment she wondered whether they were words from any of the revealed books. Then the words dissolved and transformed into a great gush of energy running straight from the woman's heart into Sarab's. This current enclosed her in warmth; light engulfed her and receded, encouraging the current to flow to its fullest extent, and this surge and ebb rocked her like a child.

"And now, your role is to give her the last push so she can go. Tell her it's all right that she's leaving," the austere woman encouraged Raphael, not unkindly.

"But I can't. My God, how can I let her go? We're in love, she's so young, she's barely twenty-two; we have a new life waiting for us, we were going to leave Paris to live by the ocean. I promised her the ocean."

"Her soul is deeply embedded within yours, and you are holding it back. Her soul can't leave for fear of tearing yours apart. You have to set her free. Don't be selfish, my son."

Raphael approached Sarab's bed and watched her shallow breathing; it stopped for a moment, then started again fitfully. There was a long pause between every inhalation and exhalation. He didn't know what he could do. Despite his profound resistance to the idea of hurrying her along her path, the words came gushing out involuntarily, burning from the depths where their souls cleaved together and realized the necessity of her journey.

"You can go, my darling. If your body has given up, we have to surrender it." His words were inaudible, like the inhalation and exhalation of light and air.

Images circled her bed—her brother Sayf, all the comrades and hostages who had been killed or mortally wounded, everyone who breathed their last in the hospital or inside the siege. All of them flowed around her like a refreshing light, touching her cold feet and cheeks. They pressed her numb hands, and it was no longer a source of grief to her that she was dying among strangers. They weren't strangers any more. There was no longer any concept of being a stranger, a foreigner, or an exile here; they were all a single essence flowing with the name of God, who was running through their existence like a rising river, a river of living light, encouraging her through His radiance to immerse herself in His river and flow into it.

Tears streamed over Raphael's cheeks and his heart exploded in agony.

I love you.

He stopped himself from saying it, for fear those words would hold her back and prevent her absolute release. He swallowed his tears.

Her face quivered with a delicate smile, the gentlest smile.

Her lips trembled with something resembling words, and he brought his ear close to her mouth, to catch what she was saying.

A gentle breath wafted over his cheek as she sank into the river.